Praise for *Blood Safari*

'Meyer, who writes in Afrikaans, is far and away the best crime writer in South Africa. The action is as exciting as any reader of thrillers has a right to demand. The writing is fluent and coherent and full of insight into the problems of South Africa. As Meyer writes, money and poverty and greed do not lie well together. But they make a hell of a thriller.' *Guardian*

'Pulsating and gripping' *The Sunday Times*

'*Blood Safari* is my first exposure to the man billed by his publishers as the "king of South African crime thrillers". For once the publicity spinners are not guilty of hyperbole – Meyer is simply excellent . . . Lemmer is too good a character to be a one-novel phenomenon. He is a sardonic, accurate observer of South African foibles, especially those of the Afrikaner. It is all rendered with enough wry, dry humour to make the reader laugh out loud.' *Business Day*

Deon Meyer lives in Durbanville in South Africa with his wife and four children. Other than his family, Deon's big passions are motorcycling, music, reading, cooking and rugby. In January 2008 he retired from his day job as a consultant on brand strategy for BMW Motorrad, and is now a full time author.

Deon Meyer's books have attracted worldwide critical acclaim and a growing international fanbase. Originally written in Afrikaans, they have now been translated into several languages, including English, French, German, Dutch, Italian, Spanish, Danish, Norwegian, Swedish, Russian, Finnish, Czech, Romanian, Slovakian, Bulgarian, Japanese and Polish.

Also by Deon Meyer

Dead Before Dying
Dead at Daybreak
Heart of the Hunter
Devil's Peak

blood
safari
deon
meyer

Translated from Afrikaans by K. L. Seegers

HODDER

First published in Great Britain in 2009 by Hodder & Stoughton
An Hachette UK company

First published in paperback in 2009

6

A CIP catalogue record for this title is available from the British Library.

ISBN 978 0340 95358 7

Typeset in Plantin Light by Hewer Text UK Ltd, Edinburgh
Printed and bound by CPI Group (UK) Ltd, Croydon, CR0 4YY

Hodder & Stoughton policy is to use papers that are natural, renewable
and recyclable products and made from wood grown in sustainable forests.
The logging and manufacturing processes are expected to conform
to the environmental regulations of the country of origin.

Hodder & Stoughton Ltd
338 Euston Road
London NW1 3BH

www.hodder.co.uk

PART ONE

I

I swung the sledgehammer in a lazy rhythm. It was Tuesday, 25 December, just past noon. The wall was thick and stubbornly hard. After each dull thump, shards of brick and cement broke off and shot across the plank floor like shrapnel. I felt sweat tracking through the dust on my face and torso. It was an oven in there, despite the open windows.

Between hammer blows I heard the phone ring. I was reluctant to break the rhythm. In this heat it would be hard to get the machine going again. Slowly, I put the long handle down and went through to the sitting room, feeling the shards under my bare feet. The phone's little screen displayed JEANETTE. I wiped a grimy hand on my shorts and picked it up.

'*Jis.*'

'Merry Christmas.' Jeanette Louw's gravelly voice was loaded with inexplicable irony. As ever.

'Thanks. Same to you.'

'Must be good and hot out there . . .'

'Thirty-eight outside.'

In winter she would say, 'Must be nice and cold out there,' with undisguised regret about my choice of residence. 'Loxton,' she said now, as if it were a faux pas. 'You'll just have to sweat it out, then. What do you do for Christmas in those parts?'

'Demolish the wall between the kitchen and the bathroom.'

'You did say the kitchen and the bathroom?'

'That's how they built them in the old days.'

'And that's how you celebrate Christmas. Old rural tradition, huh?' and she barked out a single, loud 'Ha!'

I knew she hadn't phoned to wish me Happy Christmas. 'You've got a job for me.'

'Uh-huh.'

'Tourist?'

'No. Woman from the Cape, actually. She says she was attacked yesterday. She wants you for a week or so, paid the deposit already.'

I thought about the money, which I needed. 'Oh?'

'She's in Hermanus. I'll SMS the address and cell phone number. I'll tell her you're on your way. Call me if you have any problems.'

I met Emma le Roux for the first time in a beach house overlooking the Old Harbour of Hermanus. The house was impressive, three new Tuscan storeys of rich man's playground with a hand-carved wooden front door and a door knocker in the shape of a lion's head.

At a quarter to seven on Christmas night a young man with long curly hair and steel-rimmed spectacles opened the door. He introduced himself as Henk and said they were expecting me. I could see he was curious, though he hid it well. He invited me in and asked me to wait in the sitting room while he called 'Miss le Roux'. A formal man. There were noises from deep in the house – classical music, conversation. The smell of cooking.

He disappeared. I didn't sit down. After six hours' drive through the Karoo in my Isuzu, I preferred to stand. There was a Christmas tree in the room, a big artificial one with plastic pine needles and mock snow. Multicoloured lights blinked. At the top of the tree was an angel with long, blonde hair, wings spread wide like a bird of prey. Behind her the curtains of the big windows were open. The bay was lovely in the late afternoon, the sea calm and still. I stared out at it.

'Mr Lemmer?'

I turned.

She was tiny and slim. Her black hair was cut very short, almost like a man's. Her eyes were large and dark, the tips of her ears slightly pointed. She looked like a nymph from a children's story. She stood for a moment to take me in, the involuntary up-and-down look to measure me against her expectations. She hid her disappointment well. They usually expect someone bigger, more imposing – not this general average of height and appearance.

She came up to me and put out her hand. 'I'm Emma le Roux.' Her hand was warm.

'Hello.'

'Please sit down.' She gestured at the suite in the sitting room. 'Can I get you something to drink?' Her voice had an unexpected timbre, as if it belonged to a larger woman.

'No thanks.'

I sat down. The movement of her petite body was fluid, as though she were completely comfortable inside it. She sat down opposite me. Tucked up her legs, at home here. I wondered whether it was her place, where the money came from.

'I, ah . . .' She waved a hand. 'This is a first for me, having a bodyguard . . .'

I wasn't sure how to respond. The lights of the Christmas tree flicked their colours over her with monotonous regularity.

'Maybe you could explain how it works,' Emma said without embarrassment. 'In practice, I mean.'

I wanted to say that if you order this service, you ought know how it works. There is no reference manual.

'It's simple really. To protect you I need to know what your movements are every day . . .'

'Of course.'

'And the nature of the threat.'

She nodded. 'Well . . . I'm not exactly sure what the threat is. Some odd things have happened . . . Carel convinced me . . . You'll meet him in a moment; he's used your service before. I . . . there was an attack, yesterday morning . . .'

'On you?'

'Yes. Well, sort of . . . They broke down the door of my house and came in.'

'They?'

'Three men.'

'Were they armed?'

'No. Yes. They, um . . . It happened so fast . . . I . . . I hardly saw them.'

I suppressed the urge to raise my eyebrows.

'I know it sounds . . . peculiar,' she said.

I said nothing.

'It was . . . strange, Mr Lemmer. Sort of . . . surreal.'

I nodded, encouraging her.

She looked at me intently for a moment and then leaned over to switch on a table lamp beside her.

'I have a house in Oranjezicht,' she said.

'So this is not your permanent home?'

'No . . . this is Carel's place. I'm just visiting. For Christmas.'

'I see.'

'Yesterday morning . . . I wanted to finish my work before packing for the weekend . . . My office . . . . I work from home, you see. About half past nine I took a shower . . .'

Her story did not flow at first. She seemed reluctant to relive it. Her sentences were incomplete, hands quiet, her voice a polite, indifferent monotone. She gave more detail than the situation warranted. Perhaps she felt it lent credibility.

After her shower, she said she was dressing in her bedroom, one leg in her jeans, precariously balanced. She heard the garden gate open and through the lace curtain she saw three men move quickly and purposefully through the front garden. Before they disappeared from her field of vision on the way to the front door, she had registered that they were wearing balaclavas. They had blunt objects in their hands.

She was a modern single woman. Aware. She had often considered the possibility of being the victim of a crime and what her emergency response could be if the worst happened. Therefore, she stepped into the other leg of her jeans and hastily pulled them up over her hips. She was half dressed in only underwear and jeans, but the priority was to get to the panic button and be ready to sound the alarm. But not to press it yet, there was still the security gate and the burglar bars. She didn't want the embarrassment of crying wolf.

Her bare feet moved swiftly across the carpet to the panic button on her bedroom wall. She lifted her finger and waited. Her heart thumped in her throat, but still she was in control. She heard the squeal of metal stubbornly bending and breaking. The security door was no longer secure. She pressed the alarm. It wailed out from the ceiling above and with the sound came a wave of panic.

Her narration seemed to draw her in and her hands began to communicate. Her voice developed a musical tone, the pitch rising.

Emma le Roux ran down the passage to the kitchen. She was fleetingly aware that burglars and thieves did not use this method. It fuelled her terror. In her haste she collided with the wooden back door with a dull thud. Her hands shook as she pulled back both bolts and turned the key in the lock. The second she jerked open the door she heard splintering in the hall, glass shattering. The front door was breached. They were in her house.

She took one step outside and stopped. Then turned back into the kitchen to grab a drying cloth from the sink. She wanted it to cover herself. Later she would scold herself for such an irrational act, but it was instinctive. Another fraction of a second she hesitated. Should she grab a weapon, a carving knife? She suppressed that impulse.

She ran into the bright sunlight with the drying cloth pressed to her breast. The neatly paved backyard was very small.

She looked at the high concrete wall that was meant to protect her, keep the world out. It was now keeping her in. For the first time she screamed 'Help me!' A distress call to neighbours she did not know – this was urban Cape Town, where you kept your distance, pulled up the drawbridge every night, kept yourself to yourself. She could hear them in the house behind her. One shouted something. Her eye caught the black rubbish bin against the concrete wall – a step to safety.

'Help!' she called between the undulating wails of the alarm.

Emma didn't remember how she made it over the wall. But she did, in one or two adrenalin-fuelled movements. The drying cloth stayed behind in the process, so that she landed in her neighbour's yard without it. Her left knee scraped against something. She felt no pain; only later would she notice the little rip in the denim.

'Help me.' Her voice was shrill and desperate. She crossed her arms across her bosom to preserve her decency and ran to the neighbour's back door. 'Help me!'

She heard the dustbin overturn and knew they were close behind. The door opened in front of her and a grizzled man in a red dressing gown with white dots came out. He had a rifle in his hand. Above his eyes the silver eyebrows grew long and dense, making wings across his forehead.

'Help me,' she said with relief in her voice.

The neighbour rested his eyes on her for a second, a grown woman with a boyish figure. Then he raised his eyebrows and his gaze to the wall behind her. He brought the rifle up to his shoulder and pointed it at the wall. She had almost reached him now and looked back. A balaclava appeared for an instant above the concrete.

The neighbour fired. The shot reverberated against the multiple walls around them and the bullet slammed into her house with a clapping sound. For three or four minutes after that she could not hear a thing. She stood close to her neighbour, trembling. He did not look at her. He worked the bolt of his rifle. A casing clinked to the cement, noiselessly to her deafened ears. The neighbour scanned the wall.

'Bastards,' he said as he aimed along the barrel. He swung the rifle horizontally to cover the whole front.

She didn't know how long they stood there. The attackers had gone. Her hearing returned with a rushing sound, then she heard the alarm again. Eventually he slowly lowered the rifle and asked her in a voice full of concern and eastern Europe, 'Are you all right, my darlink?'

She began to cry.

2

Her neighbour's name was Jerzy Pajak. He led her into his house. He asked his wife, Alexa, to call the police, and then they clucked over her in Polish accents. He gave her a light blanket to cover her embarrassment, and sweet tea. Later they walked with her and two policemen to her house.

The steel security gate hung askew and the wooden front door was beyond repair. The coloured policeman was the more senior of the two, with stripes on the shoulders of his smart uniform. She thought he was a sergeant, but because she was unsure, she addressed them both as 'mister'. He asked her to check whether anything had been stolen. She said she would finish dressing at the same time. She still had the multicoloured blanket draped over her shoulders and the temperature in the city was rising. She walked up to her room and sat for a moment on the white duvet on her double bed. It was over an hour since she had made it. She didn't believe they were burglars. She had had enough time to come to a conclusion and develop suspicions.

She dressed in a green T-shirt and trainers. After that she walked through the house to satisfy the sergeant and went to report nothing missing. While they settled themselves in a circle in the sitting room, Pajaks on the couch, she and the policemen on chairs, he questioned her carefully and sympathetically in good, regulation Afrikaans.

Had she been aware of anyone watching her or her house lately? 'No.'

'Have you noticed a car or any other vehicle unusual in the area?'

'No.'

'Any people loitering in the street or behaving in a suspicious manner?'

'No.'

'You were in your bedroom when they came in?'

She nodded. 'I was dressing when I heard the gate. It makes this noise. Then I saw them running to the front door. No, not running. Walking fast. When I saw the balaclavas, I . . .'

'I assume you couldn't see their faces.'

'No.'

The Pajaks couldn't understand the Afrikaans, but their heads followed the interrogation from one side to the other, like spectators at a tennis match.

'Skin colour.'

'No . . .'

'You seem unsure.'

She thought they were black, but she didn't wish to offend the other policeman. 'I can't say for sure. It happened so fast.'

'I understand, Miss Le Roux. You were scared. But anything could help.'

'Maybe . . . one was black.'

'And the other two?'

'I don't know . . .'

'Have you had any work done on or around your house lately?'

'No.'

'Are there any items in your house of exceptional value?'

'Just the usual. A few pieces of jewellery. A laptop. The TV . . .'

'A laptop?'

'Yes.'

'And they didn't take it?'

'No.'

'You must excuse me, Miss Le Roux, but that is unusual. Listening to what happened here, this is not the typical modus operandi of a burglar. Breaking down the doors and pursuing you into the backyard . . .'

'Yes?'

'It sounds as though they meant to attack you personally.'

She nodded.

'One has to look for motive, you understand.'

'I understand.'

'And that is usually of a personal nature. In most cases.'

'Oh?'

'Forgive me, but was there a relationship that went bad?'

'No,' she said with a smile to mask her relief. 'No . . . not that bad, I hope.'

'One never knows, miss. So there was a man in the recent past?'

'I can assure you, mister, it's more than a year since I was in a serious relationship and he was a Brit who went back to England.'

'The break-up was friendly?'

'Absolutely.'

'Since then has there been anyone who might be unhappy over a break-up?'

'No. Definitely not.'

'What is your line of work, Miss Le Roux?'

'I'm a brand consultant.'

She saw his confusion and elaborated. 'A brand consultant. I help companies to position their brand of products in the market. Or reinvent them.'

'Which company do you work for?'

'I work for myself. My clients are companies.'

'So you have no employees?'

'No.'

'And you work with big companies?'

'Mostly. Sometimes there are smaller ones . . .'

'Has anything happened at work that might have upset people?'

'No. It's not . . . I work with products, or the perception of the company brand. It wouldn't upset anyone.'

'An incident? With your car? With someone doing a job for you? Gardener, domestic?'

'No.'

'Is there anything you can think of? Anything that could have led to this?'

This was the question that she was not ready to answer yet.

'So I said "no", but I don't believe it was the truth,' Emma told me. The floor lamp beside her cast a soft, sympathetic glow over her euphemism.

I did not respond.

'I . . . I didn't want . . . I wasn't sure whether they were connected. No, I . . . I didn't want them to be connected. Anyway, it was something that happened a thousand kilometres from the Cape and it might have been Jacobus, or it might not, and I didn't want to bother the police with something that could have been my imagination.' She suddenly stopped talking and looked at me and smiled slowly, as if she were weary of herself. 'I'm not making any sense, am I?'

'Take your time.'

'It's just . . . it doesn't make sense. You see, my brother. . .' She stopped again, drew a breath. She looked at her hands, then, slowly, up at me. Emotion shone in her eyes, her hands made a small hopeless gesture. 'Mr Lemmer, he died . . .'

It was the sum of her body language, her choice of words and sudden change of gear which triggered the alarm in my head. As if she had practised this phrase, this offer. There was the tiny flicker of manipulation, as if she wished to distract my attention from the facts on the table. It only made me wonder: why should that be necessary?

Emma le Roux would not be the first client to blatantly lie about a threat with that little frown of absolute sincerity. Not the first to embroider misty eyed, or exaggerate in order to justify the presence of The Bodyguard. People lie. For a million reasons. Merely because they can, sometimes. This was one of the confirming phenomena of Lemmer's First Law: Don't get involved. It was also one of the primary sources of Lemmer's Second Law: Trust nobody.

3

She recovered quickly; I had to concede that. When she received no response, she shrugged off the emotion with a shake of her head and said, 'My brother's name was Jacobus Daniël le Roux . . .'

She said he disappeared in 1986. Her sentences were less fluent now, her narrative cursory, as if the details were a fountain from which she dared not drink. She had been fourteen at the time; Jacobus had been twenty. He was some kind of temporary game ranger, one of a few soldiers on compulsory military service who volunteered to help the Parks Board in the battle against elephant poaching in the Kruger Park. And then he just disappeared. Later they found signs of a skirmish with ivory poachers, cartridge casings and blood and the remains of the campsite the poachers had left behind in their haste. They searched and tracked for two weeks, until the only meaningful conclusion was reached: Jacobus and his black assistant had been killed in the confrontation, and the poachers had taken their bodies with them out of fear for the reaction they would cause.

'It's been more than twenty years, Mr Lemmer . . . It's a long time, you see. That's what makes all this so difficult . . . Anyway, last week, on the twenty-second, something happened that I haven't mentioned to the police . . .'

That Saturday evening, just past seven, she had been in the second bedroom of her house. She had fitted it out as an office with a built-in desk, filing cabinets and bookshelves. There was a television set and a stationary exercise bicycle and a felt notice-board with a few happy social photos plus sober newspaper clippings from the business pages affirming her success as a brand consultant. Emma was busy on her laptop, examining spreadsheets of statistics that required concentration. She was vaguely aware of the TV news headlines, which brought on only a feeling of déjà vu. President Mbeki and the members of his alliance were at loggerheads, a suicide bomb in Baghdad, African leaders complaining about G8 conditions for debt relief.

Later she could not recall what it was that made her look up. Perhaps she had just finished a graph and needed to shift her focus for a moment, perhaps it was pure coincidence. Once her attention was fixed on the TV screen, it was only seconds before a photograph appeared. She heard the newsreader say, '. . . involved in a shooting incident at Khokovela near the Kruger National Park in which a traditional healer and three local men died. The remains of fourteen protected and endangered vultures were found at the scene.'

The photograph appeared in black and white. A white man in his early forties stared deadpan at the camera, as people do when ID photographs are taken.

He looks like Jacobus would have. It was her abrupt, instinctive thought, purely an observation, and a touch of . . . nostalgia, almost.

'The Limpopo police are searching for a Mr Jacobus de Villiers, also known as Cobus, an employee of an animal hospital at Klaserie, to help them with their enquiries. Anyone with information can contact the police station at Hoedspruit . . .'

She shook her head. She grimaced. Coincidence.

The newsreader moved on to commodity prices and she returned her attention to the computer screen and the large amount of work awaiting her. She drew the pointer over a block of data. She selected the graph icon.

What would Jacobus have looked like at . . . forty, would he have been forty this year? Her memories of his features were based mostly on the photographs in her parents' home; her own recollection was less reliable. But she did remember her brother's incredible intensity, his spirit, and his overwhelming personality.

She turned the graph into multicoloured towers of data meant to bring insight about sales trends in relation to the competition.

Coincidence. Strange that the TV photo man should also be called Jacobus.

She selected more blocks of data.

Jacobus was not such a common name.

She needed to make a pie graph of this, with wedges of market share to demonstrate that her client's salad dressing was the slow horse, last across the line. The problem was hers to solve.

The remains of fourteen protected and endangered vultures were found at the scene.

That would have upset Jacobus.

She made an error compiling the graph and clicked her tongue at herself. Coincidence, pure chance. If you absorbed a thousand pieces of information every day for twenty years, it would happen at least once, maybe twice, in a lifetime. The numbers would conspire to tease you with possibilities.

She suppressed this vein of thought for nearly two hours, until she had processed all the data. She checked for new emails and turned off her computer. She fetched a clean towel from the linen cupboard and climbed on the exercise bicycle, cell phone in hand. She read SMS's, listened to her messages. She pedalled systematically harder, watched the television absent minded, channel-surfing with the remote.

She wondered how much like Jacobus the photo really was. She wondered about her ability to recognise him. Imagine if he hadn't died and walked in here now? What would her father have said about that news item? What work would Jacobus be doing if he were alive? How would he have responded when faced with fourteen dead rare vultures?

More than once she forced her thoughts away to other things, plans for tomorrow, preparations for a few days at Hermanus for Christmas, but Jacobus came back to haunt her again and again. Just minutes after ten o'clock, she dug into one of her cupboards and brought out two albums. Swiftly flipping through one, not dwelling on the pictures of her parents, or the happy family groups. She was looking for a particular photograph of Jacobus wearing his bush hat.

She removed it, put it aside and studied it.

Memories. It took considerable willpower to suppress them. Did he look like the man on TV?

Suddenly she was sure. She took the photo to her study and dialled enquiries to get the number of the police station in Hoedspruit. She looked at the photo again. Doubt crept back. She called the Lowveld number. She just wanted to ask whether they were sure it was Jacobus de Villiers and not Jacobus le Roux. That was all. Just so she could get this idea out of her head and enjoy Christmas without the frustration of longing for her deceased family, all of them, Pa and Ma and Jacobus.

Eventually, she spoke to an inspector. She apologised. She had no information, didn't mean to waste his time. The man on TV looked like someone she knew, also called Jacobus. Jacobus le Roux. She stopped then, so he could react.

'No,' said the inspector with the exaggerated patience of someone who handles a lot of weird phone calls. 'He is De Villiers.'

'I know he is De Villiers now, but his name might have once been Le Roux.'

The patience diminished. 'How can that be? He's been here all his life. Everybody knows him.'

She apologised and thanked him and ended the call. At least now she knew.

She went to sleep with the longing unstilled, as though her losses had been renewed after all these years.

'And then, yesterday afternoon, I was standing outside with the man who was replacing my front door. The sergeant, the policeman, had found someone from Hanover Park, a carpenter. I heard the phone ring in the study. When I picked it up there was static on the line, I couldn't hear very well, I thought he said "Miss Emma?" It sounded like a black man. When I said "yes", he said something that sounded like "Jacobus". I said I couldn't hear him. Then he said "Jacobus says you must . . ." and I said I couldn't hear, but he didn't repeat it. I asked "Who is this?" but the line went dead . . .'

For a moment she drifted off in her thoughts, her focus far away, then she came back, turned her head to look at me and said, 'I'm not even sure that's what he said. The call was so short.' She was speaking more rapidly, as if she were in a rush to finish. 'I drove over here last night. When Carel heard the story . . .'

She left it at that. She wanted a response from me, an indication that I understood, an assurance that I would protect her from everything. This was her moment of buyer's remorse, like someone who has bought a new car and reads the advertisement again. I am familiar with it, this moment when you commit yourself to the unwritten part of the contract that says 'I accept unconditionally'.

I nodded my head sagely and said, 'I understand. I'm sorry . . .' and made a semicircle with my hands to show that I included everything – her loss, her pain, her dilemma.

There was a short silence between us, the agreement sealed. She expected action now, some sort of guidance.

'The first thing I must do is inspect the house, inside and out.'

'Ah, of course,' she said, and we rose.

'But we're only staying here for one night, Mr Lemmer.'

'Oh.'

'I have to know what's going on, Mr Lemmer. It . . . I find it all so disturbing. I can't just sit here and wonder. Is it OK for us to travel? Can you travel with me? Because I'm going to the Lowveld tomorrow.'

4

It was dark outside, but the street lights were bright. I walked around the house. It was no fortress. There was burglar-proofing on the ground floor only, subtle enough not to offend the aesthetics. The weakest point was the sliding glass doors that opened on to the big veranda overlooking the sea. Tuscan pillars, corners and protuberances offered four or five alternatives to access the windows on the first and second storeys.

Inside, I knew, was the usual alarm system with motion sensors and a connection to a local private security firm. Their blue-and-white sign was prominently displayed beside the garage. It was holiday home security, designed as an optimistic deterrent and to keep insurance premiums down.

The house was about three years old. I wondered what had been here before, what did they knock down to build this excess and splendour, and what that had cost.

Lemmer's Law of Rich Afrikaners: If a Rich Afrikaner can show off, he will.

The first thing a Rich Afrikaner buys is bigger boobs for his wife. The second thing a Rich Afrikaner buys is an expensive pair of dark glasses (with brand name prominently displayed), which he only removes when it is totally dark. It serves to create the first barrier between himself and the poor. 'I can see you, but you can't see me any more.' The third thing the Rich Afrikaner buys is a double-storey house in the Tuscan style. (And the fourth is a vanity number plate for his car, with his name or the number of his rugby jersey.) How much longer will it be before we outgrow our inherent feeling of inferiority? Why can't we be subtle when Mammon smiles on us? Like our rich English-speaking compatriots whose nose-in-the-air snootiness so offends me, but who at least bear their wealth in style. I stood in the dark and speculated about Carel-the-owner. Apparently he was already a client of Jeanette's. The Rich Afrikaner does not use bodyguards, only home security – high fences, expansive alarms, panic buttons, and neighbourhood security companies with armed response. What requirements did Carel have for protection?

I had my answer at the dining table, later.

When I entered the room, most were seated at the big table. Emma did the introductions. She was apparently the only one who was not part of the family.

'Carel van Zyl,' said the patriarch at the head of the table, his handshake unnecessarily firm, as if he needed to prove something. He was a big man in his fifties, with fleshy lips and broad shoulders, but the good life had already left its mark on his cheeks and midriff. There were three younger couples – Carel's children and their spouses. One of them was Henk, who had met me at the door. He was seated beside his wife, a pretty blonde with a baby on her lap. There were four other grandchildren, the oldest a boy of eight or nine. My seat was beside his.

Carel's wife was tall and attractive and unbelievably well preserved. 'Feel free to take off your jacket, Mr Lemmer,' she said with exaggerated warmth as she placed a plate of steaming turkey on the table.

'Mamma . . .' said Carel reprovingly.

'What?' she asked.

He made a pistol of his hand and pushed the finger barrel down his shirt. He wanted to tell her I was wearing a firearm, and would be reluctant to show it.

'Oh! Sorry,' she said, as though she had committed a social blunder.

'Come, let's ask the blessing,' said Carel sombrely. Everyone held hands and bowed their heads. The boy's hand was small and sweaty in mine, his father's cool and soft on the other side. Carel prayed with comfortable eloquence, and in bullet points, as though God were a fellow member of the board.

'Amen' echoed around the table. Dishes were offered, children encouraged to take vegetables. There were short silences: a secret consciousness of the stranger in their midst and a subtle insecurity about the correct form of interaction. I was a guest, but also an employee, an intruder with an interesting job. The boy watched me with unashamed curiosity. 'Have you really got a gun?' he asked. His mother hushed him and said, 'Don't mind him.'

I forked turkey on to my plate. The hostess said, 'It's just leftovers.' Carel said, 'It's delicious, Ma.'

Someone introduced the weather forecast as a topic and conversation began to flow – plans for the next day, how the children could be kept occupied, whose turn it was to braai. Emma did not join in. Her attention was on her food, but she ate little.

I became aware of an unnatural geniality between them, despite my presence. There was no conflict here, no fraternal rivalry, and none of the usual banter between couples. It was rather like one of those ideal families portrayed on an American TV programme. It was emanating from the way Carel had the final say, the casting vote. Their submission was barely noticeable, interlaced with a cheerful, practised pattern of interaction, but it was there, bowing to the benign despot – the one with the wallet and the fortune.

How did Emma fit into all this?

Once the plates were emptied and a discussion of the next day's golf had ended, Carel decided that it was time to engage me. He waited for a moment of quiet and gave me an intimate smile.

'Now we know what the ghosts looks like, Mr Lemmer.'

For a fraction of a second I didn't know what he was talking about. Then I got it. He had had previous dealings with Body Armour but had the wrong end of the stick.

To all appearances Jeanette Louw is a lesbian in her fifties with big bottle-blonde hair, a dreadful smoking habit – Gauloise was her brand of choice – and an outspoken preference for seducing recently divorced, hurting, heterosexual women. But hidden behind that front was a razor-sharp intellect and a brain for business.

She had been the legendary regimental sergeant-major of the Women's Army College in George, before taking her package seven years ago. After months of market research she had opened her own business on the sixteenth floor of a luxury office building in the Cape Beachfront area. On the glass double doors, through which you could see Jolene Freylinck, the manicured receptionist, BODY ARMOUR was printed in bold, masculine letters and the explanatory 'Personal Executive Security' below in slim sans serif.

Initially, her clients were foreign businessmen, the senior executives of international corporations who came to find out how a quick buck could be squeezed from Africa. Their embassies had whispered in confidential reports that the country was stable enough for investment, but safety on the streets was not quite up to Western standards. Jeanette aimed her marketing at the diplomats, the economic attachés and consuls, the embassy clerks and switchboard operators. Would their important visitors prefer to avoid the long list of personal threats, the muggings, car hijackings, assaults, rapes, abductions and break-ins? Body Armour was the answer. The first few clients went home safely and her reputation grew. Gradually the whole spectrum from East to West had hired her specialists: Japanese, Koreans, Chinese, Germans, French, Brits and Americans.

Then the foreigners began to make movies in the Cape, and the pop stars of the world came to sell their concert tickets to the boere and her client list took on a new dimension. Snapshots of Jeanette with Colin Farrell, Oprah, Robbie Williams, Nicole Kidman and Samuel L. Jackson preened on her walls. She would sit behind her desk and tell you about the big ones that got away. Will Smith and his huge entourage, including his own American bodyguards who travel around him like African praise singers. Sean Connery had earned her eternal admiration by turning down her service with a 'Do you think I'm a fucking wimp?'

As with similar services the world over, Jeanette's portfolio of hand-picked freelance bodyguards took on a two-part character. First, there were the deterrents – those highly visible, muscle-bound, thick-necked, steroid-bulked colossi that accompany the famous and keep hoi polloi at bay through visual intimidation. Their sole qualifications were the intimidating size of their torso and limbs and the ability to scowl in a menacing manner.

In the other branch of Jeanette's service were those whose job was to manage more subtle but also largely imaginary threats. They had to flatter the client's ego with a curriculum vitae reflecting both official training and high-profile experience. They preserved the illusion of danger by moving in the periphery, incessantly observing and evaluating. Sometimes they worked in teams of two, four or six with tiny concealed ear- and microphones. Sometimes they worked alone, depending on the size of the client group, the financial means, or the nature of the risk. They had to blend into the environment the client was moving through, appearing only to whisper polite suggestions at convenient moments. The client expected that, because film and television had set the standard of behaviour. (I had a Scandinavian businesswoman who insisted I wear an earphone complete with a trailing wire disappearing down my collar, despite the fact that I was working alone and had no one to communicate with.)

Consequently, Jeanette Louw would ask prospective clients or their agent: 'Do you need a gorilla, or an invisible.' In the world of the rich and famous it was recognised terminology.

But Carel-know-it-all hadn't got it quite right. His mistake told me something – his knowledge was only fragmentary.

'When you hire a bodyguard, Jeanette asks you if you want a ghost or a gorilla,' he explained to the rest of the table. 'We have only used the gorillas for the celebrities who come to make ads.'

I couldn't think of an appropriate response. The situation was strange to me. The employee didn't usually sit at the same table as the employer – it was socially unacceptable. Add to that my own lack of enthusiasm for small talk. But Carel didn't require a response.

'The gorillas are the big guys,' he said. 'They look like nightclub bouncers. But the ghosts are the real pros. The ones that guard state presidents and ministers.'

They stared at me, the whole table.

'Is that your background too, Mr Lemmer?' Carel asked. It was an invitation, but I turned it down with a mere nod, slight and unenthusiastic.

'There you are, Emma. You're in good hands,' said Carel.

Good hands. I suspected that Carel did not have first-hand experience of the hiring process at Body Armour. It was something he left to subordinates. If he had handled it himself, he would have known that Jeanette had a price list and I wasn't anywhere near the top. My place was in the bargain basement, the one that didn't like teamwork, the one with a secret history and defective public relations.

Did Emma know? Surely not. Jeanette was too professional. She would have asked, 'How much would you like to spend?' and Emma would have said she had no idea of the cost. 'Anything between ten thousand rand a day for a team of four and seven hundred and fifty for a solo operator.' Jeanette would have explained the choices without mentioning her twenty per cent cut, plus administrative charge, unemployment insurance, income tax and bank transfer fees.

What did a brand consultant earn? How big a chunk of that was R750 per day, R5,250 per week, R21,000 a month? Not small change, especially for imaginary threats.

'I'm sure I am,' said Emma with a distant smile, as if her thoughts were somewhere else.

'There's more ice cream,' said Carel's wife hopefully.

He invited me to his playroom. He called it his den.

'Invited' in the broadest possible sense. 'Shall we have a chat?' were the words Carel used, a grey area between invitation and order. He went first. A mounted kudu head stared out over the room. There was a billiard table and a cane bar, bottles on a shelf, along with a small cigar humidor. The pictures on the wall were of Carel-and-gun posing with dead animals.

'Drink?' he asked, and moved behind the bar counter.

'No, thanks,' I said, leaning against the billiard table.

He poured for himself, two fingers of brown, undiluted liquid. He drank from the glass and opened the humidor. 'Cuban?'

I shook my head.

'You're sure? These are class,' he said complacently. 'They age them for twenty-four months, like wine.'

'I don't smoke, thank you.'

He selected a cigar for himself, stroking his fingers down the chunky cylinder. He snipped the end off with a large instrument and put the cigar in his mouth. 'Your amateur trims it with that cheap rubbish that crimps it here at the end.' He held up his clipper for my inspection. 'This is what they call a .44 Magnum. Makes a perfectly round hole.'

He reached for the box of matches. 'And then you get the fools who lick cigars before they light up. That comes from the days when you bought local cigars in the corner café. If the moisture content is properly maintained, you don't lick them.'

He struck a match and allowed the flame to burn strongly. Then he held it to the cigar. He inhaled in short, rapid puffs while rotating the cigar in his fingers. White clouds of smoke floated up around him and a rich aroma filled the room. He shook the match. 'They say the best way to light a cigar is with a Spanish cedar spill. You take a long thin strip of cedar, set that alight first and then use it to light the cigar. It has a pure, clean flame that does not influence the flavour of the cigar. But where would we get Spanish cedar? I ask you.' He smiled at me as if we shared the same difficulty.

He drew deeply on the cigar. 'Cuban, nothing can touch them. The Jamaican is not bad either, nice and light, the Dominican somewhere in between, Honduras is too wild. Nothing touches the cream of old Fidel's crop.'

I wondered fleetingly how long he could maintain a monologue in front of a bored audience, but then I remembered that he was a Rich Afrikaner. The answer was: infinitely.

He drew an ashtray closer. 'Some fools think you shouldn't tap off a cigar's ash. Total myth. Bullshit.' He chuckled. 'The guys smoke cheap cigars and then say the bitter taste is the result of knocking off the ash.'

Carel sat on a bar stool, cigar in one hand, drink in the other.

'There's a great deal of bullshit in the world, my friend, a great deal of bullshit.'

What did he want?

Another puff on the cigar. 'But let me tell you one thing, there's no bullshit in little Emma. None. If she says there are people out to harm her, then I believe her. Do you understand?'

I was not in the mood for this conversation. I did not respond. I knew he didn't like it.

'Don't you want to sit down?'

'I've been sitting too much today.'

'She's like a daughter in this house, my friend, like one of my own. That is why she came to me about this thing. That's why you're here. You have to understand, she's gone through a lot in her life. Deep waters . . .'

I tried to temper my annoyance by thinking how fascinating a man like Carel van Zyl was.

Self-made Men all share a personality type – driven, smart, hard working and dominant. When the wealth grows and people start to defer to their power and influence, every Self-made Man makes the same mistake. They believe the respect is for them, personally. It polishes their self-esteem and tones down their personality towards geniality. But it remains a thin veneer; the original dynamo is still at work behind the self-deceit.

He was accustomed to being the centre of attention. He did not like standing on the sideline of this event. He wanted me to know that he was responsible for my involvement; he was the father figure serving Emma's interests, therefore he was actually in control, and the arbiter of my services. He had the right to interfere and to be a part of this. Above all, he had Knowledge. And he was about to share it with me.

'She came to work for me after she graduated. Most men would have seen just a pretty little thing, but I knew she had something, my friend.' He punctuated his sentence with the cigar.

'I've employed a lot of them, account managers, and they just see the glamour and the long lunches with clients and the fat pay cheques. But not Emma. She wanted to learn; she wanted to work. You would never say there was money behind her; she had the ambition of someone from a poor background. Ask me, my friend, I know. In any case, she had been working for me for about three years when the thing with her parents happened. Car accident, dead on impact, both of them. She sat in my office, my friend, poor little thing, crushed, I'm telling you. Crushed, because she had no one left. That's when she told me about her brother. Can you imagine? So much loss. Turbulent times. What can you say?'

He reached for the bottle and unscrewed the cap.

'But she's strong, that one. Strong.'

Drew the glass nearer.

'I only heard about the size of the estate later. And let me tell you now . . .' He poured two fingers. 'This is all about the money.'

A dramatic silence, cap back on the bottle, a sip from the glass, a short pull from the cigar. 'There are a lot of vultures out there, my friend. A lot. The bigger the fortune, the quicker they sniff it out. Ask me, I know.'

He gestured with the glass: 'Out there is somebody with a scheme. Someone that's done his homework, someone who knows her history and wants to use it to get at her money. I don't know how. But it's about the money.'

He brought the glass to his lips again and then put it down on the counter with finality. 'All you have to do is work out the scheme. Then you have your man.'

At that moment I could have told him Lemmer's First Law. I didn't.

'No,' I said.

It was not a word he was used to hearing. His reaction proved that.

'I'm a bodyguard. Not a detective,' I said before I walked out.

My room was beside Emma's. Her door was shut.

I showered and set out clothes for the next day. I sat on the edge of the bed and sent Jeanette Louw an SMS: IS THERE FILE AT SAPS GARDENS RE ASSAULT/BREAK IN ON E. LE ROUX YESTERDAY?

Then I opened the bedroom door so that I could hear and I switched off the light.

5

Nobody followed us to the airport.

We travelled in Emma's Renault Mégane, a green cabriolet. My Isuzu pick-up stayed in Carel's garage. 'There is more than enough space for it, Emma.'

He had ignored me this morning.

'Do you drive, Mr Lemmer?' she asked.

'If it's acceptable to you, Miss Le Roux.' It was our last formal exchange. While I was familiarising myself with the automatic gearbox and the startling power of the two-litre engine between Fisherhaven and the N2, she said, 'Please call me Emma.'

This was always an awkward moment because people expect me to reciprocate, but I never volunteer my first name. 'I'm Lemmer.'

Initially, I watched the rear-view mirror with extra attention, because that was where the amateurs would be – visible and keen. But there was nothing. I varied the speed between 90 and 120 kilometres per hour. Ascending the Houw Hoek Pass, I wondered about a white Japanese sedan in front of us. Despite the precautions I had taken, it maintained the same speed as we did and my suspicion grew stronger as we descended the other side of the pass when I pushed the Renault up to 140.

A few kilometres before Grabouw, I decided to make certain once and for all. Shortly before the T-junction, I put on the indicator, slowed down as though I intended to turn off and watched the white car. No reaction, it kept on going. I put off the indicator and accelerated.

'Do you know the way?' Emma enquired politely.

'Yes, I know the way,' I replied.

She nodded, satisfied, and rummaged in her handbag until she found her sunglasses.

Cape Town International was chaos – not enough parking owing to the building additions, too many people, a beehive of anxious Christmas season travellers on their way to somewhere and keen to get the journey over as quickly as possible. Impossible to spot shadows.

We checked in Emma's large suitcase and my black sports bag.

'What about your firearm?' she asked on the way to Departures.

'I don't have one.'

She frowned.

'Carel just assumed,' I said.

'Oh.' Not happy. She wanted the assurance that her protector was suitably equipped. I kept quiet until we were through the baggage scanner, when we waited at the Nescafé coffee shop for a table to become vacant.

'I thought you were armed,' she said with faint concern.

'Guns make things complicated. Especially travelling.' It wouldn't help to tell her that my parole conditions forbade the possession of a firearm.

A table became available and we sat down. 'Coffee?' I asked.

'Please. Cappuccino, if they have it. No sugar.'

I went to stand in the queue, but in a position to see her. She sat with her boarding pass in her hand, staring at it. What was she thinking? About weapons and the level of protection she expected? About what lay before us?

That's when I saw him. His eyes focused intently on Emma. He weaved between the tables. Big, white, neat beard, mustard T-shirt, pressed jeans, sports jacket. Early forties. I moved, but he was too close to intercept. He reached out a hand to her shoulder and I blocked him, gripped his wrist and swung back his arm, got my weight against his back, pressed him up against the pillar beside Emma, but without violence. I didn't want to attract attention.

He made a noise of surprise. 'Hey,' he said.

Emma glanced up. She was confused, her body taut with fright. But she recognised beard-face. 'Stoffel?' she said.

Stoffel looked at her, then at me. He pulled back, trying to free his arm. He was strong, but uncoordinated. An amateur. I stayed fluid, gave him a bit of leeway.

'Do you know him?' I asked Emma.

'Yes, yes, it's Stoffel.'

I loosened my grip and he jerked his arm away.

'Who are you?' he asked.

I stayed very close to him, intimidating him with a look. He didn't like that. Emma stood up, holding her hand in the air apologetically. 'This is all a misunderstanding, Stoffel. Nice to see you again. Please sit down.'

Stoffel was indignant now. 'Who is this guy?'

Emma took his hand. 'Come say hello, it's nothing.' She pulled him away from me. He allowed it. She offered her cheek. He kissed it quickly, as if he still expected me to do something unexpected.

'Coffee?' I asked in a friendly tone.

He didn't reply immediately. He sat down, slowly and solemnly, so he could restore his dignity. 'Yes, please,' he said. 'Milk and sugar.'

There was a little smile on Emma's face, the anxiety forgotten. She glanced fleetingly at me, as though we shared a secret.

The flight to Nelspruit was on SA Express's fifty-seater Canadair jet. I sat beside Emma, on the aisle; she sat by the window. The plane was nearly full. There were at least ten passengers who, according to age, gender and level of interest, could qualify as members of Emma's imaginary opponents. I had my doubts. To place someone on a plane as a tail is overkill, because the point of departure and arrival is known.

Before we took off she said, 'Stoffel is an attorney.' I hadn't sat with them over coffee. There were only two seats at the table and I preferred to stand for a wider view and a final chance to stretch my legs. I expect Stoffel wanted to know who I was and she had avoided the question.

'He's a good guy,' she said now. And added, 'We dated, a few years ago . . .' With nostalgia that indicated a history. Then she took the flight magazine out of its slot and flipped it open.

Stoffel, the ex.

My assumption had been otherwise – I thought he was a business acquaintance, or the husband of a friend. He hadn't struck me as the kind of man she would be attracted to. And their interaction was so . . . friendly. But I could picture it: they meet at one of the social or cultural watering holes where the rich gather after sundown. He is well spoken and intelligent, with a cutting self-mockery and a fund of judicial inside stories that he tells with flourish. His attention to Emma would be subtle, he would have a method with women, a recipe he had perfected over twenty bachelor years. She would find it pleasant. When he procured her number from a mutual acquaintance four or five days later, she would remember who he was. She would accept the invitation to the top-ten restaurant. Or the art exhibition, or the symphony concert. She would know from the start that he was not really her type, but she would give it a chance. By her mid-thirties she would have learned enough about people in general and men in particular to know that her type had complications. A woman like Emma would be attracted to the *Men's Health* cover man – a finely sculpted Greek god only half a metre taller than she was. So that they would make a fine picture as a couple.

Her sort was a metrosexual with a dark fringe, pale eyes and the perfect smile. The sporty, fit, outdoor kind that went jogging on the beach with his Staffordshire terrier, and parked his old, second-hand Land Rover Defender in front of Camps Bay's hot spots, the spade prominent on the rack along with the jerrycans. After four or five relationships with clones of Mr Men's Health she would know that the soulful silences and the laconic devil-may-care chats were mostly camouflage for self-absorption and average intellect. So she would allow the Stoffels of the world a chance, and after a month or so of entertaining, albeit unexciting dates she would gently tell him it would be better if they were only friends ('you're a good guy') while secretly she wondered why this sort of man could not set her heart alight.

We took off into the south-easter. Emma put the magazine away and stared out of the window at False Bay, where the white horse breakers galloped into the shore. She turned to me.

'Where are you from, Lemmer?' With apparent interest.

A bodyguard does not sit with his client on planes. The bodyguard, even on a solo mission, forms part of the greater entourage. Usually he travels in a separate vehicle, always in a seat, to perform his duties anonymously and impersonally. No intimate contact and conversation, no questions about the past. It is a necessary distance, a professional buffer, so ordained by Lemmer's First Law.

'The Cape.'

It was not enough to satisfy her. 'Which part?'

'I grew up in Seapoint.'

'It must have been wonderful.' What an interesting assumption. 'You've lost the accent.'

'That's what twenty years in the public service does for you.'

'Brothers and sisters?'

'No.'

Some part of me enjoyed this, the attention, the interest. I felt like her equal.

'And your parents?'

I merely shook my head, hoping it would be enough. It was time to shift the focus. 'What about you? Where did you grow up?'

'Johannesburg. Linden, in fact. Then I went to Stellenbosch University. It was such a romantic idea, compared to Pretoria and Johannesburg.' She stopped for a second, thoughts drifting off. 'Afterwards, I stayed in the Cape. It's so different from the Highveld. So much . . . nicer. I don't know, I just felt at home. As if I belonged. My dad used to tease me. He said I lived in Canaan while they were in exile in Egypt.'

I couldn't think what next to ask. She got in first. 'I understand from Jeanette Louw that you live in the country?'

My employer would have had to explain why it would take six hours for me to report. I nodded. 'Loxton.'

She reacted predictably, 'Loxton . . .', as if she ought to know where it was.

'In the Northern Cape. Upper Karoo, between Beaufort West and Carnarvon.'

She had a way of looking at you, a genuine, open curiosity. I knew what the question on her tongue would be. 'Why would you want to live there?' But she didn't ask it. She was too politically correct, too aware of convention.

'I wouldn't mind having a place in the country one day,' she said, as though she envied me. She waited for my reaction, for me to tell her the reasons, the pros and cons. It was a subtle way of asking the 'Why would you live there?' question.

I was rescued by the steward, who passed out blue cartons of food – a sandwich, a packet of savoury snacks, a fruit juice. I avoided the bread. Emma only drank the juice. While she forced the straw through the tiny foil-sealed hole with her delicate fingers she said: 'You have a very interesting job.'

'Only when I can squeeze the Stoffels of the world against a pillar.'

She laughed. There was also a touch of something else, faint surprise, as if seeing something contradictory to the image she had built up of me. This average man who had been a disappointment in the conversation department had a sense of humour.

'Have you guarded any famous people?'

That's what everyone wants to know. For some of my colleagues, interaction with celebrities gives them valuable attention currency. They would answer 'yes' – and deal a few names of film stars and musicians like cards on the table. The questioner would pounce on one name and ask, 'Is he/she nice?' Not, 'Is she a good person?' or, 'Is he a man of integrity?' But nice – that all-inclusive, meaningless, lazy word South Africans just love to use. What they really want to know is whether fame and fortune have turned the subject of the discussion into a self-centred monster, news that they can pass on as part of the eternal market forces of information that determine social status.

Or something like that. The standard answer of B. J. Fikter, the only other Body Armour employee that I can work with tolerably, is, 'I can tell you, but then I'd have to shoot you.' It was an affirmation that still afforded status, but the worn-out joke avoided revealing any details.

'We sign a confidentiality clause,' I told Emma.

'Oh.'

It took a while for her to come to the realisation that she had tried all the possible subjects without success. A merciful quiet descended. After a while she took out the magazine again.

6

Kruger Mpumalanga International Airport was a surprise, despite the pretentious name. The airport building, set between green hills and chunky rock formations, was modern and new. And attractive. It had an African theme of giant thatched roof and ochre walls, yet was not kitsch. The heat out on the runway was oppressive, the humidity high. I switched on my cell phone as we walked to the arrivals hall. There was an SMS from Jeanette. FILE EXISTS.

Inside the terminal it was cooler, quite bearable. We waited for our luggage. I stood half behind Emma. There was a sensual curve to her jeans and the slope of her lovely neck and shoulders which set off the powder-blue camisole to best advantage. But shifting my focus away, to compare her to the larger, coarser people surrounding her, I noticed that she seemed vulnerable. She had a tender fragility that cried out for protection, or at least compassion, despite the subtle self-assurance of the beautiful and wealthy career woman.

On the plane she had been charming, correct, humble, an altruist. I am interested in you as a person, Lemmer, even though you are a hired hand.

So many facets.

Lemmer's Law of Small Women: Never trust them. Not professionally, nor personally. From an early age they learn two Pavlovian tricks. The first is a product of people's reactions: 'Ah, aren't you a cute little thing,' especially if the little face is round and the eyes large. People treat them like precious little pets, so they learn to exploit that with mannerisms and gestures that emphasise their cuteness, and allow them to sharpen their manipulative skills into a social blade. The second is the feeling of physical helplessness. The world is big and powerful; they are delicate and relatively weak. The bigger, fuller woman's curves of breast and thigh are beacons for male interest; the silhouettes of small women attract less attention. For survival, self-defence and to stand their ground, they are forced to resort to other means. They learn to use the power of their intellect; they learn to manipulate, to play a continuous mental game with the world around them.

Jeanette had confirmed the existence of the case file. There was truth in Emma's story. But how much truth? Did it answer enough of the questions? If her life truly was in danger, why had she opted for Body Armour's cheapest option, when, according to Carel, she had inherited grandly?

Should I give her the benefit of the doubt and assume that Carel had been exaggerating? Or didn't Emma believe that she was in real danger – despite being a small woman with a predisposition to that? Perhaps she was financially conservative. Or just stingy. Or too modest or self-conscious to bear the presence of two to four men with firearms around her.

Or she could be playing a game.

Our luggage arrived. We went over to Budget Rent-A-Car. My phone rang while Emma was completing the forms. I recognised the number, moved a distance away and answered.

'Hello, Antjie,' I said.

'Where are you?' said Antjie Barnard in her deep, incredibly sensual voice.

'Working. I'll be away a week or so.'

'That's what I thought. What about your turn for irrigation? It's hot here.'

'I'll have to ask you to do it.'

'Then I will. If I don't see you before then, Happy New Year.'

'Thanks, Antjie, same to you. Look after yourself.'

'What for?' She laughed and rang off.

When I turned, Emma was right behind me, with the light of new information shining in her eyes. I said nothing, just took the key of a white BMW 318i that she held out to me. It was parked outside in the sun. I loaded our bags in the boot and did a 360-degree reconnaissance. Nobody was interested in us. I got in and started the engine so the air conditioner could kick in. Emma unfolded a map on her lap.

'I thought we should go to Hoedspruit first,' she said. Her index finger sought out the road. I noticed that she wasn't wearing nail polish. 'Here, past Hazyview and Klaserie, it looks like the shortest route. Do you know this part of the country, Lemmer?'

'Not well.'

'I'll navigate.'

We drove. There was more traffic than I had expected, pick-ups, 4×4s, trucks and minibus-taxis. No sign of anyone following. Through White River the contrast with the Cape was sharp – here the colours of nature were bright and over the top in the foliage of the endless trees, the blood red of nearly every flower, the deep dark mahogany of the people manning stalls along the roadside. Ugly, amateurish signs shouted names, prices and directions to campsites, guest houses and private game farms.

Emma gave directions; we found the R538 and drove on, initially in silence.

When the question eventually came, it was no surprise. No woman can suppress her curiosity over certain things.

'Was that your . . .' An instant of hesitation to indicate that the term would be broadly inclusive: 'friend?'

I knew what she meant, but feigned ignorance.

'The one who phoned just now?' Emma's tone was in chit-chat mode, that neutrally friendly style that indicated mere curiosity, a matter of interest. It was not necessarily untrue. That is how women's brains work. They use such information to colour in the picture. If you have a girlfriend, you can't be a total psychopath. The art is to answer them in such a way that you avoid the annoying follow-up questions. What does she do? (To determine your and your girlfriend's status.) Have you been together long? (To gauge the degree of the relationship.) How did you meet? (To satisfy their craving for romance.)

I just grinned and made a non-committal noise. It worked every time, because it said to them she was not the sort of friend they had in mind and that it actually was none of their business. Emma took it bravely.

We drove through Nsikazi, Legogoto, Manzini, little villages, a continuous monotony of poor houses and restless people wandering about in the incredible baking heat, children squatting on their haunches beside the road, swimming in a river under a bridge.

Emma looked to the left, at the horizon. 'What mountain is that?' She was determined to pursue a conversation.

'Mariepskop,' I said.

'I thought you didn't know this area.'

'I don't know the roads.'

She looked at me expectantly.

'When the ministers come to the Kruger Park for a weekend, they fly into Hoedspruit. There's a military airport.'

She looked at the mountain again. 'How many ministers have you guarded, Lemmer?' Carefully adding: 'If you can talk about it . . .'

'Two.'

'Oh?'

'Transport and Agriculture. Mostly Agriculture.'

She glanced back at me. She didn't say a word, but I knew what she was thinking. Not exactly high risk. Her bodyguard – an unarmed former minder of the Minister of Agriculture. I knew she felt really safe.

'I'm looking for Inspector Jack Phatudi,' Emma said to the constable in the Hoedspruit charge office.

The hefty policewoman had an inscrutable expression. 'I do not know that man.'

'I think he works here.'

'No.'

'He is investigating the Khokhovela murders.' Emma's voice was light and friendly, as if she were talking to a loved one.

The constable looked at Emma without comprehension.

'The traditional healer and three other men who were killed.'

'Oh. That one.'

'Yes.'

The policewoman moved slowly as if the searing heat were holding her back. She pulled a telephone closer. The phone might have been white once. It was battered and coffee coloured now. She tapped in a number and waited. Then she spoke in staccato sePedi – phrases like bursts of machine-gun fire. She put the phone down.

'He is not here.'

'Do you know where he is?'

'No.'

'Will he be coming back?'

'I do not know.'

'Is there somewhere I can find out?'

'You will have to wait.'

'Here?'

'Yes.' Still without inflection.

'I . . . uh . . .' Emma looked at the hard wooden bench against the wall, then back to the constable. 'I'm not sure . . .'

'They will phone,' the constable said.

'Oh?'

'To say where he is.'

'OK,' said Emma with relief. 'Thank you.' She went over to the bench. Her skin had a sheen of perspiration. She sat down and gave the constable a smile of patient goodwill. I stood beside the bench and leaned against the wall. It wasn't as cool as I had expected. I watched the constable. She was busy writing up a dossier. She did not perspire. Two black men came in and went up to the desk. They spoke to her. She scowled and upbraided them in short bursts. They answered apologetically. The phone rang. She held up a hand. The men stopped and looked down at their shoes. She answered the phone, listened and then replaced the receiver.

'He has gone back to Tzaneen,' she said in Emma's direction. But Emma was gazing out through the door.

'Lady!'

Emma jumped and stood up.

'He has gone back to Tzaneen.'

'Inspector Phatudi?'

'Yes. That is where his office is. Violent Crimes.'

'Oh . . .'

'But he will come tomorrow. Early. Eight o'clock.'

'Thank you,' said Emma, but the constable was busy with the two men again, talking to them as if they were boys who had been up to no good.

She navigated the way to the Mohlolobe Private Game Reserve with a printout of their web page in her hand. 'There are so many places here,' she said as we passed the dramatic entrance gates of the Kapama Game Reserve, the Mtuma Sands Wildlife Lodge and the Cheetah Inn, each a variation on the postmodern Lowveld theme of rough stone, thatched roof, animal motif and fancy lettering. I suspected that the room rates were directly proportional to the subtlety of these portals to Eden.

Mohlolobe's unique selling point was a pair of slender, tasteful elephant tusks moulded from concrete to guard the entrance. There was a gate guard wearing a uniform of khaki and olive green. He wore a wide-brimmed hat that was marginally too big for him and carried a clipboard with a couple of sheets of paper. On his chest was a metal name tag. It read Edwin. Security Official. 'Welcome to Mohlolobe,' he said on my side of the BMW with a glittering white smile. 'Do you have a reservation?'

'Good afternoon,' Emma answered. 'It's in the name of Le Roux.'

'Le Roux?' He consulted his list, eyebrows raised hopefully. His face brightened. 'Indeed, indeed, Mr and Mrs Le Roux, you are most welcome. It is seven kilometres to the main camp, just follow the signs, and please do not leave the vehicle under any circumstances.' He swung open the big gate and waved us through with a flourish of his arm.

The dirt road twisted through thick mopane forest, here and there a piece of open grassveld. A herd of impala trotted into the undergrowth in annoyance. 'Look,' said Emma. And then she inexplicably pressed her hand over her mouth, and stared, entranced. Hornbills swooped from tree to tree. A herd of buffalo chewed the cud and stared in boredom. Emma was silent. Even when I pointed at the heaps of digested grass and said, 'Elephant dung.'

Mohlolobe Main Camp smelt of big money. The thatched roofs of the guest units were disguised along the banks of the Mohlolobe river, paved roads, hidden lighting, forced joviality from the staff in their khaki and olive uniforms. This was Africa for the rich American tourist, eco-friendly five-star luxury, an oasis of civilisation in the wild, cruel bush. I followed the signs to reception and we got out into a wall of heat, but inside the building it was suddenly cool. We walked down the passage to the reception desk. There was an Internet room on the left. They called it 'The Bush Telegraph'. An expensive curio shop on the right was 'The Trading Post'.

A pretty blonde waited at reception. On the olive green of her shirt was a name tag. Susan. Hospitality Official. 'Hi. I'm Susan. Welcome to Mohlolobe,' with a big smile and a well-concealed Afrikaans accent. Sue-zin, not Soe-sun as it would have been pronounced in Afrikaans.

'Hi. I'm Emma le Roux and this is Mr Lemmer,' she said, equally friendly, to Sue-zin.

'You wanted a two-bedroom suite?' the blonde enquired discreetly.

'That's right.'

'We're going to give you the Bateleur,' as if she were doing us a big favour. 'It's right in front of the waterhole.'

'That would be lovely,' said Emma, and I wondered why she didn't speak to the woman in Afrikaans.

'Now, I just need a credit card, please,' she said, looking at me. When Emma took out her purse there was a little moment when Sue-zin looked at me in a new light.

The Bateleur suite was understated luxury, but all Emma did was nod in satisfaction as if it more or less lived up to her standards.

The black porter (Benjamin. Hospitality Assistant) carried in our travel bags. Emma pushed a green banknote into his hand and said, 'That's fine, just leave them here.'

He showed us the secrets of the air conditioning and the minibar. When he left Emma said, 'Shall I take this one?' and pointed at the bedroom to the left of the sitting room. It was furnished with a double bed.

'That's fine.'

I took my bag to the other room, on the right, two single beds with the same creamy white linen as Emma's. Then I took stock. The wood frame windows could be opened, but were kept closed because of the whispering air conditioning. Every bedroom and the sitting-cum-bar-room in the centre had a sliding door on to the veranda at the front. The locking mechanism was unsophisticated, not good security. I opened it and walked out on to the veranda. It had a polished stone floor, two couches and chairs in ostrich leather, two mounted binoculars and a view of the waterhole, now deserted apart from a flock of pigeons that drank restlessly.

I walked around the building. Three metres of lawn, then the bush. Designed and situated for privacy. Not a single other unit, each named for some kind of eagle, was visible. Bad news from a bodyguard's perspective.

In theory, however, if anyone wanted to get at Emma, they would have to avoid the main gate, scale two metres of game fence and walk seven kilometres through the veld in lion and elephant country. Not much ground for worry.

I went back in; the cool was refreshing. Emma's door was shut; I could hear the whisper of a shower. For a brief moment, I visualised her body under the stream of water, then went to seek out the cold water in my own bathroom.

7

We walked in twilight to the Mohlolobe's Honey Buzzard Restaurant. Emma seemed a little down. She had been quiet at dinner the previous night in Hermanus. Maybe she wasn't a night person, or perhaps it was the heat.

While we sat in candlelight at the table she said, 'You must be very hungry, Lemmer.'

'I could eat.'

A waiter brought menus and the wine list. 'Sometimes I forget about food,' she said.

She passed me the wine list. 'You're welcome to have wine.'

'No, thanks.'

She studied the menu for a long time and without enthusiasm. 'Just a salad, a Greek salad,' she told the waiter. I ordered a bottle of mineral water for the price of a small car – and the beef fillet with green pepper sauce and mashed potato. We looked around at the other people in the room, middle-aged foreigners in groups of two or four. Emma tugged the white linen serviette out of its imitation ivory ring. She twirled the ring round and round in her delicate fingers, examining the fine leaf pattern engraved on it.

'I'm sorry about earlier . . .' she said, looking up. 'When I saw the impala . . .'

I remembered the moment when she had put her hand over her mouth.

She turned her attention back to the ring in her hand. 'We had a game farm in the Waterberg. My dad . . .'

She took a deep breath and exhaled slowly, trying to gain control over the emotion behind the words.

Deon Meyer

'Not a big farm, only three thousand hectares, just a piece of land with some buck so we could go there on weekends. My dad said it was for us, for his children, so we wouldn't be total city kids. So we would know what klits grass is. Jacobus was never in the house when we were on the farm. He would sleep outdoors and walk and just live outside . . . He always had two or three friends there, but in the late afternoon when the sun went down he would come and fetch me. I must have been nine or ten; he was nearly out of school. He would go walking with his little sister. He knew where to find the buck. All the little herds. He would ask me, what do you want to see, sis, what buck? Then he would teach me about them, what their habits were, what they did. And the birds, I had to learn all their names. It was fun, but I always felt a little bit guilty because I wasn't like him. It was like he only came alive when he was on the farm. I didn't always feel like going to the farm, not every weekend and every holiday . . .'

She went quiet again until our food came. I tackled the steak with a passion. She pushed her lettuce around restlessly with her fork, and then put it down.

'My dad . . . for him the worst thing was that they never found Jacobus. Maybe it would have been better for him if there had been a . . . a body. Something . . .'

She lifted the serviette from her lap and pressed it to her mouth. 'He sold the farm. When there was no more hope. He never talked to us about it; he just came home one day and said the farm has been . . . it was the first time . . . today, when I saw the buck. It was the first time since then, since Jacobus died.'

I didn't say anything. My expressions of sympathy had never been reliable. I just sat there, aware that I wasn't especially privileged. I was merely the only available ear.

Emma picked up the serviette ring again. 'I . . . Last night I was thinking maybe I'm making a big mistake, maybe I so badly want to have something of Jacobus somewhere that I can't judge this impartially. How can I be sure it isn't my own emotion and longing? I miss them, Lemmer. I miss them as people and I miss them as ideas. My brother and mother and father. Everybody needs a family. And I wonder, did I come here searching for that? Did the man on TV really look like Jacobus? I can't be sure. But I can't just . . . that phone call . . . if you asked me now what the man said, what I definitely heard? That's what you need a father for, to ask him, "Dad, is this the right thing?" '

My plate was empty. I put down the knife and fork in relief. Now I didn't have to feel guilt that the food was good and I was enjoying it while she struggled with her emotions. But I couldn't answer her question. So I said, 'Your father . . .' Just a little encouragement.

She enclosed the ring with her hand, lost in thought. Finally, she looked up at me and said, 'He was the son of a stoker.'

A waiter took my plate away and she pushed her salad towards him and said, 'I'm sorry, the salad is great. It's just my appetite.'

'Not a problem, madam. Would you like to see the dessert menu?'

'You should have some, Lemmer.'

'No thanks, I've had plenty.'

'Coffee? Liqueur?'

We declined. I hoped Emma was ready to leave. She put the serviette ring down where her plate had been and rested her elbows on the table. 'It seems as if everyone has forgotten how poor so many Afrikaners were. My grandmother made a vegetable garden in the backyard and my grandfather kept a chicken coop between the railway lines. It wasn't allowed, but there was no other space on the property. Those little railway houses in Bloemfontein . . .'

So she related the family history, the rags-to-riches saga of Johannes Petrus le Roux. I suspected it was the telling of a familiar story, one she had heard many times over as a wide-eyed child. It was a way for her to touch the cornerstone of her lost family, to redefine herself and this investigation in the immediate present.

Her father had been the second-oldest of five children, a large family that placed heavy demands on the salary of a stoker. At fifteen there had been no option, he had to go to work. For the first year he laboured as a general dogsbody at the giant SA Railways sheds in Bloemfontein's East End, within walking distance of his parents' modest home between the sidings. At the end of each week he would hand over the envelope with his meagre earnings to his mother. Every evening he would rinse out his single work shirt and hang it in front of the coal stove to dry. At sixteen he began his apprenticeship as a fitter and turner, the area of his interest.

And thus, in time, the little miracle began. Johan le Roux and his tutors gradually realised he had an instinct for gears, a head for the many ratios and variations they had with each other and the machines that drove them. By the time he qualified as a fitter his skill was widely recognised and his solutions in a dozen different engines were saving the railways thousands.

One summer morning in 1956, two Afrikaner businessmen from Bothaville walked into the big workshop. Over the racket of hammering and filing and cutting, they shouted that they were looking for the Le Roux boy'tjie who was so good with gears. They built farm implements for the maize farmers of the Northern Free State and they needed his talents in order to compete with the expensive machinery that was being imported from America and the UK.

His stoker father was against it. The state was a reliable employer, an insurance policy against depression and war and poverty. The private sector was run by the English and Jews and foreigners, all out to cheat the boere, in his opinion; a risky existence. 'Pa, I can design my own stuff. I can draw up the plans myself and cut the forms and put the machines together piece by piece. I can't do that in the Railways,' was his argument. At the end of the month he left by train for the little town on the Vals river, where the gods prepared to smile on him.

He was everything his new employers had hoped he would be – hard working, dedicated and ingenious. His ideas were innovative, his products successful; his reputation became known in wider circles. It was barely a year later that he met Sara.

This moment is a crucial one in the Le Roux story, as it is in many family histories I have heard over the years. When Emma presented it, there was the old amazement at destiny, the fate that determined a chance crossing of paths for her future parents and so decided her genetic blueprint.

The small industrial area of Bothaville is to the north of the town, on the other side of the railway line. To reach his boarding house in the town centre, Johan le Roux had to use the pedestrian bridge at the station and walk down the platform. Sweaty and begrimed, carrying his tin lunch box, he followed his usual path one late afternoon. In passing, he glanced inquisitively through the windows of the brightly lit, jam-packed station tearoom. And spotted the pretty young woman sitting there. He was stopped in his tracks. It was a magical scene: the petite girl in the gay hat and snow-white blouse, with red lips, holding a cup of tea in her delicate hands.

For a long time he stood on the twilit platform watching out for her, torn by the knowledge that she was meant for him, but that his oil-stained overall was not going to make a good impression. Nor could he risk going home to change; by the time he returned she might have left with the train.

Eventually, he opened the door and made his way through the tables to where she sat. 'I'm Johan le Roux,' he said. 'I look a lot better when I've had a bath.'

She looked up and to her eternal credit she saw the man behind the workman, the gentle smile, intelligent eyes and the zeal for life. 'I'm Sara de Wet,' she said, holding out her hand without hesitation, 'and my train has been delayed.'

He offered to buy her another cup of tea. For an immeasurable instant she hesitated, she would tell her children, like someone teetering at the top of a precipice. She knew with absolute certainty that her 'yes' or 'no' was a fork in the road through her life. 'Yes, please, I would like that,' she answered. In the hour before the drawn-out whistle of her train called her away, they had exchanged life stories and taken the first steps on the road to love. She was the elder of two daughters of the only lawyer in Brandfort, on her way to Johannesburg to work as a typist for a mining company. She had a secretarial certificate from a Bloemfontein college – and a nervous excitement about the great adventure awaiting her in the city. He wrote his address on the back of the tearoom account (now a yellowing, barely legible fragment of history that Emma preserved in an old family Bible) and said she could write to him if she liked.

She had. At first they corresponded for a month or three and then the long-distance romance took shape. Once a month he would go up for a weekend, every week he received a long letter and sent one off. Every now and then, just to hear her voice, he would ring her over the crackling country telephone lines of Bothaville.

Until a year later, when the men from Sasol appeared at his workshop door. It was 1958. Their plant had already been operating for three years, but some of the gears on the coal lines would just not work smoothly. They had come looking for a contractor to maintain and improve them, and rumour had it that Johan le Roux was the master of gears.

The contract he negotiated was large enough for him to open his own business in Vanderbijl Park, but not so generous that he could ask for her hand. He had to wait until 1962, when his debts were paid off. But in those four years they saw each other at least every weekend, and could talk on the phone every day.

In 1963 they were married in Brandfort and together they ran Le Roux Engineering Works – he in the workshop, she on administration and accounts. Three years later Jacobus Dawid le Roux was born and Sara became a full-time mother and housewife. By 1968 they were ready for another child, but Johan le Roux's growing reputation brought yet another revolution to their life. This time it was a long black sedan at the workshop door – and three white men in black suits and hats who had come to see him. They were from the newly formed Arms Development and Production Corporation, the predecessor of what later became Armscor in 1977. He had to sign an oath of silence before they told him about the artillery pieces and armoured vehicles that had to be designed and built. Since they had already established by careful enquiries that he was a good Afrikaner, they had come to offer him the gearing contract.

This new income stream had two consequences. The first was that Johan and Sara le Roux grew rich. Not overnight and not without merit, for the state is an unsympathetic client and it took long hours of blood and sweat. But over a period of nearly thirty years, Le Roux Engineering grew to an industry with three giant workshops and a separate building in Johannesburg for research, management and administration.

The second consequence was that they had to wait until 1972 before they could think of another child. That was the year Emma Le Roux was born. On 6 April, a birthday she shared with the entire Republic in those days.

'Then they moved to Johannesburg so my father didn't have to travel so much.'

My own intuition was that Big Bucks no longer felt entirely at home in the middle-class greyness of Vanderbijl Park. Linden was the neighbourhood of the up-and-coming wealthy Afrikaner in those days.

'And that was where I grew up,' with an apologetic wave of her hand that said 'that was my fate'. I could see the earlier heaviness had lifted, as if the telling of her story had somehow freed her. She smiled a little self-consciously, and checked her watch. 'We must be up early tomorrow.'

We went outside. The night was an incubator of heat and humidity. Far off to the west there was lightning. While we followed the brightly lit pathways back to the Bateleur suite, I considered her story. I wondered whether she ever thought about the source of her wealth, built on the foundation of apartheid and international sanctions and now so wholly politically incorrect. Was it a guilty conscience which made her place so much emphasis on her parents' poor background?

Was the origin of her wealth the reason she had a career, the reason she did not simply live off her interest?

At our suite I asked her to lock her bedroom door from the inside – which, we were soon to find out, was bad advice.

My cell phone beeped in my pocket. I knew it was Jeanette Louw's daily 'EVERYTHING OK?' text. I took it out and sent back the usual 'EVERYTHING OK'. Then I walked around the building one more time before going to bed. My own bedroom door remained open. I lay in darkness and waited for sleep. Not for the first time, I chewed over the advantages of a respectable family history.

8

Emma's cry penetrated the thick sand of sleep: 'Lemmer!'

I was on my feet and in the sitting room before I was wholly awake, not even sure her cry had been real.

'Lemmer!' Pure terror.

I rushed at her door, slammed into it. Locked. 'I'm here,' I said, hoarse with sleep and frustration.

'There's something in the room,' she shrieked.

'Open the door.'

'No!'

I hit the door with my shoulder, a dull thud, but it stayed shut. I heard a strange, vague sound inside.

'I think it's a . . . Lemmer!' My name was a frightened scream.

I took a step back and kicked the door. It splintered open. Her room was pitch black. She shrieked again. I banged my palm where the light switch should be and it was suddenly bright and the snake lunged at me, a huge, grey, hissing, wide-mawed monster, the inside of the mouth as black as death. I recoiled into the sitting room. Emma screamed for me again, and for a fleeting moment I saw her in the double bed, pillow and duvet, everything piled up in front of her for protection. The snake lunged at me, striking again and again, the hollow hiss of pure rage. I tripped over a chair, and the snake's fangs bit into the material millimetres from my leg. As it pulled loose, venom sprayed in a bright mist. I rolled off the chair, across the floor. I had to get a weapon, a club. I grabbed the lamp off the corner table, swung it, and missed.

The snake was incredibly long, three metres, maybe more, streamlined and lethal like a spear. I leapt behind the other armchair, trying to keep it between us; the snake came over the top, its front end lifted high. The lamp was too heavy, too clumsy, I smashed it against the wall to get rid of the shade, hit a painting, glass and wood shattered, Emma screamed. The snake struck and I hit, grazing its neck. I leapt to the right to get away. Swiftly, it came again, unmanageable, terrifyingly determined, as though my blow had released a deeper rage, a long, thick, elastic projectile, the black eyes relentless, the maw aggressively gaping.

I shook with adrenalin. It struck, pain stabbed my foot, I hit back with the lamp, the metal where the bulb had been struck the reptile's neck, knocking the head against the wall. For a moment, it was off balance. I struck again. The lamp-stand was long and heavy. It hit the snake's body where it slid across the tiled floor, and seemed to break something under the gunmetal scales. The snake recoiled, twisted around itself. I hit again and again and again, the head evading me. I saw a line of blood on the floor. It was my foot. The venom would dull me; I must finish it now.

I lifted the lamp high over my shoulders, smashed it down violently. Missed. Gripped it like a baseball bat, swung, hit, swung, grazed the head. Missed. It was retreating now. I held the lamp-stand like a sword, trying to trap the head against the floor. Once, twice unsuccessful, the third thrust of the point was behind the head, I bored it into the tiles. Its long body wound up the lamp and around my arm. With my bleeding foot I tramped the neck down, lifted the lamp again and stabbed the head with all my fear and loathing and revulsion. The snake was coiled around my leg now, the long supple muscle convulsing one last time. As it relaxed, I jerked my foot away and smashed down one last time to totally pulverise the coffin head.

She sat on top of the toilet in my bathroom. I sat on the floor, still in my sleeping shorts. My foot rested on her lap. She carefully extracted the splinter of glass.

'I'm bleeding on you.'

'Just keep still.' Strict, the same schoolmarm who had ordered me to 'Sit down, Lemmer' a few minutes ago. I noticed her hand still had an obvious tremor. She pulled the shard out with her fingers and put it carefully on the windowsill. It hadn't been the snake's venomous fangs after all. She rolled paper off the toilet roll and pressed the bundle hard against the cut. The blood soaked through it.

'Hold this tight,' she said, and pushed my foot towards me. She got up and went out. I couldn't help noticing the imprint of her nipples against the big T-shirt she wore for pyjamas which hung to above her knees and exposed her shapely calves. I kept the toilet paper pressed to the cut. My hands were steady. She was away for a while and then I heard her bare feet moving through the disarrayed sitting room with its overturned chair, broken painting and the pieces of the lamp. The snake lay outside on the veranda. Its long scaly body was still supple and smooth when I'd dragged it out. I felt guilty, despite the circumstances, about the indignity, the sharp contrast between that deadly coil and this lifeless ribbon.

Emma was carrying a small leather bag. She sat down again, unzipped it and took out a pair of scissors. Picking up one of the white facecloths, she began to cut.

'Someone put that snake in my room, Lemmer,' she said in a matter-of-fact tone.

I just looked at the scissors and facecloth.

'That's what woke me. The window . . . when it slammed shut. Or something. I just went to have a look. The window is shut, but not latched.'

Deftly she cut a long spiral out of the cloth. 'Give me your foot.' I put it on her lap again. She took off the bloodstained paper and inspected the cut, which had stopped bleeding. She took the facecloth bandage and began to wind it around the ball of my foot. 'Someone must have unlatched the window from inside last night. While we were at dinner. It's the only way, you can't open the window from outside.'

I said nothing. She wouldn't want to know how improbable her theory was. How would you handle a reptile like that? How do you slip it through the slot of a half-open window?

How would 'they' know we were staying here? How would they have got here from the main road in the night with a three-metre venomous snake and known exactly which window was Emma's?

Emma took a tiny silver safety pin from the leather bag and pinned the bandage securely. She tapped her palm on my toes. 'There you go,' she said, satisfied with her handiwork. I took my foot off her lap. We both got up. At the bathroom door she stopped and turned to me with a solemn expression on her face.

'Lemmer, thanks. I don't know what I would have done without you.'

I had nothing to say. I waited for her to leave.

'How do you do it, Lemmer? Do you run?'

'I beg your pardon?'

'There's not an ounce of fat on you.'

'Oh.' I was caught off guard. 'Yes . . . I run. That . . . sort of thing . . .'

'You must tell me about "that sort of thing", some time,' and she left with a little smile on her lips.

As I lay on my bed in the dark again and waited for elusive sleep, I pondered the way she viewed the alleged conspiracy with such calm assurance. To her it was completely real, an accomplished fact, an unfortunate reality that she had to live with. It didn't make her hysterical, merely pragmatic. Someone wants to kill me – I hire a bodyguard. Problem solved.

It was somehow flattering, her childish trust, her belief in my abilities. But I gained no satisfaction from it, coming as it did from the same woman who was entangled in imaginary plots. Whereas I had initially guessed she was lying, now I suspected her of fantasy, illusions born out of yearning.

I lay in the darkness for a long time listening to the noises of the bush, the nocturnal birds, a hyena. Once I imagined I heard a lion roar. Just as I began to descend into sleep there was another sound: the soft tread of Emma's bare feet through the sitting room, past me to the other single bed beside mine. There was the rustle of linen and then all was quiet.

I heard Emma breathe out slowly, a sigh of comfort. Or relief.

9

Greg. Hospitality manager. He had thin blond hair and his red complexion did not respond well to the sun. His olive-and-khaki uniform was a little tight around the waist. 'My most sincere apologies, this is totally unacceptable, we will move you, of course, and there will be no charge for your accommodation.' He looked down at the lifeless snake.

It was very early and the veranda was packed. Beside the dead reptile stood Dick. Senior Game Ranger.

'It's a black mamba, awesome animal,' Dick said to Emma, as if the snake belonged to him. He was her type and he knew it – a thirty-something Orlando Bloom clone, tanned, a big conversationalist. Once he realised that Emma had been alone in the double bed behind lock and key when the incident with the snake had occurred, he focused all his attention on her.

The black ranger (Sello. Game Ranger) and I looked at the dead animal. The morning was hot already. I hadn't slept much. I didn't like Dick.

'You don't have to move us,' Emma said to Greg.

'Most feared snake in Africa, neurotoxic venom, lung failure within eight hours if you don't get the anti-venom. Very active, especially this time of year before the rains. Very aggressive when confronted, the best thing is to step back . . . ' motormouth Dick said to Emma.

The best thing is to step back. What did he think we'd done? Invite it to dance?

'Then we will have the place sorted out. As good as new by lunchtime. I'm very sorry,' said Greg.

For the first time Dick looked at me. 'You should have called us, dude.'

I just looked at him.

'I don't think that was an option,' said Emma.

Greg gave Dick a stern look. 'Of course it wasn't.'

Dick tried to regain lost ground. 'Just a pity it had to be killed, such an awesome animal. They are very territorial, you know, and they usually avoid contact with humans, unless they're cornered. Hunts by day, mostly. Far out, man, real far out, never happened before. How the hell did it get in? They're so damn agile, can get through the smallest of holes or gaps or pipes, who knows? Sello, do you remember that one we found in the anthill last month? Huge female, maybe four metres, one minute she was there, the next she was gone, just slipped away somewhere.'

'We'll have to go for breakfast,' said Emma.

'And that will be on the house too,' said Greg. 'Please, if there's anything . . .'

'Mamba in the bedroom,' said Dick, shaking his head. 'It's a first for us, but hey, it's the bush, right. Africa is not for sissies . . . I suppose it had to happen some time or other. Radical. Just such a pity . . .'

Inspector Jack Phatudi was a block behind the desk, a bodybuilder who resisted the urge to boast, since his snow-white shirt fitted loosely. He had a permanent frown on his broad forehead, unfriendly grooves that broke the glossy sheen of his shaven head. His skin was the darkest shade of brown, just short of black, like exotic polished African wood. In the pressure cooker of an office he was the only one not perspiring.

He held the twenty-year-old photograph of Jacobus le Roux between his thick, strong fingers and said, 'This is not him.' He irritably pushed the photo back across the surface of the government-issue table.

'Are you absolutely sure?' asked Emma. We were sitting opposite Phatudi. She left the photo lying on the table.

'You cannot ask me that. Who can say they are absolutely sure? I do not know what he looked like twenty years ago.'

'Of course, Inspector, I . . .'

'How will this help me?'

'I beg your pardon?'

'The suspect has killed four people last week. Now he is gone. Nobody knows where he is. You bring me this photograph from twenty years ago. How will it help me find this man?'

She was momentarily halted, yielding to his onslaught. 'Well, Inspector, I don't know,' she said pleasantly. 'Perhaps it won't help you. And I don't want to waste your time. I have too much respect for the role of the police. I was just hoping that you might be able to help me.'

'How?'

'I saw the picture of the man on television for just a few seconds. Would it be at all possible to see it again, to put it next to this one . . .'

'No. I cannot do that. It is a murder docket.'

'I understand.'

'That is good.'

'May I ask you one or two questions?'

'You can ask.'

'The television news said the man, Jacobus de Villiers, worked at an animal hospital . . .'

'The TV people, they don't listen. It is not a hospital, it is a rehabilitation centre.'

'May I ask what the name of the centre is?'

He was reluctant to name it. He adjusted his bright yellow tie, rolling the huge shoulders under the white shirt. 'Mogale. Now you will go show your photograph there?'

'If it's OK with you.'

'You will make trouble.'

'Inspector, I assure you . . .'

'You do not understand. You think I do not want to help you. You think this policeman is difficult . . .'

'No, Inspector . . .'

He held up a hand. 'I know you think that. But you do not know the problems. There are big problems here. Between your people and the black people.'

'My people?'

'Whites.'

'But I don't know anybody here.'

'It does not matter. There are big problems. The people, they fight all the time. There is much tension. The black people, they say the whites are hiding this Cobie de Villiers. They say the whites, they care only for the animals. These men who died, they have families. These families are very angry. The animals are wild animals. They belong to the people. They are not the animals of the whites.'

'I understand . . .'

'So when you go and ask questions, you will just make trouble.'

'Inspector, I give you my word that I will not make trouble. I am not here about the killings. I am truly sorry for the families of those men. I have lost my whole family too. I just need to talk to the people who worked with this man. I will show them the photograph, and if they say it isn't the person I am looking for, I will go home, and I will never bother you again.'

He scowled at her. It was an intense look, as if he could turn her from her course by willpower. Emma looked back at him with ingenuous sincerity.

Phatudi gave in first. He sighed deeply, pulled the file towards him, flipped it open and took out a photograph that he shoved angrily across to the one Emma had brought. The two pictures lay neatly side by side.

Emma leaned over to study the photographs. The inspector watched her. I sweated and studied the poster on the wall. It advised people not to commit crime.

They sat like that for a minute or two, the tiny Emma and the rock of a detective, in dead silence.

'It is Jacobus,' said Emma, but to herself.

Phatudi sighed.

Emma picked up both photos and held them out to me. 'What do you think, Lemmer?'

Me?

The photo of Jacobus le Roux was in black and white, a young soldier in a bush hat smiling at the camera. The same high cheekbones as Emma, the same slightly prominent eye teeth. There was an intensity, an urgency, he wanted to get the photo session over with because there was a world out there waiting. An easy self-confidence, liking the camera and what it was capturing. My father is rich and life awaits me like a ripe pomegranate.

In Phatudi's photo Cobie de Villiers was in colour, but colourless – an enlargement of what could only be an identity-book photograph. De Villiers seemed weary of life. No smile, just an expressionless face and dull eyes, a forty-year-old man without prospects. The only possible similarity was in the cheekbones, but it was vague, necessitating a leap of faith, or hope.

'*Ek kan nie sê nie.*'

'*Dis reg,*' said Inspector Jack Phatudi, also in Afrikaans, ''*n Mens kan nie sê.* You can't say.'

Emma looked at him in surprise. 'And all the time we've been speaking English,' she said.

He shrugged his shoulders. 'I speak sePedi, Tshivenda and isiZulu too. You came in here speaking English.'

Emma put the photos down on the table, turned around so that Phatudi could view them. 'Look at the eyes, Inspector. And the shape of the face. Take this one and add twenty years. It is Jacobus . . . it could possibly be Jacobus.'

He shook his head. 'What kind of word is "possibly"? Do you know what my job is, Mrs Le Roux? I have to make a case against this man.' He tapped the picture of the hapless Cobie de Villiers. 'I have to find him and I have to take him to court and my case must prove that he is guilty beyond reasonable doubt. Reasonable doubt. Those judges, they shout at you. They will shout at me if I talk about possibly. Do you understand that?'

'I understand that. But I don't want to take anyone to court.'

He scooped up his photo and put it back.

'Is there anything else?'

'Inspector, what happened to the people that were killed?'

The scowl deepened. 'No, Mrs Le Roux, that is *sub judice*. I can't tell you.'

In the BMW Emma studied the map with great concentration. I aimed the air conditioner's cold blast at my forehead. A great relief. Emma glanced up. 'Can we stop at a garage? I want to find out where the Mogale rehabilitation centre is.'

I pulled away. 'Right, Mrs Le Roux.' I echoed Phatudi's address without thinking and she laughed in astonishing clear musical notes.

'The inspector is an interesting man,' she said. When her laughter had subsided, as an afterthought, she added, 'You are too.'

Categorised with the detective. I wasn't sure that it was fair, but I wasn't going to react.

'Look, there's an Engen filling station, let's ask there . . .'

I put on the indicator and turned off.

10

The centre lay against the lower slopes of the Mariepskop. The mountain, with its forbidding mass of red rock cliffs, was a powerful figure of authority guarding the plains.

Mogale Rehabilitation Centre was displayed in fancy green lettering together with a logo of a raptor's head and an invitation to enter. Plus a programme:

TIMES OF OUR REHAB TOURS
Mondays to Saturdays:
* 1st Tour starts at 09h30   * 2nd Tour starts at 15h00

'We're just in time,' said Emma as she got out to open the gate.

I drove through. Beyond the gate was another notice. *Wild Animals. Please remain in your vehicle.* Emma got in again. A kilometre further on she said, 'Look' and pointed out a swarm of vultures gathering at a carcass. 'I wonder if they feed the birds here?'

The centre was spread out – cages, gardens, lawns and covered parking for vehicles. *Visitors: Please park here.* A young man in khaki and green, apparently the standard uniform of the Lowveld, waited impatiently at the gate. We got out.

'We're about to start the tour,' he said, but not in any unfriendly way. He was a head taller than me, with broad shoulders and an athletic self-confidence. Emma's type.

He led us to a thatched building that was a lecture hall. Several rows of tiered wooden benches descended towards a stage. The audience was already seated, people great and small, with cameras slung around necks and cool drink cans in hand. There was a wilderness scene painted on the wall behind the stage: raptors and vultures in the sky, a leopard, hyenas and buck in the long grass between the thorn trees. The young man positioned himself centre stage. 'Good morning, ladies and gentlemen, and welcome to the Mogale Rehabilitation Centre. My name is Donnie Branca, and I'll be your guide this morning.'

He looked at us and said, 'Vultures.' For an uneasy moment, I thought he was referring to his audience.

'They're not cuddly, they're not cute. As a matter of fact, we think of them as disgusting beasts – squabbling and squawking at a stinking carcass, fighting over decomposing meat. Carrion eaters with beady little eyes, scrawny necks and hooked beaks, often covered in blood and gore and guts up to their eyeballs. Pretty revolting. So most people don't care much for vultures. Well, let me tell you, here at Mogale, we not only care for them, but we love them. With a passion.'

There was something about the tone and manner of Donnie Branca's words that was vaguely familiar. He spoke smoothly and easily, with conviction and zeal.

He said vultures were the big game of the feathered kingdom, an indispensable link between mammals and birds in the broad spectrum of nature. They were an ecological necessity, the cleaners of the veld capable of consuming rotting carcasses from head to tail before diseases could incubate that would create havoc up and down the food chain. Vultures were part of the balance, he said, a perfect, delicate balance that had determined the cycle of life in Africa for a hundred thousand years.

'Until we humans disturbed the balance.'

Branca allowed his words to sink in before continuing. He explained that the problem with vultures was that public and private game reserves could not fence them in. Many birds patrolled areas that were four or five times greater than the Kruger National Park. And that was where the trouble began. They would nest in mountains and valleys, in trees and forests where their ancestors had brooded for thousands of years, but humans had taken over these areas. There was an incorrect perception that vultures preyed on the farmers' small stock and poultry. So, they were shot.

'And then there's the belief among the local people that vultures have magic powers. They believe that vultures have supernatural eyesight that is not only able to find food over vast distances, but is so good that they can actually see tomorrow. In other words, see into the future. Since we started a National Lottery in South Africa, sangomas, as witch doctors prefer to be called, have been selling vulture heads for a small fortune to eager gamblers who believe that they are lucky charms that will enable them to see into the future, their talisman to predict the winning numbers.'

Beside me, Emma was listening with intense concentration.

'The market for vulture parts has skyrocketed in the past few years. Take a guess what a vulture head is now selling for. Five hundred rand? A thousand bucks? Try ten thousand rand. But the sangomas buy the dead vultures from poachers for maybe two or three hundred rand a piece. And how do the poachers capture the vultures? They poison them. They set out a carcass laced with a deadly poison and they kill a hundred or two hundred birds at once, but they are on foot and they can only carry off ten or twenty, so the others are just left to rot.'

The audience murmured their displeasure, but Donnie Branca was far from finished. He began to quote statistics of losses, every species a learned chorus in English, Afrikaans and Latin. The magnificent bearded vulture/lammergeier/*Gypaetus barbatus*, which historically nested in the mountains of Lesotho, was entirely extinct in that country. 'Completely annihilated. Nothing left, not one, not a single bird.' On the South African side of the border only nine breeding pairs remained. 'Nine, ladies and gentlemen. Nine.'

I realised of whom the man reminded me. There had been a lay preacher in jail, a born-again armed robber from the Cape Flats by the name of Job Tieties. Bible in hand, he would preach at night, to himself and a handful of approving brothers. His voice carried through the cells with that same urgent, evangelistic fervour.

The Cape vulture/Kransaasvoël/*Gyps coprotheres*, once so numerous in Africa, was totally wiped out in Swaziland, on the critically endangered list in Namibia, and there remained only two thousand breeding pairs worldwide. 'Two thousand. Imagine just two thousand people left in the whole world. Just try and imagine that. A century ago, there were one hundred thousand Cape vultures in South Africa. This incredible bird with a wingspan of two and a half metres that can spend the whole day gliding on the thermals over the African veld, covering seven hundred and fifty kilometres effortlessly – that's the direct distance between Bloemfontein and Cape Town. Just two thousand breeding pairs left. A travesty, a tragedy, a disaster. Why? Why should we worry that they are disappearing, these disgusting, ugly, dirty birds?'

Because nature was a delicate piece of engineering, he said. It was God's timepiece, where every little gear, every tiny spring, was of vital importance to keep perfect ecological time. 'Allow me to explain: every vulture had its place, its function, its role to play. Different vultures consumed different parts of the carcass – the body and beak of each was adapted for a specific task. The hooded vulture/Monnikaasvoël/*Necrosyrtes monachus* would be the first to feed. Its sharper, smaller beak could rip open the hide of the dead animal. It would be a hurried affair in order to snatch a few strips of meat before the larger, dominant scavengers arrived. But it was indispensable; without it the others could not get at the innards.'

The Cape vultures were the riff-raff of carrion. Eternally soaring high above the African veld, they would look for the lions and hyenas, crows, ravens and jackals that would indicate a carcass was ready. Then, they would swoop down in huge flocks, spiralling towards the earth in wide circles and gathering in rowdy bunches close to the feeding ground to be sure it was safe. And so the maul would begin, the great scrum to get at the carcass. Its bald neck marked it as an internal feeder. The giant beak and strong tongue shaped like a trowel would tear out great chunks of meat – it could swallow a kilogram of carrion in three minutes.

'But the king of the carcass is the lappet-faced vulture/Swartaasvoël/*Aegypius tracheliotos*. It stands a metre high.' He indicated with his hand above the ground. 'It has a wingspan of almost three incredible metres, just about twice the size of any other vulture, and it does not take shinola from any of them. Lappets can travel up to one thousand, one hundred kilometres through the sky, arrive late at the carcass, and then dominate. But here's the interesting thing: despite their size and their attitude, they don't compete for food with other species, because they are specifically adapted to eat the skin and ligaments – and they are the only ones to do so. Isn't that something?'

Heads nodded in wonder around us. I had to concede; he was good.

Nature wastes nothing, Donnie Branca said. There was even a vulture to clean up the bones: the lammergeier. Frequently, it would be first at a kill, but would wait nervously at the side until there were bones available. Small bits of bone would be swallowed whole: 'it's sometimes comical to see the bone go down sideways in the throat'. The lammergeier would take larger bones up into the air and drop them from a great height to shatter on the rocks, so that it could pick them up and swallow them.

'If we poison them, if Escom's power cables kill them when they dive into them, if the farmers shoot them or take away their breeding grounds, the ticking of God's clock will stop. Not only for them, ladies and gentlemen, but also for all of nature. Rotting carcasses breed blowflies and disease, which spreads to mammals, reptiles and other birds. Often to human beings as well. Food chains get broken, the delicate balance is disturbed, and the whole system comes crashing down. That's why we care for vultures at Mogale, that's why we love them. That's why we sit with poisoned birds through many nights to nurse them back to health, that's why we detoxify them, mend their wings, feed them with great patience and release them back into the wild. You can't breed them in captivity, but you can heal them, save the injured and the sick. You can go out and educate farmers and sangomas, talk to them, plead with them, explain to them that nature is a finite resource, a delicate, fragile instrument. But it takes facilities and manpower, training, food, dedication and focus. And all of these things cost money. We get no financial aid from the government. Mogale is a private initiative, kept alive by volunteers working long hours, seven days a week – and contributions from people like you.

People who care, people who would like their children to see a Cape vulture spread its awesome wings and ride the African thermals ten, twenty, fifty years from now.'

Donnie Branca stopped for a short, meaningful moment. I was ready to give him money. 'We also have breeding programmes for servals, wild dogs, leopards and cheetahs,' said Branca. Beside me, Emma shook her head and said softly, 'No.'

I looked at her in surprise. 'Poor branding,' she whispered. 'I'll explain later.'

Then Donnie Branca invited us to view the animals with him.

II

Emma stood in the big cage with a huge glove on her right hand, holding a strip of meat. The Cape vulture flew up from the ground with the noise of a spinning windmill and landed on the glove with extended talons. Its giant wings, spread wide for balance, dwarfed her, and it was so heavy that she had to support her outstretched arm with the other.

'Hold that meat as tightly as you can,' Donnie Branca said, but to no avail. The beak took hold of the strip and pulled it effortlessly from her grasp.

I stood behind the other visitors at the door to the cage, watching the childlike wonder on Emma's face.

'*Jislaaik*,' she said, and the vulture flew off her hand, stroking her short hair with its long wing feathers. The crowd applauded.

Donnie Branca stood at the gate, just beyond the collection box, to thank the visitors and wish them goodbye. Emma made sure we were at the back. Branca smiled at her and put out a hand. 'You were a real trooper with the feeding,' he said.

'Mr Branca.' She shook his hand.

'Call me Donnie.' He liked her.

'My name is Emma le Roux. I would like to talk to someone about Jacobus de Villiers.'

It took him a second to change gear. The perfect white teeth disappeared. 'Cobie?'

'Yes,' said Emma.

Branca looked at her as if seeing her for the first time, with much-diminished interest. 'Are you from the papers?'

'I'm a consultant from Cape Town. Jacobus is my brother.' She zipped open her handbag.

'Your brother?'

Emma took out her photo. She handed it to Branca. He took it and studied it intently.

'But Cobie . . . I thought . . .' He passed the picture back to her. 'I think you should talk to Frank.'

'Frank?'

'Frank Wolhuter. The manager.'

Frank Wolhuter's office did not have air conditioning. It smelt strongly of animals, sweat and pipe tobacco. He got up and offered Emma his hand, blue eyes scanning her up and down. He was as sinewy as biltong, with a Jan Smuts goatee and thick grey hair long in need of a trim. He introduced himself with the happy smile of a man expecting good news.

'Emma le Roux, and this is Mr Lemmer.'

'Please, sit down. What can I do for you good people?' He must have been well into his fifties, his face deeply lined with character built by a life in the sun and wind.

We sat.

'I suspect Cobie de Villiers is my brother,' Emma said.

The smile froze and then systematically crumbled. He stared at Emma and eventually said, 'You suspect?'

'I last saw him twenty years ago. I believed he was dead.'

'Miss de Villiers . . .'

'Le Roux.'

'Of course. Mrs Le Roux . . .'

'Miss.'

'Le Roux is your maiden name?'

'Le Roux was Jacobus's surname too, Mr Wolhuter. It's a long story . . .'

Frank Wolhuter slowly sank back into the worn brown leather chair. 'Jacobus le Roux.' He seemed to taste the name. 'You must excuse me, but under the circumstances you may find me somewhat sceptical.'

Emma nodded and opened her handbag. There was no need to wonder why. The photograph appeared. She put it on the desk and pushed it towards Wolhuter. He put a hand in his shirt pocket and drew out a pair of reading glasses which he placed on the bridge of his nose. He took the photo and studied it at length. Outside, a rehabilitating lion roared in its pen. Birds screeched. It wasn't unbearably hot inside, perhaps because the curtains were half closed. Emma watched Wolhuter patiently.

He put the photo down, took off the glasses, placed them on the table, pulled open a drawer and took out a pipe with a long straight stem. Next a box of matches. He bit the pipe stem between his teeth, struck a match and held it to the tobacco. He sucked the pipe alight with practised ease and blew smoke at the ceiling.

'Ag, no,' he said, and looked at Emma. 'That's not Cobie.'

'Mr Wolhuter . . .'

'Call me Frank.'

'Did you know Jacobus when he was twenty?' I was amazed at the tone of her voice, so reasonable and pleasant.

'No.' Sucking his pipe.

'Can you say with absolute certainty that that is not his photograph?'

Wolhuter merely looked over his pipe at her.

'That is all I'm after. Absolute certainty.' She smiled at him. It was a pretty smile. I was sure he would not be able to resist it.

Frank Wolhuter worked on a big ball of smoke and then said, 'Tell me your long story, Miss le Roux,' but his eyes were narrowed, an unbeliever.

She said nothing about the attack. A smart move, since I hadn't found it all that convincing. But this time she told her story in chronological order. Maybe she was learning. She began in 1986, the year her brother disappeared. And how, twenty years later, she saw a face on television and received a mysterious phone call. It was in the same hesitant style of incomplete sentences, as if even she didn't totally believe in what she was saying. Maybe she was too afraid to believe. When she had finished, Wolhuter passed the photo to Branca.

'I've seen it,' the younger man said.

'And what do you think?'

'There is a similarity.'

Wolhuter took the photo back. He looked at it again. Gave it back to Emma. He put the pipe back in the still-open drawer.

'Miss le Roux . . .'

'Emma.'

'Emma, do you have an identity document with you?

A little frown. 'Yes.'

'May I see it?'

She glanced at me and then put her hand in her bag. She took out an ID book and gave it to Wolhuter. He opened it at the photo.

'Do you have a business card?'

She hesitated again, but dug out her purse, snapped it open and brought out a visiting card. Wolhuter took it between his lean fingers and studied it. He looked at me. 'You are Lemmer?'

'Yes.' I didn't like his tone.

'What is your interest in the matter?'

Emma drew in a breath to answer, but I was quicker. 'Moral support.'

'What is your profession?'

It was his manner which led me to make a mistake. I tried to be clever. 'I am a builder.'

'A builder, you say?'

'I do up houses, mostly.'

'Do you have a business card?'

'No.'

'And what do you intend to build here?'

'Friendships.'

'Are you a developer, Lemmer?'

'A what?'

'Frank . . .' said Emma.

Wolhuter tried to silence her with a good-natured 'Just a sec, Emmatjie . . .', using the Afrikaans diminutive. Bad choice of words.

'I am not Emmatjie.' For the first time since I had met her, there was ice in her tone. I looked at her. Wolhuter and Branca looked at her. She sat up straight, cheeks lightly flushed. 'My name is Emma. If you don't like that, try Miss le Roux. Those are the only two acceptable options. Are we all clear?'

I wondered fleetingly why she needed a bodyguard.

Nobody said a word. Emma filled in the vacuum. 'Lemmer is here because I asked him to be. I am here to find out whether Cobie de Villiers is my brother. That is all. And we shall do that with or without your help.'

12

Wolhuter raised a bony hand and slowly rubbed his goatee. Then his face eroded into a wary smile. 'Emma,' he said, with respect.

'That's right.'

'You're going to need that attitude. You have no idea what a wasp's nest you're sticking your head into.'

'That's what Inspector Jack Phatudi said too.'

Wolhuter gave Branca a meaningful look. Then he asked Emma, 'When did you speak to him?'

'This morning.'

'What do you know about him?'

'Nothing.'

Frank Wolhuter shifted his body forward and leaned his forearms on the desk. 'Emma, I like you. But I see from your card that you are from Cape Town. This is another world from Cape Town. You won't like me saying it, but let me tell you that Capetonians do not live in Africa. I know. Every year I go to Cape Town and it's like visiting Europe.'

'What has all this to do with Jacobus?'

'I'll get to that. First, let me paint you a picture of Limpopo, of the Lowveld, so you can understand the whole thing. This is still the old South Africa. No, that's not entirely true. The mindset of everyone, black and white, is in the old regime, but all the problems are New South Africa. And that makes for an ugly combination. Racism and progress, hate and cooperation, suspicion and reconciliation . . . those things do not lie well together. And then there's the money and the poverty, the greed.'

He picked up his pipe again, but did nothing with it.

'You have no idea what's going on here. Let me tell you about Inspector Jack Phatudi. He is from the Sibashwa tribe, important man, nephew to the chief. And by a mere coincidence the Sibashwa are in the middle of a big land claim. The acreage they want is part of the Kruger Park. And the Sibashwa are no great fans of Cobie de Villiers. Because Cobie is what some would call an activist. Not your usual greeny, your typical bunny-hugger. No. He doesn't do protest marches or shout from a podium. He's undercover, he's quiet, he's here and he's there and you never see him. But he's relentless, never gives up, never stops. He'll listen, and he'll eavesdrop, and he'll take his pictures and make notes – and before you know it he knows everything. He's the one with the evidence that the Sibashwa have already signed an agreement with a property developer. We're talking hundreds of millions. So Cobie went and gave this information to the National Parks people and their lawyers, because he believed that if the Sibashwa's land claim succeeded it would be the beginning of the end for Kruger. You can't build a bunch of houses and think it'll have no impact. You can't . . .'

He cut himself short. 'Don't let me preach to you. The fact of the matter is, the Sibashwa don't like Cobie. Even before this vulture affair he's had trouble with them. Gin traps for leopards and wire snares for buck and their dogs forever running around and causing havoc. They know that it's Cobie that reports them to the authorities, Cobie that shoots their dogs. They know him. They know what he's like. That's why they poisoned those vultures, because they knew someone would phone Cobie. It was an ambush. They wanted Cobie there so it would look as though he had shot those people, the sangoma and the poisoners. But it wasn't Cobie. He couldn't. He can't kill anything.'

'I know,' said Emma, with feeling. 'Then why is he hiding?' The right question to ask.

'The sangoma who was shot is Sibashwa. But they wanted him out of the way, because he was just as opposed to the development. He wasn't stupid. He knew everything would change the minute the big money began to flow. It would be the end of their way of life, their culture and traditions. So how do you solve the problem? You get rid of Cobie and the sangoma, two birds with one stone. Why do you think all the witnesses to the shooting are Sibashwa?'

'It's all too convenient,' said Branca.

'Exactly,' said Wolhuter. 'How objective will Inspector Jack Phatudi be in his investigation? Assuming he's not part of the whole thing in the first place. And why did they break into Cobie's room the night before last? Why didn't Jack Phatudi run up here with a search warrant? Because they're looking for the copy of the developer's contract. They want Cobie's photographs and diaries, all his evidence. Not for the courts. They want it to disappear. Just like they want Cobie to disappear. They want to take Cobie out with a ridiculous accusation, and if they get that right, Donnie and I are next in line; because we oppose the claim and we know about the development. This land claims mess . . .'

He angrily picked up his matches as his voice rose.

'Frank . . .' said Branca soothingly as though he knew what to expect.

'No, Donnie, I won't keep quiet.' He struck a match, sucked angrily on the pipe and looked at Emma through the smoke.

'Do you know how many there are that want a piece of Kruger? Nearly forty. Forty bloody land claims against the game reserve. What for? So they can destroy that, too? Just go and see what the blacks have done with the farms they got here in the Lowveld. With their land claims. I'm not a racist, I'm talking facts. Go and have a look at what it looks like. It was prime land; successful, productive white farmers had to get off, and now it's a wasteland, the people are dying of hunger. Everything is broken – the borehole pumps, the irrigation pipes, the tractors, the pick-ups, and all that money the government put in, gone. Wasted. And what do they do? They say "give us more" and they do nothing and half of them have moved back to where they lived before the whole thing started.'

His pipe had gone out. He struck another match, but it never reached the pipe. 'These are the same people that want a piece of Kruger, because their great-great-grandfather had three cows that grazed there in seventeen-something. Give it to them and see what happens. Chop up the park in forty bits of tribal land and that's the end, I'm telling you, we can all pack our bags and move to Australia, there'll be nothing left here anyway.'

He leaned back in his chair. 'And it's not just the blacks. Greed has no colour.'

He jabbed his pipe stem at me. 'That's why I get edgy when a man comes in here and says he's a builder. There are a lot of them sneaking around here. White guys. Skinny little city slickers in collar and tie, with dollars signs in their eyes and "Development" on their business cards. They feel nothing for conservation. They haven't come to uplift the disadvantaged. They come here and seduce the people. They create these visions of pots of gold at the end of the land claim rainbow. The people are so poor, they want to believe in it, they are blinded.'

'Golf estates,' said Donnie Branca in great distaste.

'Picture that,' Frank Wolhuter said, his deep voice passionate again. 'Go and look at the Garden Route. See what the golf estates have done there. All under the banner of conservation. Show me one thing they have conserved there. Trashed, yes. Wasted. They use more water per hectare than any other kind of development in the world, and now I hear they are going to develop golf estates in the Little Karoo, because there's no more land left on the coast. With what water, I ask you? The only water is underground and that is a finite resource, but develop they will, because the money calls. And here? A golf estate in the Kruger Park? Can you picture that? Can you see how it would ruin the fauna and flora and the water resources, here where we have a terrible drought every other year?'

'What will be left for our children?' Branca asked.

'Nothing,' said Wolhuter. 'Except eighteen holes and a few impala beside the eighteenth green.'

Then they fell silent and the sounds of the animals in the pens filtered through the curtains like an approving audience.

Emma le Roux stared at the opposite wall for a long time before taking her ID book and putting it away in her bag. She left the visiting card on the desk. 'Where is Jacobus now?' she asked.

Wolhuter's anger was spent, his voice calm. 'I can't tell you.'

'Can you give him a message?'

'No, I mean I don't know where he is. Nobody knows where he is.'

'Maybe he's gone back to Swaziland,' said Donnie Branca.

'Oh?'

'That's where he comes from,' said Wolhuter. 'Are you from Swaziland too?'

'No,' said Emma.

Wolhuter raised his hands in a gesture that said 'there you are, then'.

'How long have you known Jacobus?'

'Let's see now . . . Five . . . no, six years.'

'And are you sure he's definitely from Swaziland?'

'That's what he said.'

'Does he still have relations there?'

Wolhuter sank back into the chair. 'Not that I know of. I sort of had the impression that he was an orphan. Donnie? Did he ever speak of his people?'

'I don't know. You know Cobie. Not a great talker.'

'Where in Swaziland?'

Wolhuter shook his head. 'Emma, you have to understand. We don't ask people for their CVs when they come and work here. Most of them are temporary. There's always an oversupply of volunteers. They do the tour and get all bright eyed, especially the young people and the tourists. It's a peculiar thing; I think the churches see a lot of it. From the start I say board and lodging is on the house, but no pay. You work for the cause and we see how it goes. We need the extra hands, but they don't last. Two months or so of sweeping bird shit out of the cages and dragging stinking carcasses out to the vulture restaurant and their eyes stop shining, the excuses begin and they move on. But not Cobie. He was here three, four days and I knew he would stay.'

'Did you ask for a CV?'

'For a job that pays nothing?'

'Did he work for six years without salary?'

Wolhuter laughed. 'Of course not. By the time we put him on the payroll, I knew him. A man's character tells you more than a CV.'

'Where was he before he started work here?'

'He worked for a man near the Swazi border. Heuningrand.'

'Heuningklip,' said Branca. 'Stefan Moller's. Stef. Multimillio-naire, but he does fantastic work.'

'What sort of work?'

Wolhuter looked at Branca. 'You know more than I do, Donnie.'

Branca shrugged. 'There was this article in *Africa Geographic* . . . about Moller buying three or four farms beside the Songimvelo Game Reserve. Abused land, overgrazed, overcropped, eroded, scrap lying around. Moller put a lot of money in to fix it. He called it "healing the land", or something like that. It's a private game reserve now.'

'Jacobus helped with that?'

'So far as I could tell.' Branca shrugged again. 'Cobie's a broad-strokes kind of guy. He just said he was there.'

'What else did he say?'

After an uncomfortable silence it was Wolhuter who tried to explain. 'Emma, I don't know how you do things in Cape Town, but here we respect a man's right to keep his business to himself. Or not. Donnie and I are different. We're talkers. Sometimes I get sick of hearing my own stories. I was a game warden for Natal Parks Board all my life, and if you would come and sit by the fire with me tonight I would tell you stories until the sun came up. Donnie's people are from Portuguese Mozambique, and that's an interesting history. Donnie tells it beautifully. But Cobie's differ-ent. He'll sit there and if I'm telling stories about animals he'll soak up every word. Then he asks questions about it, non-stop, to the point of rudeness. Like he wants to suck you dry, hear everything, learn everything. When we talk about other things he switches off, just gets up and goes. He's just not interested. It took me a long time to get used to that. We all tell stories about ourselves – most of us. It's how we tell the world who we are, or who we would like to be. But not Cobie. He doesn't really care how people see him, or don't see him. He lives in a narrow world . . . one-dimensional . . . and people are not part of that dimension.'

'Cobie doesn't like the concept of people,' said Branca.

Emma waited for him to explain.

'He calls humanity the greatest plague the planet has ever known. He says there are too many people, but that's not the real problem. He says that if a man must choose between wealth and conservation, wealth will always win. We will always over-exploit, we will never be cured.'

'That's why we know so little about Cobie. I can tell you he grew up somewhere in Swaziland; I think his father was a farmer, because now and then he mentions a farm. I know he only has Matric. And he worked for Stef Moller before he came here. That's all I know of his history.'

'And there was a girlfriend,' Branca said.

That made Emma sit up. 'A girlfriend? Where?'

'When he worked at Stef's. He said something once . . .'

'How do I get to Stef Moller's?'

13

The barrel of a gun changes everything.

It was quiet in the car when we drove away from Wolhuter and Branca. I pondered the way Emma le Roux had spoken just before we left. She had smoothly and expertly explained their mistake in brand positioning – no hesitant, incomplete sentences, no break in rhythm. With that lovely musical voice and the light of assurance shining in her eyes she had told them that Donnie Branca's lecture to the public was outstanding, but it had one great failing. If they put that right the donations would increase considerably.

That got their attention right away.

She explained how branding worked, brand name positioning. Every product represents an idea in the mind of a client, a single concept. Take vehicle manufacturers: one occupies the position of 'safety' – Volvo. One occupies 'driving pleasure' – BMW. One represents 'reliability' – Toyota. But no brand name can have more than one position. The human mind does not allow it. When a brand tries that, it fails, without exception.

At Mogale, she had said with knowledgeable enthusiasm, the same principle applied. Vulture rehabilitation was perfect. It was original, unique, strong, fresh, decidedly different – everything required for strong positioning. Branca's lecture was the perfect pitch – it entertained, educated, was emotional, and spoke straight to people's hearts. Until he mentioned the other animals, the cheetahs, wildcats, leopards and wild dogs. Then, Mogale became just another brand trying to be everything to everyone.

'You have two choices. Give the mammal programmes another brand name, or leave them out of the lecture entirely. You make the donors soft on vultures. They sit there thinking, "How much can I give to this amazing cause?" but then you go and multiply their choices suddenly, for no reason, and they don't know how their money will be spent. If this was my concern, I would shift the other animals out, away from the raptors, set up another centre with another name, where the lecture and the tour focus on one species only.'

On the way out I considered it confirmation of my suspicion that she was – lying is not the exact word – about the other stuff, the attack, Jacobus.

It was my job for twenty years to spot threatening behaviour in people. The best indicator of that was a break in rhythm. Someone out of step with the flow of a crowd, someone whose breathing, movement or facial musculature danced to a different tune. The rhythms of speech – everyone has their own, but when there were great and sudden changes, it meant tension and stress, the bosom buddies of the lie.

Why she should lie, and about what, I could only speculate. People have many inexplicable, complex or simple reasons to lie. Sometimes they do it simply because they can. But Emma needed a motive.

The next item to occupy my mind was the formulation of a new Lemmer Law on Animal Fanatics, but I never got that far. When we drove out of Mogale's gate the silver Opel Astra was parked across the road, noticeably and blatantly waiting for us.

There were two men in it, a black man in the driver's seat, a white man in the passenger's. But it was the barrel of a rifle that got my adrenalin pumping. It was propped vertically in front of the passenger, the barrel obscuring his face. The shape of the sight and muzzle identified it as an R4.

Emma was occupied with the road map, so she didn't see them.

The firearm is the bodyguard's single biggest problem; the unarmed bodyguard's greatest fear. But that wasn't my only concern. There was the possibility that I was wrong about Emma, about the threat, about her relationship with the truth. That had to wait, however.

I turned on to the tar road and drove off. In the rear-view mirror the Astra followed. No discretion. Two hundred metres behind us. A bad sign.

I accelerated gradually. I didn't want Emma to know yet.

The road to Klaserie was straight and wide. Beyond 130 kilometres per hour the Astra dwindled, but then it began to close the gap. Past 150 and it was still there.

'We'll have to go through Nelspruit to Barberton and then take the R38,' Emma said, deep in thought. 'That seems to be the shortest route.' She looked up and said, 'We're not in that much of a hurry.'

I lifted my foot from the accelerator. I knew what I needed to know.

She looked across at me. 'Are you OK, Lemmer?'

'I wanted to see what the BMW could do.'

She nodded, trusting me, and began folding the map.

'What did you think of Wolhuter and Branca?'

Even if there hadn't been an armed threat on our heels, that would not have been my topic of choice. I didn't like Wolhuter and company. There is a Lemmer Law that states that he who needs to say 'I'm no racist, but . . .' is one. I knew for a fact that Wolhuter and Branca hadn't told her everything they knew and I didn't want to be the one to break that news to her. In my humble opinion, the Mogale Rehabilitation Centre was an ecological rearrangement of the deckchairs on the *Titanic*, like most green initiatives. But none of these things were important right now.

I had to deal with the Astra problem, and that meant telling her about it.

'Emma, I'm going to have to do something and I am going to need your help.' I kept my voice even.

'Oh?'

'But please, you must do exactly as I ask, without hesitation and without question. Do you understand me?'

She wasn't stupid. 'What's going on?' she asked in an anxious tone, and then she looked back. She spotted the Astra. 'Are they following us?'

'The other thing you must do is stay calm. Breathing helps. Breathe slowly and deeply.'

'Lemmer, what's going on?'

Calmly and slowly, I said, 'Listen to me. Stay calm.'

'I am calm.'

Arguing would be no help. 'I know you are, but I want you to be even more calm. As calm as . . . as a cucumber.' Not very original. 'Or a tomato, or a lettuce leaf or something,' I said, and that worked.

She laughed, short and nervously. 'I think that's the longest sentence you've spoken to me yet.' Her anxiety had diminished. She took a deep breath. 'I'm OK. What's going on?'

'The Astra has been behind us since the gate at Mogale. Don't look back again. I'll have to deal with it. Shaking them off isn't an option. Opels can keep up and I don't know the roads that well.'

'Go to the police.' So easy. Why hadn't I thought of that?

'We could, but the nearest police station is sixty kilometres away. And what would we say to them? What complaint would we have? The problem is, the passenger behind us has a rifle with him. An R4. He went to the trouble of showing it to us. That has me thinking why – and I don't like any of the possible answers. The best thing I can do is to take the gun away from him. Then we can hear their story. But in order to do that, you must help me by doing what I ask. OK?'

Her reaction was not the one I expected.

'Why is it that you can talk now, Lemmer?'

'I'm sorry?'

'For two days you pretend to be this silent, stupid type with nothing to say and no conversation, and now it comes pouring out of you.'

Silent and stupid. I'll have to suck it up.

'There I was, crying in front of you last night, and you sat there like a brick wall.'

'Maybe this isn't the best time . . .'

'A builder? You can tell Wolhuter, but not me?' Bitterly.

'Can we talk about this later?'

'Absolutely.'

'Thank you.'

She did not react, just stared at the road.

'There's a filling station up ahead. We passed it this morning. If I remember correctly, there's a café too. I'm going to stop at the petrol pumps and we're going to get out and walk straight into the café. Not too fast, not too slow. Briskly, like people in a bit of a hurry. Right?'

'OK.'

'The important thing is that we must not look at the Astra. Not even glance.'

She didn't respond.

'Emma?'

'I won't look.'

'You must wait for me in the café. Stay there until I get back. That's very important.'

'Why in there?'

'Because it's a brick building that will shield you from a bullet. It's public. There'll be other people around.'

She nodded. She was tense.

I took my cell phone out of my pocket. 'Type in your number. Call your phone.'

She took it and typed the number.

'Press "call".'

It took a while before her phone rang.

'You can hang up now.'

I took my phone back and put it in my pocket.

'I didn't have your number.'

'Oh.'

'Remember the breathing. Remember the cucumber,' I said. Then I spotted the petrol station and put on the flicker.

She didn't look for the Astra, despite what I'm certain was a strong temptation to do so. Together, we walked up the stairs to the café and went inside. There were three customers and a short fat woman behind the counter. The place smelled like salt and vinegar.

'Stay near the back.' I pointed at the corner where the drink fridges stood. A stopwatch was ticking in my head.

Thirty seconds.

I looked for the back door. A white wood partition allowed access to a small kitchen where a black woman was slicing tomatoes. She looked up in surprise. I put a finger to my lips and walked past her to the wooden door that I hoped led outside. I turned the knob and it swung open.

Outside, there were four or five cars in various stages of decay or repair. Two men stood at the open bonnet of one. They heard my footsteps as I passed them on the way to the edge of the mopane forest beyond.

'The toilet is that way,' one of them called.

I stuck a thumb in the air, but kept on without looking back, not rushing but focused. It was oppressively hot in the bright sun.

One minute.

They must not see me from the Astra, which was all that mattered. The garage and café buildings were between us.

I reached the treeline, walked another twenty metres straight on and then looked around for the first time. The bush was dense; I was invisible. I turned ninety degrees to the right and began to run. My foot burned where the glass shard had sliced it the previous night. There wasn't much time. Hopefully, R4 and his mate had stopped. They would consider the situation and make a decision. The logical one would be to wait a while. Four, five, six minutes, to see whether we came out. That was all the time I had.

I ran far enough that the building would no longer hide the Astra. I turned right again, towards the road. Jogged now, back to the edge of the bush. Had to check where they were.

The Opel was visible through the long grass and trees. It was parked across the road, a hundred and twenty metres from the petrol station. The doors were still shut, but vapour trailed from the exhaust pipe.

Two minutes.

I would have to cross the road behind them. I jogged back deeper into the trees, turned parallel to the road, zigzagging between tree trunks in the dense growth. I counted steps in time with the seconds. Anthills, thick grass, trees.

Do you remember that one we found in the anthill last month? That was Dick this morning, talking about the black mamba. It put a spring in my strides.

Three minutes, seventy metres.

I found a footpath. Cattle spoor. I accelerated. Ninety metres, a hundred, a hundred and ten, hundred and twenty. Heat and damp in my shoe. The cut was bleeding again. I swerved towards the road. Dropped back to a jog, then to a walk. Sweat ran down my face, down my chest, and my back.

The bush opened up suddenly. I stopped. The Astra was thirty metres to the right, its rear facing me. The engine idled. They were watching the filling station.

Momentarily, I hesitated, breathing as deliberately and slowly as possible.

Four minutes. They'd be getting restless.

The sound of a car approached from the left. I could use that. I waited for it and when it was directly in front of me, I bent over and ran across the road behind the vehicle. It was a pick-up with railings and a bored-looking brown cow on the back.

I turned right towards the Astra and ran alongside a fence, hopefully in the occupants' blind spot. I wiped sweat from my eyes. Twenty metres, ten, five, and then the driver turned his head, a black man, he looked into my eyes, his mouth made an 'O', and he said something. The passenger door opened and then I was there and opened it wider. The R4 was swinging around, I grabbed the barrel with my left hand, the sight scraped deep into my palm, blood and sweat made it slippery, I got a grip and jerked violently up and away. I hit the white man on the nose with my right hand as hard as I could. It was a forceful blow, pain shot up my arm and I felt his cartilage break. His grip on the rifle slackened.

It was an R5, the shorter version of the R4. I got both hands on it and jerked it from his grasp. He made a noise as I hit him above the ear with the folding butt.

I spun the weapon around, cocked it and pressed my thumb against the safety catch. It was on. I clicked it off and pointed the rifle at the driver.

'Afternoon, *kêrels*,' I said.

The white man brought his hand unsteadily up to his bloodied nose, now bent against his left cheek.

14

I called Emma. She answered in an anxious voice. 'Lemmer?'

'You can come now. I'm standing at the Astra, about a hundred metres left of the garage,' I said, and then put the cell back in my pocket.

I saw her leave the café and jog in my direction. The men lay in the grass in front of me, side by side, face down in the dust, hands behind their backs. I kept the R5 pointed at the black man; the white would give us no trouble.

Emma approached. Her eyes widened as she took in the scene, the bloody crooked nose. I held an ID card out to her, the black sergeant's. 'They are policemen,' I told her. 'Jack Phatudi's men.'

'Police?' She angrily wiped the sweat from her forehead and took the card.

'You're in deep shit,' the white constable said.

'Watch the language, buddy. You're now in the presence of a lady,' I said, and moved closer to him.

'Why were you following us?' asked Emma.

'To protect you,' said the black sergeant.

'From what?' Emma asked.

I had asked the same question – and received the same silence.

'Get up,' I said, and took out the R5's magazine. They got to their feet, the constable with more difficulty than the sergeant. I turned the rifle around and passed it butt first to Crooked Nose. I put the magazine in my pocket. 'Your pistols are in the car.'

'You are under arrest,' said the sergeant.

'Get Jack Phatudi on the phone.'

'Are you resisting arrest?' he asked without much conviction.

'Call Phatudi, and let the lady talk to him.'

He wasn't a big man, twenty centimetres shorter than I am, and skinny. He was unhappy and I suspected he didn't relish calling the inspector and explaining.

'Just give me his number,' said Emma, cell phone ready in her hand.

He preferred this option. He recited the number. Emma keyed it into her phone while I went over to the constable.

'Let me help you with your nose,' I said.

He stepped back. 'I'm going to lock you up, you fu. . .' He bit the word off and looked at Emma.

'Suit yourself.'

'Inspector?' Emma spoke into her phone. 'This is Emma le Roux. I'm standing beside the road near Klaserie with two of your men who say that you ordered them to follow us.'

She listened. I could faintly hear Phatudi's voice, forceful and angry, but couldn't make out the words.

'Who?' she asked eventually, worried. It became a one-sided conversation. Now and then Emma interrupted with questions and statements:

'But how, Inspector? I haven't . . .'

'That is just not true.'

'Why didn't you inform us?'

'Yes, but now one of them has a broken nose.'

'No, Inspector. You were the one that had nothing to say this morning because it was *sub judice.*'

'I am sure we will survive without your protection.'

'Thank you, Inspector,' with the same icy tone as when Wolhuter had called her 'Emmatjie'. She passed the cell phone to the black sergeant. 'He wants to speak to you.'

'There are people who are angry with me,' Emma said as we drove towards White River.

I had no idea what Phatudi had said to his sergeant. The conversation was in sePedi. When it was finally over, the black sergeant had looked away into the bushes and said, 'You must go,' with extreme dissatisfaction.

Now Emma sat with her legs tucked up, her feet on the passenger seat of the BMW, arms encircling her knees. 'That's what Phatudi said. There are people who have heard that Jacobus is my brother and that I have brought a lawyer to get him off. Can you believe it? He said he's heard all sorts of rumours and he's worried about our safety. One of the rumours is that I know where Jacobus is. Also that I want to lay the blame for the murders on others. That I'm working with Mogale to derail the land claim. So I asked him who was saying all these things and he couldn't answer me. But he's the only one who knows why I'm here.'

And all the people who'd been present in the charge office in Hoedspruit. She seemed to have forgotten them.

She shook her head angrily and looked at me. 'Why does it have to be like this, Lemmer? Why is there still so much hate in this country? When are we going to move on? When will we get to a stage when it's not about race or colour or what happened in the past, but just about right or wrong?'

When we are all equally rich or equally poor, I thought. When everyone has the same land and possessions. Or when nobody has anything . . .

She wasn't finished. 'But it's no use talking to a brick wall. You've probably signed some clause that forbids you to talk about stuff like that.' Her hands began to gesture angrily. 'What's your story, Lemmer? Are you always so sullen, or is it just that you don't like me? I must be very boring after all the important and famous people you've looked after.'

I suspected the real source of her frustration was that her contrived cuteness was not working as it ought. Not on Phatudi, not really on Wolhuter, and also not on me. Welcome to the real world, Emma.

'I appreciate that you're angry,' I said.

'Don't patronise me.' She dropped her knees, turned her shoulders away from me and stared out of the window.

I kept my voice courteous. 'To do my job, I have to keep a professional distance. That's one of the fundamental principles of my vocation. I wish you would understand; this is an unusual situation. Ordinarily, the bodyguard would not even travel in the same vehicle as the client, we never eat at the same table, and we are never included in conversation.'

And I could tell her about Lemmer's First Law.

She took a while to process this. Then she turned back to me and said, 'Is that your excuse? Professional distance? What do you think I am? Unprofessional? I have clients too, Lemmer. I have a professional relationship with them. When we work, it's work. But they're human beings, too. And I had better see them as human beings and respect them as such. Otherwise, there's no point in what I do. Last night we weren't working, Lemmer. We sat at a table like two human beings and . . .'

'I'm not saying . . .'

But she was on a roll. The anger made her voice deep and urgent. 'Do you know what the trouble is, Lemmer? We live in the age of the cell phone and the iPod, that's the trouble. Everyone has earphones and everyone lives in this narrow little world where nobody wants to hear anybody else, everyone wants to listen to their own music. We cut ourselves off. We don't care about anyone else. We build walls and security gates, our world gets smaller and smaller, we live in cocoons, in tiny safe places. We don't talk any more; we don't hear each other any more. We drive to work, each in his own car, in his own steel shell, and we don't hear each other. I don't want to live like that. I want to hear people. I want to know people. I want to hear you. Not when you speak as the strong, silent bodyguard. As a human being. With a history. With opinions and perspectives. I want to listen to them and test my own against them, and change if I should. How else can I grow? That's why people become racists, and sexists and terrorists. Because we don't talk, we don't listen, because we don't know, we live only in our own heads.' All that in complete, fluent sentences, and when she had finished she made a gesture of frustration with her small, fine hands.

I had to admit that she nearly had me. For a moment I wanted to submit to the temptation and say, 'You're right, Emma le Roux, but that's not the whole story.' Then I remembered that when it came to people, I was a disciple of the Jean-Paul Sartre school of philosophy and I merely said, 'You have to admit that our work is somewhat different.'

She shook her head slowly and shrugged in despair.

We drove in silence for over an hour, through White River and Nelspruit, then the sublime landscape beyond the town – the mountains, the vistas, and the winding road up the escarpment to Badplaas, to the entrance of the Heuningklip Wildlife Preserve. No decorated entrance, just a tall wire gate in the game fence and a small sign with the name and a phone number. The gate was locked.

Emma called the number. It was a while before someone answered.

'Mr Moller?'

Apparently it was. 'My name is Emma le Roux. I would very much like to speak to you about Cobie de Villiers.'

She listened, said, 'Thank you,' and disconnected the call.

'He's sending someone to unlock the gate.' She was irritated.

Ten minutes of silence passed before a young white man in blue overalls arrived in a pick-up. He said his name was Septimus. He had a squint in one eye. 'Uncle Stef is in the shed. Follow me.'

'Ah, my dear, I have to honestly say that it doesn't look like Cobie,' said Stef Moller, multimillionaire, apologetically and carefully, as he passed the picture back to Emma with grimy fingers.

He stood in a large corrugated-iron shed alongside a tractor that he had been working on when we entered. A muddle of tools, spares, drums, cans, steel shelving, workbenches, tins, paintbrushes, coffee mugs, empty Coke bottles, old tyres, a plate with breadcrumbs, the smell of diesel and lucerne. The standard farm shed. There was something that tugged faintly on my subconscious. Perhaps it was the contrast between expectation and reality. There was oil on Moller's bleached T-shirt and jeans. He was close on sixty, tall and almost totally bald. Strong workman's hands. His eyes were large and they blinked behind large gold-rimmed spectacles. His speech was painfully slow, like a tap dripping. He didn't look like a rich man.

Emma took the photo without a word. She couldn't hide her disappointment. The day had begun to take its toll.

'I'm sorry,' said Moller sincerely.

'It's OK,' said Emma. She didn't mean it.

So we stood in silence in the gloom of the shed. The zinc roof creaked in the heat. Moller's eyes blinked as he looked from me to Emma, and back to me.

Rather reluctantly, she asked: 'Mr Moller, how long did he work for you?'

'Just Stef, my dear.' He hesitated as if it were a weighty decision. 'Perhaps we should have something to drink up there.' He pointed a dirty fingernail towards the house.

We went out and I couldn't rid myself of the feeling that I had seen something vital.

The homestead was without character, a white house, bleached corrugated-iron roof, built in the unimaginative seventies, perhaps, and fixed up a bit later. We sat on a veranda made of paved cement blocks. I satisfied my hunger from a big bowl of biltong and drank three glasses of Coke. Moller apologised for bringing the refreshments himself on a tray. 'There's only Septimus and myself, no other labour. I'm afraid there's only Coke, will that do?'

'Of course,' Emma replied.

He related his story for Emma. I could see that he liked her in a shy, apologetic way.

He said that he remembered Cobie de Villiers well. 'He turned up here in ninety-four, March, I think, in a beat-up old Nissan 1400 pick-up.' He spoke in a measured, unhurried way, like a man dictating to a dim secretary. 'In those days I didn't lock the gate. He came knocking on the door.'

When Moller answered the door, he found a young man standing with his baseball cap in his hand who said, 'Oom, I hear you are making a game reserve,' using the unique Afrikaans term of respect for elders.

Moller said that was so.

'Then I would really like to work for you.'

'There are lots of game farms with jobs for game rangers . . .'

'They want guides to take the tourists around, oom. I don't want to do that. I want to work with the animals. That is the only thing I can do. I heard you don't go in for tourists.'

There was something about Cobus, a simple determination, and a strong conviction, which appealed to Moller. He invited him in, and asked for references.

'Sorry, oom, I don't have any. But I have two hands that can do anything and you can ask me anything about conservation. Anything.'

So Moller asked him whether it would be a good thing to plant ilala palms on the reserve.

'No, oom.'

'Why not? They are good food. For the fruit bats. And the monkeys and elephants and baboons like the nuts too . . .'

'That's true, oom, but it's a Lowveld tree. It's a bit too high above sea level here.'

'And tamboti?'

'Tamboti is good, oom. This is its area. Plant them near the rivers, they like water.'

'Are they good for the game?'

'Yes, oom. Guinea fowl and francolin eat the fruits and the kudu and nyala like the leaves that drop off.'

He put him to the final test. 'Tamboti makes good firewood.'

'Just don't barbecue on it, oom. The poison makes people sick.'

He had heard enough. That night Cobie de Villiers moved into a renovated labourer's cottage and for three years worked harder than Stef Moller had ever seen anyone work before – from dawn till late at night, seven days a week.

'He knew just about everything about nature. I learnt from him. A lot.'

'Did he ever talk about his past? Where did he get all that knowledge?'

'Ah, my dear . . .' Stef Moller took off his glasses and began to polish them on his dirty T-shirt. His faded blue eyes seemed vulnerable without the protection of the thick lenses. 'People.' He put the glasses back on. 'They come here, but they're not interested in how we healed the veld. They ask other questions. Where did I come from? How did I make my money? I don't like that. You shouldn't judge a man by how many mistakes he's made in his life, you should judge him by how much he's learned from those mistakes.' He stopped, as if he had answered her question.

Emma took it to mean that he had not. 'Why did he leave?'

Moller blinked rapidly. 'I don't know . . .' He shrugged. 'He didn't say. He asked for two weeks' leave. And then he left. He didn't even take all his things. Maybe . . .' He looked away into the distance, where the sun hung low over the green hill.

'Maybe what?' Emma prompted him.

'The girl,' Moller said quietly. 'It might have had something to do with the girl. The last few weeks before he left . . .' His thoughts drifted off, then he pulled himself back. 'That's when he came to ask for leave. The first time in three years. I thought he wanted to take her somewhere, but then she came looking for him a while later. We didn't see him again . . .'

'Where did he go?'

'He didn't tell me. He didn't tell anyone.'

'When was this?'

He didn't hesitate. 'Ninety-seven. August.'

Emma sat still, as if the information was enlightening. Then she opened her handbag and took out a pen and a sheet of paper. It was the web page printout of the Mohlolobe Private Game Reserve. She turned it over on the table and wrote something on the back. She looked up at Moller again.

'I would like to talk to the girl.'

'She worked at the resort.'

'What was her name?'

'Melanie,' he said, the Afrikaans pronunciation, with a long 'a'. With just a hint of disapproval in his voice. 'Melanie Lottering.'

Emma wrote that down too.

Moller blinked and said with admiration, 'You really believe that he's your brother.'

Her voice was barely audible as she answered. 'Yes.'

*   *   *

Emma picked up her bag and was ready to leave, but she hesitated and said very carefully: 'Would you mind if I asked you one question about the reserve?'

He nodded. 'You want to know why. You want to know what the point is if there are no tourism facilities.'

'Oh dear, is that what everyone asks?'

'Not everyone. Some. But I understand. It must be difficult to grasp when someone behaves differently. People expect you to spend money in order to make more. You develop a game reserve so other people will pay to see it. If you don't do that people wonder what you're hiding. It's only natural.'

'I didn't mean it like that.'

'I know you didn't. But most people think like that. That's one of the reasons I lock the gate at the entrance. They used to come in here and ask questions. Mostly, they didn't understand my answers and went off shaking their heads. Or maybe they did understand, but didn't like the answers. They wanted the right to see, to enjoy, to drive around in the reserve and show the animals to their children.'

Moller looked in the direction of the gate and said, with nostalgia, 'Cobie understood.' Then his gaze returned to Emma. 'But let me explain to you, and you can make up your own mind.'

Blinking, he organised his thoughts. 'Up till ten thousand years ago, we were hunter-gatherers. All of us. On every continent and island. We moved around in small groups in the search for food and water, depending on the availability. We were part of the balance of nature. We lived in harmony with the ecology, in the same rhythms. For a hundred thousand years. The principle of "make hay while the sun shines" was in our genes. When there was abundance, we enjoyed it, because we knew that the hungry years would come. That's nothing unique, all animals are like that. Then we discovered how to domesticate cattle and goats and we learned to sow grass seed and after that everything changed. When we stopped moving on, we made villages. We multiplied and we sowed and our cattle and sheep and pigs grazed in one area. We lost the rhythms of nature. Are you following me so far?'

Emma nodded.

'I'm not saying that what happened was wrong. It was inevitable, it was evolution. But it had enormous implications. The academics say the place we first began to farm was in the Middle East, the fertile crescent of Iraq in the East, through Syria and Israel to Turkey. Go and see what it looks like today and it's hard to believe they call it the Fertile Crescent. It's just desert. But ten thousand years ago it wasn't desert. It was grassland and trees, a temperate climate, good soil. Most people believe that the climate changed and that's why there's nothing there today. Oddly, the climate is just about the same. It became desert because people and their agriculture exhausted the Middle East. Overgrazed, over-farmed and over-utilised. Because of that urge to utilise abundance fully, there might never be a tomorrow . . .'

Moller wasn't the natural evangelical speaker that Donnie Branca was. His voice was softer, the tone infinitely courteous, but his belief in what he said was equally immovable. Emma sat transfixed.

'We can't change history. We can't wish away all the technology and agriculture and we certainly can't change human nature. The peacock with the longest, most colourful tail has the best chance to get a mate; whereas we rely on the number of cattle in our kraal, or the name of the car in our garage. That's why money controls everything. People are not truly capable of conservation, though they make all the right noises. It's just not in our nature. Whether we're talking about pumping oil or chopping down trees for firewood, the environment will be the loser. The only way to keep a proper ecological balance today is to keep the people out. Completely. The entire concept of public game reserves is failing, regardless of whether they are national, provincial or private game parks. Do you know how many rhino have been shot for their horns in game parks this year?'

Emma shook her head.

'Twenty-six. Twenty of them were in Kruger. They arrested two game rangers – the very people who are supposed to be protecting them. In KwaZulu two white men drove into the

Umfolozi Game Reserve in broad daylight, shot two rhino, cut off the horns and drove out. Everybody knows there are rhino there. That's why I lock my gates. The less they know, the greater the chance that my animals will survive.'

'I understand.'

'That's why I don't want tourists here. Once that starts, it gets harder to control. The accommodation in Kruger is insufficient, the demand continues to grow. Now they are going to build more. Where does it stop? Who decides? Certainly not the ecology, that's for sure. The pressure is political and financial. Tourism has become the lifeblood of our country, a bigger industry than our gold mines. It creates jobs, brings in foreign currency, it's become a monster that we must keep on feeding. That monster will consume us, one day. Only the places like Heuningklip will remain. But not for ever. Nothing can stand in the path of man.'

15

In the Aventura Badplaas holiday resort's barbecue restaurant we waited for the manager to track down Melanie Lottering's current place of work.

I ate a plate of vegetables and salad, which was all that I could tolerate after all the biltong I'd eaten at Moller's. Emma ordered fish and salad. Halfway through our meal the manager returned with a scrap of paper in his hand.

'She still works for Aventura at the Bela-Bela resort. They also have a spa.' He gave the note to Emma. 'She's married now, her surname is Posthumus. These are the numbers.'

Emma thanked him.

'She was very good with the guests. I was sorry to see her go.'

'What sort of work did she do?'

'Beauty therapist. You know, herbal baths, massage, thalasso treatments, full-body mud wraps . . .'

'When did she leave?'

'*Jislaaik*, let me think . . . about three years ago.'

'How far away is Bela-Bela?'

'Quite a way. Just over three hundred kilos. The shortest route is via Groblersdal and Marble Hall.'

'Thanks a lot.'

He excused himself and Emma took out her cell phone and began to call Bela-Bela.

When we left it was already dark.

'This is going to be a long day, Lemmer, I hope you don't mind,' said Emma. She sounded weary.

'I don't mind.'

'I could drive if you like . . .'

'That's not necessary.'

'We can sleep late tomorrow. There's nothing more I can do.'

And then what? I wanted to ask her. Would she go back to Cape Town and wait until Cobie de Villiers came out of hiding? Did she hope someone like Wolhuter would keep her informed?

She switched on the roof light, took out the sheet of paper again and made notes. Then she turned the light off and leaned back in her seat. She sat silent for so long that I thought she was asleep. But then I saw that her eyes were open. She was staring out at the pitch-black night and the bright beam of the halogen lights ahead.

Melanie Posthumus sat on the couch of the staff house in the Bela-Bela resort with a child on her lap.

'This is Jolanie. She's two,' she said happily when Emma enquired.

'That's an unusual name,' said Emma.

'We made an anagram with my hubby's name and mine. His name is Johan; he's got a function on tonight. He's the catering manager and it's that time of the year, you know. But we call her Jollie, she's so full of sunshine, see.'

At first glance Melanie was pretty – black hair, blue eyes and a flawless complexion. The sweet Cupid's bow of her red lips was like a constant invitation. She spoke in the accent of Johannesburg's Afrikaans suburbia, with the exaggerated inflection that turned an 'a' into an 'ô'. Her use of 'anagram' was not a good sign either.

'I'll make us something to drink in a sec. First I've got to get Jollie to sleep, she's lekker tired and if it gets past her bedtime she gets her second wind and, as Johan always says, then it's pyjama drill on the gravy yard shift.'

'I know this isn't a good time,' said Emma.

'No, don't worry about that, you've come so far and I'm very curious. How do you know Cobie? I was very cross with him for ages, but you can't stay cross for ever. You have to get closure and go on with your life, you must follow your destiny.' She nodded at the sleepy-eyed child on her lap. 'It's like Brad and Angelina. They had to wait before they found each other.'

'It's a long story. I knew Cobie many years ago.'

'Like in boyfriend and girlfriend?'

'No, no, as in family.'

'I was just about to say, not you too . . .'

'I'm trying to trace him.'

'Family? That's funny, you know, he told me he was an orphan, that he didn't have any family.'

'Maybe it's not the same Cobie that I knew. That's what I'm trying to find out,' Emma said with extreme patience. I wondered how disappointed she felt that her 'brother' might have been in love with this little bird of a woman.

'Oh, OK, I was just saying . . .'

'I'm trying to talk to everyone that knew him. I need to know for sure.'

'Like closure.' Melanie nodded her head sympathetically. 'I understand completely.'

Suddenly Emma's phone rang shrilly. The baby's eyes opened and her face crumpled in dismay. 'I'm so sorry,' said Emma and pressed the button to turn it off.

Jollie-Jolanie's eyes drooped slowly shut.

'You got to know him when he was working at Heuningklip?' Emma asked in a low voice as she replaced the cell phone in her bag.

'*Jo*. That was serenity if there ever was. I was coming from Carolina way. I had a little white Volkswagen Golf, and its name was Dolfie. It never gave me any trouble. Never. So then I felt something wasn't lekker and I stopped and it was a flat tyre. Man, I couldn't even remember where the spare wheel was. Cobie came past, he'd been to the co-op to fetch some stuff with his pick-up and all he saw was this girl with her hands on her hips looking at the flat tyre, and he stopped. Now isn't that serenity?'

Only when she used the word the second time did I realise she meant 'serendipity'.

'Yes it is,' said Emma with a straight face.

'So, we began to chat. Actually, you know, I'm a terrible chatterbox and this good-looking ou was so shy and quiet and then he took out the spare and it was flat too! So then we went in his pick-up to the BP beside the resort and I asked him where he worked and what he did and so on. When he said Heuningklip, I couldn't stop asking questions, because everybody knows about Stef Moller. He's this billionaire that bought all these farms and made them nice, but nobody knows where his money came from and he lives in this little old house and he doesn't talk. And Cobie said Stef is this amazing person that just wants to heal the land so nature can balance and I said "how does that work?" and then Cobie began to explain. And that's when I fell in love, when he talked about the veld and the animals and the economy and you could see the real Cobus, the one behind the shyness. I asked him what is his favourite animal and he said "the honey badger". So I said why and we sat there in his pick-up on the road beside Dolfie and he told me stories about the honey badgers and he talked with his body like this, his eyes and hands and all.'

Melanie's blue eyes shone and she looked at the baby on her lap with a tinge of guilt. The child's eyes were shut and her mouth, a duplicate of her mother's, was open.

Melanie's voice dropped an octave when she saw that the child was asleep. She wiped the moisture out of her eyes. 'That's when I fell in love. And then he just went off. But I've got closure.'

'How long did you see each other?'

'Seven months.'

Emma encouraged her with a nod.

'At first Cobie was so shy. I waited a whole week after the flat tyre, and when I heard nothing from him I took him a gift pack from the Badplaas chemist shop to say thank you. He was back in his shell again, so I said doesn't a girl get coffee on this farm. I saw he didn't have proper curtains even in his little house and I said I would make him some, but he said no, he didn't need them. A woman just knows when an ou likes her and I could see him looking at me behind that shyness and so I knew I just needed to be patient. So I drove out there the next Saturday and measured the windows and went through to Nelspruit and bought some pretty yellow material that was nice and cheerful. The next weekend he helped me to hang it up and then I said, "You can say thank you now," and when he held me his whole body was shaking. I think it was his first time.'

It was after eleven when we drove back to Mohlolobe, four hundred kilometres on the N1 via Polokwane and then right on the R71. For a long time Emma just sat staring. Before Tzaneen her head drooped slowly to her shoulder and she slept, too tired to do battle with all the ghosts.

I looked at her and felt the urge to pity her. I felt like running my hand over her short hair and saying with great sympathy and compassion, 'Emma le Roux, you are the Don Quixote of the Cape, charging Lowveld windmills with pointless bravery, but now it's time to go home.'

Melanie Posthumus had told us that Cobie de Villiers came from Swaziland. He told her his stories in fragments. He grew up in an orphanage in Mbabane after his parents had been killed during a robbery in their farm shop. He had no family. After school he worked as an assistant game ranger, later he got a job with the company contracted to repair the environmental damage caused by the Swazi's old Bomvu Ridge iron mine. He told her wonderful stories – of how the archaeologists worked alongside them to investigate ancient history. 'It's the oldest mine in the world, you know,' Melanie said with authority. 'There were Africans taking stuff out of the ground in 40,000 DC.' She said 'dee cee' with undaunted self-confidence.

She said, 'Cobie was an outlander, you know.' The staff members at the Badplaas resort were an isolated group thrown on their own resources and they would frequently braai and dance and party together. But Cobie hadn't liked to socialise at the resort, despite the stream of invitations. Instead he would take her to the veld when she had a day off and then the 'real' Cobie would surface. It was then that he lived, that the sun shone through him and his shyness evaporated. They slept under the stars, and beside a campfire in the veld he told her that he'd found his niche with Stef Moller; he'd like to stay there for ever, there were so many plans, so much work. Moller's farms covered fifty thousand hectares. The goal was seventy thousand. That's when they could reintroduce lions and wild dogs. But not all the neighbouring farmers wanted to sell.

She was the one that began to talk of marriage, 'because Cobie was too shy'. Initially, he seemed not to hear her hints, later he began to say, 'maybe, one day'. Melanie had an explanation for that. 'He was just too used to being on his own, you know.' She had helped him lose that habit. She let him know that she would come and live on the reserve with him, keep house for him, go to the veld with him, put no social pressure on him whatsoever. Eventually, he began to build up enthusiasm for the idea – in his own quiet way.

I had my own theories about her method of igniting that enthusiasm.

'One night he came to the resort and he was too serious for words and he said before we can get married there was something he had to do. He would be away a week or two and then he would bring me a ring. I asked him what he was going to do and he said he couldn't tell me, but he had to do the right thing and he would tell me about it one day.'

She never saw him again.

'Can you remember the date?'

'It was the twenty-second of August 1997.'

Emma had brought out her sheet of paper – and the photo of the young Jacobus le Roux. Without a word, she passed the picture across the coffee table. While Melanie Posthumus was looking at it, Emma had written something more on her sheet of paper. Melanie stared at the photo for a long time until she said, 'I don't know.'

Her husband, Johan Posthumus, arrived when we were on our way to the door. He was not much taller than his wife. He had protruding ears and a slight paunch. He treated Melanie as if he still couldn't believe his luck.

As we drove off, they stood close together in the light of the veranda. He kept one hand on his wife's shoulder, the other waved us goodbye. I read relief in the gesture.

When we turned on to the N1 at a quarter past eleven that night, Emma made a single notation and then put the pen and paper away and stared out of the window for a long time. I wondered what she was thinking. Would she, like me, ponder the glorious irony of Melanie Posthumus – intellectually challenged, but blessed with an instinctive ancient wisdom, knowing precisely how to use her sexy body and pretty face to snare the reluctant Cobie de Villiers? I'd sat there listening to Melanie, the breathless chatter, the childlike naivety, and wondered: why Cobus? As a spa therapist she must have had a constant supply of more well-to-do, better socially adjusted men. What was it about her self-image and genetic requirements that made her choose the 'outlander'. (That mutation of 'outsider' was perhaps her most amusing misuse of the language. It said a lot about the emerging syndrome of quasi-intellectuals. Satellite television brought National Geographic, Discovery and the History Channel to the common crowd, so everyone was familiar with the jargon, although their terminology was frequently faulty.) Was it simply that Melanie wanted the one who didn't immediately come drooling after her like Pavlov's dog? Beautiful women do that, even those that aren't brain surgeons, because the lovely exterior often hides a gnawing insecurity.

And that led me to wonder whether Emma still believed the Cobie de Villiers of Heuningklip and Mogale was one and the same person as Jacobus le Roux. On what grounds? I tried to weigh the compulsion to track down a lost brother against the evidence of the day and came to only one conclusion – her hopes must be dashed. The evidence was against it. But then, I was an objective bystander.

Emma was no Melanie Posthumus. She was smart. She stood up for herself. I respected her perseverance, her relentless crusade to reveal the truth, to 'know for sure', as she repeatedly said. But could she see the truth when it was right in front of her nose? Could she take a step back and evaluate the facts without emotion?

Emma slept while I answered Jeanette Louw's daily 'ALL OK?' SMS with one hand. I would have liked to add 'except for my client's grasp of reality' to my 'ALL OK', but Body Armour's code of conduct didn't provide for that.

Emma didn't wake when I stopped in front of the Bateleur suite in the Mohlolobe Game Reserve at three in the morning. She was a vulnerable figure in the front passenger seat: tiny, silent, asleep.

I got out, unlocked the suite and turned on the lights. The door had been repaired, the lamp replaced and there was a giant bowl of fruit, chocolate and champagne on the table in the sitting room. I walked around checking the rooms inside, then outside, testing all the windows. Back at the car, Emma was still asleep.

I didn't want to wake her. Nor did I wish to spend the night in the car.

I stood looking down at her for a long time and then quietly opened her door and gently picked her up, her head against my neck, one of my arms around her back, the other behind her knees. She was as light as a child. I felt her easy breathing against my skin and smelled the blend of her body scents.

I carried her up the steps, and when I took her into her room, she whispered in my ear, 'The other room.' I saw that her eyes were still closed. I turned and went into my bedroom. I put her gently down on my single bed and pulled back the covers of the other. Picked her up again, put her in her own bed and pulled off her shoes. Covered her with the duvet.

Just before I turned away to go and lock the car, I caught a glimpse of the very faintest smile of contentment on Emma le Roux's face. Like a woman who has won the argument.

16

At eight in the morning, I was sitting outside on the veranda drinking coffee when Emma appeared, wrapped up in the complimentary white bathrobe, her hair still wet from the shower.

'Morning, Lemmer.' The musical tones were back in her voice. She sat on the chair beside me.

'Morning, Emma. Coffee?'

'I'll get some in a moment, thanks.'

The flaps of the bathrobe slid back to expose her tanned knees. I concentrated on the animals that I had been watching. 'Baboons,' I said, pointing at the troop on the opposite riverbank on their way to water. The males, like bodyguards, kept watch over the females and little ones.

'I see them.'

I drank my coffee.

'Lemmer . . .'

I looked at her. The idea that she might be wearing nothing under the bathrobe interfered with my concentration.

'I'm sorry about yesterday.'

'No apology necessary.'

'It is. It was wrong and I'm sorry.'

'Forget about it. It was a rough day, with the snake and everything.'

'I can't use that as an excuse. You were irreproachably professional and I respect that.'

I couldn't look at her. The irreproachably professional bodyguard was battling his imagination, which had inexplicably crept under the soft white towelling of the bathrobe.

There are certain things you will wonder about your entire life, because you can't discuss them with anyone out of fear of being branded a pervert. Like the fact that I was sitting beside her on the veranda, visualising her pubic area. That abrupt triangle of fine, dark brown curls below the smooth brown skin of her belly. All that was necessary was to reach out my hand and lift the flap of the robe and there it would be, as damp as her head, a tropical shell smelling of soap and of Emma as I had breathed it in the previous night. I focused on the baboons, feeling guilty, and wondered whether just men were like this, whether a woman, in similar circumstances, could be capable of this degree of banality.

'Apology accepted.'

It was some time before she spoke again. 'I was thinking . . . if you don't mind, let's stay another day. We can do the game drive tonight, have a good meal. And go home tomorrow.'

'That's fine.' Had she seen the light?

'I'll pay you for the whole week regardless.'

'Jeanette does the contracts.'

'I'll call her.'

I nodded.

'Let's go and get a decent breakfast.'

'Good idea,' I agreed.

I was waiting for Emma on the veranda when I heard her call me with excitement in her voice. I rose and found her in the sitting room holding her cell phone.

'Listen to this,' she said. 'Let me play it for you again.' She pressed buttons on the mobile, listened to it against her ear and passed it to me.

'You have one saved message,' the voicemail intoned, and then a familiar voice spoke. 'Emma, this is Frank Wolhuter. I believe you were right, I found something. Call me, please, when you get this message.'

'Interesting,' I said, and gave the phone back to her.

'That must have been last night, when we were with Melanie. I phoned but there's no answer. Do we have a phone book here?'

'In the drawer of the bedside table. I'll get it.'

Back in the sitting room, we looked up the number of the
Mogale Rehabilitation Centre and called. It was a long time before
someone picked up and Emma said, 'May I speak to Frank
Wolhuter, please?'

A man spoke over the connection. I couldn't hear the words, but
Emma's face registered shock and she said, 'Oh my goodness,' and
moments later, 'Oh no,' and, 'I'm so sorry. Thank you. Oh my
word. Goodbye,' and she slowly lowered the phone to her lap.

'Frank Wolhuter is dead.'

Before I could respond, she added, 'They found him in the lion
camp early this morning.'

We didn't have that breakfast. Instead we drove to Mogale. On the
way, Emma said, 'This is no coincidence, Lemmer.'

I had expected her to say that. It was a bit early to make
assumptions.

Ten kilometres from Mogale's gate an ambulance passed us going
in the other direction without lights or a siren. At the rehabilitation
centre there were four police vehicles and a handwritten notice on a
sheet of cardboard: 'We are closed to the public until further notice.'
A uniformed constable guarded the gate at the auditorium.

'They are closed,' the constable informed us.

'Who's in charge?' asked Emma.

'Inspector Phatudi.'

'Ah.' Caught off balance for a second. 'Could you please tell him
Emma le Roux is here to see him?'

'I cannot leave my post.'

'Can I go in? I have information for him.'

'No. You must wait.'

She hesitated and then turned and went back to the BMW,
which was parked under the roof next to the 'Visitors: Please park
here' sign. She stood at the front of the car and folded her arms
over her bosom. I went and stood beside her.

'Do you know the police, Lemmer?'

'What do you mean?'

'Do you know how their ranks work?'

'Sort of,' I lied.

'How senior is an inspector?'

'Not very. It's above a sergeant and below a captain.'

'So Phatudi isn't the chief?'

'Of the police?'

'No! Of Serious Crimes.'

'No. That would be a senior superintendent, or a director.'

'Oh.' Satisfied.

She nodded. We waited in the heat until it became unbearable. Then we climbed into the BMW, switched on the engine and the air conditioner. After a quarter of an hour the engine began to get hot. I turned it off and we rolled down the windows. We repeated this sequence for an hour until the uniform from the gate approached and said, 'The inspector is coming.'

We got out.

Phatudi emerged from the auditorium accompanied by our two shadows from the day before – the black sergeant and the white constable with the broken nose. He wore a white plastic strip across his nose and both eyes were purple. Neither one of them was happy to see us.

Emma went up to greet Phatudi, but he held up a hand and scowled. 'I don't want to talk to you.'

Her reaction took us all by surprise. She lost her temper. Later, I would consider this piece of her personality jigsaw puzzle and come to the conclusion that it was her way of dealing with stress – a spectacular short circuit when the wires were overloaded, as they had been the previous day, in the car. But today's was more intense, and out of control. Her head jerked up, she squared her pretty shoulders, lifted a small hand with a pointed index finger and went right up to the big policeman. 'What kind of detective are you?' She punctuated the last word with a stab of her finger on his broad chest. Her hand looked like a tick-bird pecking at a buffalo.

I hoped she had more to say than this single phrase.

'Madam,' he said, gobsmacked, arms hanging down passively at his sides while her finger drummed on him and a deep red flush crept up her neck to her forehead.

'Don't "Madam" me. What kind of detective are you? Tell me. I have information. About a crime. And you don't want to talk to me? How does that work? Is protecting your people all that interests you?'

'Protecting my people?'

'I know all about you, and let me tell you I won't let it rest here. This is my country, too. My country. You're supposed to serve everybody. No, you're supposed to serve justice and, let me tell you, I won't let it rest here. Do you hear?' Every 'you' was a finger stabbed at his heart.

The sergeant and constable just stood there in amazement.

'Protecting my people?' Phatudi gripped her wrist in his big hand in an attempt to halt the irritating poking.

'Let me go,' said Emma.

He kept hold of her wrist.

'You have ten seconds to let go of her arm, or I will break yours,' I said.

Slowly he turned his head to face me, Emma's arm still in his grasp. 'Are you threatening a policeman?'

I moved closer. 'No. I never threaten. I usually give only one warning.'

He let go of Emma's arm and stepped towards me. 'Come,' he said, and rolled his bodybuilder's shoulders.

With the big ones, you must hit hard and hit fast. Not on the body, that's just looking for trouble. In the face. You do as much damage as possible, preferably to the mouth and nose, get the blood spurting, lips splitting, and break the teeth and jaw. Give them something to think about, especially the bodybuilders, who, in any case, have a strong narcissistic streak. Make them worry about their looks. Then kick them in the balls as hard as you can.

But Emma jumped in first. I was ready, balanced on the balls of my feet, adrenalin flowing, and keen for it, when she bumped Phatudi ineffectually and said, 'No, Inspector, I'm talking to you. And I'm telling you, you have only one chance before I talk to your boss.'

That single word made the difference. He was ready to tackle me, but he stood his ground. 'Boss,' he said slowly. 'That's a white word.'

Emma had calmed down, she had her temper under control. 'The other day you talked about "your people" to me, Inspector. The whites. Remember? Don't play the race card with me. You know what I mean. Your commander or your officer or whatever. Police ranks aren't my strong point, but my rights as a citizen of this country are. And the rights of every other citizen, black or white or brown or whatever. Every one of us has the right to talk to the police, to be heard and to be served. And if you don't agree with me, you'd better tell me now, so I know where I stand.'

Phatudi's problem was his two colleagues. He couldn't afford to lose face.

'Mrs Le Roux,' he said slowly, 'everyone has the right to the services of the police. But nobody has the right to interfere with a murder investigation. Nobody has the right to make trouble and cause mischief. Obstructing the course of justice is a crime. Assaulting a police officer is a crime.' He held his thumb and forefinger a centimetre apart. 'I am this close to arresting you.'

She was not intimidated. 'Wolhuter phoned me last night. He found something that proves that Cobie de Villiers is my brother . . .'

Her interpretation of the facts.

'I came here to tell you that, because it's directly related to your investigation. So please explain to me how that is obstructing the course of justice. And if they really wanted to protect us, these two clods could have stopped us and informed us they would be following us, which I don't believe for a minute. I will not take responsibility for someone else's lack of intelligence.'

The two clods inspected their feet.

'What proof?' Phatudi asked.

'I'm sorry?'

'What proof did Wolhuter have?'

'I don't know. That's why I'm here.'

'What did he say?'

She brought out her phone. 'Listen to him yourself,' she said, and worked the keyboard to replay the message. She passed the phone to Phatudi. He listened.

'That is not what he says.'

'Excuse me?'

'He never said he had found something that proves that De Villiers is your brother.'

'Of course he said that.'

Phatudi handed her back the cell phone. With that constant scowl, he looked permanently fed up, so it was hard to read him. He stood there looking at Emma and eventually said, 'Let's go and talk somewhere cool.' He turned on his heel and headed for the auditorium.

'What did Wolhuter say to you yesterday?' he asked as we sat down.

'How did Wolhuter die?' she retorted.

It was going to be an interesting session.

Instead, a miracle took place on Phatudi's face. Crease by crease the frown was demolished. Then he started constructing a smile from the ground up. It was a captivating metamorphosis, perhaps because it was so unthinkable that he could use the same face for both expressions. When the smile reached roof level, his massive bulk began to shake and his eyes screwed shut. It took me a while to register that Inspector Jack Phatudi was laughing. Soundlessly, as though someone had forgotten to turn the sound on.

'You are something else,' he said when the quake had subsided.

'Oh?' said Emma, with not quite so much aggression.

'You are small, but you have venom.'

With that he joined the Gutsy Emma fan club, along with the late Wolhuter, the living Lemmer and the blinking Stef Moller. I wondered how calculating Emma was, how much manipulation was camouflaged by the fearless indignation. It was a new, a third Pavlovian trick that needed to be added to my Law of Small Women.

I studied her. If she was smug, she hid it well. 'Inspector, let's help each other. Please.'

'OK,' he said. 'We can try.' The improbable smile stayed strong until Emma told him what Wolhuter had said the previous day.

17

'Why must they lie? I can't understand it,' Jack Phatudi said. The frown was back in force.

'What are they lying about?' Emma asked.

'About everything. About me. About the Sibashwa. The land claims. There aren't forty land claims on Kruger. Six years ago the Commission realised that the claims were from the same families, but none knew about the others. They consolidated them and now it's just the Mahashi, The Ntimane, The Ndluli, the Sambo, the Nkuna and the Sibashwa. There were two other claims, from the Mhinga and the Mapindani, but they were turned down. That leaves eight claims. Very far from forty.'

'But you have a claim.'

'I? I am a policeman. I'm not claiming land.'

'The Sibashwa have a claim. You are a Sibashwa.'

'True, the Sibashwa have a claim. In 1889 we were driven out. My people lived there for a thousand years and then the whites came and said, "You have to go." Tell me, madam, what would you do if the government came and said, "We're taking your home, find another place."'

'If it was for conservation, I would go.'

'Without a cent in compensation?'

'No, there must be payment.'

'Exactly. That's all the Sibashwa want. In 1889 there was no such thing, just guns at our people's heads, and they said move or we shoot you. Our ancestors are buried there, a thousand years of graves, but they just took the ground and said we must go. Now the people, the Mahashi and the Sibashwa, everyone, all they are saying is, "Let us make right the wrong."'

'What about the National Park?'

'What about it? All the people, all the claims, they are not asking for land in Kruger. They say, give us land here beside the park, then we can also build lodges. Do you know the story of the Makuleke?'

'No.'

'The Makuleke had a land claim to the north of the park and they won, ten years ago. So what do you think happened? They built a lodge and they formed a committee with Kruger and everyone is happy. The Makuleke people get the profit and Kruger gets the conservation. So why can't other people do that too? That's all they want.'

'But what about the development that Jacobus knew about?'

'These people at Mogale, they take these things and make lies out of them. Many business people came from Johannesburg and they said to the people, let us build this and let us build that. The Makuleke put the management of their lodge out on concession; a white company runs it. It's just business, everyone wants to do business. Some white men had plans for golf resorts, but that won't happen. Cobie de Villiers heard stories and he went running to Kruger before the process had even begun, before the people could decide if it was good or bad.'

'What about the vultures?'

I'd been wondering when she would get to that. Phatudi didn't like the question. He got up from his chair and waved his hands. 'The vultures. Tell me, madam, who killed the animals in this country? Who hunted the quagga until not one was left? And the Knysna elephant? The black people?'

'No, but . . .'

'Look at the people of Limpopo, madam. Look where they live. Look how they struggle. There are no jobs, there is no money, and there is no land. What are they supposed to do? When the children have to eat tonight and there is no food, what do you do? You . . . the Boers did it too. Why did the Boer make Kruger Park? Because they, the whites, had killed nearly everything and they wanted to save the last few. Same with the elephants. Because the Boers were poor and ivory was good money, so they shot them. Thousands and thousands. But that's OK, because they were white and it was a hundred years ago. Today, my people are poor. The problems are socio-economic. We need to make jobs for the people, then they will leave the vultures alone.'

'Wolhuter said the poisoned vultures were an ambush, to get Jacobus there. But someone else murdered those people. Because they wanted Jacobus out of the way.'

Phatudi said something in his language, an expression of disbelief. The black sergeant shook his head.

'Inspector, my brother is incapable of killing people.'

'Then he is not your brother, madam. This Cobus, he is . . .' Phatudi tapped a thick finger against his temple. 'They saw him. Five children saw him with a firearm. He went into the sangoma's house where the people with the vultures had gone and they heard him shooting inside and they saw him come out. He was running then. The children know him from Mogale; they came there with the school. They don't know he hates the blacks. They don't know about the politics and about how De Villiers talks about "the kaffirs". They say what they saw.'

Emma didn't want to hear it. She looked away.

Phatudi sat down again, opposite Emma. His voice was gentler. 'This De Villiers, he is not like you. He can't be your brother.'

'Then why was Wolhuter murdered?'

'Who says he was murdered?'

There was a query on her face.

Phatudi pointed a finger in the direction of the animal pens. 'That lion killed him. Wolhuter went in there last night. They say he sometimes has to get the honey badger out. The lion and the badger were together in the pen when they were small, now it sometimes goes under the wire and makes trouble with the lion and then it gets hurt. This morning they found the honey badger at Wolhuter's house, so it was out of its cage. Wolhuter did the wrong thing, he didn't dart the lion with the drug first. These things happen here.'

Emma stared at Phatudi as if she were weighing every word for truth. The stare continued once he had finished speaking, until she sighed and let out a long breath that made her shoulders droop, a gesture that indicated she had no more questions.

It engendered a degree of sympathy in Phatudi. 'I'm sorry,' he said. What for? I wondered.

Emma nodded without speaking.

'Yesterday I didn't have your number. I would have told you that I'm sending my people to look after you. The community is very angry. They say if they find De Villiers they are going to kill him. When you came looking for me at the police station. Someone heard what you said. Then I started hearing the stories, how they were going to . . .' He lifted a hand to his bald head and scratched behind his ear. That wasn't the only sign that he was lying. It was in his voice, too. Up till now he had been on solid ground in all his statements, but in this explanation there was a change of gear – a faint plea that said 'believe me'.

'It doesn't matter,' said Emma.

Phatudi got up. 'Mrs Le Roux, I have to go.'

His sergeant and constable also made moves.

'Thank you, Inspector.'

Phatudi said goodbye to her. He ignored me until just before he walked out, when he looked me in the eye. I wasn't sure whether it was a warning or a challenge.

Emma and I remained behind. She put her elbows on her knees and dropped her head. She sat like that for a while. Then she murmured something.

'Excuse me?'

'I can't go in here now. I can't ask if Wolhuter left anything for me.'

On the road back to the Mohlolobe Game Reserve, Emma asked me to stop at the butcher's shop in Klaserie. She went in and came out five minutes later with a brown paper parcel.

She climbed into the car and handed it to me. 'This is for you, Lemmer.'

I took the parcel.

'You may open it.'

It was biltong, at least two kilograms of it.

'I saw how much you enjoyed it yesterday at Stef Moller's.'

'Thank you very much.'

'Only a pleasure.' But she wasn't the old Emma. The spark had gone out. We drove to Mohlolobe in silence. When we parked in front of the suite she said: 'Never mind, I'm awake,' with a wry self-deprecating smile.

She gave me a chance to check in and around the Bateleur before she went in. The midday heat had reached perfect pitch, a high, unbearably sweltering note. When I indicated that she could enter, she disappeared into her original room, leaving the door ajar. I heard the bedsprings as she lay down. I weighed up my options. Sitting on the veranda was not one of them. I picked up a magazine, *Africa Geographic*, and sat on one of the chairs in the sitting room, where the air conditioner was the most effective. A short snooze wouldn't do any harm. I flicked through the magazine, stopped at a double-page spread: 'Rough & Tough – Honey Badgers'. This was the animal that had apparently been responsible for Frank Wolhuter's death. Cobie de Villiers had associated himself with it.

I read. *To be described in the* Guinness Book of Records *as 'the most fearless animal in the world' is no mean feat, especially when the animal stands a mere thirty centimeters tall and weighs fourteen kilograms at most.*

A man who went into hiding when he was suspected of murder was not necessarily fearless.

The badger's appetite for snake seemed insatiable; we once watched a twelve-kilogram male eat ten metres of snake over a period of just three days. The author went on to describe a badger that had caught a puff adder, was bitten, but in three hours was up and about and consumed its prey.

Unfortunately there hadn't been one around the night before last.

I heard her.

I put down the magazine and listened, to make sure. Quiet sobs in the bedroom.

Damn.

What should a bodyguard do?

I sat still.

Bouts of weeping were interspersed with the sobs, the sound of total heartbreak.

I got up and went over to the doorway. I peered in cautiously. She lay on the bed, her body racked with her crying.

'Emma.'

She didn't hear me.

I repeated her name, louder, more carefully. She didn't respond. Slowly, I went in, bent down and put my hand on her shoulder. 'Emma.'

'I'm sorry,' she said through the sobs.

'No need to be sorry.' I patted her shoulder and it seemed to help a little.

'Nothing makes sense, Lemmer.'

Two hours ago she had been the wildcat. 'Never mind,' I said, but that was no comfort.

'Nothing.' She wiped her nose with a soggy tissue and abandoned herself to weeping.

'There, there,' was all I could think of to say. It wasn't very effective. I sat down on the bed beside her and she shifted, sat up and wrapped her arms around me. Then she let loose and wept as if the world would end.

It took a quarter of an hour for her to cry herself out on my chest. She clung to me initially as if I were a lifebuoy, while I continued to pat her back awkwardly, without the faintest idea of what I should say in addition to 'there, there'. But she calmed down, the sobs diminished, and her body relaxed.

Then she fell asleep. I didn't realise it at first. I was too conscious of my cramped legs, my deficiency with words, the warmth of her body against me and her scent and the dampness of her tears on my shirt. Eventually, I realised that her breathing was slow and deep and, when I looked, that her eyes were closed.

I eased her softly down against the pillows. The air conditioning had made the room cool, so I pulled the bedspread over her and crept back to my chair.

I would have to reassess my opinion of her. She might just be a lovely young woman who wanted her brother back very badly. Maybe hope had faded with every fragment of new information, but she'd held fast to it, had clung to the possibilities of conspiracies and secrets, until this morning. Now she was trapped between two equally unacceptable alternatives: her brother was Cobie de Villiers – and a murderer. Or he was neither. It would be like losing him all over again.

Or maybe I should be careful. Maybe I should rewrite Lemmer's Law of Small Women so that it read: Don't trust yourself.

I couldn't concentrate on the magazine. My hand remembered the contours of Emma's back and my heart remembered her helplessness and despair.

I was just the bodyguard, the one available. She would have cried on anyone's shoulder.

She was an intelligent, socially adjusted, extremely rich, highly educated and attractive young woman, and I was Lemmer from Seapoint and Loxton. I should not forget that.

I realised that it was the second time in twenty-four hours that I had put Emma le Roux to bed. Perhaps I should ask for a bonus.

18

Late that afternoon, Emma spent more than an hour in the bathroom. When she came out she said, 'Shall we eat?' You couldn't see that she'd been crying. It was the first time I'd seen her in a dress. It was white, with tiny red flowers, and it left her shoulders bare. She had white sandals on her feet. She looked younger, but her eyes were old.

We walked through the dusk in silence. The sun slipped away behind dramatic towers of thundercloud in the west. Lightning flickered in the snow-white cumulus. The humidity was unbearable and the heat incredible. Even the birds and insects were still. Nature seemed to be holding its breath.

Susan from reception, the Afrikaner blonde who would speak only English, intercepted us on our way to dinner. 'Oh, Miss le Roux, how are you? I heard about the mamba, we are all so sorry. Is your suite OK now?'

'It's fine, thank you very much.' Muted, clearly still depressed.

'Wonderful. Enjoy your dinner.'

As we sat down, Emma said, 'I really should speak to her in Afrikaans.'

'Yes,' I said without thinking.

'Are you a language fanatic, Lemmer, a *taalbul*?' She asked without much real interest, as if she already knew that I would avoid the question. Or it might have been part of the new depression.

'Sort of . . .'

She nodded absently, and reached for the wine list. She stared at it for a while and then looked up at me. 'I'm so silly, sometimes,' she said softly.

I saw that there were shadows under her eyes that the light make-up couldn't disguise. She tried to smile, but struggled. 'If I spoke Afrikaans to her, there would be this moment. She would say, "Oh, are you Afrikaans?" and pretend to be surprised, but we would all know that she had known all along and it would be this moment of . . . discomfort.' She attempted to smile, but didn't succeed. 'And that's typical Afrikaner. We always avoid discomfort.'

Before I could think of a response, she turned back to the wine list and said with determination, 'Tonight we are going to drink wine. What would you like?'

'I'm on duty, thank you.'

'No, not tonight. White or red?'

'I'm not really a wine drinker.'

'A beer?'

'A red Grapetiser would be nice.'

'Do you drink at all?'

'Not alcohol.' I depended on her not to ask more. As with the Afrikaans question, there was enough probability of an uncomfortable answer. I was wrong, as I had been in most of my predictions of Emma.

'Is it a matter of principle?' she asked carefully.

'Not really.'

Emma shook her head.

'What?' I said.

She waited before answering, as if she needed to gather energy. 'You are an enigma, Lemmer. I always used to wonder what it meant when I read about someone who was an enigma, but now I know.'

Maybe it was because she had referred to me as 'stupid and silent', or perhaps it was because I wanted to cheer her up, that I said, 'Explain to me what's so great about alcohol, because I don't get it.'

'Don't tell me that's an invitation to a real, actual conversation?'

'You said I'm "off duty" tonight.'

'Aah.' She put the wine list down. 'Very well.' She looked up at the candle sconce above us, drew a deep breath and spoke, slowly at first, trying to find the right words. 'I like red wine. I like the names. Shiraz. Cabernet. Merlot. Pinotage. They roll beautifully off the tongue, they sound so secretive. And I love the complex aromas. There is a mystique to the flavours.'

Then more quickly, freeing herself: 'It's like sailing on a trade route past islands of fruit and spices. You can never see the islands, but from the aromas that waft over the water, you can guess what they look like. Exotic, bright colours, dense forests, beautiful people dancing by firelight. I love the colours and the way they look different in sunlight or candlelight. And I love the flavour, because it forces me to taste, to concentrate, to roll it around my tongue and look for the goodness. And I like all the things it stands for – the bonhomie, the company of friends. It's a social symbol that says we're comfortable enough with each other to enjoy a glass of wine together. It makes me feel civilised and grateful that I have the privilege to enjoy something that has been made with so much care and knowledge and art. So, tell me what's not good about that.'

I shook my head, partly because I disagreed with her, partly because I couldn't believe I was doing this. 'Wine doesn't taste nice. Period. It's not as bad as whisky, but it's worse than beer. It's not nearly as nice as grape juice. But grape juice isn't sophisticated, even though it looks different in sunlight and candlelight. Sweet wine is the exception. But nobody drinks that in cultivated company, not even a good late harvest. Why not? Because it simply does not enjoy the same status. And there's the whole answer. Status. It's an old thing. Our civilisation originated in Mesopotamia, but grapes didn't thrive there. The Mesopotamians made beer out of grain and everyone drank it. But the rich don't want to drink what everyone drinks. So they imported wine from the highlands of Iran. And because it cost more, because the common people could not afford it, it gained status, regardless of how it tasted. So they created the myth – wine is for the cultivated tongue, for the well-to-do taste. Eight thousand years later, we still believe it.'

I liked the way she looked at me while I spoke. When I'd finished, she laughed, a short happy sound, like someone who has unwrapped a present. She was about to say something, but the wine waiter arrived and she turned her attention to him and said, 'I would like this bottle of Merlot and I want the best red grape juice that you have and bring us two extra glasses please.'

The waiter jotted his notes and when he had left she leaned back in her chair and said, 'Where have you been hiding, Lemmer?' She held her tiny hand up and said, 'Never mind, I'm just glad you're here. Are you a reader? How do you know these things?'

Four years in jail, Emma le Roux, is a lot of time on your hands. 'I've read a bit.'

'A bit? What do you read?'

'Non-fiction.'

'Such as?'

'Anything.'

'Come on. Tell me about something you've read recently.'

I thought for a while. 'Did you know that the history of South Africa was determined by grass seed?'

She raised an eyebrow, the corners of her mouth twitched. 'No.'

'It's true. Two thousand years ago there were only Khoi and San people here. They were nomads, not farmers. Then the Bantu people came down from East Africa with cattle and sorghum and they pushed out the Khoi and the San people to the western half of South Africa. Why there? Because the sorghum seed was a summer crop and the western parts are winter rainfall areas. That's why the Xhosa never settled farther than the Fish River. They needed summer rain. Four hundred years ago the Europeans arrived at the Cape with winter cereals. The Khoi couldn't stop them; the difference in technology was too great. Think about it: if the Xhosa and Zulu had winter grains, how different the history would have been, how difficult it would have been for the Dutch to establish a halfway station at the Cape.'

'Astonishing.'

'It is.'

'Where did you read that?'

'A book. Popular science.'

'And the language thing?'

'What about it?'

'You said you were a *taalbul*?'

'Yes. Sort of.'

'And?'

'Well, take Susan, for instance. She knew we were Afrikaans. She could tell from your name and surname. She could hear your accent. But she speaks English to us. Why?'

'Tell me.'

'Because she works with foreigners mostly and she doesn't want them to know she's an Afrikaans girl. There's too much baggage. She wants the tourists to like her, to think she's cute. She doesn't want to be judged and labelled by her language and its history.'

'She doesn't like the positioning of Afrikaans as a brand.'

'That's it, exactly. What I don't understand is why she . . . why we all don't do something about that position. The solution is not to hide away. The solution is to change the perception of the brand.'

'Is that possible?'

'Isn't that what you do?'

'It is, but a language is a little more complex than ketchup.'

'The difference is that everyone who cares about the ketchup will work together to change the perception. The boere simply won't do that.'

Emma laughed. 'That's true.'

The waiter brought the bottle of Merlot, a bottle of grape juice and two extra glasses. He started to pour, but Emma said thank you, she would do it herself. She slid an extra wineglass over to me. 'Just try one mouthful,' she said. 'A tiny bit, then tell me truthfully that it doesn't taste good.'

She poured for me. I took the glass.

'Wait,' she said. 'First breathe it in.' She poured herself half a glass, turned it in her hand and held it under her nose. I did the same. There were pleasant aromas, but there was also something else.

'What do you smell?' she asked.

How could I tell her? That my past was locked away in the smell of wine, memories of where I came from, who I am.

I shrugged.

'Come on, Lemmer, be objective. Can you smell the cloves? The berries? It's subtle, I know, but it's there.'

'It's there,' I lied.

'Good. Now taste it.' Then she took a sip, rolled the wine around in her mouth, looked at me in expectation. I swigged some wine. It had a dark flavour, like the smoke of a smouldering fire. She swallowed. 'Now tell me it tastes bad.'

I swallowed. 'It tastes bad.'

She laughed again. 'Truly, Lemmer? Truly?'

'Taste the grape juice. Objectively and honestly.' I poured into the spare glasses. 'You don't even have to smell it. Just taste.'

'OK,' she said with an amused smile, and we drank.

'Crisp,' I said. 'Taste the subtle fruit flavour, unmistakably grape. Young, refreshing, pure *joie de vivre*.'

She laughed. I liked that.

'Feel the way the bubbles dance on your tongue, tiny explosions of ecstatic, undisguised honesty, stripped of all pretension. This noble liquid need not pretend, need not ride on the back of eight thousand years of brand positioning. It is here, unadulterated juice, immediately delicious, pure drinking pleasure.'

She laughed loudly, nearly choking, her eyes shut and her pretty mouth open. The other diners' heads turned towards the happy notes, and they couldn't resist smiling. Lightning flashed outside the windows, thunder crashed close by, rumbling and rolling from north to south like a runaway locomotive.

Just before we ordered dessert, I inexplicably said on the spur of the moment, 'My friend who phoned, at the airport . . .'

'Antjie,' Emma replied with a mischievous twinkle. Her memory surprised me.

'She's nearly seventy years old.'

'Wonderful,' said Emma. I wished I knew what she meant by that.

*   *   *

She was tipsy when we left the restaurant. She held on to my arm. It was raining outside, a thick curtain of fat storm drops. I hovered on the threshold. She pulled off her sandals and took my arm again. 'Let's go.' We went outside and were immediately drenched. The rain was warm and the air not cool yet. Her hand held me back so we didn't walk fast. I watched her. She had turned her face up to the rain, eyes shut, and the running water turned her mascara into black tears. She let me lead her like a blind person. The white dress clung. I saw the curves of her body. Water streamed over my face, over my eyes. The rain rattled on the path, in the trees, and on the thatched roofs. It was the only sound in the night.

At the Bateleur suite she dropped my arm, threw her sandals in an arc on to the veranda and stayed out in the rain. I went under the roof, unlocked the door, sat down on one of the chairs and pulled off my socks and shoes. She stood out there with her face upturned and arms stretched to the sky. Accepting the invitation, the rain increased in intensity, and the streams of water shone in the light of the veranda.

Then lightning flashed brilliantly and thunder crashed deafeningly close. She shouted something and with a bright laugh dashed up the steps past me and through the door.

I pulled off my shirt, draped it over the arm of a chair. Turned my shoes over so the water could drain and hung up my socks beside the shirt.

I walked in through the sliding door, pulled it shut behind me and locked it. The sitting room was dark, lit only by a beam of light from her room. I thought of a shower, took one step forward, and saw the reflection in the glass of the picture on the wall.

Emma.

She had undressed. She stood beside the double bed, leaning forward with the white towel in her hair.

I stopped. I didn't breathe. I conspired in the treachery of reflective glass, perfect angles and the half-open door to her room. I looked at the golden body. Her flat stomach, feminine hips, slim legs, and dark, thick bush of pubic hair. Her breasts bobbed with every brisk movement of the towel, nipples tight and pointed. An eternity, yet too short – too soon she finished and turned half away to throw the towel over something. I saw the curve of her creamy buttocks and then she walked as unconsciously and gracefully as a lioness or a steenbok out of the picture and into her bathroom.

I was lying in my bed in the dark when she came in. The rain had stopped, the quiet was deafening. I lay there with my eyes shut, and forced my breathing to be slow and deep.

I heard her soft footsteps stop right beside me. I could feel her closeness, the heat radiating from her body, and I wondered what she was wearing.

All I needed to do was pull the sheet up so she could lie down beside me.

She was standing right next to me. Right there. I couldn't, I shouldn't, but I must. When my hand reached out, she'd already turned away and moments later the other bed creaked, linen rustled and she sighed. I will never know what it meant.

19

The day that would end so dreadfully began so well.

We slept late. I was up first and made coffee. We drank it together on the veranda. The morning was bright, new and cool. She said her head was a little sore and she laughed at herself.

Later, she phoned Mogale to check whether we could see Donnie Branca. They couldn't find him, said he would call back. We went for breakfast. Dick, Senior Game Ranger, spotted us on the way. 'The game drive will be awesome tonight,' he said to Emma.

'We might not be here tonight,' she said. 'We might be going home.'

'You'll have to stay another day. There's nothing like the Bushveld after the first real summer rain. The animals go wild. It's a once-in-a-lifetime experience. Totally awesome.'

'Awesome' was clearly one of his favourite words. He spoke exclusively to her.

'We'll see . . .'

'For you, I'll delay the drive until six. Or seven,' he flirted.

'You will?' She liked it.

'Absolutely.'

'Then we will do our best, Lemmer and I.'

'Awesome,' but a little deflated since she'd included me. 'Have a great day.'

'You too,' and she smiled at him.

The call came while we were at the breakfast table. She answered her cell phone, listened and said, 'Mr Branca,' and, 'My most sincere sympathies . . .'

She said she knew that it was a bad time at Mogale, but Frank Wolhuter had left her a message. She told him about it and then listened attentively for a long time. 'Eleven would be great, thank you.'

She put the phone down. 'He said he knew that Frank Wolhuter went through Cobie's things for the first time after we left. Frank said nothing to him, but he knows where he would have put something. He'll see us at eleven.' She looked at her watch. 'We'd better move.'

Susan came to our table and said, 'Oh, Miss le Roux, someone just left a message for you at the gate.'

'Who?' asked Emma.

'Gate security says it was a little boy.'

'A child?'

'Shall I ask someone to get the message for you?'

'No, no, we're on our way, *ons sal dit daar kry, dankie*, Susan. We'll pick it up at the gate.'

'O-kay,' said Susan, and there was a small awkward moment before she turned away from us with a swish of her long blonde hair.

The message was on a piece of paper that was probably from a school exercise book or something like that. It had faint blue lines and a red vertical margin. It wasn't in an envelope, just folded twice, with Miss Emma le Roux written on it in blue ballpoint.

We stood beside the little building at the gate where the guard, Edwin, Security Official, sat with his wide-brimmed hat and brilliant white smile. Emma unfolded the letter and read it. Then she passed it to me.

```
Miss Emma
You must better go home now. Here, it is not so
safe.
   A Friend
```

'Who brought this?' Emma asked Edwin.

'A boy.' Cautiously, as if he knew that this meant trouble.

'Do you know him?'

'Maybe.'

'Please, Edwin, I need your help. This is very important.'

'There are many boys here in the villages. I think he is one of them.'

'Which village?'

'I will try to find out.'

'Wait,' said Emma, and walked back to the BMW. She returned with a hundred-rand note in her hand. 'Edwin, all I want to know is who gave the message to the boy. He is not in trouble. I will pay him if he can tell me. And this is for you. If you can find him, I will pay you more.'

'Thank you, madam,' he said as the note disappeared into a pocket. 'Maybe I can find the boy.'

'Thank you very much.' She checked her watch. 'We're late,' she said.

She sat with the letter in her hands while we drove. She stared at it for a long time.

'Miss Emma,' she said. 'That's what the man who phoned me at my house called me.' She looked at me and then back at the note. 'It sounded like a black man over the phone, Lemmer, and this reads like English is not the writer's first language.'

I wasn't going to respond. Luckily, her phone rang again and she answered and said, 'Carel!' He must have asked how it was going, because she said, 'If you had asked me yesterday, I would have said badly, but I think I've got something, Carel. We're on our way there now. And remember that phone call I received and couldn't make out what the man was saying? I didn't imagine it.'

My friend 'Carel the Rich' of Hermanus. Apparently, he wanted a full report, because she told him the whole story, all the way to Mogale.

A pretty young Dutch volunteer with a bush hat and long legs in shorts took us to Donnie Branca, who was sitting in Frank Wolhuter's office. Emma tried to speak Afrikaans to her, but she answered exclusively in English. She said they were still in shock, the reality of Mr Wolhuter's death hadn't sunk in properly.

Branca pushed documents around on the desk. He was sombre and spoke in muted tones. Once the Dutch girl had gone he said, 'It wasn't an accident. Couldn't be. The honey badger has gone in there before, but we would dart Simba with a tranquilliser. Frank would have done that. But the dart gun is in the store. He would never have done it alone either. Phatudi says there's no evidence, but I found something just now. Come and see.'

He walked ahead of us through the interior door of the office. Behind it was Wolhuter's living quarters. In the bedroom a book-case stood open like a door. It was hinged to the wall. Behind it in the wall was a gun safe and the steel door was open. Branca stopped in front of the safe.

'Look at this.' He pointed.

The safe was two metres high and half a metre wide. It had two levels – below there was room for six weapons. There were only two hunting rifles. From the dust pattern it was clear that someone in the very recent past had removed the other four. On the top shelf there were documents and a few piles of banknotes, three thousand rand maybe, a pack of dollars, a pack of euros, maybe a thousand each. There was a rusty red stripe on the sill of the safe at the level of the document shelf. It looked like dried blood someone had smeared there by accident.

'Blood,' said Branca.

Emma leaned closer to look. She didn't comment.

'There are two safes. Everyone knows about the one in the storage shed, where we keep the other weapons. Only Frank and I knew about this one. If he had anything for you, he would have kept it here. That's why I looked here this morning, after your call. That's when I found it.'

'Do you think . . .' She stopped, upset by the various possibilities.

'Do you still have Frank's message?'

She nodded and took her phone out of her handbag. She pressed the buttons and held it out to him. From beyond the grave Frank Wolhuter repeated, 'Emma, this is Frank Wolhuter. I believe you were right. I found something. Call me, please, when you get this message.'

Branca's face was strained when he passed the phone back to her. 'After you left the day before yesterday, Frank unlocked Cobie's room. He was busy there the whole afternoon. I went to say goodbye before I left to visit my girlfriend at Graskop. That was the last time I saw him.'

Emma stared at the streak of blood. 'That night . . . Was anyone else staying here?'

Branca shook his head. 'Only Frank and Cobie and I lived here. The workers' quarters are on the slope of the mountain and the volunteers live two kilometres away in the dormitories. When I came home after midnight everything was quiet. I thought Frank was asleep – he was early to bed, early to rise. The next morning Mogoboya found him with Simba.'

Branca took out a handkerchief and used it to push the door of the safe closed. 'I'll get Phatudi to come over . . .' He made a move for the door. 'I haven't been in Cobie's room yet. Would you like to come with me?'

'Please.'

He fetched a bunch of keys from Wolhuter's office and together we walked to the little building half hidden in the mopane trees at the edge of the rehabilitation centre. Branca pointed at a broken window. 'That's where they tried to break in last week.'

'Who did?' asked Emma.

'Who knows. We think it was Phatudi's people. At night you can't see the burglar bars. Frank heard the glass break and he turned on the lights.'

He unlocked the door, first the doorknob lock, then the Yale. I wondered whether they all were as security conscious. The cottage was dark inside, the curtains drawn. Branca switched on a light.

Spartan was the word. A single bed against the wall, pine bedside cupboard, two worn armchairs and a tall built-in cupboard of faded white melamine. The walls were bare; on the floor was an old woven carpet with an African block motif. Two doors, one to the kitchen, where a square dark wooden table and three wooden chairs, an ancient electric stove and a bookshelf were visible. The other led to the bathroom. Everything was relatively tidy and clean for bachelor's quarters. A pair of jeans hung over the back of the armchair. Emma rubbed the material between her fingers while she looked about. Branca crossed to the single bed, where something lay, a book perhaps.

He picked it up and opened it.

'Photographs,' he said.

Emma went over. It looked like a small photo album, just big enough to hold photos of the regular size.

'That's Melanie Posthumus,' Emma said. 'These are Cobie's photos.'

'Who's Melanie? The girlfriend?'

'Yes.'

'Two, three, four photos. He must have liked her a lot.'

'And that is Stef Moller,' Emma said.

Branca turned the page and pointed 'And here's Frank. And me. And this was a Swedish volunteer. She liked Cobie a lot. We thought . . .'

'What?'

'Maybe, you know . . .'

'What?'

'Well, we saw her come out of Cobie's house early one morning. But she left. Like they all do.'

Branca had paged right through it. 'That's it.'

'Wait,' said Emma, and took the album from him. She opened it. 'Look here.' She pointed it at me. 'There are two pictures missing. Right at the front.'

I looked. On both sides of a page there was only transparent plastic with a white background and the faint outline where two postcard-sized photographs had been.

'This room . . . Is it exactly as Frank left it?' asked Emma.

'Must be. No one else has been in here,' said Branca.

'What about cleaners?' She went into the kitchen.

'Frank and I have a maid, but we're slobs. Cobie did everything himself.'

The kitchen wasn't big enough for everyone. Branca and I stood in the doorway. Emma inspected the bookshelf.

'So it could have been Frank who left the album on the bed?'

'Could be.'

She turned. 'Maybe he took the photos out to show me.'

'Maybe.'

'Did you look in the safe? For anything?'

Of course he had looked in the safe, just after he had removed the four rifles.

'No. When I saw the blood, I didn't want to tamper with possible evidence.'

He was lying. And he was good at it.

'Can we have a look? We can be careful.'

'OK,' he said.

They walked towards the door. I quickly scanned the bookshelf in the kitchen. There were magazines on the lower shelf, the yellow spines of *National Geographic*, a series of *Africa Geographics*. The rest were books on animals, game- and veld management. Crammed. Not an inch where the album might have fitted.

The photographs weren't in the safe. There were title deeds and records of donations and financial statements and cash.

'What's the money for?' Emma asked.

'That's the cash float. For incidentals and emergencies.'

'Is there any other place where he might have put the photos?'

'I'll have a look. In his room, maybe. But it'll take time. There's so much to do now. I don't know what's going to happen. If I find something, I'll let you know.'

'Thanks.'

We said goodbye and left. Emma wanted to track down the black child who had brought her the message.

She took out the note again, read it and refolded it. She kept it in her hand. When we turned on to the tar road, there were no policemen waiting to protect us. I did a thorough survey of any possible tails and I wondered why I felt so uneasy. I concentrated on the road, trying to ignore a voice that kept whispering that I ought to tell Emma that Branca was hiding something. That didn't work. I tried to rationalise it away: it was none of my business, it would make no difference. In all probability it had nothing to do with her search for Jacobus le Roux.

But the note in her hand worried me. It made no sense. It didn't fit into the scheme of my original suspicions.

'Why did he only send me the letter now?' Emma wondered aloud. 'We've been here three days already.'

That was a very good question. I didn't have time to think it through. At Klaserie, just beyond the railway line, something flashed in the veld to the left of us. Something that didn't fit. I slowed down as we approached the T-junction where the R351 joined the R40. Out of the corner of my eye I saw the sun reflect momentarily on metal. I was going to turn and look, but I spotted the battered blue Nissan pick-up on the left shoulder of the road just before the stop sign. Two figures were inside, the doors opening in unison.

Balaclavas on their heads, firearms in their hands.

'Hold tight,' I told Emma as I floored the accelerator and checked to the right for oncoming traffic. I had to take the left turn at speed. Just get away from here.

'What's going on?'

Before I could answer, the left front tyre burst with a dull, shuddering thud.

20

Adrenalin flips the world into slow motion.

The bonnet of the BMW dipped for a second as the tyre disintegrated. I fought the wheel, not getting the response I expected, wanting to look back, to see whether the Nissan was on the road behind us. I stepped on the accelerator again. The rear-wheel drive kicked in and the car held the line of the turn for a moment, but I was going too fast and I didn't have enough front traction. The rear swung out across the R40 towards the gravelled edge as I fought to bring it back in line.

'Lemmer!'

The tyres shrieked, the BMW spun 180 degrees, its nose facing back towards the T-junction. The Nissan was bearing down on us and I could see the gunmen – balaclavas on their heads and gloves on their hands – as it appeared.

I tried to turn the car, but something smacked into us. *Donk*.

In my peripheral vision I caught a flash in the veld. Sunlight on a gun barrel? I spun the steering wheel, hands slick with sweat, and gunned the engine.

Donk. Another tyre, the right rear, was gone. The BMW swayed and juddered.

'Lemmer!'

'Calm down!' I turned and accelerated, the nose came around, away from the balaclavas, and pointed north. A car approached us, honking desperately. It swung out just in time, the driver's face a mask of panic. I put my foot down again and the rear tyre jumped completely off. Metal rim on tar, making a wild, screeching noise, we jerked forward, away from them, thirty, forty, fifty metres.

It screeched and bucked, but the car held its line down the middle of the road and we picked up speed. Far ahead, traffic approached.

They shot out the left rear tyre, rendering the BMW wholly uncontrollable. I would have to slow down. Or we would have to abandon it. Slow was not an option. I could see them coming after us in the rear-view mirror. I aimed for the veld, drove into the long grass.

The car burst through the fence, wires whipping with whirring noises. I braked hard and made a final sideways swerve in the grass. The engine stalled and suddenly all was quiet.

'Out!'

She opened her door but couldn't get out. I unlocked my seat belt and turned to her.

'Your seat belt is still locked.' I kept my voice even while I pushed the release button.

'Out. Now.' I opened my door and jumped out. She was already on her feet. I grabbed her hand and dragged her away from the car.

'Wait,' she screamed. She turned back, dived into the car, grabbed her handbag and then reached for my hand.

A train whistled. North-west of us. I pulled her along and we ran towards the sound.

'Keep your head down,' I yelled. The grass wasn't as long here as it was near the road. Mopane trees and thorn bushes gave cover. A shot cracked behind us. It was a pistol. The bullet hummed past to the right.

The sniper with the rifle, the one that had shot out our tyres with real skill, was somewhere to the west of us. And the two balaclavas were behind us.

Another two shots. Both wild. They didn't know exactly where we were.

I heard the rumble of the train, which was now directly north of us. The railway tracks were somewhere up ahead but I still couldn't see them. I sped up, dragging Emma over an antbear hole. I jumped. Emma fell and her hand jerked out of mine. I turned and saw that she was lying stretched out. She'd tried to break the fall with her hands and her head had knocked something, a stone or stump. There was a two-centimetre wound on her cheekbone beside her eye.

'Come on,' I said, as I picked her up. Her eyes were dull. I looked back. They were moving through the grass and bushes, running towards us.

'Lemmer.'

I pulled her by the hand. 'We have to run.'

'I've . . .' She held a hand to her ribs, breathless. '. . . hurt something.'

'Later, Emma. We've got to keep moving.' Her mouth was open, breathing hard. Her cheek bled. We were too slow.

The train.

The racket filled my ears as it came into view. It was a diesel locomotive, pulling a thundering brown centipede of freight cars. There was barbed wire between us and the railway service road, then another metre up a slope to the tracks.

I dragged her towards it. There was no time to climb the fence. I grabbed her with both hands around her chest.

'No,' she cried, gasping at the pain in her ribs, I lifted her over the wire and she fell to the ground on the other side. I ran, jumped and vaulted over three metres farther down. She tried to get up. They were coming. Sixty or seventy metres. There were two of them. They stopped and waved their arms at someone. Then I saw him, directly to the south. The man with the rifle. A big man, white, in camouflage gear and a baseball cap. He dropped to the ground. The balaclava looked at us and started running again.

I reached Emma. She was curled up, her lips forming 'Lemmer', but the train drowned out the sound. She looked bad. Blood from the wound on her cheek ran down her neck. The cut was deep. But the more serious problem was her ribs.

There was no time.

I put my left hand behind her back, held her tight and sprinted up the bank. Her handbag stayed behind in the grass. We ran alongside the train, but it was moving too fast. Still, it was our only chance. I put out my right hand, waited for the next freight car and grabbed when metal hit my hand. Lots of pain, but no luck. I'd wait for the next one. I grabbed again, got hold of a metal rod, and let the momentum jerk us up. I clung to her and swung her. She was too much weight on my arm, but I managed to bring her up with me between the cars. We landed on metal and my head banged against something. Still, I held on to Emma. My feet scrabbled for a foothold as I fought for balance. I dragged her in, pulled her tight against me, her hands gripping my shoulders. She screamed something I couldn't hear.

We were going to make it.

I looked into the veld. The balaclavas stood still.

Sniper Man lay there on his belly, weapon in front of him, set up on its tripod. The rifle barrel and the telescope above it followed the train's movement.

There was a puff of smoke from the weapon and then he was gone, out of the field of vision. Emma jerked in my arms and fell, flopping away from me. I grabbed her, got the thin material of her T-shirt in my fingers and held on.

It tore and I saw the exit wound high on her breast. He'd shot her. Rage exploded in me. The material ripped some more and she fell away in slow motion, eyes closed. Then she was gone, just the rag of T-shirt in my hand.

I jumped off the train. Too long in the air, stone and grass flashed past, and then I hit the ground, landing too hard on my shoulder. A hammer blow of agony went through me. I was rolling and something stabbed me. I continued to roll and hit something else. Finally, I came to a stop, but I couldn't get up. I had to find Emma. My shoulder must be dislocated. My right arm was all wrong. It was to the front and side of me. I couldn't breathe, but I tried to get up, bellowed, as I fought to breathe. I stumbled, walked and fell. Got back up on my feet.

There she lay. Deathly still.

'Emma,' but I couldn't get the word out.

She lay on her face. There was blood at the back of her head. Blood on her back. That was the bullet wound. I turned her over with my left hand. She was gone, her body limp. Oh Jesus, please. I pressed my chest to hers, pushed my left hand behind her back, held her to me, and stood up. She hung over my shoulder, lifeless. Was she breathing?

The train had gone.

They were coming.

I had to run. Carrying Emma.

Stumbled. How would I get over the fence? I ran down the other side of the track away from them. I had to get over the wire, but I couldn't.

Ahead of us there was a gate. Similar to a farm gate, it was an entrance to the service road. We must get over there. I would have to press down on the gate, swing over and jump. I ran, staggering and stumbling. I would have to use my right arm, but would it hold? I pressed my good arm on the gate, swung my legs and Emma over. It was an unreal moment in the air, the arm wasn't going to hold. It gave and my right hip hit the top of the gate. We toppled over and I landed on my back with Emma on top of me. She was heavy now. I got to my knees and noticed that my left hand was slippery with blood from Emma's back.

I made it to my feet, my legs wobbling beneath me.

The treeline was twenty metres away. I heard them shouting behind me. We had to reach the trees. My knees complained, my shoulder was all to hell, the pain a wave building to a crest. You must live, Emma le Roux, you must live.

There was a footpath into the trees. A game path. I jogged, staggering, through the mopanes. Don't follow the path, because that's what they'll do. I swerved to the right. I could smell smoke, burning wood. Were there people near by?

Look where you step, I told myself. Don't make a noise, get deeper into the bush. I had no more breath, my chest was on fire, legs numb, shoulder dislocated. The trees opened up and there were the huts, a humble place, with five women around a fire. Three children playing in the dust, one wrapped up on a woman's back. Cooking pots. They were stooped over the pots. The women heard me and looked up with wide eyes. They saw a crazy white man with a bleeding woman over his shoulder.

I heard the balaclava calling behind me. Too close. We weren't going to make it.

I ran towards the middle hut. The door was ajar. I ran in and shoved it closed with my hip. There were two mattresses on the ground and a small table with a radio on it. I laid Emma down and turned to face the door. When the first one came through, I would have to take his gun. With one hand? It wouldn't work but it was my only option.

I tried to listen. It was deathly quiet. There was a crack in the door. I peered through it and saw them emerge from the bush, surprised by the huts. They halted when they saw the women, swung the guns and said something in a native language. No response. I couldn't see the women at the fire. Balaclava shouted something, threatening and commanding. A woman's voice answered him. They stared at her for a minute and ran off.

I listened. A child wailed. Then another. Women's voices consoled them.

Had the women sent them on a wild-goose chase?

I went over to the mattress. Emma lay too still. I held my ear to her mouth. She was breathing. Jerkily, unevenly. Not good. There was too much blood on her chest, her hair, her neck, her cheek. I had to get her to a hospital.

The door opened. The woman stood there warily.

'*Is hulle weg?*' I asked.

No reaction.

'Have they gone?'

She said something I couldn't understand. She looked at Emma.

'Doctor,' I said.

'Doctor,' she said, and nodded.

'Quickly.'

Another nod. 'Quickly.'

She turned and called out to someone with urgency in her voice.

21

His name was Goodwill and he drove like a maniac.

He seemed too young to have a licence. The Toyota Hi Ace was four years old and had 257,000 kilometres on the clock. At first he argued with me. 'The clinic in Hoedspruit is shit, we must go to Nelspruit. To the hospital.'

'There's no time.'

'There will be time, I will drive fast.'

'No, please.'

'No doctor in Hoedspruit, just nurses. They know nothing.' He turned right at the junction where we had been attacked. 'Trust me.'

I hesitated.

'Then you'd better hurry.'

'Watch me.' He sped.

I held Emma tightly in my arms in the middle seat and Goodwill drove with his hazard lights tick-tocking, tyres squealing and horn blaring. I felt her jerk, felt the little spasms in her body as life seeped away. I said to her, 'Emma, you must not die, please, Emma, you must not die.'

The doctor jerked my arm back into the socket and I wanted to *bliksem* him right there, punch him in the face, it was such incredible agony, but then it was quickly gone. He stepped back and said, '*Jissie*, pal, I thought you were going to hit me.' He was in his fifties and as round as a barrel.

'Fuck it, Doc, I nearly did.'

He laughed.

'Phone, Doc. I have to know.'

'I told you.'

'You said we have to get my arm back in, then we could phone.'

'Later.'

'Now.'

'It's no use. She's in theatre.'

'Where is the operating theatre?'

'Let me give you an anti-inflammatory.' He took a syringe out of a drawer. 'And something for the pain. I must put something on that cut as well.'

'What cut?'

'The one on your right biceps.'

'Doc, where is the theatre?'

'Sit here.'

'No, Doc . . .'

He got angry. 'Listen to me, pal. If you want to hit me, now's the time, because I'm going to get tough with you. Just look at you. You're trembling like a reed, hyperventilating, you're in shock, bleeding and as dirty as a pig. You want to go and mess around in theatre like that? They'll throw you out, let me tell you. Get your butt in this chair so I can inject you and clean up that wound. Then you're going to take a pill to calm you down. And then you're going to clean yourself up and wait until they come out and tell us what's up.'

I stood there glaring at him.

'Your arse in the chair.'

I went over to the chair. I sat.

'Lean forward. Loosen your belt.'

I did as he said.

'Bend over more, pal, I have to reach your butt.'

He stood behind me, pulled down my pants and wiped a spot with cotton wool and alcohol.

'Is she your wife?' The needle went in. Unnecessarily rough.

'No.'

'Hang on. Sit still. Another one for the pain. Is she your girlfriend?'

'No.'

'Family?' He fetched another syringe.

'No. She's my client.' I felt the needle go in.

'Your client, huh?' He tossed the syringe in a rubbish bin and opened another drawer.

'Yes.'

He took out a plastic container of pills. 'The way you're carrying on, you seem to care a hell of a lot for your clients. Here's a pill. Go and clean up, then take it.'

I had lost my cell phone. My wallet was in the BMW. I asked the rotund doctor if I could borrow money from him for the public phone.

'Use this one,' he said, and took me to his office. In a silver frame on his desk was a photo of a woman. She was beautiful, elegant and slim. She had long red hair streaked with grey.

'How do I get a line?'

'Press zero,' he said, and closed the door behind him as he left.

I made the call. Jolene Freylinck, the manicured receptionist, answered on the second ring in her deep, sexy voice.

'Body Armour, good morning, how may we be of assistance?'

'Jolene, it's Lemmer.'

'Hi, Lemmer, how's it going?'

'I've got to talk to Jeanette.'

No hesitation. 'I'm putting you through.'

Recorded music, Jeanette's choice. Sinatra sang 'My Way' while I waited. Only two phrases, the part where he says he bit off more than he could chew, before Jeanette interrupted, 'You've got trouble.' A statement of fact.

I described the trouble.

'And how is she?' she asked when I had finished.

'Critical.'

'Is that all they will tell you?'

'That's all.'

'Lemmer, you don't sound good. How are you feeling?'

'There's nothing wrong with me.'

'I'm not so sure of that.'

'Jeanette, I'm fine.'

'What are you going to do?'

'I'm staying here with her for now.'

For five seconds she was quiet. Then she said, 'I'll call you.'

'My cell phone is gone.'

'What's your number there?'

I don't know how long I sat at the doctor's desk with my head in my hands. Ten minutes maybe. Or half an hour. I tried to think. My head wouldn't cooperate. The door opened. A man and a woman came in. He had silver hair and wore an expensive grey suit. 'Grundling,' he said, and put out his hand. He smiled. He had sharp teeth. He looked like a great white shark. 'I am the hospital administrator, and this is Maggie Padayachee, our client services manager. We are here to offer you our assistance.'

Maggie's grey suit was darker. Her black hair was in a bun. Her teeth were less sharp.

'Emma . . .'

'I can assure you that Miss le Roux is receiving the best medical treatment possible. However, our managing director has just called from Johannesburg and asked us to give you every assistance as well.'

'In any way we can,' said Maggie.

Jeanette Louw. Who knows people in high places. She had been busy.

'I need to get to the theatre.'

They ignored that. 'We have a hospitality suite we would like to offer you. And you need a change of clothing, obviously,' said Maggie.

'I will leave you in Mrs Padayachee's capable hands, Mr Lemmer. Just so you know, we are at your service any time.'

'Please, I have to talk to Emma's . . . Miss le Roux's doctor.'

'Of course.' Soothing voice. 'But they're still in theatre. Let's make you comfortable first. Do you have any luggage we can fetch for you?'

*   *   *

The hospitality suite had a sitting room, a bedroom and a bathroom with a shower. Luxurious. Air conditioning. Original oils. Kelims.

There was a set of hospital pyjamas and a dressing gown on the bed. Slippers on the floor. The bathroom had a toothbrush, toothpaste, razor, shaving cream and deodorant. I wondered exactly what Jeanette Louw had said to the managing director of SouthMed.

I took off my shirt. It was stained with Emma's blood. So much of it, dry and dark red now, like wine.

My torso looked like an abstract painting in sombre shades of red, black and purple. My ears rang. My heart thudded. The pain had backed off, thanks to the injection. I undressed and got into the shower. I was cold. I turned the taps open wide and turned my back to the stream. My body shook.

Emma mustn't die.

She must not.

I had never lost a client.

What had I done wrong? The train. I should never have jumped on the train, but there had been no other way.

I should never have doubted her. I should have believed her. Three men. Balaclavas. The same as the attack in Cape Town. Why? Why cover their heads? Why hadn't the sniper worn a balaclava? And the gloves. Why the gloves?

I ought to have spotted the sniper sooner. I should have climbed deeper between the freight cars. I should have held Emma behind me. I should have taken the bullet. I should have held her tighter.

She couldn't die. I must finish up, I had to guard her. They would come back. She was dead, I knew it. Because I wasn't good enough.

I had to protect her.

I contacted the theatre from the phone in the sitting room. 'I need to know Miss le Roux's condition, please.'

'Who is this speaking?'

'Lemmer. How do I get the operating theatre?'

'You're calling from the VIP suite?'

'That's right.'

'I'll call you back.'

They were soon knocking on the door. I opened it in the hospital pyjamas and dressing gown. It was Maggie and the rotund doctor. 'Dr Taljaard is worried about you.'

'I'm fine.'

'Fine my arse,' said Taljaard. 'Did you take the pill I gave you?'

'Dr Taljaard . . .' said Maggie sternly.

'Don't Dr Taljaard me. Did you take the pill?'

'No, Doc.'

'I thought not. My name is Koos. I don't like "Doc". Come on. I'm giving you another injection. Lie on the bed. Maggie, you wait outside.'

'Dr Taljaard, he's a VIP.'

'That's your problem. Those eyes of his are my problem, they're wilder than a wild dog's. Come on, pal, lie down. If you won't listen, you have to take the pain.'

'Please, Doc, I don't want . . .'

'Hey!' he said. Fierce. 'You have a hearing problem?' Threatening.

I didn't know what to do. I just stood there.

He closed the door. 'Let's be reasonable.' He spoke quietly in an easy tone. 'I don't know what happened, but you have trauma, and it's not physical. Right now your brain is not working properly and you are going to make a fool of yourself. You'll be sorry later. Let's get you a little calmer. I've just come back from the theatre. No news yet. However, the fact that they're still busy should be good news to you.'

'I have to protect her.'

He steered me towards the bed with a firm hand. He never stopped talking.

'There's nothing you can do right now. Lie down. Face down. That's it. Just a quick injection, we'll use the right buttock this time, left one's a bit over-utilised. Let's get this gown up. That's good. Here we go, this will sting just a little. There you go, easy as that. No, don't get up yet. Lie still for a minute. Give the stuff time to kick in. It will make you relax. A bit sleepy, too. Wouldn't be a bad idea to have a little rest. Don't you think? Just a little breather, just to catch your breath.'

A great weight sat down on me.

'Come, let's get these slippers off. Ugly mothers, anyway. Let's get you under these blankets. Wait, shift up a bit, just a bit more, there you are. Sleep tight, pal. Sleep tight.'

22

The pain dragged me from sleep. Pain in my shoulder, in my arm, right hip, left knee. I didn't know where I was at first. The dressing gown was twisted uncomfortably around me. Behind the curtain the window was dark. The sitting-room light shone through the crack in the bedroom door.

There was someone in the sitting room. I heard a quiet deep voice.

I got up. My legs felt unreliable. I straightened the dressing gown. Checked my watch: 19.41. I had slept nearly six hours. Where was Emma? I opened the door. Inspector Jack Phatudi was sitting there. He was talking on his cell phone. He frowned at me. He said, 'I have to go,' and folded up his phone.

'Martin Fitzroy Lemmer,' he addressed me.

I went over to the room's phone and picked it up. I saw my black sports bag beside Phatudi's chair. Had he brought it?

'She is critical, Martin. She is in a coma and they don't know if she will make it. They won't be able to tell you more than that.'

I put the phone down. 'She needs protection.'

'I have two people at the door of the ICU.'

'Those two?'

'Yes, those two. Come and sit down. We need to talk.'

'What are your arrangements for controlling access to her? Do they know what they're doing?'

'Do you think we're morons because we're black, Martin?'

'No, Jack, I think you're morons because you behave like morons. Besides, one of your morons is white. The arrangements?'

'There is a list of two doctors and four nurses. They are the only people allowed access to her.'

'Put me on the list too.'

'Why? When did you become a doctor?'

'She's my client.'

'Client? You are Martin Fitzroy Lemmer, who served four years of a six-year sentence in Brandvlei for manslaughter. Tell me, what kind of service do you provide to a rich young woman like Emma le Roux?'

I didn't answer. He had done his homework.

'What happened today? Road rage again, Martin? Tell me about it.'

My head felt thick. My body ached.

'Sit down here.'

I stood.

'We took your prints off the R5.'

'Congratulations.'

'Why are you with Emma le Roux?' His tone was reasonable.

'I am employed by Body Armour, a company that provides protection services. She hired us.'

'Not very good protection, Martin.'

He wanted to provoke me. He used my first name to annoy me. 'It was an ambush, Jack. They shot out the tyres with a rifle. How do you prevent that?'

'Who did?'

'I don't know.'

'You're lying.'

'You were the one that sent people because you were concerned for our safety. You tell me who they were.'

'The people I was worried about don't lay ambushes with high-velocity rifles. What happened?'

'We were on our way back from Mogale. They were waiting for us. Shot out the tyres. I couldn't control the car. So we ran for it. There was a train. We jumped on the train and they shot Emma.'

'How many were there?'

'Three.'

'Describe them.'

'They were too far away.'

'Not good enough.'

'They were wearing balaclavas. They were men, that I know. They were never closer than fifty or sixty metres.'

'And you got away? Miss le Roux was shot and your shoulder was dislocated?'

'We were lucky.'

'Lucky? Tell her that.'

'Fuck you, Jack.'

'Are you going to assault me now, Martin? Are you going to beat me to death like you beat a twenty-three-year-old articled clerk to death?'

'The articled clerk had three mates, Jack. It was self-defence.'

'That's not what the court said. You have an anger management problem. I could see that yesterday.'

'You threatened Emma physically. She asked you to let her go. That's police brutality.'

'Where have you been?'

'What?'

'Where have you and Miss le Roux been since you arrived in our area?'

'To Mogale, Badplaas and Warmbad.'

'What were you doing in Badplaas and Warmbad?'

'She went to talk to Cobie de Villiers' former employer and his fiancée.'

'And?'

'And nothing. They know nothing.'

'What else?'

'What do you mean, "what else"?'

'Something must have happened. Someone is angry with you.'

'You were the one who was angry with us, Jack. It makes me wonder.'

'What about the message?'

'What message?'

'You know what I'm referring to.'

'I have no idea.'

'The woman at Mohlolobe said somebody left you a message at the gate. The gate guard said he gave the letter to Emma le Roux. What was in the letter?'

'I don't know. She didn't say.'

He leaned forward, chin propped on his hand, like the Thinker.

'I want to shower, Jack.'

He waited before responding. 'Why did she need you, Martin?'

'What?'

'Why did she hire a bodyguard to come and look for her brother? It's not that dangerous in the Lowveld.'

'Ask her.'

'I'm asking you.'

'I don't know.'

He got up slowly and stood right in front of me. 'I think you're lying.'

'Prove it.'

'I know your type, Martin. Trouble magnets. We don't need more trouble here. We have enough. I'm watching you.'

'*Jissie*, Inspector, you make me feel so safe.'

He scowled at me and turned those big shoulders and went to the door. He opened it and then he said, 'Next time it won't be four years, Martin. I'll put you away for a long, long time.'

Only once I had showered did I spot the envelope on the bedside cabinet. The room must have been a hive of activity while I slept.

I tore it open. It was neatly typed under the letterhead of SouthMed Clinics.

Dear Mr Lemmer

We have brought your luggage, which you will find in the lounge. Miss Le Roux's bags are in safe keeping. Should you need them, please contact me.

You are welcome to use our restaurant facilities on the ground floor at your leisure. Also, a Ms Jeanette Louw called, and asked that you call her back once you feel up to it.

Dr Koos Taljaard, who has been treating you, is at
your disposal. His telephone number is 092 449
9090. The surgeon in charge of Ms Le Roux's care is
Dr Eleanor Taljaard, and you can reach her on
extension 4142.

Should you need any assistance, please do not
hesitate to call me on 092 701 3869.

Very best wishes

Maggie T. Padayachee

Client Services Manager

I recognised the trauma surgeon immediately. It was her picture in
the silver frame on Dr Koos Taljaard's desk.

'I'm Eleanor,' she said in a lovely modulated voice. She was
taller than me.

'How is Emma?'

'Are you Mr Lemmer?'

'Oh, sorry. Yes. I . . .'

'It's understandable. Miss le Roux is your client, I believe.'

'That's right.'

'Can you help us to contact her next of kin?'

'No. I mean . . . There aren't any.'

'Not any?'

'Her parents and her brother are dead. There is no one else.'

'Dear me. An employer? Colleagues?'

'She works on her own, a consultant.'

'Oh.'

'Doctor, tell me, please. How is she?'

'Come sit down, Mr Lemmer.' She steered me by the elbow to
an office. On her desk was a photo of Koos. In a silver frame. He
looked rotund. She sat down. I sat opposite her.

'All I can tell you at the moment is that her condition is very
serious. It's the injury to the brain that makes it more complicated.'

'What brain injury?'

'There was a direct trauma to the brain, Mr Lemmer.'

'What sort of injury?'

'Look, the details are not important . . .'

'Doc, the details are important.'

She looked at me, sighed, and said, 'It is typical coup-contre-coup. The problem is that she is not stable enough to scan yet. I suspect an epidural haematoma. Possible brain damage. Can you tell me how the injury occurred?'

'Doc . . .'

'Eleanor.'

'She fell. Her eye was bleeding . . . here . . .' I pressed my fingers to my cheekbone.

'No. The zygomatic wound is superficial. I'm referring to the parietal trauma.' She dropped her head and indicated with her hand the left rear of her skull. 'This is the parietal bone of the cranium. It protects the parietal lobe of the brain. The impact must have been severe.' She assumed I didn't understand the medical terms, not knowing that I had previous experience.

'We were on a train. When they shot her, she fell. She fell off a train. It was travelling fast.'

'Dear me . . .'

'I didn't see how she landed.'

'Who on earth . . . ?'

'I don't know.'

She wanted to pursue the topic, I could see that. But she reconsidered and gathered her thoughts. 'Mr Lemmer . . .'

'They just call me Lemmer.'

'When this type of injury occurs, the impact is so great that the brain literally bounces back and forth against the sides of the cranium. The first impact we call the coup, the second is the contrecoup, when the opposite side of the brain rebounds against the cranium. Usually the injury is to the cerebral cortex. That's the outermost layer of the cerebrum, between one point five and five millimetres thick. The bruising varies according to the nature of the impact. The process is popularly called concussion. The Afrikaans term *harsingskudding* describes it well, like a brainquake. Are you with me?'

'I understand.'

'Concussion appears in varying degrees and symptoms. Light concussion can make you dizzy for a second, serious concussion can leave you unconscious. Miss le Roux's injury is serious. She has lost consciousness, which is not a good sign. With this type of injury, where an object or a fragment of skull has not penetrated the brain, unconsciousness is usually a symptom of brain damage. Not always, but usually.'

'Doc . . .'

'Please don't call me "doc". My name is Eleanor. You need to understand, Lemmer, it is impossible to know yet whether there will be permanent brain damage, or what the nature of the damage will be, if there is any. The area of the brain that is injured determines that. Miss le Roux is in a coma and the best indicator of the degree of possible damage is the length of time she remains comatose. But there are two good signs. She doesn't have bilateral dilation of the pupils. That means both pupils respond to light – they contract when we shine a light on them. Statistically only twenty per cent of brain trauma patients with normal pupillary response die. So there is hope, but I must reiterate: we don't know whether there is epidural haematoma. In common terms: bleeding on the brain. Once she is stable enough, we will do a CT scan.'

'What is the other good sign?'

'In cases like this, we use the Glasgow coma scale. The scale runs from three, which is very bad, to fifteen, which is normal. The position of a patient on the scale is determined by their best response in the first twenty-four hours after the injury. We are not working with exact science here, but the good news is that Miss le Roux is outside the three to four zone. Currently, she is six on the scale, and we hope she will show improvement in the next twelve hours. The Glasgow scale tells us that thirty-four per cent of patients who register between five and seven will live, with or without a mild degree of handicap.'

Thirty-four per cent.

'You can give us some information that might help us, Lemmer. How soon after her fall did you get to her?'

'I'll have to think about it.'

'One minute? Two, four, five?'

I shut my eyes. I saw the sniper in the grass, the sights of the weapon tracking us, the shot inaudible over the noise of the train, only the white vapour from the barrel, like the mist on your breath on an icy morning. Emma jerking in my arms . . .

'The gunshot wound, Eleanor? What about the wound?'

'Explain the trajectory.'

'About thirty degrees, shooting from below.'

'That's what saved her. The bullet missed the lungs and arteries. But the bullet wound is not our primary concern.'

How long did it take me to reach her?

How long had I waited after she fell, after the T-shirt had torn?

I was jumping again. The train on my left was a rust-brown blur, the grass, the sleepers, the gravel beside the tracks flashed past. I was suspended in air. I hit the ground. Shoulder first, a hard impact, sudden pain, face in the grass, winded, something cut my arm. I rolled over and over and then lay in the grass, looking at brown earth. How long had I lain like that? I didn't know. How long was it before I could get up?

How far from me were the balaclavas at that stage? The motion of the train had taken us farther from them – a hundred, two hundred metres? Was it more? The sniper was the reference point. It must have been more than three hundred metres. When I saw them next, they were closing in. How long had they stood still?

'I really don't know,' I said. 'Maybe two minutes before I reached her. Though it might have been more.'

'When you reached her, was she unconscious?'

'I think so. Why?'

'There is a general rule for coma patients – the shorter the time between trauma and coma, the more serious the condition.'

'So, it's bad news.'

'Yes, Lemmer, it's bad news.'

She would not allow me to see Emma. I had to wait until the next day. Her husband wanted to see me before he went home. She called him. Dr Koos came in and kissed his wife on the forehead.

'I know what you're thinking, pal,' he said to me. 'You are wondering how an ou like me could get such a sexy creature for a wife.'

'No, Doc . . .'

'Does he call you "doc" too?' he asked his wife.

'All the time.'

'I'll inject him till he stops.'

'Thank you, darling.'

'We have names. She's Eleanor and I am Koos. Repeat after me . . .'

'How did an ugly ou like you get a wife like that, Koos?'

'That's more like it. And the answer is: I have no idea. How are you feeling? Your eyes are not quite so manic, at least.'

'He listens to me when I talk. That's why I married him,' she said.

'Naaa, it's because I'm so good at kissing, et cetera.'

'Never mind the "et cetera". There's a patient present.'

'OK, pal, you must be feeling really sore.'

'I'll survive.'

'Oh, tough guy? It doesn't work on women.'

'Sometimes,' she said.

'But not as good as a perfectly performed French kiss . . .'

'Koos!'

He grinned and took a plastic container of pills out of the pocket of his white coat. He put it on the table in front of me. 'Take two tonight before you go to sleep and one after every meal from tomorrow on. It will ease the pain and help you sleep well. But no more than three per day. When you don't hurt any more, throw the rest away.'

'OK, Doc.'

'There we go again. He's tough, but he's no rocket scientist. Maybe because he's in love. It screws up your head.'

'You think he's in love?'

'Definitely.'

'You sound better,' said Jeanette Louw over the phone. I could hear she had a Gauloise between her lips.

'They injected me with something. I slept for six hours.'

'I know. I told them they'd better do something. You should have heard yourself. How is she, Lemmer?'

I told her.

'Doesn't sound good.'

'I know.'

'It's not your fault.'

'I'm not so sure of that.'

'Stop shitting me. What could you have done?'

'I should have taken the threat seriously. I should have believed her.'

'What would you have done differently?'

I didn't know. I didn't want to think about it. 'There are things I need.'

'What?'

'Two invisibles. A car. Money. And a firearm.'

It didn't take her long to put two and two together. 'You're going after them.'

'Yes.'

Another pause. I heard her draw on the cigarette and blow out the smoke, two thousand kilometres away.

'Will ten thousand do?'

PART TWO

23

I didn't recognise the police guards at the door of the intensive care unit. The two youngsters looked wet behind the ears. Phatudi's clods must be on day shift, but these boys didn't look any better. They sat staring at me with their pistols safely clipped in their holsters until I reached them. One stood up then.

'No entry.' His eyes were bloodshot from lack of sleep.

'My name is on the list.'

'Who are you?'

'Lemmer.'

He took a folded sheet of paper from his breast pocket and opened it out.

'Martin Fitzroy?'

Fucking Phatudi. 'Yes.'

'Wait here.'

The balaclavas could have eliminated them in about four seconds.

I waited. At a quarter past seven Dr Eleanor Taljaard came out of Emma's ward. She looked tired. I wondered when she had last slept. She said there were 'positive signs'. 'She's still in the coma, but is responding more strongly to external stimuli. Her Glasgow index is eight now.'

'How much will that improve her chances?'

'Ask me again after we've done the CAT scan tonight.'

'More or less?'

'Lemmer, it's guesswork.'

'I know that.'

'Well, I'd say more than fifty per cent.'

'That's an improvement on yesterday's thirty-four per cent.'

'It is. Let's not get too excited about it. There's a still a lot of work to do. You can be of help.'

'Really?'

'She needs stimulation, Lemmer. Your voice is the only one she knows. I want you to talk to her.'

'Me? Talk to her?'

'Yes.' With great patience. 'I want you to sit in the chair beside her bed and talk to her.'

'For how long?'

'As long as possible. You have all day.'

'All day!'

'Of course, you can eat and drink when you need to, but the more time you spend talking to her, the better.'

'What do I say?'

'Whatever you like. Keep your voice level and speak only loud enough for her to hear you. Talk to her.'

Life is not fair.

Eleanor saw exactly how keen I was.

'Come on, Lemmer, she won't know what you're saying. Get a book and read to her. Or tell her the story of a film you've seen. Anything. She needs you.'

She seemed lifeless and fragile, pale and forlorn. They had shaved off her hair. There were bandages around her head and chest, wires connected to her, a drip in her arm, monitors and machines making soft electronic noises. Her left hand lay on top of the bedlinen, very still. I wanted to reach out and touch it.

I sat beside her on the bed. I didn't want to look at her. I looked through the glass on the other side of her. Eleanor Taljaard stood out there watching me. She nodded at me. I nodded back. I looked at Emma.

'I'm sorry,' but it was too quiet, she wouldn't be able to hear me. I cleared my throat. 'Emma, I'm so sorry.'

Only the electronics of her life functions answered me.

What should I say to her?

'I, um, the doctor said you can hear me.'

The whole day? Impossible. Where could I get a book? A magazine? A woman's magazine might be the solution.

'They say you are a little better this morning. They say there's a good chance you will recover. You must *vasbyt . . .*'

Vasbyt. What kind of fucking word was that? How could I tell someone in a coma to hang in there? I'm a moron.

'Emma, they said I must talk to you because you know my voice.'

Tell her what you need to say.

'It was my fault, Emma. I should have believed you. That was the mistake I made. I'm so sorry. I thought I was smart. Thought I knew people, thought I knew you. I was wrong.'

She just lay there.

'I'll fix it. I promise I'll fix it.'

How? How was I going to fix it?

'I don't know how yet, but I will.'

Then I sat back and was quiet.

I looked up at the glass window. Dr Taljaard was gone. Emma and I were alone. I could see the slow movement of her chest, breathing in and out.

I gathered my thoughts slowly and carefully and said, 'I have to keep talking. You know I'm not good at this. The thing is, I don't know what else to say to you. They didn't give me any time to think. I hope you understand. I'll go and buy a magazine in a while. What do you read? I wonder. There's such a choice nowadays . . . It rained again this morning. Not thunderstorms like the other night, only soft rain. I was outside just now. The first time since we . . . It's not so hot now.'

Could I go out to buy a magazine?

'Dr Eleanor Taljaard seems to know what she's doing. She's about fifty. Her husband also works here. His name is Koos. They are an interesting couple. He's shorter than she is. They seem to get along very well.'

Say something.

'I will tell Jeanette Louw to refund you your money.'

Don't talk about the injury.

What do women like?

'Remember when I said I was a builder? There at Wolhuter's place? I was trying to be clever, but it wasn't a complete lie. I'm busy doing up my own house. At Loxton.'

This was the right topic.

'It's an old house. No one is really sure when it was built. I think it must be between ninety and a hundred years old. It's the last house on the left as you drive out to the town dam. The previous owner was a Muslim. He was the electrician in town for a year or two. The people nicknamed it the Al Qaeda house. You know, tongue in cheek. But there wasn't enough work there and he left. Maybe he didn't feel at home without his own people. Now they talk about Lemmer's house. It's kind of ironic because it is my first house. I had a flat in Seapoint before. Before that I always rented, because we were six months in Pretoria and six months in Cape Town when I worked for the minister.

'In any case, I'm busy renovating my house. It wasn't in a bad state. There were a few cracks in the walls and the garden was very neglected, because the Muslim had been away for two years when I moved in. But the layout is peculiar. All the old houses in Loxton are built with the kitchen and bathroom side by side at the back. When you want a bath you have to walk from the bedroom down the passage and through the kitchen. They didn't build showers at all. I don't know why, water is so scarce in the Karoo. The old folk only built baths.

'At the moment I'm breaking down the wall between the bathroom and the kitchen. I've converted one of the smaller bedrooms into a bathroom. It was quite a job – I had to move all the pipes and plumbing. It took me about a year between working jobs for Jeanette. I think the new bathroom looks good now. I've got ceramic tiles on the floor and a big shower and basin and a toilet behind a little wall that I built.

'In p . . . I learned bricklaying previously. Perhaps I should tell . . .

'Maybe later. Anyway, I rebuilt the wall three times before it was right.

'When the new bathroom was ready, I started on the wall between the kitchen and the bathroom. I want to make one big room including the small bedroom beside the kitchen. A kind of big living space for eating and cooking and entertaining. Not that I can actually cook . . . Or do much entertaining. But in Loxton the people are different. They knock on your door and say, "We've come for coffee." And then you chat.

'There's an old Aga stove in the kitchen. It's lovely and warm in winter. When I have finished taking down the walls, it will be one big room with the stove in the centre.

'There's a coloured woman who is teaching me to cook. Her name is Agatha. She says the stove is in her name. She comes twice a week to clean and wash and iron clothes and then she shows me what to do with a leg of lamb or ribs in the oven. The meat that comes out of that Aga melts in your mouth and the delicious aroma fills the whole house. Sometimes she brings her grandson along. He's three. His name is Ryno. She says he's named after a character in *7de Laan*, the Afrikaans soap opera. Do you ever watch it? I started watching it with Agatha. She gets personally involved in that soapie.

'I must be boring you a lot.

'When I worked for the government there was never time for TV. I have a satellite dish now. It was just for the rugby to start with. But you know how poor the rugby was . . .

'Life is very boring in Loxton. But that's what I want. That's why I moved there. But that's another story.

'In any case, the old sitting room at the front is my bedroom now, with the new bathroom alongside. The house has a veranda facing the street. There are no houses across the street. Just the commonage. Karoo veld. Koppies. The commonage is ten thousand hectares. Can you believe that? Some people keep sheep on the commonage. Oom Joe van Wyk said I should get myself some sheep. He said I mustn't worry about the slaughtering, there is a butcher in town again for the first time in seven years. And a restaurant and a coffee shop . . . the Rooi Granaat. You should taste the fig liqueur that Tannie Nita makes, Emma, it's better than any wine.

'I've got the garden going too. There is still irrigation by water furrow in Loxton. My turn is on Tuesdays at three o'clock. When I'm not there Agatha or Antjie Barnard leads the water from the water furrows. There's an old pear tree in the garden. I pruned it back and it bears well. I planted a saltbush hedge all around the boundary fence, and three peach trees and an apricot. Agatha said I should plant a fig tree, because it's best suited to the Karoo and she could make jam. I planted four close to the kitchen. The rest is lawn and a few flower beds.

'I enjoy the gardening.'

I looked at my watch. A quarter to eight in the morning.

The whole day.

I looked at her hand. The shape of the slender wrist and fingers.

'Emma, I don't know what else to tell you.'

Outside, behind the glass, a nurse walked past.

'I want to start a herb garden too. And a vegetable garden. The soil is good. Oom Wessel van der Walt has a vegetable garden on both his plots and the plots in Loxton are big, seldom smaller than a thousand square metres. Oom Wessel bought two plots long ago. When he retired he built on one. A lot of people in town are retired, but more and more of them are from Cape Town or Johannesburg. To get away. From whatever. They came and opened guest houses and a restaurant. There's a couple who do freelance writing for magazines and a guy who designs websites. And a few holiday houses.'

The door opened. A nurse came in, a young black woman. She smiled at me.

'Good morning,' she said, and came over to Emma.

'Good morning,' I said.

She took readings and noted them on a chart.

'Just carry on,' she said. 'I'll be finished soon.'

'Do you think she understands what I say?'

'No.'

'Do you think she will remember anything?'

'No.' Then mischievously, she said: 'So if you want to say anything important, you will have to wait until she wakes up.'

I wondered what Dr Koos had been telling the staff.

'Can I go out to get a magazine? To read to her.'

'You can, but do you know which one to buy?'

'No, I'll just get a woman's magazine.'

'But which one?'

'An Afrikaans one.'

'Which Afrikaans one?'

'Does it matter?'

She looked at me sternly. 'Of course it matters.'

'Why?'

'Shame,' she said. 'You're not good with women, are you?'

24

'If I tell you why I went to live in Loxton, I will have to tell you the whole story. Right from the beginning.'

When she wakes up and Phatudi talks to her she will find out who I really am anyway.

She doesn't understand and she won't remember either.

Tell her.

'Emma, I was in jail.'

She just lay there.

'I was in jail for four years.'

I leaned back in the chair and shut my eyes.

'When I came out, I didn't want to stay in the city. The city has turned into a place that brings out the worst in us. I'm not making excuses. I had choices and I made the wrong ones. But you have to know your weaknesses and you have to protect yourself from them. I went looking for a place that could protect me. I just drove. I took the back roads, from the Cape to Ceres. Then to Sutherland and Merweville and Fraserburg and Loxton.

'Did you know there are mountain passes in the Karoo? Did you know there are places where you can stop and get out and see for a hundred kilometres? There are gravel roads that run through rivers that have water in them all year round. In the Karoo.

'I didn't know that.

'In Loxton I was filling up at the Co-op and Oom Joe van Wyk came and talked to me. The pumps at the Co-op are at the back; you have to drive through the gates. I got out to stretch my legs and he approached me. Put out his hand and said he was Joe van Wyk and asked me how many kilos the Isuzu had, because he farmed only with Isuzus and his last one had lasted seven years and four hundred thousand kilometres. Now the children were farming and he and his wife lived in town and he still drove an Isuzu, but a Frontier, because there had to be room for the grandchildren. So who was I and where did I come from?

'That's how it should be. The other day you talked about people not hearing each other. I wanted to say I was different, I wanted to say I don't want to be heard, I want to be left alone. I think hell is other people. The Jean-Paul Sartre way. But I would have been lying. I don't really believe that.

'What I should have said was that you were wrong. I don't want to be heard, Emma, I want to be seen. On the one hand it scares me: to be seen. On the other hand it's what I long for most. Because it never happened. The city is one reason. People don't see each other in the city.

'In Loxton, somebody saw me. But that's not why I went to live there. Not the main reason. I wanted to be in a place where I was safe.

'I've got a problem with my temper. That's the trouble with me, Emma. I needed to find a place where I would not be provoked.

'But there were other reasons too.

'I believe everyone must belong somewhere. I think it's in our blood.

'In prison I tried to study for a degree. It wasn't the first time. I must be the longest enrolled student in the history of Unisa. I have completed eleven subjects, but not all for the same qualification. I would start a course and a year or two later I'd want to do something else. When I was in jail I read and studied to try and understand what was going on in my life. It didn't help. You are what you are. The answers aren't in books. They're in you.

'But there were things in the books that made me think. Like the desire to be part of something. Even though you know you can't really be. They say we lived in tribal bands in ancient times. Later in tribes. All the people were related to each other. Somewhere I read that if two people walked into each other in the forest in New Guinea, they would discuss their genealogies for hours to try and prove a relationship. Otherwise they would have to kill each other.

'That's the way we are. If we are family, if we belong to the same tribe, if we have something in common, we see each other. There is peace and order. But in the city we are nothing to each other. It's everyone for himself.

'When I was a kid, in Seapoint, there were tribes. Jews and Greeks and Italians. Everyone belonged to a tribe. Except me.

'My father was an Afrikaner in Seapoint. Gerhardus Lodewikus Lemmer. Gert. Gert, the mechanic, at Ford in Main Road. That's where he met my mother. She was English. Beverly Anne Simmons of the Spares Department.

'She was a slim, petite woman.

'Her father was Martin Fitzroy Simmons. My English grandpa. I never knew him. But I inherited his names.

'When you told me your parents' story. How your father did all those things. My father wasn't like that. For thirteen years my mother kept telling him he should start his own business but he wouldn't. "You're a good mechanic. You can make a fortune." He said he went to work and he went home and the worries were the Englishman's, the man who owned the dealership. If you own your own business, the worries are yours. He didn't want the worries. Then my mother said he was just poor white Afrikaner trash, she hadn't married him to live in a two-bedroom flat in Seapoint for the rest of her life.

'They must have loved each other. In the beginning anyway. I know he loved her. I could see it.

'I've only once talked about them before, Emma. It's hard for me. I don't want to. There are times when I don't even want to think about them. Each was as bad as the other. Each in his or her own way. My mother was a manipulator and a slut and my father was a coward and a violent man. What do you do when your parents are like that? What do you do when other people talk about their parents and you sit there with this hatred inside you? For what they did to each other. And to you. They were like two different chemical substances that were harmless on their own, but as a combination they were explosive.

'English was the language of domestic fights, of arguments and baiting, screaming and swearing at each other. They always spoke English to each other. My mother refused to speak Afrikaans. "It's such a common language," she used to say, and then my father would speak only Afrikaans to me and she would fight with him about that too. On the other hand, they fought about everything. Money, work, his drinking and her unfaithfulness, about his lack of ambition and her desire for status. About the food she cooked and the household tasks that he didn't do. About her spendthrift ways and his stinginess, about every conceivable thing.

'I thought it was normal. It was all I knew. For five days of the week they would argue and bicker every night. Every night they would take potshots at each other until something hit home and that became the subject, the point of argument they focused on until they began to rant and swear.

'I don't know how old I was when I began going off on my own. Seven, maybe. When it was time for them to come home I would wander round the streets or go and sit by the sea. But when I got home and she asked, "Where were you?" and he said, "Leave my son alone" I would become the new focus of disagreement.

'While I walked around Seapoint I would see other people. Tribes and groups sitting on pavements and in gardens and on balconies, all laughing and chatting. I would stand there like a child without a cent gazing through a sweet-shop window.

'He hit me for the first time when I was nine years old. It was like a dam wall breaking.

'He never trusted her, he always suspected something was going on. He hinted and accused her, but he never had any proof. She was too sly for that. But that night she was reckless. And he was drunk. He was standing at the window and he saw one of the Bardini brothers who had the ice-cream shop on Main dropping her off with his motorbike. He saw her kiss the man goodbye, how he held her bottom while they kissed. How she looked back at the Italian as she walked away and laughed. Then my father knew what she had done and when she came in he said, "And now you're fucking the dagos?"

'And she said, "At least they know how to fuck," and he called her a whore and she threw an ashtray at him that smashed against the wall and he wanted to hit her. He went up to her and lifted his hand and she said, "Don't you dare," and he turned around and hit me on the side of my head and she screamed, "What the hell are you doing?" and he said, "Will you do it again?" and she said, "Damn you, what are you doing?" and he hit me again and shouted at her, "Not me. You. You are doing this."'

I stopped talking, because I didn't know how the fuck I had come to be talking of this.

'I'm sorry, Emma.'

I shifted in the chair. I leaned forward. I wondered whether I could hold her hand.

'I didn't mean to go on like that . . .'

Her skin seemed to have become transparent. I could see the dark blue of her delicate veins.

'But that's who I am.'

With every beep of the machine her heart pumped blood through her arteries to her brain, where they still didn't know how much damage there was.

'I think I understand today. How it all fitted together. From that day on, my father hit me. A lot. And hard. The trouble with violence is that it begets more violence. In people, in communities, in countries. It's like this evil you let loose, you can't get the genie back in the bottle. But it doesn't help to stand in the dock and tell the magistrate that it was your father who made you like that.'

I felt the hem of the hospital sheet. It was softer than I expected.

'The thing that I could never understand, was why he didn't hit Bardini. Why didn't he go round to the ice-cream shop and drag the man out of there and beat him up? The answer is that my father was a coward. And that is one thing I swore I never would be.

'My father's strategy worked for a while. He told her if she didn't want him to hit me she would have to stop whoring. She would behave herself for two or three months, but I don't think she could live without the attention of other men.

'Only as an adult did I try and piece together her story. I collected all the photos of her as a child and later ones with my father. I remembered what she used to say about her youth, when she was going at it with her husband. "Daddy loved me, Daddy adored me." She talked about her father like that, the middle-class Englishman from lower Rosebank. He was a clerk in the provincial administration. She had been a pretty child. Petite, with blonde hair and large eyes. On every snapshot she was smiling cheekily at the camera, always conscious of herself. And smug.

'They met at the garage. My father was twenty, with a dark fringe and brooding eyes. He had a girl in Parow, a serious relationship; there was talk of getting engaged. That, I think, was the start of the trouble. My mother wanted the attention of all the men and here was one she couldn't have. She kept on until she got it.

'By the time I was five, she wasn't young and cute any more. I don't know if it was the pregnancy or just the passing of time. Perhaps the souring of their marriage. At thirty she was tired. Worn out, and it showed on her face and her body and she knew it. She tried to regain the attentions of men with make-up, hair dye and tight clothes. They were the candle and she was the moth. It was irresistible, an unavoidable reaction, the way a leg jerks when you bang the knee.

'We went through the cycles. She would be faithful and reasonable and calm would prevail. Then they would start fighting and she would go off looking for attention until some man wanted something more and she would give in and sleep with him somewhere. Even in our flat. Once I came home from school in the morning, I can't remember why, maybe I was sick. I had a key and I went in and heard them. My mother and Phil Robinson, the rich Brit who owned the hotel on the seafront. A hundred hotel rooms, but they had to come to our flat.

'When she saw me she screamed, "Jesus Christ, oh, Jesus Christ, Marty, go away, go away," but I just stood there staring until she climbed off and came and shut the door. Later, when Robinson was gone, she begged me not to tell my father. "He'll just hit you again."

'That's my history, Emma.

'Poor white Afrikaner trash. Just like my mother said.

'My father was a drinker of wine. That's what the smell of wine really brings to mind. The sour smell of his breath when he was drunk and beat me because my mother had gone.

'When I was thirteen, she left. My father beat me then because she wasn't there. And because he wanted to make me "tough, so you can handle life and all its shit".

'He succeeded.

'I've thought about this a lot. What he did to me. The biggest thing is, it takes the fear away. Fear of getting hurt. And of hurting. That was the important one. Feeling pain is something that becomes ordinary afterwards. You get used to it. But causing hurt, it's like a thing that has to get out.

'There was a karate club in Seapoint, in the Anglican church hall. My father sent me there. My problem was with control. I could never understand why we had to hold back, why we weren't allowed to hit the other guy.

'I looked for trouble. At school, in the streets. And I got it. I liked dishing it out. For the first time I was the one causing pain. Drawing blood. Breaking. It is like being outside of yourself. Or inside something else, another world, another state of being. Time stands still. Everything disappears, you hear nothing and you see nothing except a red-grey mist. And this object in front of you that you want to destroy with everything you have in you.

'When I was in Matric, I beat up my father for the first time. After that, things went better for a while.

'I wanted to get out then. Get away from him and from Seapoint. My karate sensei was a policeman. He wanted me for the police karate team. I joined because you have to go to Pretoria. It was far enough. They spotted me there and recruited me to be a bodyguard. I was one for ten years. One year with the Minister of Transport. He retired. Eight years with the white Minister of Agriculture. The last year was with the black Minister of Education.

'My first year . . . The Minister of Transport was an incredible man. He saw me. He saw everybody. Maybe he saw too much – felt too much. Maybe that was why he shot himself. But I often used to think: why couldn't someone like him have been my father?'

25

I talked to Emma Le Roux for four hours before Dr Eleanor Taljaard came to tell me to go and eat.

I didn't tell Emma everything. I didn't tell her about Mona.

I wanted to. I had the words in my mouth.

It's a funny thing, letting all these monsters loose in my head. It's an avalanche, a dry river after rain, a trickle, a stream, a flood that sweeps everything with it.

But when I came to Mona there wasn't enough momentum, the clouds suddenly dried up. Mona of Pretoria. Mona of Muckleneuk. A full-bodied woman four centimetres taller than me.

I sat there, next to Emma, and thought about it. The Mona Chronicles. I met her in the summer of 1987, one year after I became a bodyguard. She worked in a salon in Sunnyside and I had to have a haircut. She said, 'Why don't you let it grow a little?'

'It wouldn't help,' I said.

I sat down and she put the number-one comb on the clippers and drew it back and forth over my head, without saying a word. I watched her while she worked. She had thick brown hair and a pretty face with rosy cheeks. Her skin was smooth and healthy. And her body. She was wearing a loose-fitting dress, but she couldn't hide the generous curves of her breasts and hips. Her ring finger was bare.

She walked away from me to fetch something. A colleague made a remark, I couldn't hear what it was. Mona laughed. It was a wonderful sound, musical, clear, genuine, originating deep inside her, and she surrendered herself to it. I followed the direction of the sound and saw how the laugh slowly invaded her body until the beautiful melody owned her.

When she was finished and had dusted and washed me off, I asked her what her name was and she said, 'Mona.'

'Can I take you out for a pizza on Friday, Mona?'

'Who are you?'

'I'm Lemmer.'

She looked at me for two heartbeats and then she said, 'You can.'

I picked her up at her flat in Berea Street and we ate in Esselen Street. Neither of us was much good at conversation, but it was a comfortable time, as if we knew each other. We were single-child city kids who had never grown up.

I remember she asked me, 'Why are you so skinny when you eat so much?'

'Exercise.'

'What kind of exercise?'

'Fifty pull-ups, sit-ups and push-ups in the morning, the same at night. And fifty kilometres a week.'

'Why all that?'

'For my work.'

She shook her head slowly. 'Thank God I'm a hairdresser.'

I wanted to hear her laugh again. More than that: I wanted to conjure it up out of her, I wanted to be the reason the melody played, because it was the sound of happiness, of contentment, of everything that was good and right in the world.

I took her back to her flat that night and she invited me in and I stayed for nine years. I had to work to hear her laugh. I had to search within myself for a sense of humour, make room for someone who could be daft and light hearted, ready to joke or tease, because Mona's laughter was not programmable. It was elusive and unpredictable, like the numbers in the state lottery. But when I hit the jackpot, the reward – to see her overwhelmed by joy – was great.

Mona changed me without knowing that she had. There is only so much room for baggage. If you bring in humour and light-heartedness, you must throw rancour and melancholy overboard. And then you travel easy. And light.

There were other lessons too. Mona accepted her own weaknesses with cheerful resignation. She was the one who tried to teach me that regret does not pay, we are what we are and there's no sense in hiding that. It was only much later that I was able to master that lesson.

It was an easy relationship. She didn't make demands, she just lived every day for itself. When I told her I would be away with the minister for three or four days she would genuinely say, 'I'll miss you.'

When I returned, her smile was real and she held out her arms and laughed happily when I carried her with some effort to her massive double bed. Then I would undress her and caress her wonderful body inch by inch, until desire flamed up in her, like a she-bear coming out of hibernation. Her body would hum and she would open herself up to me as if opening the doors to wonderland. When I went into her, her face showed intense pleasure without shame. I became addicted to that, as I was to her laughter.

With Mona nothing was conventional.

When I had to accompany the minister to Cape Town for six months the following February, she said, 'I have to tell you something.'

'What?'

'You can do what you like down there.'

'What do you mean?'

She looked out of the window and said, 'Lemmer, I can't . . .'

'Can't what?'

'I can't do without sex for six months.'

'I'll come and visit you.'

She said it didn't matter. If I met someone in the Cape, that was fine. She just didn't want to know about it. When I came back after six months and still wanted to live with her, she would be here. If I didn't want to, that was fine too. But she would not promise to be faithful. Not when I was so far away.

'Why not?'

'There is a type of man I can't say "no" to.'

'What type?'

'Your type.'

'What kind of man would that be?'

She wouldn't say.

'Come with me to Cape Town.'

'This is my place. Right here.'

For nine years she was my summer wife. My house and haven in Pretoria. We never fought. We never talked about the six months that we didn't see each other. Then I took the golden handshake and I knew I would have to go to Cape Town, to Seapoint. I would have to go and find myself.

Once more I said, 'Come with me.'

Once again she said she could not.

Three years after I left her, she called me, the night before I was found guilty and all the papers were full of it. She said, 'Now you know.'

'Now I know what?'

'What type of man I meant.'

I told Emma why I left government service.

'In 1998 they said they had to increase the number of black bodyguards. We could choose a severance package, or a transfer. A transfer to where? They couldn't say. So I took the package.

'I bought myself a flat in a block between Fort and Marine Streets in Seapoint, just a kilometre from where I grew up.

'I looked for my father. I couldn't find him. Nobody knew where he had gone. The Ford dealership was still there with the same name. New owners. The whole of Seapoint was full of new people. The Italians had gone, and the Greeks. Of the Jews, only the women were still there, old ladies walking along the seafront alone or in groups waiting for their children to come and visit them. There were Nigerians and Somalis, Russians and Romanians, Bosnians, Chinese, Iraqis. New tribes that I could not be part of.

'I started a karate dojo at Virgin Active in Greenpoint. In the mornings I taught self-defence to English and Afrikaans women; in the afternoon, JKA karate to kids – South Africans and all the other tribes of Seapoint. I did that for nearly two years. It was a job. At the gym the women called me "Lemmer" and the children called me "sensei". I was neither happy nor unhappy.

'But I began to see things. I had a new perspective, because for the first time in over thirteen years I was a civilian again. The Man on the Street.

'I saw the new wealth. I saw the new consumerism, the frenzied buying of brands and status and just-because-I-want-it. I saw it in everyone. White, black and brown. Did they want to hide the past behind a wall of possessions? Or was it the present they wanted to hide?

'The biggest surprise was the new urban aggression, an attitude of "I'll take what I want", of "don't stand in my way". I noticed it on the roads first, the lack of consideration. The absence of the chivalrous, the charitable, the community spirit. Lawlessness too, as though there were no rules any more. Or rather as if the rules were not for everyone. Driving through red lights. Driving slowly in the right lane – or fast in the left. Cell phones to ears on the freeway, and the glare they gave you of "just try and say something". As though this country had become a place where you did as you pleased, took what you could before it all went to hell. Or before someone else took it.

'And the moaning and groaning and gnashing of teeth. Everyone was unhappy, irrespective of race, colour or creed. Unhappy with the government, with each other, with themselves. Everyone pointing fingers, blaming, complaining.

'I couldn't understand it. The Russians and the Romanians and the Bosnians would collect their children after the evening karate class and they would say, "This is a wonderful country. This is the land of milk and honey." But the South Africans complained. They drove smart cars, lived in big houses and seafront flats, they ate in restaurants and bought big flat-screen TVs and designer clothes, yet no one was happy and it was always someone else's fault.

'The whites complained about affirmative action and corruption, but they forget that they had benefited from the same for fifty or sixty years. The blacks blamed apartheid for everything. But it was already six years since it had been abolished.

'The loneliness. In the evening I would walk down the passage in my block of flats to my door, following the pizza man, who was delivering boxes to lonely fat women who opened their doors with frightened eyes and who ate alone while looking for friends on TV. Or the Internet. In the morning a woman would occasionally invite me for coffee and then would sit and tell me how lonely her marriage was. Sometimes I was lonely enough to relieve their need. But then they would stop coming. That's when I formulated Lemmer's Law of Lonely Moms.

'I knew something was going to happen. Not a conscious knowing, just a vague premonition. A city sucks you in systematically, changes you, squeezes and polishes you, so you become like the rest. Lonely, aggressive and selfish. Also, you are aware of who you are on a certain level, of the things that lie dormant inside. The things you are capable of, the things that being a state bodyguard had channelled and suppressed. But you don't think about them or talk about them, you are just aware of the tension, a growing unease.

'You must think I'm rationalising, Emma. You must think I'm making excuses. I did what I did; I can't get away from that. I sat in front of my lawyer, a big man by the name of Gustav Kemp, and I tried to explain to him why it wasn't my fault. He said, "*Kak*, man. You play the hand life deals you and you take your punishment like a man." He gave me a day to think it over, and if I still thought I was innocent he would organise another lawyer to represent me.

'He remained my lawyer.

'So what happened had to happen. Sooner or later. In prison I thought about that day a lot, how I should have seen it coming, all the signs were there. In me. In other people's eyes when they bump into you on the pavement or give you the finger in traffic.

'But hindsight is always perfect vision. We are like the proverbial frog in water that keeps heating up.

'That evening . . .

'I had to go to Bellville for a JKA grading meeting. I was in a hurry after the karate class. I showered and changed and ran down the Virgin Active steps to my car. There were four of them busy with Demetru Niculescu, one of my students. He was a Romanian, fifteen years old with bad acne and a floppy fringe. The men were between twenty-two and twenty-five, that smartass age when you are nobody, but know everything. Four whites with gym-built muscles and a gang mentality who were taunting Demetru.

' "Show us some moves, karate kid."

' "Hey, nice pimples, dude. Grow them in the dark like mushrooms?"

'When Demetru opened his mouth they homed in on his accent.

' "Where the fuck are you from?"

' "Seapoint."

' "Bullshit, dude. What's your nationality?"

' "South African."

' "Your daddy in the Russian mafia?"

'That was all I heard. I said, "Leave the kid alone."

' "Whoo, it's the karate master. Now I'm scared."

' "Go home, Demetru."

'He left, relieved.

'The biggest one heard my accent. "Hey, Dutchman, are you going to show us some moves?"

'I walked away. He followed me. "I'm talking to you, Dutchman." The others shouted, "Chickening out? We won't hurt you, Chop Suey."

'I heard the big one's footsteps behind me. I knew if he touched me there would be trouble. He followed me right into the car park. I felt his hand on my shoulder and I turned and there he was up close, taller and bigger, and I was ready, really ready.

'I said to him, "I will kill you," and I knew and he knew it was the truth.

'Something shifted in his eyes, I saw the flicker of fear. That's what stopped me at that moment. I hadn't expected that. But I suppose it was also what made him drive after me, that moment when he lost face.

'So I turned away, got into my car and drove off. Never even looked back.

'I wanted to go through the Waterfront to save time. There was traffic at the circle near the BMW Pavilion, a long queue. I felt another car bump me from behind. Not hard. A nudge. Then I saw them in the mirror, in a Volkswagen Golf GTi. They shouted and gestured. So I got out.

'I should never have got out, Emma. I should have kept on driving.

'They got out too.

' "We're talking to you, arsehole."

' "Who the fuck do you think you are?"

' "Fucking hairy back cunt."

'The big guy was the driver of the Golf. Vincent Michael Kelly. Vince. Twenty-four years old, an articled clerk at KPMG. One point nine metres tall, ninety-five kilograms. I would learn all that in court.

'I inspected the rear end of my car. There was no damage.

' "Hey, he's talking to you."

'All four approached. Vince came up to me. "Got a hearing problem, rock spider?" He shoved me in the chest. There was only bravado showing in his eyes now.

'Steroids were mentioned during the court case, but we couldn't prove anything. I think they did it because there were four of them, because they were young and strong. I was shorter and smaller than them. It creates a visual illusion. But I think it was because at the gym Vince was momentarily not the man he thought he was. He had come so that he wouldn't have to live with that moment.

'He pushed me and I hit him. Not hard. Just enough to bring him to his senses. But it didn't. Then the others pitched in. I tried, Emma. Part of me knew what would happen if I let go. I tried. But we are what we are. That's what I learnt, that night. It doesn't matter what they say, it doesn't matter how hard the prison psychologists try, we are what we are.

'That's why I moved to Loxton, Emma. That's why I went looking for a tribe of my own. I had to avoid these situations. Try and avoid the possibility of trouble. If I had to stand in that street at the circle, if they came at me again, I would do exactly the same, go to that place, that other world.

'If it had been just one guy, I wouldn't have lost myself. Not even then. But there's something about two or three or four that gives you new rights, at least in your own mind. Switches off the warning lights. And there was this frustration too, about who I am and where I came from and thirteen years of repression.

'I let it all loose.

'The big one, Vincent, he . . .'

Even though she could not hear, would not remember, I chose my words carefully. 'He died,' I said. 'They charged me with manslaughter. With extenuating circumstances. A six-year sentence. I did four.'

For a long time I sat beside the bed without speaking. Ten, maybe twenty minutes.

Aware of what went unsaid.

Vince falling and hitting his head against the Golf. I had hit him, in rage and hate, with everything I had. Three, four, five times. He whiplashed backwards and the back of his head had connected with the right front corner of the car. I can still hear the sound, that hollow, hard, clear sound.

He was in a coma for four days. Brain damage. Kemp used words like parietal and epidural haematoma with great disapproval. And then Vince died.

And the other thing. The thing I had not told Kemp, the lawyer, or the judge, not anyone.

How sweet it was.

Those moments, those minutes when I released myself, when I could kick and hit, could inflict hurt, could break and *bliksem*, that was where I belonged. When I killed Vince and hammered the other three until they begged for mercy, the tumblers of the universe were lining up perfectly. I felt at one with the world, whole and complete, good and right. It's a terrible thing. It intoxicates. It's addictive.

And so terribly sweet.

26

Dr Eleanor Taljaard came and chased me out just after twelve. She looked rested and professional. 'I have work to do here and it's lunchtime. Koos is waiting for you in the restaurant. Maggie left a message. It's in your room. You can come back at two.'

'OK, Eleanor.'

'You did well.'

Had I?

The restaurant was full. 'Sunday,' said Dr Koos Taljaard. 'Conscience day. They visit the sick.'

Over a meal of tasteless chicken schnitzel with cheese sauce he told me they had been in Nelspruit for sixteen years – at the Provincial Hospital first, then the SouthMed Clinic.

'In all those years we never had a patient falling off a train because of a bullet wound.'

I just looked at him and carried on chewing.

'What happened?' he asked.

'Someone was angry with us.'

'But why? What could make someone so angry?'

'I don't know.'

He looked at me in disbelief. 'It's true,' I said.

'People don't usually react like that,' he said.

'I know.' The question was: who did? And why?

In my room there was another typed letter from Maggie T. Padayachee. And a car key.

Dear Mr Lemmer
Budget Car Rental has delivered a silver Audi A4
for you. It is parked near the gate.

Also, a Ms Jeanette Louw called and requested
that you kindly return her call at your convenience
- on her cellular phone.
Very best wishes
Maggie T. Padayachee
Client Services Manager

I phoned Jeanette.

'Thanks for the car.'

'A pleasure. They tell me her condition has improved.'

'That's what they say.'

'And you? How do you feel today?'

'There's nothing wrong with me.'

'The flights are full, Lemmer. The entire country is flying off somewhere for New Year. We can only come tomorrow.'

'We?'

'I'm bringing Fikter and Minnaar.'

'Oh.' Not usual for her to come. She heard my surprise.

'You know what the Cape is like in the holidays. Full of Gautengers and foreigners. I haven't been to the Lowveld for a long time.'

'What time are you coming?'

'We'll be there by lunchtime. I'm bringing your Christmas present. I hope it's what you wanted.'

'Thanks.'

'It's the least I can do.'

Strange thing to say, I thought.

'She's stable enough to do the scans this afternoon,' Eleanor Taljaard said when I was back at the intensive care unit by two o'clock. 'You're on duty until four.'

I sat down. Emma was still pale and wan under the sheets.

'Hello, Emma.'

They had replaced the bag of fluid dripping into her vein. It hung fat and transparent above her bed.

'I went for lunch. Chicken schnitzel. It wasn't Mohlolobe's standard. Then I phoned Jeanette Louw. They'll be here tomorrow, she and two bodyguards. They will look after you here, Emma. Until I've finished.'

Finished. Finished what? I hadn't the faintest idea where to begin. Sitting here beside a woman I barely knew, with the urge to smash someone's head in, and I had no idea how I was going to do it.

I wanted to go and lie on my bed, shut my eyes and think about where Emma and I had been, about every little thing that had happened. I hadn't believed her when I should have. Not listened, not looked, nor paid attention. Now there were things in my head, things that didn't quite make sense, but I couldn't get a grip on them. Like soap in the bath, they slipped out of my grasp when I closed my hand on them. I must think. The whole thing just didn't make sense. Not enough to kill Emma le Roux. What had she done to cause that? What evil had she interfered in?

Gloves? In summer? In the Lowveld? Gloves and balaclavas, but the sniper had not worn them.

In Cape Town there had been three, but all three were covered then. Had they also worn gloves? Understandable, since they didn't want to leave fingerprints. But in the veld?

Why only yesterday? Why had they waited? Did they have to come up from the Cape first?

I tried to arrange the events in sequence. Emma said the news report about Cobie de Villiers had been two days before they attacked her in the Cape. Three days before Christmas. The twenty-second. Saturday, 22 December.

Two days. Why the delay between the call to Phatudi and the attack in the Cape? What did it mean?

We had arrived here on 26 December. One, two, three, four days before the ambush.

Did it mean anything?

I must talk to Emma. I couldn't just sit here and think. She must hear my voice.

Where was I last? Jeanette. On her way.

'Jeanette . . .' I said.

'I had been in Loxton for two months when the phone rang. It was Jeanette Louw asking if I was looking for work.

'I hadn't much in the bank. I had sold the flat in Seapoint for a big profit, but my legal fees and buying the Al Qaeda house ate up most of it. So I asked, "What kind of work?" and she explained.

'I asked her how she knew about me and she said, "There are one or two of your old colleagues who speak well of you."

' "I've just come out of jail."

' "I don't want to marry you, I want to offer you a job." Then she explained how it worked, how much she paid and, "You should know, I'm a lesbian and I don't take shit from anyone. When I call, you come. Immediately. If you get up to shit, I'll fire your butt. Immediately. But I never drop my people. Are you interested?"

'So I accepted, because I looked around my house and I knew how much needed to be done. I hadn't even begun to break down and rebuild. The place was empty. I had a bed and a table in the kitchen with two chairs. I bought the table in Victoria West at an auction and I got the two chairs from Antjie Barnard as a present.

'Antjie. Now there's a character. I called her "Tannie", "Aunt", showing respect for one's elders, and she threatened to hit me with her walking stick.

'That's another story. Antjie Barnard came knocking on my door in Loxton, four o'clock on a Sunday afternoon. She was wearing big walking boots and a wide-brimmed hat. She said, "I'm Antjie Barnard and I want to know who you are." She was sixty-seven then and you could see she was a lovely woman, beautiful perhaps when she was young, green eyes of an unusual shade, like the sea at the South Pole. She put out her hand and I shook it and said, "Lemmer. Pleased to meet you, Tannie."

' "Tannie? Tannie? Am I married to your uncle?" The walking stick lifted ready to beat me. "My name is Antjie."

' "Antjie."

' "That's right. What do I call you?"

' "Lemmer."

' "Right then, Lemmer, stand aside so I can come in. You have coffee, I expect."

'I told her, "I don't have chairs."

' "Then we will sit on the floor."

'And we did, coffee mugs in hand. She pulled out a packet of long cigarettes, offered one to me and asked, "What is a man like you doing in Loxton?"

' "Not for me, I don't smoke."

' "I hope to God you drink," she said, and lit one for herself with a slender electronic lighter.

' "Not really."

' "Not really?"

' "Actually, I don't drink at all."

' "Sex?"

' "I like sex."

' "Thank God. A person must have a sin. Not bad sins, Lemmer. Good sins. Otherwise you don't live. Life is too short."

' "What are the good sins?"

' "Gossip. Eating. Smoking. Drinking. Sex. What do I do with this ash?"

'I fetched her a saucer. When I came back she asked, "Was it a good sin that brought you to Loxton?"

' "No."

' "Was there a woman involved? Children?"

' "No."

' "Then it doesn't matter. We all have our secrets and that's fine."

'I wondered what her secret was.

'Two weeks later she came knocking again, this time late on a Tuesday. "Bring your pick-up, I've got some chairs for your table." We drove to her house, a perfectly restored Victorian Karoo house with white walls and a green roof. The furniture inside was tastefully antique. Down the passage was a row of black-and-white photographs of Antjie Barnard and her life. I looked at them and she said, "I was a cellist." An understatement, because the images in frames told a story of an international career.

'The same afternoon we initiated the chairs in my kitchen over coffee – and a cigarette for her.

' "And this ashtray, Lemmer? Have you taken up smoking?"

' "No."

' "You bought it for me."

' "I did."

' "That's my trouble."

' "What?"

' "Men. They can't leave me alone."

'I laughed. Then I saw she was serious.

'She looked at me with those clear, piercing eyes and said, "Can you keep a secret, Lemmer?"

' "I can."

'Those eyes measured me again.

' "Do you know why I'm here? In Loxton?"

' "No."

' "Sex."

' "Here?"

' "No, you idiot. Not here." Then she told me how she grew up in Bethlehem in the Free State in a typical conservative Afrikaans home, how her talent for music quickly outgrew the coaching available in that town. She was sent to the Oranje Meisieskool in Bloemfontein so she could take cello lessons at the university. At seventeen she won an international bursary and studied in Vienna. At twenty she married an Austrian, at twenty-eight an Italian, at thirty-six a German, but concert tours were no good for marriage.

' "Men liked me too much, and I liked men too much."

'At fifty-five she had had enough. Enough money, enough memories, enough strange cities and hotel rooms and fair-weather friends. So she came back to the Free State and bought herself a house in Rosendal near Bethlehem.

' "Then I met Willem of Wonderkop. A farmer. Sixty years old, married, but a Man with a capital 'M'. We couldn't keep our hands off each other. One Wednesday evening he told his wife he had to go to a church council meeting, but instead he came to me and we made love like a pair of twenty-year-olds, wild and abandoned. We fell off the bed and I broke my arm and he broke his hip and there we lay, naked, guilty and in big trouble.

' "What could I do? I couldn't carry him and he couldn't stand up. I had to get help. I had to choose between the preacher and the two gays who ran the coffee shop. Either way we were done for because nobody gossips like gays and ministers. So I chose the gays, to save him his place on the church council.

' "When my arm came out of plaster, I got in my car and went looking for a place where the people wouldn't know the story. That's how I ended up in Loxton."

'She never asked me about my past. I told her I had been a bodyguard for the government. When I had to be away for two or three weeks I would tell her where I would be. Of course, then the whole town knew. They never say so, but there is some pride that someone from Loxton was guarding important and famous people from the evils of this world.

'But I am not yet truly one of them. There is hope. At Easter this year I was having tea with Oom Joe and all his children and grandchildren were there when Antjie came in. Oom Joe introduced her to his children, "And this is our Antjie Barnard."

'Maybe, in four or five years, if nobody finds out why I went to prison, they will introduce me as "our Lemmer".'

27

After four, when they came to collect Emma for the scan, I fetched the keys of the Audi and went out to find the car.

The car park was chock-a-block full, but I found the car near the entrance, as Maggie T. had promised. It was a two-litre manual sedan, silver, with satellite navigation. Jeanette was not stingy. I got in and drove to Klaserie.

I took the byroads, turned off unexpectedly, accelerated, memorising every vehicle in front and behind, but nobody followed me.

The BMW was no longer beside the R40. Only the deep ruts remained in the long grass, muddy now after the rain. I locked the Audi and walked the four hundred metres back to the T-junction. I felt the aches in my body. From the stop street I walked west to the flyover where the R351 went over the railway line. If I were to set up an ambush, how would I do it?

The two tar roads made a triangle with the railway line. In the middle of the triangle was a rise with rocks and trees. That is where I would position my sniper, because he could see the junction at the stop street. I climbed the wire fence and walked through the veld and up the slope.

How had they known we would come this way?

How had they known we were going to Mohlolobe – and not Hoedspruit? Was it because we drove this route every day? Because the western route to Hoedspruit was just about as far?

Or had they covered both alternatives?

I stood on the rise and looked down. Perfect panorama. You could see the traffic for two kilometres on the R351. Plus at least a kilometre on the R41 north. It was two hundred and fifty metres from the T-junction, equidistant from both roads. A manageable distance for a sniper, wind wouldn't be a great factor, gradient perhaps twenty degrees.

Still, he would have to know his job. On a moving vehicle, a tyre is not a big target.

Trouble is, there are hundreds of them here. Men who can shoot, who can drop a strolling steenbok at three hundred metres with a telescope – place trophy shots where they will.

But how did they know we would turn left at the stop, to the north? How had they known we were going to Mohlolobe – and not to Nelspruit? If I had turned right, he wouldn't have got in the second and third shots.

Too many questions. Too many variables. Not enough information.

Where would he have lain in wait? I searched between the trees and rocks for the best spot – room to stretch out on your belly, unhampered vision, scope to swing the rifle through ninety degrees. Enough cover.

I had seen something flash in the seconds before he fired. I drew a line from approximately where we had been on the R351, searching for the logical spot.

There. I jumped down from a rock into a hollow he might have used. No tracks, the rain had seen to that. Grass stems were bent, a couple broken. I lay down, holding an imaginary rifle in my hands. This spot would work – shoot him there, keep an eye on him, see that he isn't stopping, follow him with the scope, around the corner, wait until the BMW stabilises, fire another shot, another one, see the BMW leave the road. Once we had exited the car he hadn't been able to shoot at us because there were trees interfering with his line of sight, and long grass. He would have followed our progress here and there. If he had a radio with him, the others could have given him directions, but he wouldn't have been able to shoot. Would have had to stand up, because this rock directly to his left would have blocked his field of vision.

He had stood up and watched us with naked eyes. Saw us running; saw Emma fall, there, saw the other two running towards us. He would have had to get moving too. Radio in one hand, rifle in the other?

He had only the rifle in his hands when I saw him.

Had he picked up the casings? Was there time?

The bullet casings would have shot out to the right. That way. Rocks and grass. He would have had to look quickly. Three tyres. But there had been more than three shots. One had hit the car. At least four. Could there have been more? Four casings that he had to find, but he was in a hurry, he had to keep an eye on us, he had to shoot us, it was his job, his assignment.

I divided the potential five square metres into quadrants and searched through the grass centimetre by centimetre, between the rust-brown stones, starting with the most likely quadrant. Nothing. None in the second and the third.

The last quadrant, to the right and slightly behind the sniper. Nothing.

Then I saw it, just outside the imaginary line I had drawn. The casing lay deep in the cleft between two rocks, half hidden by grass.

I broke a twig off a tree and poked it into the cleft, lifted out the casing, letting the stick slide into the open end.

Bright and new, 7.62, the longer NATO calibre, standard bullet, mass-manufactured locally.

I rotated the stick so the casing dropped into my shirt pocket.

What had been so odd about the rifle?

I had seen it only for a moment, that awful second or two, behind Emma. He had been lying in the veld on his belly, a big man with a baseball cap and the rifle and tripod and telescope.

It wasn't big. Was that what was strange? A smallish sniper rifle.

Could be. But there was something else. It wouldn't come to mind. He had been too far away.

A tripod meant it wasn't a hunting rifle.

Firearms had been recently removed from the safe that Donnie Branca opened. Was there a connection?

I would have to find out.

I walked down the slope to the place where the BMW had stopped in the grass. The fence was still broken. Traffic drove past on both tar roads. The sun was setting on the Mariepskop side. My shadow stretched long across the green sweetveld.

I tried to follow the route Emma and I had run. I found the antbear hole where she had fallen. Then we turned towards the railway tracks. I scanned the grass for my cell phone. The chances of finding it were slim.

This was where I helped her over the wire just before the railway tracks. Stood here, looked up, saw the two balaclavas waving their arms at the sharpshooter. He dropped to the ground.

So he could take aim at us? In this long grass? Couldn't be.

Why had he dropped flat? Fallen, tripped perhaps? No, it wasn't like that, it was deliberate. What for?

This time I climbed through the fence. We had run south beside the train. Emma's handbag must have dropped here. Right here.

It was lying in the grass, not obvious, but easy enough to see. If Phatudi's men had been here they would have found it. They couldn't have been here at the railway track, then.

I picked up her bag and opened it.

It smelled of Emma.

All her things seemed to be there. Cell phone too.

I closed the handbag and walked back to the Audi.

'There doesn't seem to be haemorrhage,' said Dr Eleanor Taljaard in her office. 'And there's no indication that the skull fracture has damaged the brain tissue directly. I'm optimistic.'

I couldn't hide my relief.

'But we're not home free, Lemmer, you must understand that.'

'I know.'

She wanted to say more. I saw her hesitate, reconsider.

'What is it, Eleanor?'

'You must be realistic, Lemmer. With coma patients, survival is always our first priority, and her prognosis looks good.'

'But?' I said because I knew what was coming.

'Yes. There is always the "but". She could survive, but remain in a coma, for an indefinite period. Months. Years. Or she could wake up tomorrow and . . .'

'And what?'

'She might not be the same.'

'Oh.'

'I don't want to give you false hope.'

'I understand.'

'You can talk to her again, this evening. If you want to.'

'I will.'

Then I went up to my VIP suite and sat on the bed with Emma's handbag. I needed her notes, which she had been making sporadically since we arrived.

I unzipped the bag. The scent of Emma le Roux. She might never wake up. Or be the same. The scent when I carried her into the suite, her warm body, her face in my neck. 'The other room,' she had whispered. That smile after I had laid her down, the one that said, 'Look what I made silent, stupid Lemmer do.'

It had been ten months since I held a woman against me.

Let me concentrate on the handbag.

I looked inside it, couldn't immediately see the notepaper. I would have to unpack the bag.

It wasn't a big handbag, but the contents were impressive.

1 cell phone. I put it on the bed.
1 photo of Jacobus le Roux.
1 Afrikaans book, *Equatoria* by Tom Dreyer.
1 letter of unknown origin – the one Emma received from the Mohlolobe gate guard.

A small black zip-up bag. I opened it up. Cosmetics. I zipped it shut.

1 cell phone charger.
1 purse. A few hundred in cash. Credit cards. Emma's own business cards.
1 sheet of paper, a web page printout with a map of Mohlolobe. On the back were Emma's notes. I put it on one side.

Was there something else in the dark depths of the handbag that could help me?

One shouldn't go through a woman's handbag, but what if . . .

1 spectacle case with dark glasses.

1 plastic tampon container.

1 small black address book, somewhat dog-eared, listing names and telephone numbers, here and there an address and a birthday; not recent.

1 pack Kleenex Softique white three-ply tissues. *Care on the move.*

2 bank slips. I didn't look at them. Not my business.

2 old shopping lists, short and cryptic, groceries.

9 business cards. Jeanette Louw's was one of them. The others were unfamiliar advertising and marketing managers.

7 cash slips. Three from Woolworths Food, one from Diesel jeans, two from Pick and Pay, one from the Calitzdorp Guest House. On the back was a recipe for 'Calitzdorp Apple Tart'.

1 note from the manager of the Badplaas resort with Melanie Posthumus's contact numbers.

1 Bluetooth earpiece for the cell phone.

1 packet of contraceptive pills.

1 packet of Disprins, the chewable sort. Unopened.

1 small round plastic tub. Mac Lip Balm.

1 small flat river pebble.

1 Mont Blanc black pen.

1 Bic ballpoint pen.

1 packet of matches from the Sandton Holiday Inn.

1 half-used pencil.

3 stray paper clips.

That was the sum total. I replaced everything except the notes, the photograph and the cell phone. I pressed the cell phone button. The screen lit up. YOU HAVE FOUR MISSED CALLS.

I manipulated the keys. MISSED CALLS. CAREL (3). UNKNOWN (1). YOU HAVE 1 NEW VOICE MESSAGE. PLEASE DIAL 121.

I dialled.

'Emma, this is Carel. Just wanted to know how it's going. Call me when you can.'

I saved the message, turned the cell phone off and put it back in the handbag.

Should I phone Carel? Tell him what had happened?

I knew what his reaction would be. 'Weren't you supposed to protect her?'

No. Let Jeanette do it.

I picked up the sheet of paper with notes on it. There were fewer than I expected. Just single notations in Emma's small precise handwriting.

August 1997: Jacobus left Heuningklip.
22 August 1997: Jacobus left Melanie.
27 August 1997: Pa and Ma in accident.
Began work at Mogale in 2000?

Five days after Cobie de Villiers disappeared, Jacobus le Roux's parents died in a car accident.

Five days.

Coincidence? Perhaps. But Emma hadn't thought so. She had underlined this entry twice. My belief in coincidence had been severely dented in the last two days.

If it hadn't been coincidence, what had Cobie's disappearance to do with the accident?

Where was he going when he left Heuningklip? What had Melanie Posthumus said? Before we got married there was something he had to do. He said he would be away for two weeks and then he would bring me a ring. Something like that. When she asked him what he was going to do, he wouldn't say. Except that it was the right thing to do and one day he would tell her.

The right thing.

What did it all mean? What had Emma thought?

Not enough information. Not enough to jump to wild conclusions and improbable theories.

I had an idea. I found the pen in Emma's handbag, picked up the sheet of paper and drew up a table of all the dates and incidents I could remember.

1986: Jacobus disappears in Kruger Park. Age +/– 19?
1994: Cobie starts work at Heuningklip. 27?
22/8/1997: Cobie disappears. 29?
27/8/1997: Parents die.
2000: Cobie arrives at Mogale. 32?
21/12/2006: Cobie disappears after sangoma murder. 38?
22/12/2006: Emma phones, gets phone call.
24/12/2006: Attack on Emma in Cape Town.
26/12/2006: To Lowveld.
29/12/2006: Emma shot.

Eight years between the disappearance of Jacobus le Roux and Cobie de Villiers' appointment at Heuningklip. Let us assume it is the same man. Even though Phatudi, Wolhuter, Moller and Melanie all say the photo of Jacobus does not look like Cobie. Could someone change so much in eight years? I looked at the photo again. Jacobus was more of a boy than a man. Does someone really change that much between the ages of nineteen and twenty-seven? Hard to believe. Yet Emma had seen similarities.

Eight years after he went missing after a shoot-out with poachers in Kruger Park, he reappears. And only two hundred kilometres from where he disappeared. He told Melanie he had grown up in Swaziland. Kruger was not far from Swaziland. Less than a hundred kilometres away. Did that mean anything?

Eight years.

Why eight years? Why 1994? The Year of the New South Africa. He works for Moller for three years and then he is gone again, invisible, for another three years, nearly, appearing again at Mogale. Why? Why not in Namibia or Durban or Zanzibar? If Jacobus and Cobie were the same person and he had reason to disappear, why did he keep coming back to this area? What kept him here?

Six years at the rehabilitation centre and then the incident with the vultures. Was there significance in these time gaps? Three years at Heuningklip, three years missing, six years at Mogale. Coincidence?

Poachers. Twice he disappears because poachers are shot at. In 1986 he shoots at ivory poachers, in 2006 he is suspected of shooting vulture poachers. Twenty years between the two incidents, but the similarities remain.

What the fuck did it all mean?

I had no idea.

I removed the book from Emma's bag and took it to read to her.

The bandages on her head and shoulder were fresh and less bulky than the previous ones. Yet she seemed just as vulnerable.

'Hello, Emma.

'I found your handbag. Everything is still in there. Your phone and purse too. I looked at your notes. I think I understand better now. But there's nothing . . . Nothing makes sense. What bothers me most, Emma, is why he looks so different. Why would his face change so much between eighty-six and ninety-four? It's the one thing that still makes me doubt that he's the same man. I know you thought differently. You believed. Maybe it was that phone call you received. And then you realised that he left Heuningklip just before your parents died. Maybe there was something else, something you didn't tell me.'

She just lay there, the woman whose naked body I had seen two days before in the reflection from the glass of a picture, so perfect, so alive.

I looked down at the book in my hands. It had a green cover, a close-up photograph of a leaf. There was a bookmark in it. I opened it at that page.

'I thought I might read to you, Emma.'

And so I began. It was a description of a unicorn hunt. And the hunter becomes the hunted.

28

Jeanette Louw had spent the greater part of her adult life in uniform. I suspect she couldn't do without it. She had developed a type of uniform for her new role as owner and managing director of Body Armour. It consisted of men's suits, expensive designer wear from some or other shop on the Cape Town Waterfront, with demure shirts and multicoloured ties. In office hours the big blonde hair would be tied back with something to match the tie.

Through the glass of the hospital main entrance, I saw her approaching. Today's suit was black, the shirt cream and the tie yellow with a blue dot pattern. She had the remains of a white Gauloise between her fingers which she flicked into some shrubs, creating an arc of sparks, before entering the building. A few steps behind came B. J. (BeeJay) Fikter and Barry Minnaar, grey, lean men, unobtrusive, as they should be, each with a black sports bag in his hand.

I rose to meet them.

'There's nothing wrong with you,' she said, perspiring.

'You should see the wounds when I'm naked.'

'God forbid. How is she?'

'Stable.'

I shook hands with Fikter and Minnaar.

'Where can we talk?'

'In my VIP suite.'

'It's our VIP suite now,' said B. J.

'But you aren't VIPs like me.'

'Of course not. It stands for Very Insane Person.'

'Very Important Peasant,' said Barry Minnaar.

'Jealousy,' I said. 'It's an ugly thing.'

B. J. got carried away. 'Very Insecure Piss . . .'

'OK!' said Jeanette Louw. She shook her head, 'Fucking men,' and we went into the hospital.

I told them everything. When I had finished, Jeanette asked, 'How are we going to handle her protection?'

'I will do night shift,' said B. J. Fikter. 'Barry can do days.'

'Do you have firearms?' I asked.

They nodded.

'Do the police still have people at her door?' Jeanette asked.

'Yes. They aren't going to like our presence.'

'Fuck them,' said Jeanette. 'I have a paying client.'

'Good argument.'

Jeanette looked at Fikter and Minnaar. 'Call me if you have trouble.'

Another silent 'yes'.

'Where are you going to be?' I asked.

'I'm going back to Cape Town. It's too damn hot and humid here.' She stood up. 'Come, Lemmer, walk with me. I have a present for you.'

She said goodbye to Fikter and Minnaar and we went out through the hospital corridors to her rented car. The heat was as it had been when I arrived. Unbearable. My eyes swept the car park from the right, past the exit in the middle to the left. It was only half full this Monday after 2 p.m. A quiet day. Birds sang somewhere.

'This heat,' said Jeanette, and wiped her forehead.

'Not for Cape sissies.'

'Loxton is also in the Cape.'

'Northern Cape,' I said haughtily. Then I spotted the Jeep Grand Cherokee six rows to the left of the entrance, two people in front, two hundred metres north-east of us. Two men, I thought. Why were they just sitting there?

'Arse-end of the world.' Suddenly serious. 'Lemmer, tell me, how do you feel?'

'A few bruises, Jeanette. A day or two, and I'll be the old Brad Pitt clone you've come to adore.'

Not even a hint of a smile. 'Are you sure?'

'Yes.'

'What about your head? On Saturday you were shell-shocked.'

The two in the Jeep just sat there. It might be nothing. Just two people waiting for someone. Or not. They seemed to be watching us.

'Saturday was a rough day. There's nothing wrong with me.'

'All right, then . . .'

'Don't look left. I think we have visitors.'

She was an old hand. She kept her eyes on me. 'How do you want to handle it?'

'Might be nothing, but I want to make sure. Where's your car?'

'That way.' She nodded to the right, north-west.

'Good. Did you bring a firearm?'

'I did.' We kept walking, seeming relaxed, chatting.

'What did you see?'

I deliberately looked in another direction. 'Black Jeep Grand Cherokee, not the latest model, the previous one. At eleven o'clock, facing us, a hundred metres, a little more perhaps. Two in front, too far to say any more.'

'Police don't use Jeeps.'

'That's pretty sharp for a lady . . .'

'The pistol is in my luggage in the back. It's the Glock 37, ten .45 GAP rounds in the magazine. Yesterday I shot a two-centimetre grouping at twenty-five metres. At fifteen metres it was less than a centimetre. It kicks very little and likes rapid fire. I brought you two magazines and a hundred rounds. You'll have to put the magazine in if you want to use it now.'

'I do.'

'What can I do?'

'Fit the magazine without them seeing and pass the Glock to me. Then get in the car. Keep the engine running and wait for me.'

'Fine.' Cool as ice. No reproaches that I had suddenly found my tongue.

We reached the hired car, a white Mercedes C180. She pressed the remote and the car beeped and flashed its lights.

'Civvies,' said Jeanette, and nodded in the direction of an old man and woman getting into a Corolla between the Jeep and us.

'I see them.'

She opened the boot of the Mercedes and began to open her suitcase. 'The Glock's numbers have been filed off, but you have parole conditions.'

'I know.'

'I'll put it beside the suitcase.'

She stood back. I bent and picked up the Glock. Keeping my body between the pistol and the Jeep, I pulled my shirt out of my trousers and pushed it into my belt under the shirt.

'See you.' I turned and began to walk towards the Jeep, not too fast, not too slow. I looked elsewhere, hoping they would think I was looking for my car. I would have preferred to have the Glock behind my back where it was easier to take out.

Seventy-five metres. I looked at the Jeep in my peripheral vision. Too far for detail, but they were still there.

Behind me the old man started the Corolla.

Sixty metres.

I heard the Jeep's engine fire. Petrol engine, the V8 growl, unmistakable. Lifted my shirt, put my hand on the pistol butt and began to run.

The Jeep shot out of the parking bay and swung left. They wanted to go to the exit. I ran to cut them off, couldn't get the Glock out because of the civilians, didn't want anyone to call the police. Looked at the Jeep. They would have to drive fifty metres towards me before they could take the exit. I might make it. I sprinted. My knee objected and my ribs weren't keen on the idea either.

The Jeep accelerated, the driver was nearest to me. I couldn't make out much, but I thought he looked like a white man. Passenger. Where was the passenger? He was hiding, head bent down. I was still twenty metres short when they took the left turn for the exit with screeching tyres. I wouldn't make it, it was too far.

I focused on the driver, had a good look, then the licence plate number. TWS 519 GP. I turned around and ran back towards Jeanette. The Corolla was approaching, the old man in no hurry. He and his old lady stared at me running around the car park, looking worried, wondering what was going on.

I saw Jeanette driving the Mercedes towards me. I looked around; the Jeep was almost at the exit. Come on, Jeanette, come on. Then the Corolla was in her way, she tried to pass, but the old man turned towards the gate right in front of her. Jeanette braked, the ABS kicked in and she just missed them. I reached the Mercedes, jerked open the door and jumped in.

'Grandpa and fucking Grandma,' she said, and put her foot down, a Gauloise between her fingers, swerved around the Corolla and raced towards the gate. The old couple's eyes were wide. The Jeep was gone.

'Did you see which way they went?'

'No. I was watching you brake for Grandpa. But I got the licence plate number.'

'I should bloody hope so.'

She stopped at the gate. We could go only left or right down the road.

No sign of the Jeep.

'Fuck,' she said.

'Not in front of the children,' I said.

Behind us the old man honked. Jeanette stiffened for a second. The she laughed, her loud bark, and shook her head. 'Now Grandpa is in a hurry. What do you want to do?'

'Nothing we can do. Besides, I got what I wanted: a face and a number. Let's go back.'

Grandpa honked again, sharply and irritably. Jeanette drove off and made a U-turn back into the car park.

'Nothing like a bit of adrenalin to brighten up the afternoon,' she said. 'Did you recognise the face?'

'No, but I know him now. What I want to know is, why weren't they here yesterday?'

'Probably didn't know where you were.'

'Or they were waiting to see if Emma would make it.'

'You'll have to tell B. J. and Barry.'

'I will.'

She parked. I took out the envelope from one of Maggie T.'s letters. 'There's a bullet casing in the envelope. Do you know someone who can look at it? Anything. Fingerprints, type of rifle . . .'

'Maybe. Give me the Jeep's licence number too.' She took a pen out of her jacket pocket. I repeated the number and she wrote it on the envelope. Then she got out. So did I. I looked around very thoroughly. Nothing. Jeanette went around to the boot. She opened it, rummaged around and turned to me with a white-and-blue plastic shopping bag.

'Extra magazine, a hundred rounds, shoulder holster. I assume you haven't found your cell phone?'

'No.'

'There's a new one in there. I want to know what's happening. Pay-as-you-go with four hundred rands' worth of airtime. And money. Ten thousand in hundred-rand notes. It's a shithouse full of money, Lemmer. I want receipts.'

'I'll do what I can.'

She handed me the bag formally.

'Thanks, Jeanette.'

'Nothing to thank me for. Now listen up. Get these motherfuckers, no matter what it takes. But you stay out of trouble with the police. If they catch you with the Glock, you're going back to jail. You know that.'

'Yes, Mother.'

'Lemmer, I'm serious.'

'I know.'

'OK,' she said and turned away.

'Jeanette . . .'

She stopped irritably and wiped away perspiration. 'What?'

'If she's so rich, why did she take the cheapest option?'

'Who? Emma?'

'Yes.'

'You think you're the cheapest option?'

'I know I am.'

She shook her head. 'You know nothing. She came in and said she wanted the best. Money no object.'

I waited for her to laugh, tell me she was joking. It didn't happen. She saw my confusion. 'I'm serious, Lemmer.'

'And you gave me the job?'

'I gave you the job.'

'You're pulling my leg.'

'In this heat?'

She stood for a moment and then she opened her door. 'Goodbye, Lemmer. Happy New Year.'

'No kiss or cuddle today?'

'Fuck off, Lemmer,' she said, and got into the Merc, but she couldn't hide her smile. Then she drove off without once looking back.

I walked to the hospital reception desk and asked them what their phone number was. I keyed it into my new cell phone. Then I went to intensive care, where Barry Minnaar was already on duty opposite the two policemen. 'Lonely already?' he said as I approached.

I nodded in the direction of the Law. 'Did the SAPS have anything to say?'

'A lot. They phoned their boss.'

'Phatudi?'

'That's the one.'

'He'll huff and puff, but he won't blow the house down.'

Barry took a folded document out of his shirt pocket. 'Copy of Le Roux's contract. Phatudi can huff all he likes.'

'We met some friends in the parking lot. Black Jeep Grand Cherokee, TWS 519 GP. Driver is white, short dark brown hair, thirty-something. Passenger hid his face.'

'Did you say goodbye?'

'Didn't have time. I think the friendship is over.'

'Good thing you told me.'

'I need your numbers, Barry,' I said with my cell phone ready.

He gave them to me. Then I fetched my stuff from the VIP suite.

29

The guard at the Mohlolobe gate was new. Sidney. Security Official. I asked him when Edwin would be on duty again.

'Edwin is gone.'

'Gone?'

'Yes, sir.'

'What do you mean?'

'Nobody knows where he is.'

I drove in and went to reception. It took half an hour because I had to wait for a herd of elephants to cross the road. Four bulls, eight cows and four calves. They were in no hurry. They looked down at the Audi with utter disdain for *Vorsprung durch Technik*.

Sue-zin was at her post, helping a middle-aged American settle his bill. She flipped her blonde hair over her shoulder with practised ease, smiled with those perfect teeth as she said, 'Of course, Mr Bradley, it's a pleasure, Mr Bradley.' As he walked away she looked up and saw me. The smile turned into a concerned frown.

'Meneer Lemmer!' She addressed me in Afrikaans, amazingly. She came out from behind the desk.

'Hello, Susan.'

'We were so shocked to hear about Miss le Roux . . .' She came and stood close to me.

'Oh. Who told you?'

'Inspector Phatudi was here.'

'Naturally.'

'How is she?'

'A little better.'

'Is she going to be OK?'

'It's too early to tell.'

Susan put her hand on my arm. 'And you, Mr Lemmer, are you OK?' With heartfelt concern. She was good, I had to admit.

'I'm fine.'

'We don't even know what happened.'

'They wanted to hijack the car.'

Her hand went from my arm to her mouth. 'A carjacking. Around here!'

'Susan, I'm looking for Edwin, the man at the gate.'

She hesitated and then said more formally, 'You should speak to Greg.'

'Where can I find him?'

She took me to Greg. The hospitality manager's office. He was the plump one with thinning blond hair and a red complexion.

'He's in there,' she said. 'See you later?'

'Thanks, Susan.'

She walked away. Her bottom was pert in the khaki trousers. She knew it.

Greg wasn't really happy to see me. He was edgy and his hands rearranged the desk incessantly. At first he made sympathetic noises about 'the accident', but his heart wasn't in it. No wonder they kept him in an office. I asked him where I could find Edwin. His hands got busier.

'The police are also looking for him, but he's gone.'

'Gone where?'

'Nobody knows. He didn't turn up for work yesterday, so I sent someone to go and find him, but he's not at home, either. Maybe it's just New Year. Sometimes, staff disappear when you need them the most.'

'Where does Edwin live?'

'I'm sorry, I can't provide that information. Company policy.'

'I might be able to locate him for you.'

'I'm sorry. I can't.'

'OK,' I said, and turned away.

'Mr Lemmer . . .'

'Yes.'

'I'm really sorry, but there is the matter of Miss Le Roux's account.'

'I'm sure she will settle it once she has recovered.'

'I see. But with all due respect, we hear that she's in a very serious condition.'

'She is.'

'So what am I to do?'

'I'm sure company policy will cover it, Greg. Happy New Year,' I said, and left.

The passage was empty. I stood for a moment outside his door. I heard him say 'Shit', and then he picked up the phone and dialled a number.

'Inspector Phatudi, please.'

I didn't wait to hear his report.

On the gravel road back to the gate the dust was so thick behind the Audi that I became aware of a vehicle behind me only when it honked urgently. I looked in the rear-view mirror. Through the cloud of dust I vaguely saw headlights flashing. I stopped and got out, the Glock ready behind my back. A short-wheelbase Land Rover stopped behind me. Dick, Senior Game Ranger, the Orlando Bloom clone, got out and came up to me with a big smile.

I pushed the Glock into my belt.

'Hey, man.' He held out his hand as though we were old friends.

'Hi, Dick.'

We shook hands. 'How you doin'?'

'I'm OK. How are you?'

'Mind if we get in?' He waved an arm. 'Lion country, like.'

I hadn't thought a senior game ranger would be afraid of lions, but I said, 'Sure.' We got into the Audi. He didn't see me take out the Glock and lower it between the seat and the door.

Dick took off his hat and held it on his lap. His fingers fiddled with the brim. 'I heard about the whole thing, man. Hectic. How is Emma?'

'She's stable, they say.' Had he chased after me to ask about Emma?

'Terrible, man. Terrible thing. And now Susan tells me it was a carjacking?'

'Yes.'

'Hectic.'

'Dick, you didn't come after me to ask about Emma.'

'Well, sort of . . .'

'What can I do for you?'

He grinned. 'It's just . . . she's a cool chick, you know, Emma . . .'

'She is.'

'You, like, work for her?'

'Yes.'

'What's your job?'

'I'm a bodyguard.'

He looked at me with new regard. 'Awesome, man.' And then, 'I just wanted to make sure that you two, you know . . . that you're not a couple, like.'

'No, we're not.'

'Is she involved, or anything?'

'Not as far as I know.'

'You think I can go visit? At the hospital?'

'She's in a coma, Dick.'

'I heard. But I mean, when she's better.'

Dick. Senior Game Ranger. Had a thing for Emma le Roux.

'I'm sure she will appreciate it very much.'

'You know Susan really likes you?'

I suppressed the urge to laugh – my ribs still hurt too much. Dick had it all worked out. He and Emma, Susan and me, two happy couples. 'She's a nice girl.'

'She's hot, bru'.'

Did he have first-hand experience?

'I'm sure.'

He didn't hear me, he was thinking about Emma again. He gazed out at the veld and the mopane trees. 'It's funny, you know, with Emma . . . I just thought there was this, like, connection.'

'Oh?'

'Man, she's just, like, radical, like really beautiful. You know? And there, bru', you know what I mean, she's like really there. You get a lot of chicks that's good looking, they're, like, way out there. But Emma. She's there . . .'

Something else occurred to him. 'Why would she need a body-guard? Is she famous, or something?' He seemed worried that it would affect his chances.

It took me a while to realise that there could be an advantage in Dick's great interest.

'No. Just careful. Do you know why she was here, Dick?'

'No.'

'She's looking for her brother.'

'Hectic, man. Did she find him?'

'No, but I'm going to try. You can help.'

'Just say the word, bru'.'

I had been upgraded. From 'man' to 'bru''. 'Do you know Edwin, the gate guard?'

'I know him.'

'Do you know where he lives?'

'Sure. About half a kay from the Acornhoek train station. It's about twenty kays from here. You take the Nelspruit road until you see the sign. I could show you, but I'm on duty. Anyway, you can't miss it. Turn left just past the Acornhoek station, and he's on the left. In front of the house, he's got this low concrete wall with like half a wagon wheel motif and he's painted it pink. Radical, bru'.'

'I'll find it. Do you know what his surname is?'

He thought hard. 'No. I know I should, but I don't.'

'It doesn't matter. One other thing, there's a possibility that Emma's brother worked at Mogale. The rehabilitation centre. I'm looking for information about the place.'

He shook his head. 'That's the funny farm, bru'.'

'Oh?'

'Bunch of weird dudes, let me tell you.'

'Tell me.'

'Radical, man. They're radical.'

Like a pink concrete wall? Or Emma's beauty?

'In what sense of the word, Dick?'

'Like in cuckoo, bru', like hectic radical, you know?'

I didn't know. Dick spoke a language that would take a while to unravel. 'Can you be a little more specific?'

'I don't have, like, proof, bru'. But you hear stuff.'

'Like what?'

'Like . . . well, let me tell you.'

30

Dick said that two years earlier, only a couple of months after he had started at Mohlolobe, there was a message for him at reception from a man by the name of Domingo Branca. The content was informal and friendly: would he like to meet other young people in the district? Come and have a drink on Saturday night at the Warthog Bush Pub, a local watering hole at the airfield beside the Guernsey gravel road.

There had been four of them. Donnie Branca and Cobie de Villiers from Mogale, David Baumberger of Molomahlapi Private Game Reserve and Boetie Strydom of the Makutswi Wildlife Ranch. Initially it was a light-hearted evening. They welcomed him to the Lowveld, enquired about his background, gossiped about their respective employers, swapped stories about the sexual opportunities tourists provided, the oddest places and circumstances where they had offered these services, and the scandalous state of rugby.

The typical conversation between young unmarried men.

Branca was the leader of the group; that was obvious from the beginning. Baumberger was the clown, Strydom the experienced one who had grown up in the area and De Villiers had said practically nothing.

Quite a few hours and beers later, Branca had steered the conversation in another direction. It was only a year later, when he heard the other stories, that Dick realised how skilfully it had been done. From gossip, sex and rugby to animal stories, conservation, concern over ongoing development, the multiplication of game farms, the competition, the poor management of the National and Provincial Parks, land claims, the growing threat to the ecosystem. It was done carefully, without radical statements, no direct accusations or politically incorrect remarks. Just a polite testing of the water: where did Dick stand with regard to all these questions?

Dick didn't actually stand anywhere. He was just a lapsed surfer from Port Elizabeth who had found a career and a job that suited his chosen lifestyle like a glove. He was outdoors all day, he thought nature was 'cool' and he liked the way tourists hung on his every word when he shared the information he had picked up along the way.

'I went back to the pub the next weekend, but they weren't there. And later, I sort of clicked – it was, like, I flunked a test, you know. And they never invited me again.'

In the months after that he began to hear the rumours. Nothing concrete, a bit here and a fragment there, from diverse sources and places. First there were the anonymous warning letters to farmers, communities and businesses about the damage they were doing to the environment. Later, the letters became threatening. They were always signed with the initials H. B.

Then there were more than letters.

Photographs of black game wardens cooking a buck over a fire were delivered to the Kruger Park management. Things happened in the night. An entire community's dogs were poisoned at Ga-Sekororo between the Lagalameetse Nature Reserve and the Makutsi Conservancy. Intimidating shots were fired at night on the tribal lands of a group that had a land claim against a famous game farm.

Nobody knew who was responsible. As always, there were theories and accusations, blame and denial. The letters H. B. were responsible for most of the speculation. Hendrik Bester, the banana farmer, was harassed so much that he considered selling his land and moving away. People fought over whether it was a Latin, Afrikaans, English, sePedi or Venda abbreviation.

The incidents began to escalate. Two suspected poachers were severely injured by leopard gin traps on the footpaths used by the people of Tlhavekisa near the Manyeleti Game Reserve. A sawmill burned down outside Graskop. It had been polluting a wetland. Two men from Dumfries were badly beaten up and tied to the impala that they had poached in the Sabi Sands Game Reserve. Dogs were shot dead in the veld. A man and a woman who specialised in the slaughter of animals for traditional medicinal purposes were assaulted. Like the impala thieves, they told of the terrifying silence and efficiency of the night-time attacks. Not a word was said to them. The attackers were masked. Two methods whereby people are identified in this part of the world, skin colour and dialect, were effectively neutralised. There were not enough incidents to create panic or hysteria. They were sporadic, spread over months, two provinces and thousands of square kilometres. The stories took time to loosen tongues and fire speculation. The only clue was the abbreviation.

H. B.

The most stubborn rumour held that it stood for honey badger, or honey badgers, since they were a group. Who had first promulgated that theory was unclear.

There were so many rumours about who was behind the H. B. front that Mogale and its people were lost in the hubbub. Sometimes they came under the spotlight. Maybe because they made no secret of their opposition to development, habitat damage and informal poaching. Maybe because they never spoke up to condemn the H. B. activities. Maybe because their tame honey badger was the most famous in the province. But since Cobie de Villers had been identified by eyewitnesses as the broad-daylight murderer of three vulture poisoners and a sangoma, the focus of suspicion was fully on Mogale. The death of Frank Wolhuter had launched a new series of rumours. That Frank had been the brains behind H. B. but had got cold feet and been murdered by his followers. That a reaction force from the black community had killed him. That a branch of the State Intelligence services had been responsible for his execution.

'It's crazy, bru', the shit that's flying around.'

'Why has the shit not hit the newspapers?'

'Some of the local rags had stuff, but nobody really knows what the fuck is going on.'

'Why "honey badger"?'

'Dunno, bru'. Your guess is as good as mine. Maybe because a honey badger is a very, very tough little dude, takes shit from nobody and nothing. Moves around sort of on its own, invisible, in the undergrowth, takes care of scary stuff like snakes. And it's a total survivor. Awesome symbol, don't you think?'

'Awesome,' I agreed. I wondered what he would say if I told him that the honey badger was Cobie de Villiers' favourite animal. 'But you said that night in the bush pub there were other people besides the Mogale lot.'

'I think it's a network, bru'. A society, like. But Mogale runs it. Not that I have proof. But that Cobie guy is a fuckin' fruitcake.'

'Oh?'

'Dude never says a word, but you look into his eyes, like, and its, like, radical, man. Fruitcake.'

'You don't support their cause in the least?'

'Fuck, no, bru'. I mean, look around you. We're in the middle of a nature reserve right next to the biggest fuckin' game park on the globe, thirty-five thousand square kays when the whole cross-border Limpopo Park thing is all wrapped, bigger than Holland, dude, a hundred and forty-seven mammal and five hundred and seven bird species. Does it look like we need shit like shooting people?'

'I get your point. But the question is, why don't they see it that way?'

'No offence, bru', but that's the way you are.'

'Me?'

'No, the Afrikaners. Always one or two radicals who have to have their secret society. Do you know how many are out there? You guys have, like, a predisposition. Have you heard of these fucks calling themselves the Verbondsvolk. And the Dogters van Sion?' His pronunciation was off.

'No.'

'It's all over the place, bru'. They have this dead prophet dude who saw the future, they tore out all the chapters of Paul from the

Bible and they believe they are the chosen chinas. Fuckin' pre-disposition, that's what you have.'

'Fair enough.'

'Did you know there's a Boere-Mafia in Nelspruit?'

'No.'

'They control everything, man. You can't develop a single hectare if they don't get their cut.'

'I thought the ANC controlled the city council in Nelspruit.'

'Bru', it's money that makes the world go round. It can buy anything.'

One thing didn't make sense. 'Dick, if the Afrikaners are behind all this, why would they use an English name?'

'You've lost me, bru'.'

'The H. B. is an abbreviation for an English term. Honey badger.'

He just shook his head in amazement. 'Radical, man, totally radical.'

There was nothing I could say to top that.

I drove away thinking about the way people surprise you.

First Jeanette Louw. Former sergeant-major, tough as nails, never pulls punches, take-me-as-I-am, wouldn't allow a euphemism or a sympathetic word over her lips. But when I asked for a car, I got an expensive Audi A4 – she could have got me a Nissan Almera or a Toyota Corolla.

I asked for a firearm and she got me a black-market Glock with the numbers filed off. She tests it on the range and brings it in person. She could have sent it with B. J. and Barry. 'There's nothing wrong with you,' she said when she saw me. But in the car park she orders me, in her usual despotic way, 'Lemmer, *tell me*, how do you feel?' With a concern in her eyes bordering on the maternal.

Jeanette. Who said, 'She came in and said she wanted the best. Money no object. So I gave you the job.'

I still thought she was bullshitting me.

Then there was Dick. Senior Game Ranger. My first impression was of an arrogant, irritating little English-speaking fool. Then he races after me because he has a thing for Emma and shows his true colours: harmless and . . . naive seems to fit.

His attraction to Emma didn't surprise me. He was her type and he must have an instinctive feel for that. His interest was obvious from the first time he saw her. I just hadn't expected him to go to so much trouble. Even finding out whether Susan would be available to keep me busy while he made up to Emma. Were the opportunities for a pretty young blonde so limited in this corner of the Lowveld that she would be interested in Lemmer of Loxton?

And the wonderful irony. While Dick spelled out the possibility of Susan, all I could think of was the black mamba of jealousy that I nursed in my bosom. The urge to grab him by the collar of his green-and-khaki shirt and tell him to keep his 'senior game ranger hands off Emma'.

People. They surprise you.

Like Donnie Branca standing on his little podium and speaking with so much knowledge and passion about the African vultures' battle for survival. Now he might be an eco-terrorist lying in wait to beat up poachers in the dead of night, his hands and face covered to hide his identity. Could he be one of the attackers at the train? Is that why they wore balaclavas and gloves? To disguise their ethnicity?

Maybe.

But Branca was not one of them. I had studied him in detail. I knew his way of moving, his walk, his posture and his measurements. He was athletic, supple, fit. The balaclava men were both shorter, their movements less sure of foot. Not clumsy, but there was an aura of unfamiliarity in the veld; this was not their natural habitat.

Branca could have sent them. They could be part of the network Dick spoke of.

But why would Emma le Roux pose a threat to them? Why would the H. B. group send three masked wonders to the Cape because a small young woman made a phone call to Inspector Jack Phatudi? How would they even have known about the call? What would they have wanted to do to her? What for?

All the different possibilities were paralysing. The Cape Town attack and the train incident could be two different groups. Or the same group. Each option had its own set of questions and implications. Jack Phatudi was part of something, or not. Or perhaps part of something else. Cobie de Villiers was Jacobus le Roux. Or not. The Jeep had a Gauteng registration. Which might be false. Or not.

Nothing made sense. The road sign to Acornhoek prevented me from wrestling with the problem any longer.

I turned left at the railway station as Dick had indicated, and suddenly there were police vehicles everywhere and the dusty street was too narrow to make a U-turn.

There were five SAPS pick-ups parked and a horde of blue uniforms standing around in groups. The Audi stood out like a nun at a sex therapy workshop. They looked at me suspiciously. The pink concrete wall was a startling beacon. Jack Phatudi stood on the threshold of the humble brick house. He shouted, waved his arms and a uniform ran in front of me and held up a commanding hand. Stop.

I pulled off the road and got out. The heat was stifling, not a tree near by for shade. Phatudi approached with a measured tread, through the little gate in the concrete wall.

'Martin,' he said with great dislike.

'Jack.'

'What are you doing here?' Very aggressive.

'I was looking for you.'

'For me?'

'I wanted to ask you some questions.'

'Who told you I was here?'

'Your office,' I lied. 'What's going on here?'

'Edwin Dibakwane is dead.'

'The gate guard?'

'Yes, the gate guard.'

'What happened?'

'Don't you know?'

'How would I know, Jack? I've just come from Mohlolobe.'

'What were you up to there?'

'Our account wasn't paid. What happened to Edwin?'

'You know.'

'I don't.'

'Of course you know, Martin. He was the one who gave you the message.' He came closer. 'What happened? Wouldn't he tell you where the letter came from?' Phatudi came right up to me. There was terrible anger emanating from him. Or was it hate? 'So you pulled his fingernails out, didn't you? Because he wouldn't tell? You tortured him and shot him and threw him away in the Green Valley plantation.'

The black constables closed in, a cordon of suspicion.

'Someone pulled his nails out?'

'Did you enjoy that, Martin?'

I had to stay calm. There was an army of police. 'Shouldn't you call the SouthMed Hospital first, Jack, and check my alibi?'

He raised his arms and I thought he was going to hit me. I was ready for him. But his movement was just a gesture of frustration. 'For what? Trouble? You are just trouble. You and that woman. Ever since you came. Wolhuter dead, Le Roux in hospital. And now this. You have brought us this trouble.'

'Us, Jack?' Mustn't get angry. I took a deep breath. 'Tell me, why didn't you tell Emma about the masked men who shoot dogs and tie dead impala to people? Why didn't you mention the Honey Badgers the day before yesterday when I told you that the men who shot Emma were in balaclavas? Don't tell me you didn't make the connection, Jack. You had trouble long before we turned up.'

If I thought I would calm him down with that, I was mistaken. He puffed up like a toad, struggling to form his words in his rage. 'That is nothing. Nothing. Edwin Dibakwane . . . he has got children. He . . . You . . . Who does that? Who does that to a man? All he did was hand over a letter.'

I didn't have many options. I was aware of the antagonism of the policemen surrounding me. Phatudi's argument that Emma and I were responsible for Edwin's death was not completely groundless. I held my tongue.

He looked at me with complete revulsion. 'You . . .' he said again, and then bit off his words and shook his head. He flexed his great hands. He turned and walked back towards the little house, stopped and glared at me. Then he came back to me, pointed a finger at me, put his hands on his hips and looked down the road towards the station. He said something in a native language, two or three bitter sentences, and then he directed himself to me again. 'Order,' he said. 'That is my job. To keep order. To fight the chaos. But this country . . .'

He focused on me again.

'I told you. You don't know what it's like here. We have troubles. Big troubles. This place. It's like the veld in drought. Ready to burn. We beat out the fires. We run from one fire to the next fire and we beat out the flames. Then you turn up here and want to set everything on fire. I'm telling you, Martin, if we don't stop it, the fire will burn so big and fast and far that everything will be burnt up. Everything and everyone. Nobody will be able to stop it.'

Some of the policemen nodded their heads in agreement. I was almost ready to see his side of it. Then he got personal.

'You must leave. You and that woman.' He spat out the words. With hatred. I could not let myself react. 'You brought your trouble here.' His index finger was a gun pointing. 'We don't want it. Take it and leave.'

I heard the anger rising in my voice. 'It's your trouble that came to her. She didn't want it. It came and fetched her.'

'Fetched her? She saw a photo on TV.'

'She phoned you about it and two days later three men in balaclavas broke down her front door to kill her. What was she supposed to do, Jack?'

He came a step closer. 'She phoned me?'

'The same evening that it was on the TV news she phoned you and asked whether the man you were looking for might be Jacobus le Roux. Remember?'

'Lots of people phoned. Lots.'

'But she is the only one that was attacked because she phoned . . .'

'I don't believe you.' Arrogant. Taunting. He wanted me to lose my temper, lose control.

I pulled my new phone out of my pocket and offered it to him. 'Call your colleagues in Cape Town, Jack. Ask them if there is a case file. Monday, twenty-fourth December. Attack at the house of Emma le Roux at ten o'clock in the morning. Call them.'

He ignored the cell phone.

'Come on, Jack, take the damn phone and call them.'

Phatudi's deep frown was back. 'Why didn't she tell me?'

'She didn't think it was necessary. She thought asking for help reasonably would be enough.'

'She only asked about the photos.'

'She also asked you about the vulture murders.'

'That was *sub judice*.'

'*Sub judice*? Why? To protect your arse?'

'What?' He stepped closer.

'Careful, Jack, there are witnesses here. She sees the TV news. Twenty-second of December. She phones you. You say Cobie de Villiers can't be Jacobus le Roux because everyone knows him and he's been here all his life. That's enough for her. She drops the whole idea, doesn't mention it to anyone. On the twenty-fourth of December they break into her house, and she's lucky to get away. That afternoon someone phones her and says something about "Jacobus". The connection is bad; she can't hear properly. She hires herself a bodyguard and comes here. You know what happens here.'

'So?'

'So the only connection with the attack on her is you, Jack. The call she made to you.'

'*Masepa*.'

'What?'

'Bullshit.'

'Bullshit?'

'I can't even remember her phoning, Martin.' But he was on the defensive now.

'Who was with you?'

'Nobody.'

'Were the calls taped?'

'We are the police, not the Secret Service.'

'Did you tell anyone about her phone call?'

'I told you, I can't remember her phoning. There were . . . I don't know, fifty or sixty . . . Most of the calls are nonsense.'

'Why didn't you tell her about the Honey Badgers? The other day at Mogale?'

'Why should I?'

'Why not?'

'What are you saying, Martin? You want me to take responsibility for something?'

'Yes, Jack. I just don't know what it is yet, but you are part of this fuck-up, and I am going to find out. And then I'll come and get you.'

'You? You're jailbird trash. Don't talk to me like that.' He came right up to me and we stood like two bantam cocks, chest to chest. I wanted to hit him, I wanted to let all my frustration and rage boil over and I wanted to take it out on the man in front of me. I wanted to go to that other place where time stood still, the room of the red-grey mist. The door was wide open and beckoning.

Afterwards I would wonder what held me back. Was it the army of police? Hopefully, I wasn't a moron. Was I tempered by the knowledge that jailbird trash learned: that you have to come out the other side, back to reality, where you paid dearly for your pleasures? And that I couldn't afford to pay the price again? Or was it the shadow of a woman standing with her face in the rain and arms stretched up to the heavens?

I stepped back from the abyss – and from Phatudi. Small, deliberate, reluctant steps.

And I turned away.

31

Phatudi's troops laughed at me when I walked to the Audi.

As I got in I saw him standing with his chest expanded and a smile of self-satisfaction.

I turned the ignition and drove away.

Past the station I let my rage boil over and banged the car into low gear and stomped on the accelerator. The rear end slid too far around the gravel turn and I fought the wheel, brought it back, accelerated again, spinning the tyres. They found traction and shot the Audi forward, revs too high. I ran through the gears, wanted to stamp the accelerator through the floor, a hundred and fucking sixty, and there was the R40 junction up ahead. I had to brake and the car shuddered and for a while I didn't know whether I was going to make it, but I stopped in a cloud of dust. I saw that my knuckles were white on the steering wheel.

I opened the door and got out. A truck and trailer thundered past on the R40, loaded high with massive logs. I shouted at it, a meaningless cry.

A minibus taxi passed the other way, filled with black faces staring at me, a crazy white man beside the road.

I didn't know where to go. That was my problem. It was the primary source of my frustration and rage.

Phatudi had baited, taunted and angered me, but I had handled that. I could wait for him, for the right time and the right place. But the fact that my choices had dwindled to nothing, I could do nothing about.

On the way to the house with the pink concrete wall, I had had three options. Edwin Dibakwane and the letter. Jack Phatudi and the phone call. Donnie Branca and Mogale. And now I had none.

Edwin Dibakwane was dead. Someone had tortured him and shot him and left his body in a plantation. The connection between the letter and its author was broken. Scrap option number one.

No, not entirely. Dibakwane would have told the people pulling out his fingernails where the letter came from. Somebody knew. But I didn't. It was still no use to me.

Phatudi had been telling the truth. Despite everything, his surprise about the attack on Emma and the connection with the call to him was genuine. Scrap option number two.

That left me with the Mogale rehabilitation centre.

The urge to go there now and thrash Donnie Branca until he told me what was going on was consuming me. I wanted to punish somebody. For Emma.

I wanted to bash someone's skull against a wall or a rock or a clay floor, over and over again, make the brain bounce back and forth against the sides of the cranium, coup and fucking contrecoup, until his cerebral cortex was a fucking pulp. That is what I wanted to do. I wanted to twist the arms of the two masked wonders at the railway track until they popped out of their joints and I heard the ligaments snap and the bones splinter. I wanted to get that sniper, take his rifle, jam it through his teeth, put my finger on the trigger, look him in the eyes, say 'goodbye, motherfucker' and then blow his brains all over the wall.

But who were they? And where could I find them?

Branca was my last hope. What would I do if he refused to talk? What was left if I hit him and he still wouldn't speak? Because he couldn't risk it, the whole affair had gone too far – a woman in a coma, a gate guard tortured and murdered, a man dead in a lion pen and mad Cobie de Villiers couldn't take responsibility for all that. It was one thing to send threatening letters to farmers, to shoot dogs and burn down buildings. Quite another story to go to jail for life.

Scrap option number three.

I walked down the road away from the Audi and then I walked back again. I still had no idea what to do.

I opened the car door and got in. Started the car. Turned right on the tar road, in the general direction of Hoedspruit, Mogale and Mohlolobe.

I just drove. I had nothing else to do.

Past the turn-off to the Kruger National Park, the R351, I saw the handmade advertising board. WARTHOG BUSH PUB. COLD BEER!!!!! AIRCON!!! OPEN! For the first time it meant something. I thought it over for a kilometre, reduced speed and stopped. Waited for oncoming traffic to pass and then I turned around.

Time to think. Cool down. Let me go and see where they tried to recruit Dick-the-dude.

It was not a place for international tourists. One big building and six or seven small ones between the mopane trees and dust. Whitewashed walls, weathered grey thatch asking for maintenance. Three well-used Land Cruisers, an old Toyota 4×4 single-cab, two big old-fashioned Mercedes sedans, a new Nissan double-cab and a Land Rover Defender of indeterminate age. Three had Mpumalanga number plates, the rest were from Limpopo Province.

Local watering hole.

From the biggest building a cracked panel hung slightly askew. A lifetime ago someone with no remarkable artistic talent had carved out the word 'Warthog' and a caricature of the same on the dark wood. A sign in the form of a vehicle number plate was screwed below: BUSH PUB. A white-painted plank fixed neatly square to the wall promised in red letters: PUB LUNCHES! A LA CARTE DINNER! GENUINE GAME DISHES! TRY OUR MIXED GRILL! WARTHOG BURGERS!

In the window beside the large wooden door was a small faded advertisement stuck up with sticky tape like an afterthought. CHALETS AVAILABLE. I opened the door. The air conditioning was working. There was a long bar the length of the building. Wooden tables and benches filled the rest of the room. All were set. A silver banner hung from the open rafters. HAPPY NEW YEAR!!!!!!! The management was into exclamation marks.

The bleached wall was covered with graffiti. *Jamie & Susan were here. Eddie the German. Morgan and the Gang. Oloff Johannsen. Save the Whale, harpoon a fat chick. Free Mandela – with every box of Rice Krispies. Semper Fi. Naas Botha was hier.* Seker omdat Morné nie kom nie. *Make Love, Not War* = Steek, Maar Nie Met 'n Mes Nie. Cartoons, illegible signatures.

At five tables there were people in groups of eight or more. From the volume of the conversation I gathered they had begun the New Year celebrations. Behind the bar a woman was unpacking glasses from a plastic crate. When I sat down at the long bar she came over.

'What would you like?'

'Dry Lemon and ice, please.'

'On New Year's Eve?' Amused laughter lines. She was on the wrong side of forty, but not unattractive, her nose and mouth worked well together. Her eyes were light, more grey than green, hair long and curled in brown waves to her shoulders. Earrings in the shape of the moon and stars. A sleeveless faded orange T-shirt covered her large breasts. Blue jeans with a dramatic belt buckle, African beads around her neck, a cascade of bangles, pretty hands with too many rings. Long nails painted green.

'Yes, thank you.'

I watched as she went to a fridge with a sliding door. She looked good in the jeans. On the back of her shoulder she had a tattoo, an Eastern letter or sign. She took out a can of cool drink – a small one.

'Two of those, please.'

She took out another, put both side by side, took a beer glass and filled it with ice. She brought them all to me.

'Do you want to run a tab?'

'Please.'

She snapped open the cans. I saw hundreds of visiting cards stuck to the shelves of bottles in long rows. Near the ceiling hung a row of baseball caps. Tractor and car logos. Currie Cup teams. Just another country pub in search of character.

'Tertia,' she said, and put out a beringed hand. The name did not suit her.

'Lemmer,' I said, and we shook hands. Hers was cool from the cans and her eyes were curious.

'You don't look like a tourist.'

'What does a tourist look like?'

'Depends. The foreigners wear safari outfits. The Gautengers, from Johannesburg and Pretoria, bring the wife and children. They put their cell phone down first, then a fat wallet beside it. Want to show off a bit, and not miss a call.

You're working. You came in here for a reason. Waiting for someone? Could be, the way you looked around.'

Then she looked into my eyes. 'Mercenary.'

I knew what she was doing. She was waiting for me to blink, the subtle narrowing of my eyes, the downward glance. I showed nothing. 'Consultant. Military consultant.' Nothing. 'Smuggler.'

She knew then she wouldn't get it. 'OK,' she said reluctantly. 'The drink is on the house.'

'Not bad,' I said, and emptied my glass.

'How close was I?'

'Lukewarm.'

'You think you can do better, that's what.'

'May I have another?' I pushed the glass towards her.

'Come on, show me what you've got.' She went to fetch two more cans.

'Do you have biltong? Or nuts or something?'

'Maybe.' She put the cool drinks down in front of me. 'If you can do better than me.'

'Tersh,' someone called from a table. 'More wine.' A chorus of similar requests echoed around the room.

'Coming,' she said to them, and softly to me, 'It's going to be a long night.'

She went to get their wine. I poured for myself again. Watched the skill of her movements. She had the body of a younger woman and she knew it.

Another group came through the door, twelve white people, six men and six women, in their late thirties to mid-fifties. Greetings rang back and forth. There was a festive atmosphere and an air of expectancy.

Tertia fetched an order book and went to stand at the new table. She laughed along with them, touching a man's shoulder here, a woman's hand there. Acquaintances, but her body language was slightly defensive, an unconscious statement of 'I don't really belong here'. An 'outlander', Melanie Posthumus would have called her.

I thought about the game Tertia wanted to play. Wondered how many hundred-rand notes she had won from travelling salesmen. It was easy if you had enough experience of people and knew how to ask your questions and make your statements. I could do better, because I knew them. I had met women like her in the Cape, when Parliament was in session and I could wander around Long Street and St George's Mall and Green-market Square. They all had the same basic story. I had formulated a Law. Lemmer's One-Night Law of Quasi-Artistic Women. More than one night and you became an insect in a spiderweb.

She was from the country, within a radius of two hundred kilometres of here at best. Lower middle-class Afrikaans. Intelligent. Rebellious at school.

After school she left for the city with a feeling of euphoria. To Pretoria, to flee her childhood home and position, not knowing that she would carry it with her. She lived in a tiny single flat somewhere in the city centre, took a clerical position with a big company, temporary only, as she fostered vague ideas of studying art. She began to read Oriental philosophy, study astrology.

She reassessed her life. Resigned from her job, packed her Volkswagen Beetle and drove alone to Cape Town. Moved into a commune in Obs or Hout Bay and made quasi-art pieces to sell in Greenmarket Square, wore loose dresses, sandals and coloured bandannas in her hair. Called herself Olga or Natasha or Alexandra. Smoked a bit of pot, slept around a little. She did not feel fulfilled.

Some time or other in the years to come she would relax her standards and say 'yes' to the short, middle-aged small business-man or beer-bellied banana farmer who had been asking her so long and politely. So she wouldn't have to grow old alone.

32

Tertia didn't ask me to guess about her again, because the restaurant filled up and the orders streamed in. Someone turned up the music. Pop music from the seventies. She put down a bowl of peanuts on her way past. She winked and shouted, 'We'll have to try tomorrow evening.' Ten minutes later a second bar lady came on duty, ten years younger than Tertia, though I suspected her life story was not remarkably different. Red hair and freckles, smaller breasts. She compensated by not wearing a bra. Bigger earrings. They worked well together, never in each other's way.

I shifted to the corner to make way for the crowd. I watched the people. The purpose with which they drank, the frenzy of their pursuit of pleasure. I could never understand this dedication to New Year, but perhaps it was because for so long I had spent it on my own or with Mona. Or just couldn't understand the festivity of the occasion. Another mediocre year past. Gone, lost. Another one to come.

I wanted to get out. I couldn't think here.

I realised that I had no place to stay.

Unasked, Tertia brought me a plate of food. I thanked her and asked her how I could hire a chalet for the night. She couldn't hear me. She had to hold her ear to my mouth. I asked again. Her skin glistened and I smelt her perspiration and cigarettes. She laughed and frowned simultaneously. 'On New Year's Eve?' and she went off to deliver four beers to a table.

I ate the spit-braaied mutton, potato salad, three-bean salad, cheese bread and grape jam. The racket continued to escalate. She came past again and plonked a set of keys down in front of me. The key ring was a silver dolphin with a blue bead for an eye. She leaned over the bar counter, her mouth against my ear. 'Straight down the road past the garages. It's the last place on the left, with the blue door. Take the room with the single bed.'

Then she was gone.

I unlocked the blue door with my black sports bag in my hand.

A lava lamp glowed in the corner, its orange light threw long shadows across the sitting room. It was a busy room. Dark blue and green material with delicate Indian patterning swept down from the ceiling to the wall, which was hung with paintings, etchings and drawings. Mythical and fantastic figures, unicorns and dwarves. Princesses with incredibly long hair. Each was signed in big round letters: Sasha.

She was a painter, not a brilliant one, but not a bad one either. Somewhere in the gap in between.

The heavy curtains were drawn. There was a deep-pile carpet. A bookshelf stood against another wall. Sofa and two armchairs, a coffee table in the middle on which stood an ashtray, three books and a small woven basket. In the basket were more dolphins with blue-beaded eyes like the one on the key ring.

The whole room smelled of incense.

To the left were two bedrooms, to the right a small kitchen and a bathroom.

The bedroom with the single bed was somewhat more spartan. The duvet had big multicoloured blocks. There was a single painting on the wall. It was a moonlit scene, featuring a long-haired princess standing with her back to the observer and her hand stretched out to a unicorn foal. I put my bag down on the bed, unzipped it, took out the Glock and put it on the bedside cupboard. Pulled off my shoes and socks, found my washbag and put that on the bed. I picked up the cell phone and called the SouthMed Hospital. It took a few minutes before I got a nurse from intensive care on the line. She said there was no change in Emma's condition. 'But we live in hope, Mr Lemmer.'

I phoned B. J. since he was on night duty.

'All quiet,' he said.

Jeanette Louw answered on the second ring. 'South-easter is blowing us away,' she said. I could hear the wind howling. There were voices in the background, the faint rush of the sea. I wondered where and with whom she was celebrating on New Year's Eve. 'Your Jeep has a false number plate. Where are you?'

'You don't want to know.'

'Are you making progress?'

'No. But I'm working on it.'

'I'm sure it will take time,' she said.

I picked up my washbag and went to the bathroom. When I switched the light on it was blue. Every white tile was colourfully decorated by hand with patterns, fish, dolphins, shells and seaweed. On the toilet cistern there were fourteen candles. Only a bath, no shower. On the edge of the bath against the wall the bottles stood in a row: oils, creams, shampoo and herbal bath salts.

I opened the taps and undressed. I briefly considered experimenting with a bubble bath. Laughed at myself.

I got in and lay in the hot water.

In the distance I could hear the bass beat of the music – and now and again people screaming jubilantly. I checked my watch. Another two hours to midnight.

I closed my eyes and set my mind to work.

Forget about the frustration. Drop the urge to do something. Review everything. Objectively. Coldly. I arranged all the facts slowly and carefully in a row like dominoes. What had tipped the first one over; what started the whole chain of events? No matter how and where I looked, it all came back to one cause: Emma's phone call to Phatudi.

I took it step by step from there. Four key events. The attack on Emma. The murder of Wolhuter. The attack on us. The murder of Edwin Dibakwane.

The thought process brought a new perspective to bear. At first there were only actions of eco-terrorism that were within the law and relatively harmless. Then there was a systematic escalation to illegal offences like arson and assault. Suddenly the big jump to murder, the ice broken by Cobie de Villiers, with attempts to

murder Emma and the death of Wolhuter and Dibakwane following shortly after.

Why? What was the catalyst? Why so suddenly?

I didn't know, didn't fret over it.

What made the big dominoes fall? First there was a telephone
call. Then there was a second one. I sat upright in the bath and
pressed my palms to my temples. Think now. Third one? Fourth
one? No, no phone call. Or was there? How had the day gone, the
day Emma stood in the rain?

We drank coffee on the veranda. Her head was a bit sore, but her
self-mocking smile was beautiful. She had phoned Mogale. Branca
had phoned back. Two calls. But we hadn't learned about the letter
at the gate yet. Dick came to flirt, Susan came to tell us about the
letter. We saw Edwin at the gate, as large as life. Then we drove to
Mogale. Looked through Cobie's house with Branca, looked at the
blood smear on the safe and left. Then the attack.

What was I missing?

How had they known about Edwin and the message? How had
they known where we were in order to ambush us?

I went back to that morning. We get the letter from Edwin.
Emma questions him. Gives him money.

Could someone have seen us while we were talking to Edwin at
the gate of Mohlolobe? Were there eyes somewhere that saw the
letter being handed over?

Game fence, high fences, dense bush on both sides of the road.
No vehicles parked at a distance. I would have seen them. But even
if there were a hidden spy with binoculars, they couldn't have
known the contents of the letter.

We drive away. Emma stares at the letter. Reads it over and
over. Speculates over the style of writing.

Then her cell phone rings.

There was a call. Carel the Rich. She told him everything.
Everything. About the letter too, and then I knew how they did it. I
hit the bathwater with my fist, the water splashed against the fish
and seaweed. A dolphin grinned at me with an open mouth and I
grinned back, because I knew.

They were listening. The fuckers were tapping the phones and cell phones. How, I didn't know yet, and I didn't know who yet, but I knew they were doing it.

Emma's phone. Somehow or other they were listening in on her calls and her messages. Phatudi's too? Maybe. But definitely Emma's.

So many questions. How had they known they should monitor her calls? How long had they been doing it? Were they just lucky? What did it take to tap a cell phone? Did a bunch of khaki-clad bunny-huggers in the Lowveld have access to such technology? Or were they part of something bigger, something more sophisticated?

Don't worry about what you don't know. Focus on what you do. They were listening, I was sure of it. That gave me an advantage.

How could I use it?

I looked for soap to wash. There wasn't a traditional cake. I ran my fingers down the row of bottles. The two in front contained liquid soap in pump dispensers. I squirted some into my palm and washed.

How could I use my new knowledge?

How could I get them? How could I find them?

There was one way. I had to play my cards right. If I was clever and thought it through carefully, it might work. I must fetch Emma's cell phone. It was in her handbag in the VIP suite at the hospital.

Don't go looking for them.

Let them come to me.

I pulled on my shorts and lay down on the single bed with my arms behind my head and thought for forty minutes, until I had the whole thing planned.

Then I got up because I knew I wouldn't be able to sleep. My head was too busy. I went into the sitting room. Tertia's bedroom door was ajar. Or was she Sasha when she was home? I leaned against the door frame and looked in. There was a large, dramatic four-poster bed with more Indian fabric draped over it and a horde of cushions. From the ceiling hung a framework of silver birds in flight. There were more paintings against the wall, an easel and paintbrushes in the corner, heavy-duty curtains, a dressing table full of bottles and jars. A bedside cupboard with books, an exercise apparatus, one of those they advertise on morning television to keep the body in shape and stay young.

What did Emma le Roux's bedroom look like? What was her house like inside?

I sat in the orange-lava-lamp twilight of the sitting room.

Emma's home would be different from Tertia/Sasha's. More subtle. Open and clean and light. Her clothes would be white and cream, her furniture of Oregon pine with a little glass and chrome. Her curtains would be open wide to let in the light of day. At night the lamps would be bright.

How people differed.

The things that made us what we were.

I got up and went to Sasha's bookshelf. Paperbacks from end to end. Dog-eared from being read over and over, or bought second hand? *The Four Agreements: A Practical Guide to Personal Freedom. Ask and It Is Given: Learning to Manifest Your Desires. The Power of Now: A Guide to Spiritual Enlightenment.*

Searching Sasha.

Your Immortal Reality: How to Break the Cycle of Birth and Death. Earth Angels: A Pocket Guide for Incarnated Angels, Elementals, Starpeople, Walk-Ins, and Wizards.

Did she really believe this stuff? Truly? Or was it a sort of game, a way of escaping reality now and then, a form of fantasy?

The Unicorn Treasury: Stories, Poems, and Unicorn Lore. Dragons and Unicorns: A Natural History. Man, Myth and Magic: The Illustrated Encyclopedia of Mythology, Religion and the Unknown.

And then *Linda Goodman's Love Signs: A New Approach to the Human Heart.* And *Sexual Astrology: Sensual Compatibility.*

I pulled out the last book and opened it. What was Emma's star sign? She had said she shared a birthday with the old South Africa: 6 April. Another Aries, just like me. I looked in the index and found the reference. *Aries and Aries. An excellent match, with an intense sexual attraction and mutual erotic satisfaction, but it is a high-maintenance*

sensual relationship: both man and woman demand lots of sexual
attention. Potential for a long-term relationship is far above average.

A load of bullshit.

I looked up what the book had to say about the Aries woman:
Turn off the lights, and she will become a tiger, anywhere, any time.
But be warned, she is more focused on her own pleasure than on yours.

I shut the book. I went to the bathroom, urinated and then
returned to my single room. I closed the door, opened the window
in the hope that the night would cool down and turned off the light.
I had to sleep. Tomorrow would be an interesting day.

At midnight the racket woke me. I went back to sleep. Not deeply.
Restlessly.

At one o'clock I heard drunken voices and a fumbling at the
door of the chalet next door.

At half past one the blue door opened. After a while I heard taps
running in the bathroom. Between sleep and waking I couldn't
keep time. I smelt the sweet scent of marijuana, heard her in the
sitting room. A last joint before bedtime. For the New Year.

Heard the door of my room open quietly.

Then nothing. I opened my eyelids a crack.

Sasha stood in the doorway, shoulder against the door jamb and
a hand on a tilted hip. Behind her nakedness was a vague soft light.
Not the orange of the sitting room. Something else. Candles. She
stood and looked at me. Her face was in deep shadow, unreadable.

'Lemmer,' she said very softly, nearly inaudibly.

I don't like my surname. It rhymes with gemmer, or ginger. It
hints at the Afrikaans word for blades, and knife fights in back
alleys. Thanks to Herman Charles Bosman it has a certain back-
ward connotation that in my case lies too close to the truth. But it's
better than 'Martin' or 'Fitz' or 'Fitzroy'.

My breathing was artificially shallow. A familiar game, for new
reasons. I shut my eyes completely.

She stood there for a long time. Once more she said 'Lemmer',
and when my breathing did not change, she clicked her tongue and
I heard her footsteps recede.

Her bed creaked.

Searching Sasha.

A week ago I would have accepted this invitation with gratitude.

Ironic. I felt like laughing. At myself. At people. At life. A few nights ago, I was too scared to stretch out my arm to Emma. Too afraid of rejection, too scared that she would jerk back violently and say, 'What are you doing, Lemmer?' with indignation. Too aware of my status, the chasm between us and the consequences of an incorrect assumption.

Emma had stood next to me. Why had she stood beside my bed? Was it because she was a little drunk? Had she remembered the embrace when I had comforted her? Was it because she was lonely, she wanted to be held again, because I was available? Or had she been lost in thought and stood there accidentally? I wasn't her type. Neither in background, or appearance.

I knew that instant would remain in my head. I would relive it over and over when I lay in my bed at home in the silence of a Loxton night. My single bed.

From Tertia's room I heard a faint scuffling noise, like muffled footsteps.

With her standing in my doorway there had been no doubt, no question, no difference in position. I was not afraid. Just unavailable.

Ironic.

The rhythmic rustling from her bedroom could be ignored or explained away at first. It was slow and soft. But it kept on, way beyond the time frame of logical alternatives.

I pricked my ears. Was it her exercise apparatus? No. Subtler, softer, slyer.

Then the knowledge bloomed like a flower in my brain. It was the sound of a mattress and a bed gently swaying.

Endlessly.

Unhurried. Peacefully, the tempo gradually, unconsciously quickening.

A sound joined in. It wasn't her voice but her breath, forcing past her throat or nose or teeth, keeping time with growing enthusiasm.

My body responded.

Faster.

It was very hot in the room.

Harder.

Dear God.

Fiercer. My imagination conjured up the image.

I lay listening, captivated, held. What she was doing was both mean and brilliant.

I wanted to press my hands to my ears. I wanted to make some noise of my own to shut out hers. I did nothing. I lay and listened.

I visualised it. For how long I didn't know. Four minutes? Eight? Ten?

Eventually she was a machine, racing, fast, in a mad, urgent rush.

If I went in there now, I knew how it would be. Vocally she would encourage me, shout out her joys, she would move artfully, roll her hips with skill, she would turn over and offer a new sensation, she would climb on top, she would know when to withdraw so it would last longer, stretch out the hours, so that she would not have to be alone.

Just like all the rest. Desperate, lonely and meaningless.

My head told me all this. It wasn't worth it. When everything was over, my conscience would call Emma's name, but Tertia would want to be held, she would want to light a cigarette and talk about tomorrow.

I got up in one movement. It was only four flowing strides to her door. I saw her on her bed. There was a candle on the bedside cupboard. She lay on her back, knees apart, her beringed finger stroking quickly, the light flickering over her shuddering, sweating body.

She saw me. She had known I would come. Only her eyes betrayed it. Her face was taut with effort and pleasure.

She took her finger away just before I thrust into her violently.

'Yes,' she said. 'Fuck me.'

PART THREE

33

I was up at twenty to five.

I didn't stop to think. I didn't stop to wash. I took my things and crept out like a coward while she slept deeply under the starry Indian heaven. I walked to the Audi and opened the door quietly, tossed in my bag and drove away.

The sun came up beyond Hazyview, the first day of the New Year.

I stopped at a garage and used the restroom. I could smell her on me when I opened my fly to urinate. I washed my member in the basin with sweet-smelling pink liquid soap. I shaved, brushed my teeth and washed my face, but I didn't feel clean.

I drove to the hospital where Emma lay. I thought about what I must do, but my brain followed other paths.

I lay on top of and inside her and in the searing heat of the moment I said 'Sasha' and something changed in her face, a fleeting moment of intense joy, as if she had been discovered, like an island in the ocean.

She had been seen.

'Yes!' she answered with glowing green eyes.

I remembered the first time someone saw me.

It was during my first year as a bodyguard, for the Minister of Transport. It was a summer morning on his farm. I was preparing to go jogging on the dirt tracks between the cornfields. He came out of the homestead with a wide-brimmed hat and a walking stick.

'Walk with me, Lemmer,' he said, and we walked in silence up the koppie from where he could survey his whole property.

He was a smoker. He sat on top of a big rock, lit his pipe slowly and said, 'Where do you come from?' I gave him a broad outline, but he wasn't satisfied. He had a way with people. He made me open up, so that eventually, while the sun came up behind our backs, I told him everything. About my father and mother and the Seapoint years. When I had finished he thought for a long time. Then he said, 'You are this land.'

Twenty years old, still wet behind the ears, I said, 'Sir?'

'Do you know what made this land what it is?'

'No, sir?'

'The Afrikaner and the Englishman. You are both of them.'

I didn't answer. He gazed into the distance and said, 'But you have choices, son.'

Son.

'I don't know if this country has any more choices. The Afrikaner's claustrophobia and aggression and the slyness of the Englishman; these things have brought us to this. It doesn't work in Africa.'

I was dumbstruck. He was a member of the National Party cabinet.

He knocked his pipe out against the stone and said to me, '*Umuntu ngumuntu ngabantu*. Do you know what that means?'

'No, sir.'

'It's Zulu. It's where the word "*ubuntu*" comes from. It means many things. We can only be human through other humans. We are part of a whole, of a greater group. Inextricably. The group is the individual. It means we are never alone, but it also means damage to another is damage to you. It means sympathy, respect, brotherly love, compassion and empathy.'

He looked at me through his thick glasses and said, 'That is what the white man in Africa must search for. If he doesn't find it, he will forever be a stranger in this land.'

I was too young and stupid to understand what he was telling me. And I never got the opportunity to ask him about it, because he shot himself, on that same koppie, to save his family the trauma of his terminal disease. But I thought about it over the years. I studied myself and other people, remembered, questioned. I developed the talent to watch their appearance and actions for threatening behaviour, but also to guess their life stories and ask myself: 'How am I human through them?' I wondered about my inability to be part of a whole. The community is a primitive organism with a selectively permeable membrane and I could not be selected, my shape didn't fit.

Later, when I had more perspective, I wished I could talk to the minister on the koppie again. Tell him Africa was the source of *ubuntu*, that was true. In the eyes of many people I saw the softness, the sympathy, the goodwill, the great desire for peace and love.

But the continent had another side, yang to the yin of *ubuntu*. It was a breeding ground of violence. I wanted to tell him that I could recognise in others the type of man I had become, thanks to my genes and my father's relentless instruction. That absence in the eyes, like something dead inside, of the man who no longer cares about feeling pain and experiences a certain pressure to dish it out, to hurt others.

And nowhere did I see it more frequently than in Africa. In my travels with the National Party and ANC ministers I saw the world – Europe, the Middle and Far East, and my home continent. And here in the cradle of mankind, in the eyes of politicians and dictators, policemen, soldiers and bodyguards and eventually fellow jailbirds, I recognised the majority of my blood brothers. In the Congo and Nigeria, Mozambique and Zimbabwe, Angola and Uganda, Kenya and Tanzania and Brandvlei Prison. People forged by violence who spread it around like a gospel.

Sometimes I felt a deep desire to be different. To belong to the brotherhood of respect, compassion and sympathy, the astonishing support and selflessness. It was the genetic echo of my forebears who left Africa too many aeons ago, the signal was too faint, the distance too great.

I didn't fret about it. That's the way it is: a white man on the continent of *ubuntu*.

In the VIP suite B. J. Fikter told me his night had passed without incident. He was getting ready to go to bed and I took Emma's cell phone and charger and went to look for Dr Eleanor Taljaard.

She said the fact that Emma was still comatose was bad news. 'There has been no change in the last seventy-two hours, Lemmer. That's the problem. The longer the coma continues the worse the prognosis.'

I wanted to ask her whether there was anything they could do, but I knew what the answer would be.

'Eleanor, I need a place to rent for a few days, a week maybe, in the Klaserie district. Not a tourist place. Something remote. A farm or a smallholding.'

'At Klaserie?'

I nodded.

'Why there?'

'Don't ask.'

She shook her head. 'The police are guarding her. Your people are guarding her. What's going on? Is she in danger?'

'She's safe here. I just want to make sure she's safe when she gets out.'

The doctor's expression was unreadable, then she shrugged her questions off and said, 'Let me ask Koos.'

She phoned her husband and passed on my request.

'Koos said it's New Year. Only doctors and people in love are working.'

'Tell him it's urgent, please.'

She passed on my words, making notes on a writing pad with a drug logo at the top. She asked for my cell phone number and repeated it to him. When she put the phone down, she tore off the sheet of paper and said, 'Koos says he will get Nadine Bekker to call you. She's an estate agent. Just give him some time. He wants to exert a bit of pressure. He's good at that.'

'Thank you very much.' I stood up.

'Lemmer,' she said. 'I assume you know what you're doing.'

'That remains to be seen,' I said.

The only place open for breakfast was the Wimpy. I ordered a Double-Up Breakfast and had drunk the first of two large coffees when Nadine Bekker phoned. Her voice was shrill and she spoke rapidly, like someone who was out of breath and late. 'Dr Koos Taljaard said you have an emergency, but I must say that it will be a challenge to get what you're looking for. People don't want to rent in the short term.'

'I'll pay for a month.'

'That would help. Give me a little time, it's New Year, I don't know if I can contact the people. I'll call you back.'

A waiter with bloodshot eyes brought my breakfast. The cook must have been at the same party, because the eggs were rubbery and the pork sausages dry. I had to eat. I ordered more coffee to wash it down. I looked around at the handful of other people in the restaurant. They sat singly, or two to a table, conversing quietly with heads and shoulders bowed. Did I look like them? Somewhat lost, vaguely lonely, a little self-conscious that a Wimpy breakfast was the best thing we could do on this festive morning.

I had a pointless feeling of guilt that I couldn't shake off. It had to do with Emma, owing partly to her condition and my work ethic. How could I, who was supposed to be working, pursue carnal pleasure while she lay in a coma? That was the easier part to ponder and shrug off. The other part was more difficult because at the heart of it was the way I felt about her. How much had she manipulated me to like her, to sympathise with her, to give my support to her cause? How much was deliberate? How much of my discomfort had to do with the fact that I couldn't protect her and that she was the first one I had failed professionally? There was an entire minefield for my conscience.

Besides, I hadn't gone looking for anything. It just happened. It was ten months since I had been with a woman. That was why last night was so intense. It will happen; sometimes you meet a woman with the same hunger, the same anger, the same need.

My cell phone rang. It was Nadine Bekker. 'I have two possibilities for you. There are some others, but the owners are not answering their phones. When I have more time I'll be able to manage something. Do you want to have a look?'

*   *   *

She was a small woman in her fifties, a busy little bee with short bottle-blonde hair and an extravagant wedding ring on her pudgy finger. She was dressed as though she were off to church, her high heels click-clacking hurriedly across the tar road as she approached my car.

'Wait, don't get out, hi, I'm Nadine, pleased to meet you, just follow me, I'll show you the first place, it's not far.'

Business couldn't be too bad in the Lowveld property market; she drove a white Toyota Prado, but not as fast as she could speak.

The first house was near Dingleydale, east of the R40, about ten kilometres from Edwin Dibakwane's house with the pink concrete. It was right on the gravel road and a huddle of the locals' houses was in view.

I stopped behind her and got out. 'Unfortunately, this won't do.'

'I'm sorry, I don't really know what you want, usually we go through all the requirements first. Koos just said a house on a farm or a smallholding.'

'I want something more remote.'

'The other place is more remote, but it is a bit run down, if you don't mind neglected, and there is no electricity, just gas. It belongs to an advocate in Pretoria. He has a few places, but no one lives on that one, he bought it as an investment. It has a beautiful view of the mountain and there's a river.'

'I don't mind neglected.'

'Let's take a look, then. Maybe it's just what you want and the rent is less too. You will have to take it for the whole month, but you said you're OK with that.'

'I am.'

We drove on, north on the R40 and then left on a gravel road at Green Valley. Mariepskop loomed directly ahead, the slopes densely forested.

After fifteen kilometres of dusty bends she stopped at a farm gate and jumped out, indicating that I should wait. She fiddled with a bunch of keys and then shoved the farm gate open and called, 'Leave the gate open, we'll be coming out here again.'

There was a rusty pole beside the gate with a nearly illegible sign with six bullet holes in it. Motlasedi.

We drove uphill on a rough farm track. I worried about the Audi's ground clearance. Near the gate it was grassveld, but within two hundred metres the bush grew thick. We drove through a tunnel of trees, the Prado's roof scraping against the branches and leaves.

The house was over a kilometre from the gravel road. It was an aged building, sixty years or older, corrugated iron roof, yellowing lime-washed walls, a big chimney. The veranda looked out over a stream, rather than the promised river. Directly west the cliffs of Mariepskop dominated the horizon.

Not perfect, but it would do. The yard was big and open enough to see someone coming from a hundred metres off. The disadvantage was that the dense bush would afford shelter beyond that. But it was also difficult to move through. As far as I could see, there was only one workable access route, thanks to the towering mountain and the jungle across the stream.

She got out and waited for me.

'What does Motlasedi mean?' I asked.

'I don't know, but I will find out. Let's have a look inside, I don't know what it's like, the place has been shut up a long time, but there is some furniture at least. What do you want to do here, so far from everything?' She walked deftly up the three steps of the veranda in her high heels and tinkled the bunch of keys until she found the one to unlock the door.

'I just want a bit of peace,' I said.

'One needs peace, too. This is the sitting room, there is something to sit on at any rate, the kitchen is this way, gas stove and gas fridge, you'll just have to get them going, a little bit of dust here, I see, I can get it cleaned for you if you want, it will take a day, come, the bedrooms are this way, at least there's gauze on the windows to keep the mosquitoes out, but you should get something to spray or rub on at this time of the year, the mosquitoes can be a nuisance so close to the water, unfortunately just the one bathroom, there's no bedding of course, but in this heat you won't need much.' She kept up the monologue right through the house at the same rapid pace as her quick, short steps on the bare floorboards, pointedly ignoring the three big cockroaches that scurried away from us. Eventually running out of breath, she asked, 'Is this what you're looking for?'

'Yes, it is.'

'Right, then, let's go and sign the contract, it's a deposit of one thousand eight hundred and a month's rent in advance, that's three thousand six hundred in total, is that all right?'

I took out my cell phone and Emma's to check whether there was reception. One bar, a second that came and went.

'That's fine, thank you.'

34

At ten past two I was back at Motlasedi. I carried a week's supply into the kitchen in Pick 'n Pay shopping bags, lit the gas flame of the fridge and packed the Energade bottles inside. I fetched the broom, bucket, cloths and cleaning materials from the car and began in the kitchen. Then I did the sitting room, bathroom and bedroom. I sweated rivers.

When I was busy spraying four cans of insecticide throughout the house, one of the phones rang. Mine. It was Nadine Bekker.

'Motlasedi means "place of the big fight",' she said when I answered. 'Would you like to hear the story?'

'Please.'

She read to me from some source or other, in English, in too much of a hurry and without respect for punctuation, so that I had to shut my eyes and concentrate on following her.

She said a local tribe, the maPulana, were attacked in 1864 by King Mswati of the Swazis. The maPulana retreated to Mariepskop and there, nearly two thousand metres above the Lowveld plains, they prepared for the battle that would follow. They rolled rocks close to the edge and guarded the single footpath up the mountain.

The Swazi warriors waited for the thick mist that sometimes formed on the slopes of the mountain on summer nights before they ascended the path. That night the mist was so thick that every warrior had to climb with a hand on the shoulder of the one in front of him.

At the top, the maPulana sat in dead silence. They waited till the last moment before they began to roll their rock missiles down the footpath. Their strategy was deadly. The Swazi losses were great and their attack deteriorated into chaos. Finally, the maPulana swept down the mountain, cutting down any resistance, and wiped out the Swazi force in the little river south of Mariepskop.

Nadine paused in her lecture here and said, 'It must be just there where you are, they say a person can still see the bones of the Swazis if you know where to look and that's why the river's name is also Motlasedi, place of the big battle, and why the maPulana call the mountain Mogologolo, meaning 'mountain of the wind' because the Swazis only heard the wind of the falling rocks before they died. Are you settled in already? Are you happy? Phone if there is anything, I must run.'

There was no shower in the bathroom. I ran a cold bath and washed and finally felt clean.

I set the alarm in the cell phone for 16.30 and lay down on the bare mattress and slept restlessly for over an hour. Then I got up, washed my face in cold water, and took Emma's cell phone and a bottle of Energade out of the fridge.

I went and sat on the veranda overlooking the stream. The hum of insects was a blanket of sound. Birds sang in the dense forest across the brown babbling water. A commando of vervet monkeys vaulted through the treetops like ghosts. A large grey ibis landed beside the water and began to poke its long beak purposefully into the short grass.

I ran through my plan one last time. Confirmed the time on my watch: 16.43.

I called Information to get three numbers. I wrote them on Emma's paper with a pencil.

I phoned the first one at once – the Mogale rehabilitation centre.

A volunteer with a Scandinavian accent answered. I asked to speak to Donnie Branca. She said to hold on. I heard them calling him.

'Please hold, he is coming.'

Then he said, 'This is Donnie.'

'It's Lemmer, Donnie. I was there with Emma le Roux.'

'Oh. I'm very sorry. We heard about the accident.'

'It wasn't an accident and you know it.'

'I'm not sure what you mean.'

'Donnie, I think it's time we dropped the bullshit. I want you to listen to what I'm going to say to you.'

'I don't like your . . .'

'Shut up and listen, Donnie.'

He shut up. I had thought for a long time about what I wanted to say to him. It was all based on calculated guesswork, but the delivery was the key. I had to say it with aggression and self-confidence. I couldn't afford to let him know that there were gaps in my knowledge.

'I'm on a farm called Motlasedi, on the gravel road between Green Valley and Mariepskop. I'm giving you forty-eight hours to tell me where Cobie de Villiers is. If I don't hear from you by that time, I am going to pass on everything I know to the newspapers and the Commissioner of Police in Limpopo.'

I gave him a while to let that sink in.

'I know what you think, Donnie. You're wondering what I know. Let me help you: I know everything. I know about your night-time escapades, I know about the firearms you are hiding from the police, I know what Frank Wolhuter found in Cobie's house – and that it wasn't on the bookshelf, Donnie.'

Then I took the big gamble, the one I had deliberated over the longest. 'I also know that H. B. doesn't stand for Honey Badger. Forty-eight hours, Donnie. Don't contact me about anything else. You know what I want.'

I pressed the button with the red receiver icon to end the call and wiped the sweat from my brow.

I breathed out slowly.

The next call was to Carel the Rich. He must have seen her name on his screen, because he said, 'I've been worrying about you, Emma.'

'It's Lemmer. The news is not good.'

'Where is Emma?' It was more of an order than a concerned enquiry.

'She's in hospital, Carel. There was an incident.'

'An incident, what kind of incident? What's she doing in hospital?'

'Carel, if you'll be quiet, I can finish.'

He wasn't used to that tone. Astonishment kept him quiet just long enough.

'We were attacked on Saturday by three armed men. Emma was wounded and sustained a head injury. She is in the intensive care unit at SouthMed Hospital in Nelspruit. Her doctor's name is Eleanor Taljaard. Call her if you want the details of Emma's condition.'

He couldn't restrain himself any longer.

'Saturday!' he shouted at me. 'Saturday? And you're only calling now?'

'Carel, calm down.'

'That's three days! How dare you only call me now? How bad is Emma?'

'Carel, I want you to shut the fuck up and listen. I owe you nothing. I'm phoning you as a courtesy. I know who attacked us. I'm going to get them, every one. Not for you. For Emma. I am on a farm by the name of Motlasedi, on the gravel road between Green Valley and Mariepskop. It's just a question of time before I get them.'

I hoped he would ask the right question. He didn't disappoint me. 'Who? Who was it?'

'It's a long story and I haven't got the time right now. I'll tell you everything when it's over. It won't be long. I'm going to blow the whole thing wide open.'

'You were supposed to protect her, it was your job.'

'Goodbye, Carel.' I cut the connection.

He would phone back immediately, I knew. I checked my watch. Nineteen seconds and Emma's phone rang. The screen said 'Carel'. I killed the call. Waited again. This time it was twenty seconds. Killed it. Another nineteen and it rang again. My money was on three times, but Carel was a determined Rich Afrikaner. He tried six times before giving up. I could see him in his den, angry and indignant, with a cigar between his fingers. He would pace up and down and try to remember what I had said about the hospital and the doctor and then he would phone them.

It was time for me to make my third call. I keyed in the number.

'Serious and Violent Crimes Unit, how may I help you?'

'May I speak to Inspector Jack Phatudi, please?'

'Hold on.'

She put me through to an extension that rang and rang. Eventually, she got back on the line.

'You are holding for?'

'Inspector Jack Phatudi.'

'The inspector is not in. Is there a message?'

'Yes, please. Tell him that Lemmer called.'

'Who?'

'Lemmer,' I spelled out my surname for her.

'OK. What is the message?'

I lied blatantly. 'Please tell him that I know who gave the note to Edwin Dibakwane.'

'Edwin Dibakwane?'

'Yes.'

'I will tell him. How can he contact you?'

'He's got my number.'

'OK.'

To make doubly sure, I also phoned the SAPS offices in Hoedspruit to leave him the same message, but to my surprise they said, 'Please hold for Inspector Phatudi,' and then he answered with an unfriendly 'Yes?'

'Jack, it's Lemmer.'

A few seconds of silence. 'What do you want?'

'I know who gave the letter to Edwin Dibakwane.'

'Who?'

'I can't tell you now, Jack. First, I want you to apologise for yesterday. Your manners leave a lot to be desired. I hope your mother doesn't know how you behave.'

He lost his temper instantly. 'My mother?'

'Yes, Jack, your mother. I am sure she taught you better manners than that. Are you going to say sorry?'

He answered me in sePedi. I couldn't understand the words, but I gathered from the tone that it wasn't an apology.

'Then I'll say goodbye, Jack,' I said. I cut off the call and switched Emma's cell phone off.

The broad stretch of thick bush between the farm entrance and the homestead was a problem. The good news was that I would be invisible inside. The bad news was that I couldn't watch the potential access routes and the house at the same time.

I chose a hiding place just over ten metres away from the edge of the thicket, where I could see the gate and more than a kilometre of access road plus a large stretch of the boundary fence without being seen. There were no shops selling binoculars that were open in Nelspruit. I would have to make do.

I removed stones and branches so I could sit comfortably against a tree. I placed the Glock within easy reach. I opened the box of ten Twinkies, took the contents out of the plastic and arranged them on the upturned khaki bush hat I had bought at Pick 'n Pay. It was food that did not crunch or otherwise make a noise. I put the four bottles of Energade down beside the Twinkies and opened one. Not ice cold, but good enough.

I checked my watch. Just under an hour since I had contacted Donnie. Theoretically they could turn up any moment. I didn't think they would. He would have to call the other masked wonders first. They would have to discuss weapons and strategy. Up till now they had been night owls on escapades. My best guess was that they'd show up around midnight. Maybe later. In the meantime, I would wait. Just in case.

I ate one Twinkie. Drank Energade.

I read on the box that more than five hundred million of these confections were sold annually. Since 1930 Twinkies had attained cult status. President Clinton put one in a time capsule. The American Association of Press Photographers had recently held an exhibition of photos with Twinkies as the subject. People even made wedding cakes out of Twinkies.

I put the carton down. I wondered why Clinton didn't put a

cigar in the time capsule. That would have pleased Carel the Rich.

The piece of open veld out there was suddenly in shade.

The sun had set behind Mariepskop. It was going to be a long night.

35

When you're hiding, you have to sit still.

I'm not good at sitting still. Despite my best attempts to make the hollow in the tree comfortable, after an hour it was full of irritations. When I shifted my body I did it slowly and deliberately, so my movements would not attract attention.

But I knew no one was watching me. It was a lesson I learned early on in my career as a bodyguard – people can sense when someone is watching them. I was usually the one watching, on constant alert for possible risk. Nine times out of ten the object of my observation became aware of it. It's a primitive instinct, but it exists. Some people react quickly, their sense is well developed, the reaction swift and aggressive. For others, it is a slower process, a systematic awakening that is at first unsure and seeks confirmation. I had learned to watch more subtly. I experimented with sidelong glances, peripheral vision, and realised that it made no great difference. The observed feel the interest, not the focus of the eye.

In the bush around me the nightlife began to stir. It was a whole new series of noises made by insects, birds and unidentified animals, a rustling of leaves and twigs. Midges and mosquitoes showed interest, but the insect repellent I had rubbed on did its job.

Twice I stood up slowly to stretch my limbs and encourage circulation. I ate and drank, watched and listened. I was calmer now that events were set in motion and a new row of dominoes was set up. I wondered who would make the first one fall.

I thought about Emma and how badly I had read her, how prejudiced I was. I don't like rich people. It's partly envy, let me confess, but it is also experience, because I have been watching

them for the past eighteen years. First, it was the wealthy influen-
tials looking for the minister's ear, more recently it was my 'clients',
as Jeanette referred to them. The overwhelming majority of rich
people were bastards, self-important and self-obsessed.

Especially the Rich Afrikaner.

My father had saved a bunch of yellowed photos in a flat tea tin
on the top shelf of his wardrobe. Two were photographs of our
forebears: my great-grandfather and his three brothers, four
bearded men in white shirts and jackets. According to my father
it was taken at the turn of the century after the loss of the family
farm, when the Afrikaner had nothing. The four Lemmers' poverty was obvious from the cut and simplicity of their clothes. But
there was a look in their eyes of pride, determination and dignity.

Years later, I would recall that photograph when I drove to
Calvinia for the Vleisfees, the annual mutton festival. It was an
impulsive decision. I had been out of the service for one year and I
wanted to get out of Seapoint for the weekend. I read an article
about the festival and rashly set out on the Saturday morning. I
was back at home by that night because I hadn't liked what I saw:
wealthy Afrikaners fresh from the city in their brand-new shiny
SUVs, sitting and drinking, inebriated at three in the afternoon or
jerking their drunken middle-aged bodies to the beat of ear-
splitting music, while their mortified teenage children sat on the
sidelines. I stood there thinking about the photos in my father's tea
tin and knew that poverty suited the Afrikaner better.

Therefore, I admit to a prejudice against the rich, and therefore
against Emma.

But prejudice is a defence mechanism. Some prejudices are
inborn, our instinctive search for the ducks from our dam, our
nearest genetic brothers and sisters, like the New Guinea tribes-
man's continual repetition of his family tree. It is also the unwitting
origin of all the -isms, so very politically incorrect, but so very
much our nature.

Other prejudices are learned. Those that spring from experience
are just as set on protection. Like a child that learns that the
hypnotic flame can burn, so we learn with every human interac-

tion, we make thought patterns of cause and effect, we categorise and label so we can avoid the painful. We promulgate laws.

Small women equal trouble. Not only my mother; our synapses are not that easily programmed. There were others, girls at school, women that I watched in a personal or professional capacity until I could build a frame of reference that dictated that if she was small and pretty, she was trouble.

I rationalise only as much as the next man, but with Emma it must serve as extenuating circumstances. How was I to know that she was different? There was no initial evidence to the contrary. Rich, lovely and small. Why should she be the exception? It was just smart not to get involved, to keep a professional distance.

And now? Now I sat in deep darkness in the Lowveld jungle and the boundaries between personal and professional involvement had disintegrated. I needed them redrawn so that I could finish the job I started: to protect her. But now, the primary driving force was vengeance. Someone had to pay for the attack on my Emma. I wanted to find the answers to her questions and lay them at her feet in a plea for forgiveness and as an offering of attraction.

My Emma.

But yesterday I slept with a stranger.

Emma. I had carried her sleeping body into her room, I had comforted her, and I had shown her a part of myself at table that only Mona had seen before. I had held her bleeding body in a minibus-taxi with the terrible knowledge that she was dying, that much more than just my professional reputation would die with her. Koos Taljaard was right. I was in love with Emma, with who she was, despite her beauty and wealth. Despite her class and her intellect, she could ask me, 'Who are you, Lemmer?' with genuine interest and curiosity. After the Cape attack she had the courage to come looking here, believing through adversity that Cobie was Jacobus, her brother, her blood.

My Emma, to whom I was unfaithful last night.

I ought to have seen it coming. I was disappointed in myself. I should have seen the danger and the opportunity when Tertia said, 'You've been fighting, Lemmer. Bad boy.' There was a flicker in her, that observation had flipped a primitive switch in her sub-conscious with a ghostly hand. Women fear violence. They hate it. But a great percentage of them have a weakness for potential violence in a man. For the ability to physically assert over other men his right to reproduce, to protect his woman and her offspring from danger. Mona had it. During my court case there were a couple of women who came every day to listen, who sat and stared at me, who followed the testimony of the fight word by word.

And Tertia. Sasha.

I should have pushed the key with the blue-eyed dolphin back across the bar counter. I should have used my head.

I should have known that I would not be able to withstand the temptation. Because I should have known that she would have been able to cast off sexual inhibitions.

For me, for men, that potential to toss all inhibition overboard is the ultimate fantasy, the deadly noose: the woman who screams her ecstasy out loud and bucks like a wild horse, whose eyes hide nothing, who wants more and doesn't ask but takes it with demonic purpose.

Tertia wanted me because I was not overtly interested. For her it was confirmation of her power to seduce despite the march of time, although it took longer, harder hours to keep the lovely body of her prime in shape. Just like my mother. Maybe it was another way for Tertia to escape from her boring existence. Maybe it was just a need to have a body to hold at New Year. Or did she want one more dance with the devil of potential violence, the fighting man, the mercenary or military consultant or smuggler?

When she was standing in my doorway with her hips and breasts on display, I wondered how long I had known it would happen. How soon was I aware that I would get up and go to her? How much of my hesitation was merely a concession to conscience? I knew I wanted it; I was hungry for it. For the intensity and pleasure and my own urge to fuck the rage away. The rage about the unreachable Emma, the rage about my weakness and predictability and helplessness. Lemmer and Sasha. In contrast to Martin and

Tertia. In a certain way we were birds of a feather that had coupled like animals on an unlikely bed for two hours. The heat is what I would remember most. The heat of the night, the heat of her body, of being inside her, of my passion and her need. How she had cried out from gratitude or fear, over and over, oh God, oh God, oh God.

Lights at the gate broke my train of thought. Startled, I jerked back to the present dark night, the forest and the first domino wobbling.

I picked up the Glock and lay down on my belly and watched.

Somebody got out of the vehicle, which looked like a pick-up, and opened the gate, too far off to identify.

The pick-up drove through the open gate, lights on bright, and waited for the gate-opener to close it and get back in. Then it came up the track.

I avoided the bright light, trying to preserve my night vision, but I needed to know who was in the pick-up.

I hadn't expected this. Not a direct assault. Out in the open.

There must be others; this would be the decoy to attract my attention. The others would stalk up through the night in dark clothes and balaclavas with night-vision scopes and sniper's rifles. I turned my head away from the pick-up, my eyes and ears searching for stalkers. Let the pick-up arrive at the empty house, they would find nothing there.

The vehicle approached. It was dark inside the cab. I had a quick look. Couldn't see who was inside. They drove past into the tunnel of trees, the lights flickering in the branches.

The others wouldn't come in at the gate. They would climb over a fence, farther east perhaps, perhaps west. Five, ten or fifteen minutes later. I would just have to wait quietly. I checked the green phosphor of my watch hands: 20.38. Why were they so early? Why not wait until the early hours of the morning when I was fighting sleep?

Did they suspect that I was alone? Were they so confident, these experienced night stalkers, hunters of what they thought was unsuspecting prey?

The pick-up's engine was hard to hear, and then it was completely quiet. They must have stopped at the homestead. Don't go and look, don't worry about them, just wait here. Wait for them.

Faintly, I heard them calling at the house. 'Lemmer!' The last syllable stretched out. They called three times. It was quiet again.

20.43. Nothing but the night sounds.

My night sight returned to normal. I looked slowly up and down the front, holding my breath so I could listen.

Nothing.

20.51 came and went.

I couldn't work out their strategy. Why send in the pick-up for any reason besides diversion? Were there another three or four lying flat on the back, as if in a Trojan horse? That made no sense. You diverted attention so that you could surprise from another direction, another place, but if the timing was off, it fell flat. You had to keep the focus on point A while your buddies infiltrated at point B. If the focus shifted, the strategy failed.

21.02. I had to suppress the urge to get up and stalk over to a vantage point to look at the homestead. What were they up to? Why were they so quiet?

Were they inspecting the terrain? Did they have two-way radios to give the others instructions? We can see there is only one road in; you must do such and such.

I would just have to wait. There was no other way. But I was growing less sure of that. No, that's what they want. Doubt. It generates mistakes. I had the upper hand. I had to keep it.

I heard them calling again, around 21.08, my name and something else that I couldn't make out. I ignored them. The Glock's grip was sweaty in my palm and the stones and tree roots pressed uncomfortably against my legs and chest.

Silence.

By 21.12 they had been there for half an hour and there had been no movement, no sound from the boundary fence or the roadside.

Three minutes later I heard the pick-up engine again, soft at first, then growing louder. They were coming back. I saw the headlights through the bush.

The lights were plain idiotic. It deprived them of vision; they would be blind in the darkness. Why did they do it?

They stopped in the middle of the bush, switched off the lights and then the engine.

'Lemmer!'

It was Donnie Branca's voice.

'Are you there?'

The bush fell silent, the nightlife intimidated.

'Lemmer!'

He waited for a response.

'This is Donnie Branca. We want to talk to you. There are only two of us.'

I didn't look at them; I focused on the visible no man's land.

There was nothing.

'Lemmer, you've made a mistake. It wasn't us. We would never harm Emma le Roux.'

Of course you wouldn't. You are just innocent animal rehabilitators.

'We can help you.'

They spoke to each other, not quietly, but I couldn't hear what they were saying.

There was the sound of pick-up doors opening and closing.

'Lemmer, we got out. We'll just stand here by the pick-up. If you can see us, you will see that we're unarmed. Have a good look. We'll just stand here.'

Now was the time for the others to arrive; now that they believed they had my attention. I swung the barrel of the Glock from left to right, following with my eyes. No movement, no footsteps, not a twig cracking, just the silence and the insects.

'We can understand why you would suspect us. We can understand that, we can see how it must look. I swear to God it wasn't us.'

Ah, just swear to God? That will convince me.

Did they consider me a complete idiot?

But where were the others? Was there someone on the back of the pick-up? Were they creeping through the undergrowth to surprise me from behind? I turned around slowly and carefully. It would be tough to hear and see them. That would be brilliant, keep my attention and stalk me from the direction I least expect.

I heard their voices in discussion again, but devoted all my attention to the thickets around me. The front was now 360 degrees, it was getting more complicated, but they didn't know where I was or even if I was really here.

'H. B. stands for "haemoglobin",' another familiar voice said. I couldn't place it immediately and then I recognised its slow measured cadence. Stef Blinking Moller of Heuningklip.

Stef? Here?

There was a long silence. I turned around, the Glock in front of me. There was nothing to see, just the silence of the bush.

They growled something at each other. Donnie Branca called, 'We'll be on our way, then,' with disappointment. I heard one door open and I shouted, 'Wait!' and stood with my chest against a tree trunk to reduce the angles by 180 degrees.

36

'Lie down in front of the pick-up, on the ground,' I told them, and moved north in the direction of the homestead, immediately, then east, closer to them. I found another tree as partial cover.

'We're lying down.'

I moved again quickly. I wanted to approach the pick-up from behind to make sure there was no one on the back.

'I'm coming,' I called, and ran, dodging through the trees to make a difficult target. I saw the pick-up, a Toyota single-cab. I stopped for a second and swung the Glock west then north, and then I ran for the back of the pick-up, pointing the pistol at it. If they got up now I would blow them away, before they got me. I reached the vehicle; there was nobody, the back was empty. I kept running to where they lay in front of the pick-up. Stef Moller was on the left, Donnie Branca on the right, and I pressed the pistol to Moller's chest and said, 'The idea is for you to lie face down, Stef. Don't you watch TV?' and he said, 'Oh! Um, no, actually, sorry,' and he turned over. I wanted to laugh from the mixture of adrenalin and anticlimax.

I put my knee on Moller's back and pointed the Glock at the back of his head and said, 'Where are the others?'

'There's no one else, just us,' said Donnie Branca.

'We'll see,' I said. 'Put your hands where I can see them.'

He shifted his hands far out ahead. 'You've got it wrong, Lemmer. It wasn't us that attacked you.'

I began to search Moller for weapons. I found none. 'Yesterday you talked about an accident, now suddenly it's an attack.'

'I wanted to express sympathy yesterday, it was just a word. My Afrikaans . . .'

I went over to Donnie Branca and patted him where I thought he might have a weapon concealed. 'Your Afrikaans is good enough when it suits you. Put your hands behind your head and turn over. I want to see if you're armed.'

He did as I asked. 'We're not armed. We're here to talk.'

First I made sure, but he was telling the truth. 'Lie on your belly.' I sat down with my back against the front of the pick-up, between them.

'All right, then, talk.'

'What do you want to know?' asked Branca.

'Everything.'

'You said you knew everything.'

'Tell me anyway.'

It was Stef Moller who began. 'The sangoma and the vulture poachers were a mistake,' he said.

'You call that a mistake?'

'We have rules. Principles. Murder is not part of them.'

'We?'

'Hb. Capital "H", small letter "b", no point in between. *The Lowvelder* got it wrong.'

'What is *The Lowvelder*?'

'The local paper in Nelspruit. They printed it as capital "H", point, capital "B", point. That's why they talk about the Honey Badgers.'

'But Hb stands for haemoglobin?'

'Yes.'

'Why?'

'For many reasons. Haemoglobin is in our blood, in the animals' too. It carries oxygen. We need it, the planet needs it. It is the opposite of carbon dioxide. It is invisible to the eye. It has four parts. So do we.'

'And they are?'

'Conservation, combat, communication and organisation.'

'You sound like the Voortrekker Movement. Or the Broeder-bond.'

'It doesn't matter.'

'Why are you telling me this, Stef?'

'You said you know everything,' he said with extreme patience. 'Now you know we won't lie to you.'

'The sangoma thing. It was you.'

'It was Cobie.'

'Cobie is one of you.'

'Cobie got carried away. He's unstable. We realised that too late.'

'You lied to Emma about Jacobus. Both of you.'

'Not about everything.'

'Tell me from the beginning, Stef, so I can understand which parts you lied about.'

'Can I sit up?'

I considered and then said, 'You can both sit, but over there. I want to see your hands.'

They shifted two metres back and sat with their hands on their knees.

'Talk,' I said.

Moller's eyes began to blink behind the thick glasses. 'He started working for me in 1994, as I told Emma.'

'Yes?'

'I . . . We, Cobie and I, shared the same concerns. About ecology, conservation, the threats.'

'Wait, slow down. Where did he come from?'

'From Swaziland.'

'But he wasn't born there. He didn't grow up there.'

'That's what he told me.'

'You're lying, Stef.'

'Cobie de Villiers is not Emma le Roux's brother.'

'You're lying.'

'I swear.'

'Before God,' I said sarcastically, but Moller didn't get it.

'Yes,' he said solemnly. 'Before God.'

'Go on.'

'When Cobie worked for me, we talked every single day for more than three years. We talked about the environment. Sometimes all night. Someone had to do something, Lemmer. I want you to understand one thing, we are not political, we are not racist, and we serve only one thing. Our natural heritage.'

'Spare me the propaganda, Stef. Tell me about Cobie.'

'That's what I'm doing. Hb is Cobie. It's what he lives for. It's all he lives for. You have to understand that. When they poisoned those vultures, it was as though someone had murdered Cobie's family.'

He saw me shake my head and said, 'I'm not condoning Cobie's behaviour. I'm just trying to explain that his intentions were good. He and I started Hb. We were very careful. At first we were only seven or so, five in Mpumalanga, two in Limpopo. We were informal, it was only communication to start with, the exchange of ideas. It's a funny thing, Lemmer. Every month someone would join. Everyone said talking would not help any more. Something would have to be done, because we live in a world where people are everything and nature is nothing. Nobody talks about nature's rights. Everything is going backwards. That's how it started. Then Cobie disappeared. We were just getting organised. I couldn't understand it. He was more driven than I am, he felt more strongly, put more energy into it, and suddenly he was just gone. To this day, I don't know where he went. Three years later he turned up at Mogale. Maybe Donnie should tell you the rest.'

'When Cobie left you, did Hb survive?'

'It's bigger than one individual. When Cobie disappeared, there were more than thirty of us. All across the country. In the Kalahari, KwaZulu, the Karoo. But we were only focused on conservation, communication and organisation. We only added combat in 2001, when we realised that we had no choice.'

'But all that is happening, Stef, without the need for secret societies. What about WWF and Greenpeace? Why didn't you join up with Greenpeace?'

He sighed deeply. 'You don't get it, do you,' he said.

Branca couldn't stay quiet. 'We told you, Frank and I. It's chaos.'

'A few land claims and a golf estate don't sound like chaos to me.'

Branca made a gesture of futility. Stef Moller sighed and said, 'That's just the ears of the hippo. A million species, Lemmer. Do you know how many that is? How many animals and plants it represents? Have you any idea? That's how many are going to go extinct in the next forty years, just from global warming.'

I had heard this old wives' tale before. I shook my head in disbelief.

'You can shake your head. You're just like the rest of mankind. You don't want to believe it. But someone must, because it's a fact.'

'And you're going to stop global warming by sending letters and shooting dogs?'

'No. We do what we can, here. We can only try to prepare for the mess that's coming.'

'Tell me about Cobie. In 2000 he turns up again suddenly. This time at Mogale. With Wolhuter.'

'Yes.'

'Where had he been?'

'I don't know. He wouldn't say.'

'Stef, I don't believe you.'

'Truth is stranger than fiction, Lemmer,' said Donnie Branca. 'We're not lying. Cobie started working for Frank and he and I talked. He was very careful. It took nearly six months before he started to recruit me for Hb. Only then did he ask me to take a message to Stef. He asked me to tell Stef that he couldn't talk about where he was, that he was sorry, but he had to protect Hb, that was why he went back to Swaziland.'

'But Frank Wolhuter didn't want to be part of Hb.'

'We tried. Frank was old school. He was a game ranger in Natal. He worked within the system, didn't see the necessity of, shall we say, alternative action. We tried, but Frank believed our work at Mogale was good enough. We never told him directly about Hb, because we could sense that he wouldn't condone it.'

'I thought so. Let me tell you what happened, Donnie, when Emma showed you and Frank the photo of Cobie. Two things. You got scared. You sat there in Frank's office worrying about what threat it posed for Hb, because you didn't know whether Emma's story was true or not. Who was she really? What did she want? You sent her in Stef's direction so he could help assess her. So you could make a decision. You phoned him after we left. You warned Stef that we were coming. Am I right?'

'In a way.'

'The second thing that happened was that Emma's photos and story made Frank even more suspicious. He must have had his suspicions about you and Cobie anyway. Even though he told us Cobie hadn't committed the vulture murders, he wasn't sure. When Emma turned up he had to do something. He unlocked Cobie's place and searched it. He found the stuff. The photos and other proof, about Hb. I don't know what it was, but I know it wasn't in the bookshelf in the kitchen, was it?'

'No.'

'Where did Cobie hide it?'

'In the ceiling.'

'So he phoned Emma and left the message, but before she could phone back, he confronted you about Hb. He wasn't happy about it. He threatened to go to the police, or something. So you threw him in the lion camp.'

'No! Frank was my friend.' Passionate, arms waving. 'I'd never do that. I don't know what happened, I swear to you. I only looked in the safe the day after Frank died.'

'Because you had to hide the rifles you used to shoot the dogs.'

'Yes. OK. I had no choice. But when I opened the safe, I saw the blood. And I found Cobie's documents. And those photos I showed Emma. I took the album to Cobie's house and I put it on the bed, and then I searched the place to make sure there was nothing else. There was this box in his ceiling, but it was empty. I can only assume, you know, that Frank found it there, and took the contents, and put them in the safe.'

'You said Frank's death was no accident. You had a motive, Donnie.'

'Jesus, Lemmer, how can you think that? I loved the man. I respected him more than any other. It wasn't me.'

'Who, Donnie? Who?'

'Someone who didn't want Emma to see the photo.'

'What photo?'

'The one that was missing from the album.'

I looked at them, at Stef Moller and Donnie Branca, with their righteous frowns, the sincerity carved deeply on their faces in the light of the half-moon, and slowly shook my head.

'No, you're lying to me. Tomorrow I'm going to the *Beeld* newspaper with everything. You can try and tell your tall story to the journalists.'

Branca began to speak but Stef Moller stopped him with a hand in the air. 'Lemmer, please, what can I do to convince you?' he said slowly.

'Tell the truth, Stef.'

'That's what we've been doing the whole time.'

'No, it isn't. Cobie is Emma's brother. Donnie said the photo that disappeared – someone didn't want Emma to see it. Why wouldn't you want Emma to see it? Why would Frank phone Emma about it? Why do you still insist that he's not Emma's brother?'

'Because we asked him,' said Stef.

'When?'

'Three days ago. Saturday. Cobie de Villiers said he had never heard of her.'

37

I had to restrain myself. I wanted to get up and grab Stef by the throat and shake him. 'So why are you lying to me about where Cobie is?' But he must have known what my reaction would be.

'We don't know where he is, Lemmer. He phoned out of the blue. He said that he'd heard that Frank Wolhuter was dead. We must be very careful, because the people who did it are very dangerous. We must take precautions; we must arm ourselves and make sure we are never alone. I asked him where he was and he said it didn't matter. I asked him about Emma and he said he had no family, he didn't know anyone like that.'

'Did you ask him why he shot those people?'

'I didn't need to. We know it was him.'

'But Frank and Donnie swore it wasn't him.'

Donnie Branca half rose indignantly. 'What did you expect, Lemmer? Be realistic, for Christ's sake. Frank didn't believe it was Cobus. What did you want me to do? Go tell everybody, "Yes, Cobie shot them in cold blood, the bastard"? I mean, Jesus.'

'Sit down, Donnie.' But it didn't help. He was angry. He got up, walked a circle in the dark and came back to stand in front of me.

'Fuck you, Lemmer. What are you going to do? Shoot me? I'm sick and tired of you. If there's something that proves Cobie is Emma's brother, it's not our business. The stupid fuck went and shot innocent people and put twelve years' work at risk. Twelve fucking years. That's how long Stef worked to get Hb going, to make it work. You shake your fucking head when we talk about the threat to the environment. You're just like everybody. The media, the government, the fucking public, everybody is in denial. You have no idea what's happening, Lemmer. All over the world. It's a fucking mess. I dare you, go do your homework. Go look at the facts. Go read the scientific material. All of it.

Not just climate change. Everything. Loss of habitat, deforestation, population growth, pollution, land abuse, urban sprawl, development, poaching, smuggling, poverty, globalisation. And then come back and tell me that there's no crisis. Go to the media. Expose us. See if you can stop it.'

'Donnie,' Stef Moller placated him.

'Jesus, Stef, I've had enough of this fucking fool. Read my lips, Lemmer. We did not touch Frank or Emma. And if you don't believe that, you can go fuck yourself.' He stalked off to the side of the pick-up, opened the door and said, 'Come on, Stef, let's go,' slammed the door and started the engine.

Stef Moller slowly got up and walked past me. 'He's right,' was all he said. He got into the pick-up and I had to move out of the way, because it didn't seem as though Donnie Branca was going to stop for me.

I'd believed that Emma was lying to me and I'd been wrong. My belief in my built-in lie detector had been shaken. I stood in the dark and watched the red lights of the Toyota disappear in the distance and I thought Donnie Branca was telling the truth and that Stef Moller was still hiding something.

If you want to know whether someone is lying, look at his eyes. It was difficult with Moller because of the constant blinking and the thick lenses. That night I couldn't see his face in the dark and I had to listen to his voice, its rhythm and intonation. He wasn't telling the whole truth.

Or was it my imagination?

I went back to my nest.

Tall Stef Moller with his bald pate and glasses and his slow, solemn way of speaking. I thought he was harmless the day we'd met him. Even though something had bothered me in the shed, something I had missed.

Tall, dispassionate men are not high on a bodyguard's list of threats. The assassins of history have been short, busy little men.

Lee Harvey Oswald, Dmitri Tsafendas, John Hinckley, Mark David Chapman.

I hadn't expected Moller here tonight. It was his voice which had convinced me to come out from cover and call to them, because I didn't identify him with cold-blooded attacks and violence. It wasn't just an instinct. Stef Moller had an aura of the oppressed and wounded about him.

But I did know that he was lying. About something.

What bothered me about the shed?

Branca hadn't been involved in the attack on Emma and myself. I believed him.

Who was it, then?

And why was Moller lying? Had he sent someone else? Didn't he trust Branca enough, and were there other Hb troops willing to do dirty work?

The people who did it are very dangerous. We must take precautions. We must arm ourselves and make sure that we are never alone.

Had he said that with authority or a bit of fear? Even so, they hadn't brought weapons with them tonight. Or were they concealed in the pick-up?

What had I seen in Moller's shed?

I sat down with my Twinkies and Energade. I could not relax. I had to stay alert, ready.

The day Emma and I were there, the shed had been fairly gloomy, the only light coming through the double doors. There were steel shelves on the walls, big drums of diesel or oil, workbenches covered with spare parts, oil rags, tins and cans, nuts and bolts, tools and . . .

I picked up a bottle of Energade and took a swig. I shut my eyes and concentrated.

On the workbench two metres from Moller there had been a carburettor and the cover of an air filter with the broken air filter beside it and . . . a tray.

An old reddish-brown tray with a cork base and a sugar bowl and coffee mugs, that's what caught my attention.

The coffee mugs.

Why?

Because there were three of them. Three coffee mugs, two empty, one half full.

I stood up in the dark forest, bottle in one hand, Glock in the other.

There's only Septimus and myself, no other labour. That's what Stef Moller had said. But there were three ugly khaki brown mugs with their teaspoons standing upright in them and someone hadn't finished their coffee. Two people, three mugs, it didn't add up. Someone else had been in that shed when Emma phoned from the gate. Someone who didn't want to be seen.

I collected my things and began jogging to the homestead. I had a good idea who that third person had been.

I believed he was still at Heuningklip and that was why Stef Moller was lying to me.

It took nearly three hours to drive the two hundred and fifty kilometres to Heuningklip. There were heavy trucks in the mountain passes and sharp bends invisible in the night up the escarpment.

I drove through Nelspruit and wondered how Emma was, wanting to make a detour to hold her hand. Talk to her. I wanted to ask her what she had been thinking when she came and stood beside my bed, but I also wanted her to remain silent so I could preserve the possibility of multiple answers.

I turned right on the R38 just beyond the Suidkaap river and thought about Stef Moller, the shy rich man. Melanie Posthumus had said he's this billionaire that bought all these farms and made them nice, but nobody knows where his money came from.

So where had it come from? And what could it buy?

I thought myself into a corner. I was tired of thinking, I wanted action. I wanted answers to clear the whole thing up, to lift the heavy dark curtains of deceit and lies and let the light shine on everything, so I could know who to grab by the shirt and could smash my fist in his face and say, 'Now tell me everything.'

On the R541 beyond Badplaas I had to slow down to spot the Heuningklip gate in the dark, since there was no ostentatious gateway, just the ghostly game reserve behind the high game fence. I drove a kilometre beyond the little signboard and parked the Audi as far off the road as I could in the long grass. I got out, pushed the Glock into my belt and checked my watch. A quarter to three in the morning. Gestapo time.

I climbed over the gate, which was three metres high. I would have to follow the track. I couldn't afford to get lost in the thickets. There might be lions too. Melanie Posthumus had said that Cobie told her when Moller had seventy thousand hectares of continuous land, he would introduce lions and wild dogs. That was a couple of years ago.

The road wound for the three kilometres up to the humble homestead and outbuildings. I walked. I felt exposed, but on either side the grass was too long and impassable. I walked with my hand on the pistol and listened to the noises of the night. I heard a hyena chuckle, a jackal howl. Dogs barked in the distance. I didn't know whether wild dogs barked, I knew only that they hunted in packs, chasing their prey for miles and biting chunks out of them until they collapsed from loss of blood and exhaustion. Then the whole pack would join in the orgy of feasting.

I walked faster, keeping to the middle ridge where my feet made less noise.

A night bird flew up with a clatter right in front of my face, then another one, three, four, five. They gave me a fright and I stood and swore with the pistol in my hand. It took long minutes for the racket to die down.

I set off again.

At last, up the hill, there was the farmyard shrouded in darkness. Not a single light burned.

Would Stef Moller be home yet? Or did he go to Mogale with Branca?

I would search the homestead first.

I crept along the shadows. There was the house, the shed and another long outbuilding. Beyond the rise were four labourer's cottages, little buildings with off-white brick walls and corrugated iron roofs. Stef Moller had nodded in their direction when he referred to squint-eyed Seppie as his only workman.

I walked slowly across the veranda to the front door of the house and turned the knob carefully with my left hand, pistol in the right.

It was open.

If a door is going to creak, you don't want to prolong it. I pushed it open quickly, went in and closed it. No appreciable noise.

It was very dark inside. I couldn't see the furniture clearly and I didn't want to collide with any. I would have to wait for my eyes to adjust. To the right was a big room. Was it the sitting room? In front of me was a hallway. I walked down it quietly.

The first door to the left was the kitchen. There were no curtains and I could see the white enamel of an old stove. There were two more doors, left and right, both open. Bathroom to the left. Bedroom to the right.

I listened at the bedroom door. Nothing.

I went on. There were another two doors on both sides. Both were bedrooms, the one to the right was the biggest. Stef Moller would sleep there. It was impossible to see anything. I took a step into the room and stood straining my ears, but all I could hear was the beating of my heart when I held my breath.

I came out, putting the ball of my foot down deliberately, then the heel, softly, silently, until I was in the third bedroom.

It was empty. There was no one in the house. Moller was still on his way, or perhaps he was sleeping over somewhere. I walked back to the front door more quickly, since there was no one to hear me. I went out and stood on the veranda. The yard was eerily quiet. The labourer's cottages lay to the east on my left. There were about a hundred and fifty metres of open ground and crunchy gravel to cross. The tall grass was mowed to two metres from the cottages. I would just have to get there and I would have cover.

The cottages were on the side of the hill in a crooked row, clearly visible in the soft light of the setting crescent moon and stars, an amazing firmament out here where no other light burned. I would begin with the one on the left, closest to the homestead. I had a problem. Squint Septimus lived in one and I didn't want to wake him. But which one? It was impossible to say. Probably not the very first one – you don't want to sleep too close to the boss. I bet on the second one.

And the man I was looking for? The fourth or the fifth cottage?

It could be either. I began the long trek across the hard-baked open ground, pistol ready. I thanked the gods for the absence of watchdogs. I put each foot down quietly, so it would not disturb a sleeping man. I aimed for the long grass just left of the first house, taking my time carefully, wondering whether he was asleep in house number three or four, and guessing what he would say when I pressed the Glock to his temple and gently shook him awake.

Fifteen metres to the grass, then ten. I had to concentrate in order not to rush the last five. Mustn't make a noise. When I was safely there, I squatted down and stared at the windows of the first house. No curtains. Upper and lower door of wood, the paint peeling.

I walked, crouching, through the grass to the next house. Dirty white lace curtains with a long rip in them. Where was Septimus? There was Septimus, sleeping, unconscious and unimportant. I crept on another seven metres and squatted on my haunches. I saw the faded yellow curtains in the window of house number three and I remembered Melanie Posthumus saying she had bought some pretty yellow material that was nice and cheerful and I knew where he was sleeping.

I've found him, Emma le Roux, I've found the elusive pimpernel Jacobus le Roux, also known as Cobie de Villiers. Murderer, missing person, activist and enigma.

Something cast a sudden shadow beside me in the thick grass and someone pressed a gun barrel softly against my cheek and said in a very nervous voice, 'Put down the pistol before I blow your fucking head off.'

38

Sudden rage or fright stimulates the medulla to excrete the hormone epinephrine. I knew this because I had read up on it in jail in my eternal search for answers. Epinephrine speeds up the heart rate, raises blood sugar levels and blood pressure, constricts the pupils and the capillaries in the skin, so blood loss will be decreased should you be hurt. It prepares the body to better manage a physiological crisis and is referred to as the 'fight or flight' response.

The books don't say what it does to the brain, which is that it ignores the temporary madness, the red mist.

But with a delicately vibrating gun barrel at your temple, fight, flight or madness are not useful responses. All you can do is fight for control and to try to neutralise the effect of the hormone with absolute concentration by breathing slowly and deeply and sitting dead still.

That was not what the shadow beside me wanted.

He banged the barrel hard against my skull and said, 'Put the fucking thing down.'

His tone was not that of a man in control. It was filled with anxiety and a shrillness that I didn't like. I slowly lowered the Glock and put it on the grass.

'Who are you?'

I wanted to look at him, but he pressed the firearm harder to my temple.

'I am Lemmer,' I said soothingly.

'What do you want?'

'I work for your sister, Jacobus. For Emma le Roux.'

'I have no sister.'

He was a wire stretched too taut and the trembling of the barrel intensified. I couldn't see it, but I felt it in front of my ear, and I wondered whether his finger on the trigger was as taut as his voice.

'Then I've made a mistake and I'm sorry.'

That was not the answer he expected. He was dumb for two hammer beats of my heart and then he said, 'Don't lie.'

I kept my voice quiet and even. 'I'm not lying, Jacobus. I'm truly sorry. Especially for Emma. She has such a terrible desire to see her brother again. I think she really loved him.'

'I have no sister.' His voice had risen half an octave. My attempt at calming was not very successful.

'I know, Jacobus. I believe you. My work here is done. I will go and tell her that she no longer has a brother.'

'That's right.'

'May I get up now? I'll go. I won't bother you again. You can keep the pistol.'

He thought about it, and as he did, the barrel of the firearm moved a few millimetres away from my temple.

'Why did you look for me here?' Less desperate and shrill.

In an easy conversational way I kept to the truth. 'Emma and I were here last week. I saw three coffee mugs in the shed. But Stef said there was only Septimus and himself. That's what made me think someone was hiding here.'

He didn't respond.

'You heard the birds I disturbed,' I said. 'You're very good.'

'Francolin,' he said.

'You move well in the bush. I didn't hear you.'

He just stood there, indecisive, like the dog that chased the bus and caught it and then didn't know what to do with it.

'Jacobus, I'm getting up now. I'll do it slowly. Then I will walk away and I won't bother you again. My work is done.'

'No.'

I knew why he didn't like the idea. 'I won't tell anyone that you are here. I swear to God.' Maybe that worked in Hb circles. I turned my head very slowly towards him. I saw him looking at the homestead and then back at me. It was Cobie de Villiers, the man in Jack Phatudi's photograph. He was sweating and his face gleamed in the moonlight. His eyes were unsettled and he held the firearm with straight arms. It looked like a MAC 10. The cheapest machine pistol on the market, but just as effective as the expensive ones.

He didn't like me watching him. That was a big danger signal. It's harder to kill a man once you've looked him in the eye. I tried to make eye contact with him. His eyes flicked back and forth, as though he couldn't make up his mind. His mouth was half open and his breathing was rapid. I knew I had to do something but I couldn't afford to wait for his decision. He was wanted by the police and he was a fugitive killer who was very seriously considering shooting me. I waited until he looked away for a fraction of a second, then I jerked up my left hand to knock the MAC aside and swung my right leg through. Shots boomed near my ear, deafening me, and I felt a burning sensation at the back of my head. I knocked his feet from under him with my leg and he fell. The machine pistol clattered through an arc, his left arm tried to block his fall and I hit him hard with my fist against his cheek as I grabbed at the MAC with both hands.

He took the blow well, because he didn't loosen his grip on the weapon. I felt something warm run down my neck which I suspected was blood.

Cobie jerked the machine pistol back and forth. He face was distorted like that of a madman and he made a low moaning sound. He wasn't much bigger than me, but he was strong and he believed that he was fighting for his life.

I let go of the MAC and hit him again. Aiming for his jaw, I hit his eye socket. His head jerked back, but he swung the machine pistol towards me. I grabbed the barrel with my left hand and hit him against the ear with my right with no noticeable effect.

Behind us a light went on in the second labourer's cottage and I could see Cobie's anguished face. His eyebrow was bleeding.

I hit him again, as hard as I could. He jerked his head away and I connected with his chin, but with little momentum. I moved to get above him. My right hand searched for his throat as he squirmed and grabbed my forearm with his left hand.

A door opened and a beam of light shone on the ground. If it was Septimus and he was armed I was in serious trouble. I let go of Cobie and dived into the grass in search of the Glock. I saw it shining, grabbed it, and rolled back to Cobie. He was still down, but he was turning the MAC towards me. I wasn't going to make it so I dived at him. He aimed and pulled the trigger. Only the sharp click of metal. The magazine was empty. I was on him, bashing the Glock's barrel violently against his cheek, while looking at the door.

Squint Seppie stood with a hunting rifle pointing at the stars and a bewildered expression on his face. 'Cobie?' he said.

'Drop the rifle or I'll shoot Cobie,' I said.

Cobie grabbed at the Glock. He was beyond fear, desperate and mad. I banged the pistol against his head, rolled away and came up on my haunches. I gripped the Glock in both hands, pointed it at Cobie and said in the most reasonable tone I could muster, 'This is a .45-calibre, Cobie. I will shoot you in the leg first, but there are some big veins there and I can't guarantee that you won't bleed to death. It's your choice.' Then I looked at Septimus, who stood frozen with the rifle in his hand.

'Septimus,' I barked.

He looked at me with an expression of pure fear.

'Put the gun down. Now.'

'OK.'

He bent slowly and put the rifle down on the slab of cement in front of his door with great respect.

'Lie down,' I ordered Septimus.

'Where?'

'Anywhere you want, you idiot. Just away from the rifle.'

He lay down on his stomach.

I stood up and moved closer to Jacobus.

'Cobie, put the gun down.'

He was reluctant to do so, even though the MAC was empty. I didn't know whether he had another magazine in his pocket.

'Get up,' I said.

He stood up. I kneed him as hard as I could just above his navel. He fell forward, mouth agape, winded.

I jerked the MAC from his hand and flung it far out into the veld. 'That's because you wanted to kill me, Cobus. And to calm you down. Fuck knows, you're mad as a rabid dog.'

Cobie curled up like a foetus, desperately gagging for air.

I touched my head with my left hand where it hurt. I felt the wound, a long deep groove starting just under my ear. It was bleeding. One centimetre closer, one fraction of a second, and I would have been dead. I felt like kicking him again. I suppressed the impulse, went over to Squint Seppie, pushed the Glock into my belt and picked up the rifle. I took out the magazine, worked the bolt to pump out the round in the barrel and threw it and the magazine into the night. Septimus watched me anxiously with one eye. I dropped the rifle down beside him and took out the Glock again. I went over to Cobie, put my knee in his back and pressed the pistol against the back of his head.

'Septimus, look at me.'

He raised his head and looked.

'I want you to go into your house and bring me some electric cord. The longest piece you have, OK?'

'Yes.' He was unsure.

'I'm going to wait here with Cobie and if you come out of that door with anything except the cord, I will shoot him.'

'OK.'

'Off you go, Seppie. Be quick.'

He hesitated for only an instant, then scurried into the cottage. Under my knee Cobie de Villiers would not lie still.

'Jacobus, I don't want any trouble from you. I swear to God I'll shoot you if you don't cooperate. The police will give me a medal.'

'What are you going to do?' Still that manic tone.

'I'm going to tie you up, Jacobus, because you have more tricks than a monkey. And then we're going to talk. That's all. If our discussion goes well, I'll let you go and I'll leave and I won't breathe a word about you to anyone. But if you don't cooperate, I'm taking you to the police. It's your choice.'

He didn't reply. He just lay there gasping.

Septimus came out very warily. He had a length of electric cord which he carried in front of him with outstretched arms like a peace offering.

'Bring it to me, Septimus, and go and lie down on your stomach again with your arms behind your back.'

He did as I commanded with great obedience and concentration. I waited until he was lying down, picked up the cord with my left hand and pushed the Glock into my belt.

That was what Cobie was waiting for. He moved suddenly, trying to roll away and hit at me in one movement. I was expecting it. My patience with him had run out. I grabbed his hand, twisted it behind his back and pushed his wrist up towards his neck, expecting to hear the pop of his shoulder dislocating. He was tough, but not tough enough to ignore the awful pain. He went limp.

'Mad and stupid is a bad combination, Jacobus,' I said as I thumped both my knees into his back with my full weight behind them. I heard the wind explode out of him again, grabbed one hand, forced it against the other, reached for the cord and began tying up his wrists. I got off him only when I was dead sure that his hands wouldn't come loose.

'Seppie, I need more cord.'

'I haven't got any more,' he said in a small voice.

'What have you got?'

'I don't know.'

'Go and look in Cobie's house.'

'OK.'

'And hurry up, Septimus, or I will shoot Cobie. First in the left leg, and then in the right.'

'OK.' He sprang up and ran to the cottage with the yellow curtains, jerked open the door and switched on the light. He came back with an electric cord still attached to a bedside lamp.

'Break the lamp off, Seppie.'

He did that.

'Now, lie down.'

He knew the position well enough. I took my knees off Cobie, took the new cord, sat on Septimus and began to tie his wrists.

Cobie de Villiers jumped up.

'Jacobus!' I shouted to no avail. He ran away down the hill with his arms behind his back.

'I'll shoot your friend, Cobie.' It didn't seem to be much of a friendship, because Cobie disappeared into the dark.

'Fuck,' I screamed in frustration. What now? First, I had to immobilise Septimus. I worked quickly, winding the cord around Squinty Sep's ankles and making a hasty knot. 'Don't do anything stupid,' I told him. Then I kicked him lightly in the ribs, pulled the Glock from my belt and set off after Cobie.

What was driving the man?

39

The dark gave him the advantage. He knew the terrain, too. Luckily a man with his hands bound doesn't have good balance.

I couldn't see him, but I heard him fall somewhere to the right, a hundred metres or more away. Branches cracked, I heard a dull thud and I ran in the direction of the noise.

If he lay still, he had a chance, but Cobie was bent on getting away. When he staggered upright, I heard his footsteps and saw him as a dark shape against the grey of the long grass, crouched over and stumbling. I set after him and caught up. With every breath he made a noise of desperation. I tackled him from behind and he crashed down. With no hands to break the fall his face ploughed into the grass.

I jumped on him and sat on his back, stuck the Glock in his neck and hissed breathlessly, '*Jissis*, Jacobus, what the fuck is wrong with you?'

'Shoot me.' The hoarse whisper was almost inaudible, while he tried to jerk his body in a senseless attempt to get free.

'What?' I willed air back into my lungs.

'Shoot me.'

'You're crazy.'

'No.'

'You are, Jacobus.'

'Shoot me. Please.'

'Why?'

'It's better.'

'Why better?'

'For everyone.'

'Why?'

'Because.'

'Wrong answer. I'm not going to sit here and shoot the breeze with you, Jacobus. We have to see how Septimus is.' I got up, but I kept hold of his wrists where the cord was tied. 'Come.' I dragged him up, keeping his arms high enough so it hurt if he didn't cooperate.

'Shoot me.' A scream in the night, demonic and full of fear, and he jerked again, ignoring the pain he must have felt in his shoulders. That's when I realised that my plan wasn't going to work and I hit him as hard as I could on the head with the Glock.

At last the Honey Badger sank to the ground, out like a light.

I carried Cobie de Villiers over my shoulder to where Septimus meekly lay, just in time to see the light of a vehicle coming up the road from the gate.

'Who's that?' I asked Seppie while I laid Cobie down next to him.

'I think it's Stef.'

My troubles multiplied. I could handle these two clowns. But one more?

It was the same Toyota pick-up that Stef Moller and Donnie Branca had been driving earlier. The tyres crunched over the gravelled yard and he stopped in front of the homestead and got out. He would see the lights at the labourer's cottages. The question was, what would he do about it?

I felt the fatigue rising through my body. Long day. Long night. I knelt beside Cobie and shoved the barrel against his neck.

'Cobie?' Moller's voice in the dark. I heard footsteps approaching over the gravel. Then I saw him on the edge of the beam of light. He had nothing in his hands.

'No, Stef. It's Lemmer.'

He saw us and stopped.

'Come, Stef, come and sit with us.'

He hesitated, looking very concerned. His eyes blinked frantically. 'What have you done?' He came closer.

'His lights are out, but only for the time being. Come and sit down, Stef, so we can talk about your lies.'

He sat beside Jacobus and stretched a trembling hand out to the still figure.

'I didn't have a choice,' he said, and softly stroked Cobie's hair.

'You lied.'

'I promised him. I gave him my word.'

'He's a murderer, Stef.'

'He's like a son to me. And . . .'

'What?'

'Something happened to him.'

'What?'

'I don't know, but it must have been terrible.'

'How do you know?'

'I know.'

Cobie stirred. He tried to turn over, but with his hands tied it was a struggle.

'Easy, Cobie,' Moller soothed him.

'He'll have to talk, Stef. He's the one with the answers.'

'He won't talk.'

Cobie de Villiers moaned and tried to roll over. His eyes opened and he saw Stef Moller.

'I'm here, Cobie.'

Cobie saw me. He jerked. Moller held a firm hand on Jacobus's shoulder. 'No, Cobie, don't. He won't do you any harm.'

Cobie didn't believe him. His eyes flicked between us, well on his way to madness again.

'Easy, Cobie, easy. I'm here; you're safe. Easy now.'

I could see Moller had done this before, the soothing, coaxing him back from the abyss. Cobie stared at Stef, then he seemed to believe him, because he sighed deeply and his body relaxed. I caught a glimpse of their history, their relationship. Also of Moller as a person. It commanded respect, but it didn't help me. Behind a locked door in Cobie de Villiers' head there was information that I needed. Moller held the key, if there was a key.

Squint Seppie was quiet, following events with one eye.

'Stef, let me explain my problem,' I said in a conversational tone, like a parent that didn't want to upset a child, my words intended for Cobie's ears. 'I am looking for the people that hurt Emma le Roux. That's all. I'm going to hunt them down and make them pay. I'm not interested in what Cobie or anyone else has done. I don't want to involve the police. To be honest, I can't afford to. All I want is a name. Or a place where I can find Emma's attackers. Just that. Then I will leave. You will never hear from me again. I will tell no one what happened. That's the promise I am making.'

Stef Moller sat with his hand on Cobie's shoulder. He blinked slowly but he never said a word. It was Cobie's decision.

The night was perfectly silent. I looked at my watch. Twenty to five. The sun was on its way. I looked at Jacobus. He just lay there.

Moller squeezed Cobie's shoulder. 'What do you say, Cobie?'

He shook his head. No.

I sighed. 'Cobie, there is an easy way and there's a hard way. Let's do it the easy way.'

Moller frowned at me. He didn't think that was the right approach.

'No,' said Jacobus softly.

'Why not?'

'Kill him.'

'He can solve the problem, Cobie,' said Moller.

'He can't. They will kill him too.'

'No, Cobie,' I said, but I missed what he added. 'What did you say?'

'They are going to kill everyone.'

'Everyone?'

'Emma and Stef and Septimus.'

'Not if I stop them.'

'You can't.' Cobie rolled his head back and forth, with a stubborn look on his face.

My patience ran out. Utterly. I grabbed a handful of Cobie's hair and stood up. I pulled him upright by his hair.

'Don't,' Stef Moller said, trying to stop me. I shoved his arm away. Cobie made an animal noise. I ignored it.

'We tried your method, Stef. It's time to make this arsehole realise what he's doing.' I dragged Cobie behind me towards the farm track. He struggled, but not much, because I had a firm grip on his hair.

'Where are you going?' Moller wanted to know.

'Cobie and I are going to see Emma. He can explain to her why they shot her and made her fall off a train. He can make his fucking excuses to her.'

'No,' Jacobus screamed.

'Shut your face and come.' I pulled and walked fast.

'Lemmer, please don't,' Stef Moller pleaded.

'Don't worry, Stef, you're safe. It will be just Cobie and Emma and me. You stay here.'

'I thought she was in a coma.'

'Then we'll just have to wait until she wakes up.'

'No, no, no,' screamed Cobie de Villiers.

'Shut the fuck up,' I told him, and dragged the madman with his hands bound and head bent behind me by the hair.

Halfway to the gate, with day breaking over the eastern horizon, Jacobus le Roux said in his rabid voice, 'I'll talk.'

I ignored him and pulled harder on his hair.

'I'll talk.' Half an octave higher.

'You're lying, Jacobus.'

'No. I swear.'

'*Jissis*, you Hb cunts are fond of swearing. Why do you want to suddenly talk now?'

'Because it's just you and me.'

'You're going to tell Emma.'

'No, please, not in front of Emma.'

'Why not?'

He made a sound, a heart-rending bark that stopped me in my tracks.

'Why not in front of Emma, Jacobus?'

'Because it was my fault.'

'What was?'

'Ma and Pa. My fault.'

I let go of his hair. He staggered backwards and fell on his backside. His head drooped. In the morning half-light his face was bloodied and swollen from my blows. His shoulders heaved.

Cobie de Villiers wept. The sobs were soft but gradually grew louder until the veld resounded, raw and wrung out. I just stood there with the Glock in my hand and watched him, weary and suddenly sorry for this forlorn wreck.

Maybe it would do him good to cry. Perhaps it would temper his madness. The sounds rose in a crescendo and then diminished. His tears dripped dark dots into the dust.

I stood in front of him and shoved the Glock into my belt. I held his shoulder as Stef had done, and said, 'Easy now, Jacobus, take it easy.'

Around us the Bushveld awoke. Cobie looked up at me slowly. He didn't look good, but his eyes were less wild.

'Can you really stop them?'

'Not "can", Jacobus. I will. No doubt.'

I could see that he didn't believe me, but it didn't matter to him any more. I untied his hands and rubbed his wrists. He gulped and breathed deeply a few times.

'I am Jacobus le Roux,' he said with terrible emotion, as if he had waited twenty years for this chance.

'I know,' I said.

'And I miss Emma so terribly.'

Jacobus le Roux's story did not come easily.

It took nearly three hours in the telling. Jerkily, struggling, sometimes disjointed so that I had to interrupt him. Every now and then emotion would silence him and I would wait until his shoulders stopped heaving. Every time he wandered off the point to irrelevancies, I would have to draw him back to his story with extreme patience. Later, when the sun was up and the heat rapidly becoming unbearable, I took him to the cool of a shady tree. We needed water. And sleep. But now he had the urge to get it off his chest and I had the thirst to hear it, to have the whole thing make sense.

When he was completely finished, when I had asked my last question and he'd answered it with a now hoarse and exhausted voice, we just sat there in the shade of the thorn tree like two punch-drunk boxers. We stared at the veld and saw nothing.

As those lingering minutes ticked away slowly I wondered what Jacobus le Roux felt. Relief? Relief that he was no longer the only one to know. Fear of what he had unleashed? Hope, that it could end now, this nightmare of twenty years? Or despair that it would never go away.

I looked at him, at the wounds on his face, the lines of tears down his cheeks, the drooping shoulders of someone who has borne too much for too long, and I recalled the picture of the young Jacobus le Roux. A great feeling of pity washed over me and I put out my hand and rested it on his shoulder. So he would know that he wasn't alone any more.

Then I allowed the red-grey mist of rage to slowly build up, anger at the people who had done this to him and Emma. I had to control it, because I would need a cool head, but I let it flood through me, so it could drive out the exhaustion.

Before I stood up to leave, I said to Jacobus, 'I'm going to make it right.'

He looked into my eyes. I saw he was empty. There was no madness, but also no hope.

I reversed the Audi out of the long grass beside the road and drove away. There were things I had to do. Eventually, I must go back to Motlasedi – my rented farmhouse below the mountain, beside the river, the 'place of the great battle', and I knew that they would be waiting there for me.

They would have heard the cell phone conversations; they had the technology for that. They would have stalked my temporary abode in the darkest hour with their sniper rifles and their bala-clavas. They would have found nothing, but they would be waiting there to kill me.

Then they would wait for Emma, until they got to her in some way or another. They would stop at nothing.

I understood most of it now. I couldn't quite grasp the precise reasons for preserving their great secret with such relentlessness twenty years on, but I would find out.

Today.

40

The awful irony of Jacobus le Roux's tale was that his father's military influence was the start of it.

After basic training in 1985, only three national servicemen were transferred to the newly formed Nature and Environmental Conservation Unit of the army, which in total consisted of just over twenty soldiers. Jacobus was one of the chosen because Johannes Petrus le Roux, managing director of the Armscor supplier, Le Roux Engineering Works, had a word with the right general.

He hadn't felt guilty about it. That was the way life worked. It was whom your father knew that counted. It was better that someone who felt so strongly about the environment should go rather than some dumb private loafing in the bush. So Jacobus le Roux had the opportunity to live his passion at the General De Wet Training Camp at De Brug outside Bloemfontein. More than ten thousand springbuck grazed on the 17,000-hectare property.

He was a self-assured young man, intelligent, passionate, dedicated and in his element. He impressed his superiors with his knowledge and work ethic. The next offer in September 1985 was made on merit.

The colonel came down from Pretoria to inspect De Brug and over a cup of tea in a prefab building he told him about the two army units in the Kruger Park. One was a contingent of 7 SAI, an infantry battalion from Phalaborwa, which patrolled the park's border with Mozambique. The other was the more obscure ESU, or Environmental Services Unit, initially formed under the influence of the legendary former special forces Major Jack Greeff, but under the control of the Nature and Environmental Conservation

Unit. The purpose of the ESU was to halt the epidemic proportions of ivory poaching and smuggling in Kruger.

Would Jacobus be interested in joining them?

He had said 'yes' long before his cup of tea was empty. Fourteen days later he reported for six weeks' intensive training at the 5 Recce Battalion base in the Lowveld. That was where he met Vincent Mashego for the first time, his tracker, partner and future comrade.

Mashego was the opposite of Jacobus. The rich white boy was part of the ruling elite; the young black man grew up in Shatale, Mapulaneng, a member of a dirt-poor, marginalised tribe whose language, sePulane, was not taught in any school or book. His tribal name was Tao, which meant 'lion', the totem of the maPulana tribe, but he was so quiet and shy that his people called him Pego. It was the cynical abbreviation of Pegopego – the chatterbox.

Jacobus was lean and muscular and a stranger to the area. Pego Mashego was small, scrawny and tough, and he knew the Lowveld terrain like the back of his hand. The Afrikaner was there because he wanted to be, the man of the maPulana through financial necessity. But they had one thing in common: a deep love of and interest in nature.

Their friendship was not spontaneous; their differences in background, class and personality were too great. But over the six weeks of hardship a bond of mutual respect began to develop. What lay ahead of them would make the bond unbreakable.

The strategy of the ESU was to deploy two-man teams to patrol an area for a week on foot. The areas were determined by timetables and grid references. The white man in each team was the leader and carried the radio. The black man carried the rations and was the tracker. Both were armed with a rifle and they holed up in thickets and rock clefts during the day so they could hunt their prey at night, since ivory poachers were nocturnal predators.

The strategy was simple: find the poachers and radio for support. If you could not do otherwise, however, shoot them before they melted away into the bush. Shoot to kill. Let them know that it was war, because Africa could not afford to lose a thousand elephants a week. At the rate they were killed in the eighties, the elephant would have been extinct by 2010.

Team Juliet Papa, the call sign for Jacobus and Pego, was deployed in November 1985, initially in the 'safer' western parts of Kruger, where they could find their feet. Only in February 1986 were they sent farther east – and experienced the relentlessness of the ivory poacher.

Twenty years on, Jacobus le Roux was still filled with loathing when he described it to me. They came upon three dead elephants for the first time. The cow had been shot because she was too close and dangerous. The half-grown calf had been shot just for fun. The bull's head was a bloody, unrecognisable mess where the poachers had chopped the tusks out with axes and pangas. Rubbish was strewn around, the fireplace left uncovered. The disrespect was blatant and deliberate. But the offenders were long gone, back across the border to Mozambique.

Three weeks later they were involved in their first skirmish, exchanging fire with a gang of poachers in the night. They followed the blood spoor of one to the border. Scarcely a week later, Jacobus le Roux shot and killed his first man.

They had seen the thieves' fire burning at night in the dry river bed of the Nkulumbedi river, only a few kilometres from the Langtoon Dam in the north-east of the park. Whispering over the radio, Jacobus tried to call in reinforcements because the group of poachers was twelve or fourteen strong, but as usual the signal was too weak. They crept closer and saw the butchery in the flickering light of the flames. Two giant elephant bulls were plundered while the gang laughed and chatted in muted voices.

They took aim. Jacobus set his sights on a man in a torn red shirt who stood to one side giving orders. That first time, he trembled slightly, although his revulsion at the slaughter was great. His brain was reluctant to send the command to the trigger finger. Only when Pego pressed him softly in the side with an elbow did he close his eyes and fire. He opened his eyes and saw the man drop. There was no dramatic convulsing as they do in movies, just a sinking, a slow, pathetic, lifeless collapse.

Beside him Pego fired shot after shot at the fleeing chaos of men, but Jacobus only lay staring at the red shirt until everything was silent.

I stopped at the Wimpy to eat breakfast and make some calls. The waitress wrinkled her nose at me because I was dirty and smelly and after the night's work I had a streak of blood down my neck.

Before the food arrived I phoned B. J. Fikter. He said that Dr Eleanor Taljaard was not yet on duty, but as far as he knew there was no change in Emma's condition.

After I'd eaten, I washed my face in the Wimpy's spotlessly clean restrooms. I had to clean the grime off the basin with toilet paper before I left.

I looked for a telephone booth and called Jeanette. It was the one call I didn't want overheard.

'I was worried about you.' Because there was an SMS from her on my phone that I hadn't answered.

'I was a little busy.'

'Progress?'

'A lot. I might finish up today.'

'Do you need help?'

That was a good question; one I had spent time pondering during the past few hours. 'Only one thing. I want to exchange the Audi for something else.'

'Why?'

'They knew exactly where Emma and I were, without seeing us. I think it might have been electronic. I don't know how, but I'm sure they bugged the BMW.'

'When do you want the other car?'

'As soon as possible. Within the hour?'

'You'll have to go to the airport at Nelspruit.'

'I'm near by.'

'It's done. Are you looking for something specific?'

'A pick-up, if possible.'

'I'll see what I can do. Go to Budget Rent-a-Car.'

'Thanks.'

She was quiet. Then she said, 'The bullet casing. You have interesting friends.'

'Oh?'

'Ever heard of a Galil?'

'Vaguely.'

'It's the Israeli combat rifle, 5.56mm, based on the AK, quite scarce. But the one that shot at you is even more rare. It's the Galil sniper rifle. Same design, very reliable, quite accurate, but it takes a 7.62 NATO round.'

'What does it look like?' The unidentified strangeness of the rifle bothered me.

'There's a picture on the Internet. Quite small for a sniper's weapon. Folding butt. The funny thing is, the tripod is just in front of the trigger guard, but the telescope isn't above it, it's to the side.'

The light went on. 'That's right. That's what I saw.'

'My source says that it's the first time in his life that he's heard of an incident with this rifle in South Africa. The question is: what is it doing here?'

'I have a strong suspicion.'

'Do you?'

'It's a long story. I'll tell you when I get back.'

'You sound tired, Lemmer.'

'I'm just not a morning person.'

'You're lying to me.'

'I'm fine.'

'Don't get macho with me. I'll kick your butt.' Jeanette Louw. Always compassionate.

'Macho? Me? When I'm so in touch with my female side?'

She didn't laugh. She sounded concerned when she said, 'If you want help, ask.'

I didn't want help. 'I will. I swear.'

'That's a new one,' she said.

'Local habit. Jeanette, one more thing. Not urgent. There's a man by the name of Stef Moller, owner of the Heuningklip private nature reserve. Fifty-plus, very rich, but nobody knows where his money came from. Can you find out?'

'Stef with an "f" or a "p-h".'

'I have no idea.'

She sighed. 'I'll see what I can do.'

Before I drove to the airport, I found a gun shop. There were three in town, but only one was open on 2 January. It stocked an odd combination of camping gear, menswear and weapons.

The hunting knives were on display in a glass cabinet near the till. The little guy behind the counter looked as though he were still at school. Maybe he was. I pointed out the one I wanted.

'It's seven hundred rand,' he said haughtily, as though I wouldn't be able to afford it.

I merely nodded.

'How will you pay?'

'Cash.'

He took out the knife, but waited until I handed over the money before giving it to me.

I drove to the airport.

The young black woman at Budget inspected my driver's licence twice before giving me the keys and the form. We are such visual beings. She and the Wimpy waitress and the schoolboy saw a man who had sat on the ground waiting, who had spent a long night kicking and fighting, sweating and struggling, who had washed hastily, not brushed his teeth.

Stripped of all false fronts, maybe I looked like the man I really was.

'You're taking the insurance?' the Budget woman asked hopefully.

'Yes,' I said.

She gave me a white Nissan double-cab, a three-litre diesel 4x4. More extravagant than I would have liked, but it would do the job and be considerably less noticeable than the Audi.

'Do you have a map of the area?'

She brought me one. I studied it and saw it would be no help – it showed only the tar roads of the Lowveld.

'Thank you,' I said, and took it anyway.

There was a small bookshop in the foyer of the airport. I went in and asked for maps. I bought one of those that are so intricately folded that you can never get them back to their original state. At least it showed the fine network of gravel roads with an invitation to Explore the Lowveld.

I went to sit in the Nissan and consider my options. I wanted to get on to Mariepskop without passing the turn-off to my farm-house, but I saw that it was impossible. There was only one road and it ran past Motlasedi's gate.

41

In the first ten months of 1986 Jacobus le Roux became a man. To be passionate about the wonder world of nature, to be inspired and captivated by the million fine gears of God's Timepiece, to innocently and with fixed determination believe that you could protect it all, these were the things of a child.

In practice, it was an adult world of unpleasant reality: night patrols on foot in an environment where the natural predators were just as dangerous as the predators of the human species; exhausting days of lying up under cover while the mercury climbed to 45 degrees Celsius, sleep evading you, the taste of your own half-cooked food and the tepid brackish liquid in your water bottle lingering in your mouth. After five days in the veld, you and your camp fellow stank of campfire smoke, sweat and excreta. You lived in a lonely, limited, dangerous world far removed from the ease and security of your wealthy suburb.

You killed people. You told yourself it was war and you fought on the side of good, but in the searing heat of noon, as you tossed and turned on your groundsheet, searching for sleep, you saw them fall, you remembered your terrible, stunned numbness when you knelt beside the body after the firefight. You realised that you were not a natural soldier, and that something died inside you with each enemy, although it did get a little easier every time.

When Jacobus was telling his story, I became aware of the difference between us. But there was no time or desire to linger over it. But now, driving down the plantation roads below the escarpment with the air conditioning on, the prosecutor in my head was eager to point an accusatory finger. I had beaten a man to death and my greatest anguish was how I could be capable of that.

Jacobus le Roux, brother of Emma, born of the Afrikaner elite – however humble their background might be – agonised over why he could not do it.

None of this was relevant.

He told me that he was certain that he had shot dead seven people in the reserve in 1986.

In July of that year he got a fourteen-day pass and went home. For the first week he could not sleep on his soft bed and the big plates of food his mother dished up made him nauseous. His father noticed how much quieter he was, but he couldn't talk about it. His sister detected nothing amiss; she worshipped him, as always.

Physically he was in the city, but his psyche was somewhere else. His mother introduced him to a girl, Petro. She was studying Communications at RAU. She was pretty in a summer dress and he would remember her pink lipstick. She talked of things he knew nothing about. The campus, music and politics. He nodded but he wasn't listening. 'What do you do in the game reserve?' she asked, as if his mother hadn't already told her everything.

'We patrol,' he said. 'What are you going to do when you've finished swotting?'

She talked about her dreams, but he wasn't really listening, the things in his head distracted him. Like a man in a torn red shirt lying dead and somewhere people waited for him to come home.

His father took a photo of him and Emma in the sitting room of their house in Linden. They were sitting side by side, his sister had her arms around his neck and her head half bent to his chest. The lens caught them perfectly – his face was blank, she laughed in joy. His father had mailed the photo to him and he carried it with him in the little army Bible in his breast pocket. Through all that lay ahead, through all those years, until one day he put it into a photo album and hid it in the ceiling of his Mogale house where he could take it out and look at it from time to time. To remind himself that it was real.

But in those fourteen days the world his family lived in felt unreal. Literally. Like a dream. He felt like a stranger in his family home. He knew why, but there was nothing he could do. Months and years later he would blame himself for not trying harder, for not bursting the bubble and embracing them.

Because soon, his family would be destroyed.

On the back roads and through the plantations it was easier to spot anyone following. I drove past unfamiliar names on the map, Dunottar, Versailles and Tswafeng, nothing more than a few huts or a farm shop. At the Boelang tribal lands I turned left. The road deteriorated and the plantations were densely forested. There were no signboards at the road forks. I took one wrong turn and couldn't make the U, the pine trees stood right up to the road. I had to reverse for a kilometre. At eleven I finally arrived. Heat waves rose up from the plain to the right and made the horizon shimmer.

I turned left here, up the mountain to the Mariepskop forestry station. I drove past the entrance to my rented property. The gate was closed. All was quiet. They were there, somewhere in the forest or the house.

There were two officers on duty at the forestry station. They wouldn't allow me to continue without a permit. There was a radar station on top and I needed permission.

Where could I get permission?

In Polokwane or Pretoria.

I just wanted to walk. Down the mountain.

I needed a permit for that too.

Could I buy one here?

Maybe.

What would it cost?

About three hundred rand, but they had no receipt book.

'No, it's four hundred,' said the other one. 'Three hundred was last year. It's the second of January today.'

'Oh, yes. That's right. Four hundred.'

I fetched my wallet from the Nissan. I went around to the passenger side so they wouldn't see me push the Glock and the hunting knife into the back of my belt under my shirt.

Before handing over the notes, I questioned them. Where were the footpaths that led down the mountain? The paths that the maPulana had followed in 1864, when they attacked King Mswati's impis.

'Impi is a Zulu word,' said one with disapproval.

'Sorry.'

'*Mohlabani*. One soldier. *Bahlabani*. Soldiers. These are sePedi words. The maPulana defeated the Swazi's *bahlabani*.'

'I'll remember.'

Then, friendlier: 'You know the story of Motlasedi?'

'A little.'

'Not many whites know it. Come. I'll show you the paths.'

'Can I leave the car here when I walk down the paths?'

'We'll look after your car nicely.'

'I might only fetch it tomorrow.'

'*Go lokile*. No problem.'

He went ahead, around the building, past an open fire where a large pot simmered, through a garden that was neatly maintained, to the edge of the indigenous forest. He pointed a finger. 'Go in here and keep on straight. You will reach the other path that comes down the mountain. Turn right and follow the path down to the bottom of the mountain.'

'Thank you.'

'Lookout for the *sepoko*. The ghosts.' He laughed.

'I will.'

'*Sepela gabotse*. Go well.'

'Stay well.'

'*Sala gabotse*, that's how you say it.'

'*Sala gabotse*,' I said, and walked into the cool leafy tunnel.

At a clear stream running over a rock I sat and drank deeply and let the ice-cold water trickle over my head and neck and run down my back until it made me gasp for breath.

I was going down this mountain alone.

I needed to define myself. For ten years I had called myself a bodyguard. It was the government's name for my job, an empty, meaningless shell. Was Koos Taljaard a doctor before he healed someone? Was Jack Phatudi a policeman before he made his first arrest?

Ten years and never once was there any real danger to the person I had to protect. Political meetings, public appearances, social events, car trips and openings of buildings and schools. I had nothing to do. Nothing but keep myself ready, keep my body honed, skills polished, sharp as a knife that would never be used to cut anything. I had watched, oh, I had watched and observed tens, hundreds, even thousands of people with an eagle eye.

Nothing had ever happened.

The concept of being a bodyguard saved me, because after school there weren't many forks in my road – and all the others led to a bad end. I was young, violent and looking for trouble. I bore a hatred for my parents and my world and was saved only by the discipline of training and the fatherly calm and true wisdom of the Minister of Transport. The man who had once made us stop in the Eastern Transvaal so we could help a minibus-taxi change a flat tyre. He chatted with the driver and the black passengers about their lives, their hardships and troubles. As we drove off he shook his head and said the country couldn't go on like this.

But despite the fact that I had direction in those years, it was ten years of being a spectator. Ten years on the periphery, a decade of being on the edge of nothing.

An unimpressive bystander, despite my genes. My English rose of a mother was a colourless bloom, as I am. My father was dark, virile and strong, but I inherited her pale skin and red-blonde hair and skinny body. Her breasts made her body look sensational. She could colour in her face, and she did, with lipstick, mascara, powder and rouge, she could metamorphose every morning. With skill she had turned her delicate features into a sensual siren, a honeypot that the men of Seapoint swarmed around.

I once nurtured a beard for four months without Mona noticing. I had to ask her whether she saw something new. It took her five minutes to say, oh, you've a beard.

Invisible.

Defined by one incident in my life. The road-rage murder.
That's what the media called it. In the single photo that appeared
in the papers I was between my legal representatives, and Gus
Kemp mercifully hid my face with his file. Invisible.

Forty-two years old and what am I?

My head complained: you're tired. It was the lack of sleep
talking.

It wasn't important.

Today I was going down there alone because I wanted to be
something.

Like what?

Something. Anything. I wanted to make a difference. I wanted to
stop the injustice. For once I wanted to gallop on the white horse of
righteousness.

I stood up, not wanting to argue with myself any more. I took
out the Glock and checked it. Then I went carefully down the
mountain in the deep afternoon shadows.

On Sunday, 5 October 1986, Jacobus le Roux's commanding officer
called the teams together and told them they must all be out of the
bush and back at base on Monday, 13 October. They were due a
week of R&R, no passes would be issued, but they could relax at base.

That was all. No explanation. As though it was something to
look forward to.

They suspected a snake in the grass, because all around them
the recces of Five Reconnaissance Battalion were abuzz over a
possible operation. Rumours were rife. Renamo, the pro-Western
faction in the civil war, was apparently advancing on Frelimo in
two northern provinces of Mozambique. The recces might be sent
to assist them. There was also something going on with the 7 SAI,
judging by the traffic of Bedford trucks in and out of base.

The Environmental Services Unit didn't really care about
whatever was going on. It didn't affect them, and in the army if
something doesn't affect you, you ignore it.

But on Monday, 13 October, he and Pego were not back at base.
To tell the truth, they never saw the inside of the base again.

The trouble began on the twelfth, a Sunday. They planned to be back in time. They had completed the last leg of their patrol, beside the two-wheel track that ran parallel to the Mozambique border in the south-eastern corner of the reserve. At one in the afternoon they were trying to sleep deep in the reeds of the Kangadjane stream, four kilometres from the border between the Lindanda-Wolhuter Memorial and the Shishengedzim guard post. They woke at the sound of a small aeroplane. They crawled out of the reeds and looked up. The plane circled west of them around the hill called Ka-Nwamuri. Very odd, because civilian planes hadn't been allowed here for over a year. They weren't even allowed to fly over it at altitude. This one was low, scarcely five hundred metres, and only a hundred metres above the koppie, a hill towards the west.

It made a wide turn and came their way and they crept back into the reeds. Jacobus took out his binoculars to have a look. There were no identifying letters or marks on the wings. Just a plain white aeroplane. It descended as it approached and then suddenly swung north. Jacobus saw two or three faces looking down and one of them seemed familiar, but he thought he must be mistaken.

It looked like one of the government ministers. A well-known one. But the plane turned again and he couldn't see the people any more as it droned away to the north-west, dwindling in the distance until they could no longer see it.

He and Pego looked at each other and shook their heads. What was it doing here? Why had it flown over Ka-Nwamuri? They ought to take a look tonight, so they could report back the next day.

They waited till sundown, cleared up their camp and made preparations. It was just over five kilometres to the koppie. They wouldn't make quick time through the thickets, but the cover was good.

Two hours later they saw the lights for the first time, halfway up Ka-Nwamuri hill, moving lights, which blinked like fireflies in the night.

Poachers didn't behave like this. What was going on?

Jacobus tried to raise the base over the radio, but there was just the hiss of static over the ether. Pego and he whispered about the best route to take to the lights.

The area directly east of Ka-Nwamuri was too flat and open. But close by ran the Nwaswitsonstso stream, the one that made a wide curve from the west around the Ka-Nwamuri koppie. It formed the Eileen Orpen Dam before carving out a small canyon that ran towards the border. They could follow the stream to the rear of the hill – and then climb over to see what was happening on the eastern side.

It took more than an hour. At the Orpen Dam they ran into to a pride of angry lions roaring their hunger and frustration into the night after a failed zebra hunt. At last, after nine o'clock they peeped over the edge of the crest of Ka-Nwamuri koppie and saw the people below.

The lights were off, but a large campfire burned at the foot of the hill. A group of people sat around the fire. Behind them, camouflage nets covered bulky shapes.

Pego hissed softly through his teeth and said *befa*, this is bad. Jacobus directed his binoculars at the group beside the fire. They were white. In civilian clothes.

He saw the carcass hanging from the tree near the fire. Impala ram.

He and Pego whispered. They must get closer. No, said Pego, he would go, he was as dark as the night and they wouldn't see him. There was a *moshuta*, a thicket, near their camp, he would crawl into the cover of that and take a look and come back. Jacobus should stay here and try the radio again. It might work better on the koppie.

'But you will come back to me?'

'Of course, because I'm leaving the *bushwa* with you,' and Pego grinned in the dark at their old joke. He would come back because Jacobus was the one carrying the food.

'*Tshetshisa*,' said Jacobus, one of the few words he knew in Mapuleng. Hurry.

Pego disappeared into the darkness and Jacobus shifted below the crest and tried the radio again. He pressed the knob and whispered, 'Bravo One, come in, this is Juliet Papa.' He listened and suddenly there was a voice, loud and clear, so that he had to turn the volume down quickly.

'Juliet Papa, identify yourself,' but it was an unfamiliar voice, not one of the ESU radio operators.

He hesitated, because this was new. There was no procedure for this. 'Bravo One, this is Juliet Papa.'

'I hear you, Juliet Papa, but identify yourself. What are you doing on this frequency?'

That gave him a fright. Had he made a mistake? He checked the radio again, set it back on the frequency they were supposed to use and repeated, 'Bravo One, this is Juliet Papa, come in.'

The same voice replied clear as day, 'Juliet Papa, this is a reserved frequency. Identify yourself.'

He felt like throwing the radio down the hill. It worked only when it wanted to and now it was confused. He switched it off and crept back to the crest. He focused the binoculars on the thicket Pego had indicated and waited.

He saw a light moving at the bottom of the slope. They were barely three hundred metres from him. Two men with a torch. They were inspecting something on the ground. They picked it up. A rope? No, through the binoculars he could see that it was a smooth black cable.

Then he heard shouts below and he swung the binoculars towards the fire and saw figures running, armed men, uniformed men. Where had they been? Where had they come from?

Shots cracked, he jerked the binoculars away from his face, searching for the flashes of the shots in the night, but he couldn't see any.

Pego, where are you?

Down there people scurried around, away from the fire. He used the binoculars again. Everything was suddenly quiet, nobody in sight. He swung back to where the two men with the torch had been. The torch was off.

Minutes ticked past.

He keep watching the fire and trying to see something in the thicket where Pego was planning to hide, but it was too dark.

There was movement at the fire. He focused the binoculars. Two soldiers with someone between them that they were half carrying, half dragging. Others crowded around. He saw the man they had was Pego and his heart leapt in his chest because there was blood on his friend's leg, at the knee.

They dropped Pego on the ground and stood around him. Someone kicked the black man and Jacobus's heart thumped in his throat. This was trouble, big trouble, he wanted to charge down the slope and shout, 'What are you doing, what are you doing? Leave him, he's my buddy,' but he lay frozen and not knowing what to do.

42

My path down the mountain was steep and overgrown – branches, tree roots, spiderwebs. Here and there were small erosion gullies and rocks that I had to clamber down step by step while the sweat poured down me in rivers.

Above all I had to be quiet, even though I didn't expect them on this side of the river. They would have someone watching the piece of ground between the forest and the farmhouse.

I guessed the distance and knew I had come close. The house ought to be within a few hundred metres. I would have to turn south, but I had to be very careful.

Jacobus saw them drag Pego away from the circle of firelight and then come back to confer. He made up his mind. He would rescue Pego first and then they would go for help. His friend was wounded and it didn't seem as though anyone was treating him.

He crept down the western slope and switched the radio on again just to listen. He was too scared to call.

Nothing.

He crept closer around the koppie, very cautiously. How had they spotted Pego? How had they caught him, the man of ma-Pulana, Tau, the Lion, who could stalk as silently as a cat?

Jacobus was lucky. He saw the electronic device by accident. It was attached to a steel peg knocked into the ground and its thin wire was nearly invisible in the night. It had an eye facing east and he guessed what it must be: a sensor of some kind, casting an invisible beam that must not be broken.

He leopard-crawled past it and did not stand up again, staying down and moving slowly and noiselessly with a great deal of effort, carrying his rifle in his hands, ever closer, until he could hear their voices and spotted one of the sentries under a tree with an R4 in his arms. Then he knew they were army and that Pego would be safe, it had been an accident. He was going to stand up and thought, thank God, it's all a misunderstanding, when Pego screamed.

I could see them.

They were sitting on my veranda, two of them. One had been driving the jeep at the hospital, the other was the man behind the Galil, the big blond one who had shot Emma.

Blondie sat on a kitchen chair, legs stretched out and his heels propped on the veranda wall. He wore the same baseball cap on his head. Jeep man was just sitting. They were talking, but I was too far away to hear what they were saying.

They were waiting for me. There would be others too. One or two watching the road, surely.

Would that be all of them?

Jacobus continued crawling in the direction of the scream, until he could see them and smell the odour of Pego's burning flesh. Four men had tied Pego to a tree. One pressed a red glowing object against his chest and said, 'Talk to me, *kaffertjie*.' Pego screamed again and then said, 'It's the truth, *baas*, it's the truth.'

The man turned around. He was in civilian clothes, broad and strong with a bushy moustache and hair just covering his ears and collar. He said to the others, 'I believe him and that means we've got big *kak*.'

'Ask him what his name is,' the other one said, older, leaner, with a slight pot belly and gold-rimmed spectacles.

'You heard the boss. What's his name?' The man with the moustache brought the glowing iron closer.

'Jacobus.'

'Jacobus?'

'Jacobus le Roux.'

The strong man turned to the older one and said, 'I'll have to find out. I think they work out of the recce base. We must stay sharp, he might be out there in the dark somewhere.'

'I swear it was him on the radio just now,' another man said.

The older man held up a hand. 'Listen, it's manageable. Let's make sure first, then we'll take it from there.'

They walked away, back to the fire, and left Pego hanging against the tree, alone.

In mid-afternoon, I lay four metres from the babbling stream, among verdant green ferns, knowing that I would have to wait until it was dark. At least it gave me time to work out a plan, observe them and find out how many there were.

I had the upper hand. They couldn't surprise me now. They would have to sit and wait, hide and worry whether I would come, from which direction and when?

I turned carefully and retreated a few metres. I wanted to make myself comfortable. Rest and relax.

That's when I spotted the skull. It lay between two big round river rocks. It was overgrown with moss, stained brown and weathered. The jawbone was missing. I picked it up and turned it over. The eye sockets stared back at me like an omen.

Jacobus crept up from behind and first whispered in Pego's ear to be quiet before cutting him loose and catching him before he dropped to the ground. Then he dragged his friend into the shadows and pressed his lips to Pego's ear and said, 'Can you crawl? They've got alarms; that's how they caught you. We'll have to crawl. Can you do it?'

'Yes.'

With his hand he showed Pego the way to go and whispered, 'You go first, I'll look out behind.' They struggled along like that, Pego needing frequent rests, because the bullet had broken his right leg and he was tired and weak. Eventually, they reached the river and he got Pego up and supported him on his shoulder. They half ran like that, limping, and suddenly there were shots fired and flares cleaved the sky. They stumbled into the river and lay down in the shallow water under the protection of the bank.

Time is forgotten when you are afraid. They lay quietly and after a while they heard footsteps and voices, people who were not at home in the veld and who made too much noise. Then it was quiet again.

Jacobus gave Pego water from his canteen and said they had to get going again, to the Nwaswitsontso canyon near the border. They would be safe there; there was a place to hide and only one easy access below the upper dam.

Pego nodded. 'My leg. *Go etsela.* It's asleep.'

'I'll carry you.'

He did, the last kilometre and a bit. They followed the Nwaswitsontso, but near the dams he veered away with Pego on his shoulder to avoid the crocodiles.

I fell asleep in the deep hollow between rocks. I woke with a start when the sun was behind the mountain and a small neon-green frog sat centimetres from my nose, staring at me with cold, red eyes.

They found a hiding place in the Nwaswitsontso gorge where ancient waters had carved out an overhang just big enough for the two of them.

'What are we going to do?' Pego asked.

'I don't know.'

He inspected Pego's wound. It looked ugly, but had stopped bleeding. He asked his friend what the men had asked him and Pego said, 'They thought I was a terrorist. They didn't want to believe I was ESU. They said they would have to kill us both, Jacobus, I heard them.'

Pego was quiet for a long time and then he said, 'Why would the boere do that?' but Jacobus didn't know how to answer him.

They lay there and Pego slept like a sick man; his breathing was quick and his body jerked involuntarily. The maPulane groaned in his fever, and muttered strange words. Jacobus lay awake thinking until he couldn't think any more. What were those people doing here?

In the early hours he heard someone. There were footsteps barely six metres above them on the edge of the gorge. He held his hand over Pego's mouth and saw his friend's eyes open and slowly register the action overhead. His head nodded slowly. He understood.

A voice spoke in Afrikaans above them. 'Shit! I nearly didn't see the fucking cliff here.'

'It's not a fucking cliff.'

'What do you call it? Look. It's fifty foot, easy.'

'How the fuck can you tell? It's pitch dark, man.'

'Well, you tell me how far down that is.'

'It doesn't matter. We'll have to go around.'

'Fuck that. They could never get down here. Look, do you see any way down?'

'We'll have to find a spot. We can't keep walking for ever. They're doing the radio call at four o'clock. We have to be ready with that thing.'

'OK. That way. If they came past here, they would have gone that way.'

'I don't think they can be this far. They say the kaffir's leg is shot to hell.'

'Why did they have to come and fuck around here tonight?'

'I haven't even eaten yet.'

'Me neither. The civvies did. Fucking impala steaks.'

One of them kicked a stone into the canyon.

'Hear that. It's deep.'

Silence.

'Would you be able to shoot the white one?'

The other one didn't answer immediately. Boots shifted. 'In the dark it won't matter. You won't be able to see which is which. What the fuck, first I want to see how they get a guy's position just because he's talking on the radio. Come on, let's get this mast up.'

They walked away.

*　　*　　*

I sat watching the house as it grew dark, but there was no one on the veranda now. The big blond man came out and walked towards the river, not straight towards me, but at an angle. He was carrying the Galil.

He was heading for a tongue of trees. He could cover the whole yard on this side of the house from there. Clever spot. As long as no one saw you.

Make yourself at home, big fellow. Dig yourself in. Lemmer of Loxton sees you. And Lemmer of Brandvlei Maximum Security learned in prison how to wait.

See you later.

At four in the morning they called over the radio.

He heard it quietly on his hip. He picked up the radio and pressed it against his ear. 'Jacobus le Roux, Jacobus le Roux, come in.'

It was the same unknown voice.

Knowing what their game was, he did nothing.

'Jacobus le Roux, Jacobus le Roux, come in.'

Over and over, incessantly, every few minutes the same patient words.

Then: 'I know you can hear me, Jacobus. We're very sorry about Vincent. We didn't know you worked for ESU.' The voice was sympathetic and friendly. 'We know he needs medical attention. Bring him in, we can help. Are you there, Papa Juliet, come in.'

For the next half hour that was their approach, soothing promises, but Jacobus was not listening any more. He thought about what he had to do in an hour or two when the sun came up. He must find help for Pego. They must get away, or they were dead men.

What could he do? They were about seven kilometres from the H10, the tar road that the tourists used, but he would have to make a big detour to get away from these people. It wasn't going to work.

They could lay low, because tomorrow they would have to be back at base and the ESU would start looking for them. But with Pego's leg, he wouldn't be able to wait that long.

The voice over the radio went quiet for five minutes. When it came back it was different, hard and angry. 'Listen carefully to me. Forty-Seven Dale Brooke Crescent, does that sound familiar? Forty-Seven Dale Brooke Crescent in Linden, Johannesburg.'

His parents' address.

'You have ten minutes to reply. Or I will send people. People who don't give a shit. People who will slit a woman's throat for fucking fun. Ten minutes. Then I'm phoning.'

43

Jacobus le Roux used the ten minutes to make up his mind. He left the radio under the overhang, woke Pego and they climbed down the canyon in the pitch dark before dawn with great difficulty.

Then they stumbled east beside the Nwaswitsontso, over four kilometres to the Mozambique border.

He had no other choice. If he answered them, they would shoot him and Pego. But he didn't take the threat to his family seriously. His father was Somebody, his father knew Ministers, his father was a Supplier, and therefore an essential Cog in the Great Machine.

All they could do was disappear. Until these people had gone, until this affair was over.

They didn't reach the border before the sun came up.

They heard helicopters just after the sky began to change colour. The far-off rhythm of their rotors was ever closer and louder. Jacobus found shelter and through the mopane leaves he watched two planes flying back and forth in a grid pattern on their side of the Ka-Nwamuri koppie. White planes, like yesterday's Cessna, without letters or marks.

The helicopters searched for over an hour and then disappeared to the south.

Now Jacobus and Pego had to get past the Shishengedzim lookout post, and in broad daylight. The border post had a view over the canyon, but it had to be done. Pego was feverish and weak. And Jacobus was dead tired from supporting him.

He staggered the four hundred metres past the rangers' lookout post and waited for the shots. He could feel them, even though none was fired. Two or three times he looked up at the building, but there was no sign of life, nobody there, no game wardens, just the people back at Ka-Nwamuri with their cables on the slope and their electronic eyes in the veld.

He cut the border fence and they were through to Mozambique. All down the river, there was no sign of life, no animals, no people, just the searing heat and his fatigue. Six hours later, they saw women washing laundry in the river.

Pego could speak their language. He could tell them, 'Don't fear the white man, he saved my life, they are hunting him too, we just want to rest a while.'

They slept that night in the nameless hamlet. The grizzled headman called himself Rico and told them through Pego that his country was burning, Mozambique was aflame, the war was destroying everything. The locals never left their village. Now and then the elephant poachers would pass through and leave them something, money or food or clothing, in exchange for a place to rest. But look, there were no young men; they had all gone away to war, just to stay alive.

On Sunday, 19 October, Jacobus and Pego heard a dreadful noise, the night sky ripped apart from north to south, very close by, thundering and deafening. Jacobus ran out of the hut and saw a flickering red light low on the horizon.

The following day at three o'clock in the afternoon, they got the news.

Samora Machel, President of Mozambique, was dead. His aeroplane had crashed the previous night near Mbuzini, just a hundred and thirty kilometres away.

Jacobus hadn't immediately put two and two together, because the women had begun wailing and the wrinkled Rico shook his head and said, '*Uma coisa má, uma coisa má,*' over and over. Then he told Pego that the white man must go; there was big trouble coming. The white man must go.

The Mozambicans gave him clothes and a bundle of food and water and said they would take his rifle in exchange. They explained to him where to go to reach Swaziland, where he would be safe.

Pego threw his arms around his friend and said, 'Thank you, my brother, I will see you again,' and so he left, travelling first down the river to the south-east, looking for a dusty road. As he walked he slowly but surely pieced it all together.

The two-hundred-kilometre trek took him nearly a week. He walked only at night, hiding every time there were people or vehicles or aeroplanes around.

He crossed the mountain into Swaziland eight kilometres east of the Lomahasha border post. At the little Catholic church at Ngwenya Peak he washed and ate properly for the first time. The priests gave him a bed and he slept for two days. They gave him clothes because the ones he was wearing were in rags. They told him he wasn't the first white South African to arrive there. They had had two others, conscientious objectors who didn't want to do compulsory military service. There were people in Manzini who could help. He had to wait for the lorry that came on Thursdays. They couldn't give him much. They gave him SZL 20, twenty lilangeni. Go with God.

In Manzini he saw the newspapers a week after the death of Samora Machel. Fingers were pointed at the South African government. Africa and the Russians were incensed.

He phoned his father's office from a telephone booth and the switchboard put him through to his father's secretary, who caught her breath when he said, 'Hello, Alta,' and she said, 'Jacobus?'

Then the line went dead.

He tried to phone again, but it wouldn't ring. He took his coins and walked off, but the phone rang. He stopped. Looked around. There was nobody near by.

He walked back and picked up the phone. 'Hello?'

'You're in Swaziland. We're going to get you. But listen . . .'

He was frozen. It was a new voice, not the one on the radio.

'If you try to phone your father again, if you make contact with anyone, we will cut their throats. We will know. I want you to understand that.'

He was dumb.

'I want to hear you say you understand that.'

'I understand.'

'Your father drives a white Mercedes Benz, TJ 100765. Every afternoon he drives the same route from the office. Accidents happen so easily. Your mother goes to the afternoon prayer meeting at the Dutch Reformed Church every Wednesday. She leaves the house alone at twenty to seven in her Honda Ballade, registration TJ 128361. She's a soft target. Your sister walks home from school every afternoon. I think you get the message. Tell me again that you understand.'

'I understand.'

'Very good. I see that you're in Manzini. If you stay there I will send some people to talk to you. We can work this thing out.'

He realised that the man wanted to keep him on the line. Maybe there were already people here looking for him. He stopped listening.

He put down the phone and walked away, quickly, from his life.

The first one was easy because I knew where he was and I knew that he was the one who had shot Emma.

I waited until nine o'clock that night. I crept across the river in the night shadows. I approached him from behind. He lay on his stomach, quite comfortably, with the Galil on the tripod in front of him. Now and then he peered through the night sight.

Beside him lay a rucksack. There would be food and drink in it. I needed that.

It's impossible to be totally silent in the bush, never mind how careful you are. There was a distance of three metres between us when the tiny, invisible twig cracked under my foot. I saw him instinctively turn his head first, and then his upper body jerked around, but I was on my feet with the knife in my right hand. He stood up hurriedly. He did what most people would do – he tried to use his weapon, the sniper rifle. He swung it at me.

Too slow. Too late. I thumped the long blade into his heart and said to him, 'That's for Emma.'

I don't think he heard me.

I stepped back and let him fall. I dragged him to one side, picked up the rifle and lay down where he had been. I used his night scope to scan the area.

There was the Jeep Grand Cherokee, half hidden behind the house beside a Toyota Prado. Big vehicles. Enough to transport a large team. How many were there? The house seemed deserted. I swung the telescope slowly across the whole area. Then I spotted him on the veranda behind the wall. Only the top of his head protruded.

Number two.

If I were in their place, I would have deployed the others near the gate.

We would see.

I heard a voice faintly whispering.

Behind me.

I plucked out the Glock and swung around.

Nothing.

Still I heard the voice. It was a man's voice. Impossible, since there was only dense bush behind me.

I realised that the sound must have come from a radio.

I crawled over to Blondie's corpse and felt in his pockets. Nothing. I turned him over and felt along his belt. Nothing again.

The voice was more audible now. Close to him, or somewhere on him. Up top.

I felt along his body, since I couldn't see in this dark, and held my ear close to his head. I heard it clearly. 'Vannie, come in.' It was a soft, impatient whisper.

The thing was in his ear. There was a fine wire looping down. I should have known that they'd have technology. I took it off carefully. His skin was still warm. I put it in my ear. It didn't fit very well. It might have been tailor made for him.

'Vannie, don't tell me your vack isn't working.'

What was a vack?

'Frans, can you see Vannie?'

'Negative.'

'Fuck.'

Numbers three and four.

'Want me to go and see?'

'Yes, it's still early. Take him one of the spare vacks, there are some more in the back of the Jeep, in the blue box.'

'OK.'

I lay down. Vacks? I looked through the scope. The man behind the wall stood up. Frans. He jogged down the steps to the vehicles and opened the back of the Jeep.

'I can't see the box.'

'It says Voice Activated Comms.'

I got it. Vack. VAC. VACs.

'It's not here.'

'It must be there.'

'I'm telling you it's not here.'

'It's in the back of the Prado, Eric. I moved it.' A new voice. Number five.

'Thanks.'

Frans shut the back of the Jeep and went over to the Prado, opened it and rummaged inside.

'OK, I've got it. Fuck, Vannie, just don't shoot me now.'

'He can't hear you, Frans.'

'I'm just saying.'

He came jogging across the lawn to me. I took the knife and stood up.

Jacobus le Roux found work as a labourer at the Mlawula game reserve in Swaziland. He was an oddity to the black game wardens, the white Afrikaner deserter who wanted to do the work of a black man. The quiet boy who never laughed.

With great effort and patience he pieced together the bits of news and rumour. Samora Machel's plane had been off course. Somewhere there was a false beacon, a VOR, the *Times of Swaziland* speculated, along with the Russian experts.

He knew where the VOR had been. He knew who had put it there.

The newspapers said the South African government wanted Machel dead. They said he had been a thorn in their sides since

1964, when he led the first attack against the Portuguese as a guerrilla fighter for the Front for the Liberation of Mozambique, or FRELIMO. A former nurse, Machel had seen his family's land confiscated, he had seen his parents starve under Portuguese rule, he had seen his brother die in a South African gold mine, and had experienced the wide gap between medical care for whites and blacks at first hand.

And because his grandparents and great-grandparents had fought Portuguese rule in the nineteenth century, the diminutive nurse took up the struggle himself. By 1970, he had become the commander-in-chief of Frelimo, and by 1975 he was the first President of an independent Mozambique.

And, said the newspapers, he had signed his owned death warrant soon after – by allowing guerrilla forces fighting against oppression in South Africa and Rhodesia to use his country as a springboard for attacks. The two neighbouring countries retaliated by forming a rebel group called RENAMO under the auspices of fighting the Marxist Machel government, and a bitter civil war was born.

By 1986, Mozambique had reached breaking point. Kenneth Kaunda of Zambia had succumbed to boere pressure and ordered RENAMO out of his country. RENAMO's great onslaught against Machel had begun and everything was on a knife-edge, at the top of the precipice. Killing Machel was supposed to finally break the deadlock.

But Pretoria denied everything. Even the minister whose face he had seen in the little plane. Especially that minister.

That was what frightened Jacobus the most. He knew that they were lying and he knew what they were prepared to do to preserve the lie.

After five months at the Mlawula reserve, they tracked him down.

He came in from the veld and big fat Job Lindani, the Swazi manager with the ready smile, said to him, 'Don't go home. There are white men waiting for you. Boere.'

He fled again.

*   *   *

Frans had been the one driving the Jeep in the hospital parking lot. I laid his lifeless body down beside big Vannie, crushed his VAC on the ground under my foot, picked up Vannie's rucksack and the Galil and jogged through the dark to the house.

There were at least another three outside, but I suspected there were more. If there were only five they need not have come with two vehicles. I guessed at six. That meant another four. At least.

'Vannie, can you hear me now?'

In the dark house I opened the rucksack. Bottled water. Sandwiches. They smelled like chicken.

'Frans, what are you doing?'

I looked for my Twinkies. Found only the empty carton. They would pay for that too.

'Frans, come in, Frans.'

I ate and drank in a hurry. Just enough to still the hunger.

'I don't believe it.'

I picked up the Galil and went out the back door, past the vehicles, south to the dense bush where I had lain in wait the night before.

'Eric, I think we've got trouble.'

'Fuck.'

'He'll have the rifle too.'

Eric ruminated on this wisdom.

'And the VAC too, maybe,' said Eric. 'Lie dead still and shoot anything that moves.'

44

He worked in the Swazi mines, on remote farms and once on a plantation. Sometimes he just hid away in the mountains and stole to stay alive. Twice he went back to Mozambique, but there were no jobs, no means of survival. He lived in fear every day for eight years. He never stopped looking over his shoulder and developed an instinct for who would betray him, and when. He didn't blame them. If you are poor and hungry, and you have a wife and five children somewhere in a Swazi village who want more, always more, then you take every cent you can get. When you walk into the shebeen in Mbabane and meet someone asking questions, then you tell him about the strange white man who works beside you in the mine shaft, the one who speaks your language and never laughs.

In 1992 the Swazi papers were full of the Great Change in South Africa.

He found hope.

He waited another two years, until March 1994, and then took the money he had saved and bought himself a new face from a surgeon in Mbabane. He bought a Nissan 1400 pick-up and a false passport in Bulembu and drove over the border and down the mountain to Barberton.

He found a public telephone booth in the town centre and dialled his parents' home number, but before it could ring fear overtook him and he put the receiver down.

What if . . .

Wait for the elections to be over. Wait. He had waited eight years, what were a few more months.

A week later he heard about Stef Moller in a bar and drove out to Heuningklip. It was only when he wanted to marry Melanie

Lottering that he knew the time was right, it was safe enough to see his family again.

I knew where they would have to hide to see the gate and the access road. I knew from which direction they would expect me.

They would be in pairs, because that made everything easier. For me too.

I approached from the west, because they would be focused on the north, with one of the team looking south. Through the night sight I saw two of them within fifty metres of my own nest, where I had waited for Donnie Branca and Stef Moller.

I was not familiar with the Galil. I didn't know for what distance the scope was calibrated. I crawled to within two hundred metres of them and settled down. With very slow deliberate movements, I found enough shelter and took aim.

No wind. I halted the cross-hairs on the shoulder of the one looking south, took a deep breath, let it escape slowly and silently, and pulled the trigger.

Nothing happened.

I made sure the safety was off. Then I remembered that it was a sniper's weapon. It had a two-stage trigger.

I took aim again, breathed in and out, pulled the trigger, pulled again and the shot boomed. I swung the barrel towards the other, he was moving, looking at his partner. I shot him; saw him jerk.

Then it was quiet.

'Who shot now?' Eric's voice.

The last two. I wasn't sure where they were. I suspected that they would be covering the eastern front, somewhere beyond the leafy tunnel where I had talked to Donnie Branca. I got up and began to jog from dark spot to dark spot.

'Dave, come in, Dave, who was that shooting? Did you see anything?'

'Eric, can you hear me?' I said.

'Who the fuck is that?'

'My name is Lemmer and I'm watching you through the night sight of a Galil.'

I had to talk to him, a talking man can't hear.

He wouldn't talk.

'You're the only one left, Eric. Now tell me why I shouldn't pull the trigger.'

'What do you want?'

'Information.'

I couldn't see them. I was on the two-wheel track between the house and the gate. I swung the scope from left to right, slowly, but I couldn't see them. Farther east? Could be.

'What kind of information?'

'I've only got two questions. But think carefully before you answer, because you only have one chance.'

'I'm listening.'

I knew what he was up to. He would gesture to his partner, look here, look there. Their eyes would search for me. Their adrenalin would be pumping; they would be ready to shoot.

'Put down your weapons.'

I couldn't keep up searching for them. If they saw me, any movement at all, they would know I was lying.

'I said, put down your weapons.'

'OK.'

'Now get up.'

I couldn't see anything. They were closer to the gate than I thought.

'Both of you.'

I waited, stretching out the silence.

'Now what?' asked Eric.

'Walk towards the road.'

'Which road?'

'The road to the house.'

'OK.'

But I saw nothing.

Did they know I was bluffing?

I still couldn't see a thing.

Then I saw the movement, far down the road.

'We're at the road.'

'Walk towards the house.'

They approached, still too far away to recognise in the dark.

'Eric, put your hands on your head.'

Both figures did that.

'No, not both of you. Just Eric.'

One of them dropped his hands. I let them come within a hundred metres of me, then aimed at the upper thigh of the one who was not Eric. I shot and he dropped.

'What the fuck are you doing?'

'Lie down next to him.'

'Shit, Eric, my leg!'

I ran through the trees beside the road, closer to them.

The other man moaned about his leg. Fifty metres, then I dropped flat at the edge of the trees and took aim.

'Eric, I'm going to bleed to death.'

'Shut up, Kappies.'

I could see them clearly. Eric lay beside Kappies.

'You'd better help him,' I said.

Eric sat up. He just looked at his partner.

'Help me, Eric.'

Eric grabbed at his waist. For a second I thought he was going for a gun, but then I saw him taking off his belt.

'*Jissis*, Kappies,' and he strapped the belt around his leg.

'It's not working.' Kappies voice was panic stricken.

'Lie fucking still, I'm doing what I can.' Eric took his shirt off and ripped it. 'I'm not a fucking doctor.'

Feverishly, he wound the cloth strips around the wound.

'That's all I can do.'

Kappies just groaned.

'Time for answers,' I said.

'What do you want?'

'I've got just two questions. Answer quickly. If you take too long, I'll shoot him again. In the other leg this time. If you lie to me, I'll shoot you.'

'Please,' begged Kappies.

'Ask what you want to ask.'

'I will count to three. If you don't answer, I'll shoot him. It's in your hands.'

'Ask.'

'Right. Question one: who do you work for?'

He didn't answer straight away. 'One.'

'*Jissis*, Eric.'

'Two.'

It was Kappies who shouted, 'Es Cee Ay.'

'What?'

'Southern Cross Avionics,' shouted Kappies.

'Thank you,' I said. 'Now, question two: who gave the order to kill Emma le Roux?'

'What do you mean?'

Eric was trying to gain time. I fired, deliberately aiming just next to Kappies' foot. He screamed in terror.

'Please, please, it was Eric!'

'*Jissis*, Kappies.'

'It was, Eric, you fucking know it.'

'Listen,' said Eric in a rush and looking in my direction. 'The order came from the top.'

'Who gave it?'

'Tell him, Eric.'

'One,' I counted.

Silence.

'Two.'

'Shit, Eric, tell him.'

'Wernich.'

'Who is Wernich?'

'Quintus Wernich. He's the chairman.'

'Of what?'

'Of the board.'

'Where is he?'

'You said two questions.'

'I lied.'

Kappies moaned again.

'Where is he?'

'He lives in Stellenbosch,' Kappies yelled. 'We don't have his address.'

'Who were the three that attacked Emma in Cape Town?'

'Kappies, keep quiet.'

'It was Eric and Vannie and Frans.'

'Fuck it, Kappies, I should have let you bleed to death, you coward.'

'And who attacked us, at the road?'

'They did. Those three.'

'Was it you lot who threw Frank Wolhuter in the lion camp?'

'Yes.'

'You were there too, Kappies.'

'I sat in the Jeep, I swear.'

'What did you get from Wolhuter? What did he want to show Emma?'

'A picture.'

'What picture?'

'An old photo. Of Cobie and Emma, when he was still in the army.'

'Did you torture Edwin Dibakwane?'

'Who's that?'

'The gate guard from Mohlolobe.'

'We were all there. Kappies too.'

'But Eric put the snake in your house.'

Bosom buddies, obviously.

'What were you doing with the Jeep in the hospital car park the other day?'

'We wanted to put a GPS sensor on your car, but you came out.'

'How did you know which one was my car?'

'We hacked into Budget's computer system.'

'There was a GPS thing on Emma's car.'

'Yes.'

'Why did you wait so long before you attacked us?'

'We didn't think she would find anything,' said Eric.

'Then she got the letter.'

'Yes.'

I got up slowly. I left the Galil on the ground.

'You can get up now, Eric,' I said.

'You'll shoot me.'

'No,' I said. 'I'm not going to shoot you.'

Cobie told me the last part of his story under the thorn tree at Heuningklip. He spoke in a monotone, hoarse and weary. Sometimes he had to stop to control his emotions. Then he would just sit there with drooping shoulders and his head on his chest and slowly breathe in and out to gather his strength.

'I was so careful,' he said. 'Not just about their safety. I knew what it must have been like for them. For my mother thinking I was dead all these years and then suddenly I'm not. It would have . . .'

He took four or five breaths before he spoke again.

'I didn't want to phone. I didn't know if they were still listening after all these years. So I thought I should first go to my father at work. I arrived there and asked to see him, but they said he wasn't there, he was on holiday and there were no vacancies anyway.

'So I said I wasn't looking for work, I was family. So she looked at me and said "Family?" as though I were lying. I asked her when they were coming back and she said in two weeks. So I asked her where they were and she said that was private. So I said, if I leave a message, would they phone him, so she said, mister, he's on holiday, we don't bother him.

'So I asked, is Alta here, and she said who and I said Alta Blomerus and she said nobody like that works here.

'I said she was Mr le Roux's secretary and she said Mr le Roux's secretary has been Mrs Davel for the last five years now. Then she excused herself, said she had to answer the phones and that Mr le Roux would be back in two weeks.

'I asked, but is he at home, and she was in a hurry and she said no, they are not at home, excuse me, mister. And then I didn't know what to do, so I turned around and left. Then I went and did a stupid, stupid thing.'

He had taken a room in a guest house in Randburg, only a few kilometres from his family home, and lay all afternoon on the bed thinking. Then he got up and called the house number just to see whether they were there.

His mother's voice was on the answering machine. 'We can't take your call. Try us on the cell. The number is . . .' He had put the phone down and sat shaking on the bed because he heard his mother's voice for the first time in decades and it sounded just the same, exactly the same, as if he had last seen her the day before.

Then he phoned again and listened. And again and again, until he knew the cell phone number by heart. The urge grew and he began to think about cell phones, that they couldn't tap a cell phone because it had no wires and there was no space for bugs. If he was careful, if he just asked where they were, it would be safe. He would pretend to be someone else.

'I didn't sleep. All night long I just thought about what I would say. I had everything ready. I looked in the Yellow Pages for the name of a company, a steel dealer, and I thought I would say that I was Van der Merwe of Benoni Steel and that I'd like to talk to him because I wanted to do business with him and then ask when he would be back.

'I phoned at nine the next morning and my mother answered. She said, "Sara le Roux speaking, good morning." I wanted to cry, I wanted to say, "Hello, ma, it's me, ma." She said, "Hello?" and I said, "Good morning, madam, may I speak to Johan le Roux, please." She didn't say anything and I said, "Hello? Mrs le Roux?"

'Then my mother said, "Dear God, Jacobus," and it gave me a fright. I couldn't help myself, I wanted to cry. My mother, she recognised my voice after eleven years. She knew it was me. Then I cried, I couldn't help it and I said, "Ma," and she said, "My son, oh God, my son."

'But then I was terribly afraid and I turned off the phone and grabbed my things and I walked out.

'The next afternoon I bought myself a cell phone and phoned her again. It wasn't her that answered, it was the police in Willowmore. They said, "We're very sorry, sir, Mrs le Roux is dead, she and Mr le Roux, here in the Perdepoort on the N9."'

45

I knew guys like Eric.

They came from the grey mass of the middle class, always bigger and stronger than the rest. At school they were trapped in the no man's land between the in-groups of the brainy kids and the jocks. The only way out, the way to be noticed and respected, was through physical intimidation. These were the ingredients in the making of a bully.

Instinctively, they knew this strategy wouldn't work in the adult world. Instead, they would join the police or the army, where a uniform would compensate. There they discovered the Power of the Gun and became addicted to it. But the salary, the working conditions, the lack of advancement through the ranks and the constant reminders that they were still middle class left them frustrated and dissatisfied. After four or five years they would seek out opportunities in the private sector, but they would never give up telling their stories – about how rough and ready they had been in the force. You had to know how fearless they were, how tough and strong, how many guys they had beaten up and how many they had shot.

They believed their own reputation, because in groups of five or six they could assault women, torture black gate guards and fling middle-aged conservationists into lion pens. They were afraid of nothing, hard men of violence.

But take away their guns and they are nothing.

I went to meet him on the road. Big sturdy guy. I hit him in the face. He dropped and got up again.

'I'm going to kill you,' he said, full of bravado. He lifted his fists, dropped his head and looked at me from under his eyebrows. He pecked with a right. I grabbed his fist, dragged him forward and smacked him across the face with the back of my hand.

He didn't want to show he was humiliated. He danced away, a poor parody of light-footed courage.

He came at me again, more wary this time. Two, three lefts at my body. I let him hit, the blows weren't debilitating. They gave him confidence. The next one would be a right, the aspiring knockout blow, the one he would swing from below his shoulder.

His balance wasn't bad, he knew better than to telegraph with his eyes – somewhere in his youth were a few years of boxing. He struck and I let it pass left of my head and then I went away to another world, the other place. Where time stood still. Where everything disappeared, you heard nothing and saw just red-grey mist. And this thing in front of you that you lusted to destroy with all the powers within you.

I fetched the Jeep and dragged Kappies and Eric into the vehicle and dumped them off at the house. I tied each one to a bed with baling wire that I found in the back of the Prado, between more sophisticated equipment. There were radio receivers and uniden-tifiable electronic boxes with LED screens and switches, laptops, earphones, microphones and antennae, extension cords and tools. I wondered whether this was the stuff they used to listen in on the calls. One carton was labelled GPS Tracking.

I checked Kappies' wound once I had tied him securely. He would live. He wouldn't win the Comrades marathon, though. He stared at me wordlessly with frightened eyes.

Whether Eric would make it, I didn't know. I really didn't care.

Then I took off my bloodstained clothes and had a bath.

I took my sports bag and drove the Jeep to the forestry station, left it there and took the Nissan. Just after midnight, I drove to Nelspruit.

In the SouthMed Hospital car park I phoned Jeanette Louw first. She must have been asleep, but she disguised it well.

'I got them,' I said.

'Got them?'

'Four are dead. Two are in a bad way.'

'Jesus, Lemmer.'

'It's not over yet, Jeanette. I have to go to the Cape tomorrow.'

'What's in the Cape?'

'I want the address of a Quintus Wernich, chairman of the board of Southern Cross Avionics. He lives in Stellenbosch.'

Jeanette Louw said, 'Fuck.'

'You know him?'

'Jesus. He's part of this?'

'Jeanette, I haven't got time now. I'll tell you everything, but not now. You know Wernich.'

'I met him when I made a presentation of our services to Southern Cross. After all that trouble the bastard said no thanks, they had their own people.'

'Not any more, I don't think. What else?'

'I knew all about them before I talked to them, but that was months ago. Let me think . . . If I remember correctly, they made their name with new systems for the Mirage, the fighter plane. I still have the stuff here somewhere. I'll take a look.'

'Can you get Wernich's address? And book a flight for me?'

'I will.' Then she asked sharply, 'When did you last sleep?'

'I can't remember. Day before yesterday; something like that. I'm at the hospital. I'll have a quick nap now.'

'Good idea. Listen, you wanted to know about Stef Moller.'

'Yes.'

'Let me just get my notes. You must understand, what I found is mostly speculative. You won't be able to prove it.'

'I don't want proof. He's out of the picture, anyway.'

'So, for what it's worth, have you ever heard of Frama Inter-Trading?'

'Never.'

'I won't bore you with details, but in the seventies and eighties the army was smuggling ivory and Frama was the front company. We're talking about hundreds of millions of rands. In 1996 the Kumleben Commission investigated the whole business and their report said that there was possible corruption and self-enrichment on a grand scale. But as you can guess, no one wanted to point fingers. One of the names mentioned was a Stefanus Lodewikus Moller. He was Frama's auditor. He was the one that moved the money around.'

I was too exhausted to digest all that.

'Are you there?' Jeanette asked.

'I'm dumbstruck.'

'Yes, Lemmer. This fucking country. But you go and sleep your sleep, I'll call you tomorrow.'

'Thanks, Jeanette.'

'Before I forget,' she said urgently.

'What?'

'You can't take the Glock on the plane.'

'Oh, yes. I hadn't thought that far.'

'Leave it with B. J. Fikter. I'll get something for you at this end.'

I picked up my bag and went into the hospital. B. J. Fikter was on night shift. He looked fresh and alert and he took his hand off his firearm when he saw that it was me. The police constable was fast asleep opposite him.

'Ah, how pretty you look, my dear,' he said.

'And I haven't even put my make-up on yet. Any news?'

He shook his head.

'The risk is considerably reduced. I wanted to let you know. Not completely eliminated, but I don't imagine you'll be bothered tonight.'

'You got them.'

'I did.'

'Thanks for inviting your friends to the party.'

'I know you're not a party animal. You look so domestic.'

'Oh, the masks that we wear. What are you going to do now?'

'I'm going to have a sleep on the VIP couch. I just want to . . .' I gestured at Emma's room.

He said nothing, just grinned.

The black night nurse recognised me. She nodded. I could go in.

I opened the door and went over to her bed. She lay there just the same as ever. I looked at her and felt a great weariness come over me. I sat down and stretched out my hand to rest on hers.

'Emma, I found Jacobus.'

Her breathing was deep and peaceful.

'He misses you terribly. He's going to come here, maybe tomorrow. When you're better, you can see him. So you have to get better.'

You can't trust yourself when you haven't slept for forty hours. Your head is a maelstrom, your senses betray you, and you live in a world where dreams and reality are indistinguishable.

So, when I imagined that Emma's hand moved almost imperceptibly under mine, I knew that I was deluding myself.

Vincent 'Pego' Mashego took a course at the Mogale rehabilitation centre in the summer of 2003. One afternoon he was walking between the buildings and he saw a figure in the lammergeier's cage that made his heart stand still.

The man was on his haunches scraping manure off the floor and Pego stared wordlessly. It was like a dream, unreal and incomprehensible.

The man looked up and he knew it was Jacobus le Roux.

Jacobus charged out, making the lammergeier flap her giant wings. They embraced fiercely, without speaking, seventeen years after they had parted ways in a nameless hamlet in Mozambique. Jacobus took him to his little house out of fear that someone would see them and that the evil would return to claim Pego, too.

They swapped stories. In 1986 Pego had stayed in Mozambique for six months and then went home to his people. Yes, there were white men who came asking for him, twice. But that was some months ago.

He had been frightened. He couldn't tell the whole story to his family out of fear that someone would say the wrong thing somewhere. As far as they were concerned, there had just been some big trouble between him and the boere, trouble that necessitated that they should never know he had returned, trouble that dictated that he would not be Pego again, they would call him only Vincent, so he could begin a new life.

The boere hadn't kept looking for him. Maybe they thought he wasn't a danger to them. Who would believe a simple maPulana man's stories about lights and cables in the game reserve, about people shooting at him and burning him?

Only late in 1987 did he get work in a private game reserve as a waiter. The owner soon spotted his knowledge of the veld and transferred him to assistant to the field guides.

In 1990 he married Venolia Lebyane and in 1995 he saw an advertisement put out by the Limpopo Parks Board. They wanted black people with Matric who aspired to become game wardens in the provincial game reserves. He didn't have the schooling, but he went to see them in Polokwane anyway. He explained that his knowledge lay in the bush, not books. He didn't have paper qualifications, but wouldn't they give him a chance?

They had, because there were few applications. The people of Limpopo wanted work in the city, not the veld. So Vincent Mashego became a game ranger, and now he was the head of the Talamati Bushveld Camp in the Manyeleti Game Reserve alongside Kruger.

Then Jacobus told his story to Pego and the black man held him when he wept. He said he owed Jacobus his life. He would help.

Jacobus said there was nothing he could do.

There would be. Some time or other.

They had seen each other afterwards. From time to time Jacobus would travel to Manyeleti surreptitiously and sit beside a campfire with Pego. It was most like old times when they used to talk about the veld and animals. Nowadays they talked about the pressure on the environment that kept increasing, the threats, the white property developments, the black land claims, the poachers going after rhino horns and vulture heads, the greed across the spectrum of colour and race.

One more poisoning after all the others pushed Jacobus le Roux over the edge. He told me it felt as though twenty years of fear, frustration and death became too much for him in that instant. He stood among the carcasses in the veld and he couldn't carry all those burdens any more. Those magnificent creatures that he had come to know so well at Mogale, those beautiful birds that had stretched out their great wings in the winds only hours before, became the symbol of his life's futility. Inside him something broke at last. He fetched his rifle and followed the spoor to the sangoma's hut. He found them there, the vultures and the blunt knives they used to cut up the carcasses, the little piles of money and the plastic bags and those four people. So he shot them. In his madness and rage and hatred.

Only three hours later, somewhere in the veld, had he come to his senses. He realised what he had done. He fled to Pego, who hid him and told him he would help, because his wife, Venolia, worked for the police at Hoedspruit. She would tell them if they were looking for Jacobus.

Venolia Mashego had been there in the office with Jack Phatudi when a woman phoned from Cape Town asking whether Jacobus le Roux might not be Cobie de Villiers. Pego knew it was the sister. He had found Emma's number and phoned her because he wanted to repay his debt to Jacobus by saving his sister. But in the bush at Manyeleti the cell phone signal was weak and he didn't know how much Emma heard.

Jacobus had been angry with him when he heard about it. So angry that he left in the night and went to Stef Moller. But after the death of Frank Wolhuter, Jacobus phoned Pego and said he had been wrong. They must warn Emma and get her away.

It was Pego who wrote the letter and had it delivered to the gate guard, Edwin Dibakwane.

But it had been too late.

46

I was dreaming of skulls on the mountain at Motlasedi when Jeanette phoned just after eight.

'I've got you on the only direct flight. Departs fourteen thirty-five, arrives five o'clock in the Cape.'

'That's a pity.'

'Why?'

'Wernich will be waiting for news from his gang of killers. He will be very worried by now. I hope he doesn't feel a sudden yearning to travel.'

'Do you want me to keep an eye on him?'

'That would help a lot.'

'Consider it done.'

'Thanks, Jeanette.'

'Don't get ideas, Lemmer. I'm doing it for our client.'

I told Dr Eleanor Taljaard that hopefully there would be a family member visiting Emma that afternoon, someone whose voice she had waited a long time to hear.

'We need a miracle, Lemmer. You know what I told you; the longer they are in a coma . . .'

'Miracles do happen,' I said, but neither of us believed it.

I drove to the airport and waited until twenty minutes before my flight left for Cape Town. Then I phoned Jack Phatudi. They said he was busy, but I said it was an emergency and I wanted his cell phone number.

What kind of emergency?

I had found the people who had tortured and murdered Edwin Dibakwane.

They gave me Phatudi's cell phone number. He was morose and aggressive until I told him where he could find the murderers of Wolhuter and Dibakwane, the people who had shot Emma le Roux. I told him that most of them were dead, but that one, maybe two, were still alive. They were injured, but could stand up in court.

'They won't talk, Jack, but they are the people you're looking for. Do the forensics, the evidence is there.'

'Did you kill them?'

'Self-defence, Jack.'

He said something in sePedi that clearly meant he didn't believe me.

'Goodbye, Jack.'

'Wait. Where's Cobie de Villiers?'

'I'm still looking. But you can recall your men at the hospital. There's no more danger to her.'

'Where are you?'

'In Johannesburg,' I lied. 'At the airport.'

'I'm coming to get you, Lemmer, if you're lying to me.'

'Ooh, I'm so scared I'll have to ring off, Jack.'

He got angry and cut me off first. Another opportunity to build bridges between races lost.

I found Stef Moller's number on the dialled calls list on Emma's phone. When they made the first call to board, I phoned him. It rang for a long time and then Moller himself answered.

'Stef, it's Lemmer.'

'What do you want?'

'How is Jacobus?'

'Cobie.'

'How is he?'

'What do you want me to say? That he's well? After all you did?'

'How is he?'

'He's not talking. Just sitting there.'

'Stef, I want you to give him a message.'

'No.'

'Just listen. Tell him I got them. Six of them. Four are dead, two will have to go to hospital, but they will be under police guard. Tell him I'm on my way to the Cape to chop the head off the beast.'

I listened to Stef Moller's breathing for a long time before he said in his steady, measured way, 'Are you sure?'

'Tell Cobie to phone Pego's wife for confirmation.'

He didn't answer.

'Then, Stef, tell him the doctors say there is only one thing that can save Emma. Jacobus must go and talk to her.'

'Talk to her?'

'That's right. He must talk to her. Take him, Stef. Take him to Emma.'

'This is the final boarding call for flight double eight oh one to Cape Town,' I heard in the background.

'Take him, Stef. Promise me.'

'What about Hb?' he asked.

'Who?'

'Hb.'

'Never heard of them, Stef. Isn't an HB a kind of pencil?'

On the plane I thought about Stef Moller. The man who didn't want to say where his money came from. The man who sought absolution behind a locked gate by trying to compensate for his crimes against nature.

To each his own way.

I slept for two hours solid on the flight and woke when the Canadair jet touched down hard at Cape Town International. Jeanette was waiting for me in the arrivals hall. Black Armani suit, white shirt and a tie with the South African flag on it. She fell into step with me and we walked outside, shoulder to shoulder, where the south-easter blew at gale force.

'He's at their head office in Century City,' she said over the bluster of the wind.

'How many offices do they have?'

'One in Johannesburg, and the plant outside Stellenbosch. I brought you the material from my previous research. You can read it in the car.'

'The car' was a Porsche with classic lines and a small spoiler over the rear. She got in, leaned over and unlocked the passenger door for me. I pushed my bag over the back of the seat into the small space behind and got in.

'Great wheels,' I said.

She just smiled and turned the key. There were impressive sounds from the back.

'What do you call this thing?'

'Babe magnet,' she said and pulled away.

'I mean what model is it?'

She gave me a look, as though I ought to know. 'It's a nine eleven turbo, Lemmer.'

'Oh.'

'*Jissis*, you ignorant Loxton country folk. It's the nine thirty series, 1984 model. She was the fastest thing on the road in her day.'

'She?'

'Naturally, a "she". Beautiful, sexy . . .'

We drove over a speed bump. Slowly.

'. . . and without suspension?'

'Fuck off, Lemmer. Your homework is behind you.'

I turned around and picked up the small pile of documents. There was a company prospectus on top: *Southern Cross Avionics. Innovation. Dedication. Quality.* A photo of a Mirage fighter plane in flight decorated the cover. It was printed in full colour, on thick, expensive glossy paper. I began to read.

Southern Cross Avionics is Africa's foremost developer of aerospace systems, a world-class competitor driven by constant innovation, total dedication to client satisfaction, and a passion for absolute quality in our products.

'Modest people,' I said.

'Propaganda,' said Jeanette.

I turned the page. The heading read 'Our Heritage'.

In 1983, two brilliant South African electronic engineers had a dream – a dream of starting their own company based on their unwavering belief that innovative research and daring design were the cornerstones of developing aerospace systems for the future. They resigned from their jobs with a parastatal weapons manufacturer, and founded the company in a tiny warehouse in their hometown of Stellenbosch.

From these humble beginnings, and despite the tragic loss of one of the founding members in a 1986 mountaineering accident, Southern Cross has grown into a multimillion-rand concern, employing more than five hundred dedicated staff members, of which more than fifty are internationally trained world-class engineers.

On their way to success, the company had a major hand in developing a laser-based rangefinder for the Dassault Mirage F1AZ fighter plane, which permitted highly accurate fusing and aiming of unguided munitions. The success of this system was acknowledged by *Jane's Defence Weekly*, which concluded that the F1AZ's proven accuracies were within the order disclosed by the USAF for their F-15E Strike Eagle.

While much of the work done in the early years was of a classified nature, the invaluable experience of developing cutting-edge technology led to the products that can truly be called world class today.

Amongst them are the XV-700 'Black Eagle' surface-to-air missile guidance system, the XV-715 'Bateleur' air-to-air guided missile, and the revolutionary XZ-1 'Lammergeier' heavy, long-range anti-armour missile.

On the third page there was a photograph of Quintus Wernich under the heading 'Founding Father and Managing Director'. He did not smile, but there was a benevolent air to the face behind rimless glasses, a kindly paterfamilias with his short steel-grey hair.

'I thought he was chairman of the board.'

Jeanette glanced down at the document on my lap. 'He is. That thing is two years old. Look at the cuttings.'

I paged through the pile. A *Business Day* newspaper cutting read 'Black MD just the first BEE step for Southern Cross'.

The appointment of Mr Philani Lungile as managing director is just the first step in a comprehensive process of Black Economic Empowerment (BEE), says Mr Quintus Wernich, former MD and now chairman of the privately owned Stellenbosch weapons systems developer Southern Cross Avionics.

'Bloody traffic,' said Jeanette. I looked up. She wanted to turn off the N2 on to the N7 but it wasn't going to happen any time soon.

'We never have this trouble in Loxton,' I said.

'Read the one about the missile programme. I found it on the Internet,' she ordered, and lit a Gauloise.

I rolled the window down and searched through the documents. The printout came from the International Centre for Strategic Research.

South African Ballistic Missile Programme

Even today, little is known about South Africa's short-lived ballistic missile programme.

The country had been developing short-range tactical missiles and rockets since the 1960s, but only became the focus of international attention after a test launch of what the apartheid regime called a 'booster rocket' in July 1989.

Western intelligence agencies soon pointed out similarities between the South African capabilities and Israel's Jericho II missile, prompting speculation that Israel had supplied crucial technology to South Africa's development effort.

This claim was substantiated by the fact that the two countries also shared knowledge and expertise in developing electronic weapons systems for the Dassault Mirage jet fighter in the seventies and eighties – through government owned ARMS-COR and privately held companies such as Southern Cross Avionics.

I looked up, because more pieces began to fall into place.

'When I read that, I knew where the rifle came from,' Jeanette said.

I nodded.

'OK, Lemmer, tell me.'

'What?'

'Everything. What the fuck has Southern Cross to do with Emma le Roux?'

'How long will it be before we get there?'

'At this rate? Half an hour.'

'What else is in this pile?' I rifled my fingers through her cuttings.

'Do you know how the big arms deal works? The one for the new Gripen fighter plane?'

'You tell me.'

'Saab of Sweden and BAE in the UK won the contract to supply twenty-eight Gripens to South Africa. But part of the deal was that they must invest and develop locally. Southern Cross was part of that – they are also going to build systems for BAE. And there's a report that Wernich and company are courting Airbus passionately.'

'That's why they still want to keep it quiet,' I said. 'That and the black economic empowerment.'

'What, Lemmer? What do they want to keep quiet?'

'Did you bring me a firearm?'

She flicked the Gauloise out of the window and pulled the left flap of her jacket open. There was a pistol in a leather holster under her arm. 'No,' she said. 'Today I am your bodyguard, Lemmer. Now tell me everything.'

47

I didn't find the new office buildings at Century City attractive. I don't know how you would describe them. Neo-Roman? Corporate-Tuscan? Overdone, outsized pillars, sharp triangular roofs, glass and concrete, as un-African as it could be. Southern Cross was on the top storey of a five-storey block. The reception room was large and clinical.

In the middle of the room a black woman sat at a desk with a huge glass top. She had a silver laptop in front of her and a tiny telephone switchboard. She was wearing an earphone and microphone headset. It looked like something a fighter pilot would use.

Jeanette spoke to her. 'We would like to see Mr Wernich.'

She looked Jeanette up and down. 'Do you have an appointment?'

I stepped forward. 'Yes, we do. Tell him Jacobus le Roux is here to see him.'

Fingers with long nails danced over the high-tech keyboard. She spoke barely above a whisper. 'Louise, there is a Mr Le Roux for Mr Wernich.'

'Jacobus le Roux,' I said. 'Please make sure you tell her that.'

The woman looked at me as if seeing me for the first time – and was unimpressed. She listened and then told us, 'I'm sorry, it seems you don't have an appointment.'

'Come on, Lemmer,' said Jeanette, and bypassed the glass princess. 'I've been here before.'

'Lady,' the receptionist said in dismay. 'Where are you going?'

Jeanette stopped and turned. 'One thing I can tell you, my dear. I am no lady.' Then she walked on, not intimidated when the woman said, 'I'm calling Security.'

*   *   *

Glass desktops were a Southern Cross theme. Louise also presided behind one. She was white, with dark brown hair in a plait, subtle make-up and fashionable glasses. She was thirty-something and faultless. Her job description would be Personal Assistant, never Secretary. She was appointed for her efficiency, computer skills and appearance. In front of her she had only a black keyboard and a flat LCD screen. The rest of the computer was concealed elsewhere. She seemed ruffled when we strode in.

'Where is Quintus hiding, sweetheart?' Jeanette asked her, and strode past her to the door leading to her boss's office.

Louise gasped and sprang up. The grey skirt clung to impressive curves. I winked at her, just because I could. Then we were inside Wernich's office.

It was spacious, with a massive glass desktop bearing a slender laptop. A high-backed leather chair stood behind the desk, like a royal throne, and six lesser ones in the same style were arranged in front of it. On the walls, in expensive frames, hung perfectly realistic paintings of missiles and jet fighters. But the man himself stood looking out of the huge windows that stretched from floor to ceiling, offering a view of a greenish-brown canal outside. His hands were clasped behind his back.

He looked around only when Louise hissed behind us, 'I'm sorry, Mr Wernich, they just walked through.'

He stared at Jeanette for a long time and then at me and nodded slightly, apparently to himself. It was the same kindly face as the prospectus photograph, but older. He looked like a church elder, that pious yet friendly appearance of so many Afrikaner men in their late fifties. He was dignified in a dark tailored suit, a definite presence.

'Never mind, Louise, I was expecting them,' he said paternally. His voice was deep and modulated, like that of an announcer on a classical music radio station. 'Please close the door behind you.'

She turned reluctantly and went out. The door closed silently. 'Please, sit down,' Wernich said.

We hadn't expected this reaction. We remained standing.

'Please,' he said. 'Let's discuss this like adults,' and he gestured gallantly in the direction of the chairs. 'Make yourselves at home.'

We sat. He nodded in satisfaction, and turned slowly back to the big windows, keeping his back to us.

'Tell me, Mr Lemmer, my men . . . Are they still alive?' It was a conversational tone, as though we had known each other for years.

'Kappies is alive. I don't know about Eric.'

'And where are they?'

'In police custody, by now.'

'Hmm,' he said, and clasped his hands behind his back. I saw the thumbs rotating in small circles; he seemed deep in thought. 'You surprise me.'

I couldn't think of a response.

'What's the amount you have in mind?'

'What amount?'

'How much money do you want, Mr Lemmer?'

I finally caught up with him. 'Is that the way the weapons industry works, Quintus? If you can't kill, you buy?'

'A somewhat crude description. Why else would you come here?'

'You're finished, Quintus.'

'Finished?'

'That's right.'

He turned around and held open his arms, an invitation. 'Very well, Mr Lemmer. Here I am. Do what you must.' Pleasant and reasonable, we might as well have been negotiating over a second-hand missile.

I just stared at him.

'What now, Mr Lemmer? Are you just going to sit there?'

I was going to say that I was going to make him talk before I dragged him away, but he didn't give me the chance.

'You know, Mr Lemmer, the thing that astounded me most was your poor reading skills. I mean, the writing on the wall was so clear: Emma le Roux was in deadly danger, but the so-called bodyguard saw nothing, said nothing, heard nothing and did nothing. At a cost of how much per day? Such incredible incompetence. Only when it was too late did you wake up. Then you wanted to deal out retribution left and right. Actually, it does make sense. Aren't you the big, strong man that beat an innocent young articled clerk to death with your bare hands? We investigated you, Mr Lemmer. Such a pathetic, pointless life. And it doesn't improve. Now you are the jailbird who can do no better than to mislead his clients about his apparent abilities, the man in hiding in a small town so he won't be found out. The one that takes his orders from a lesbian doing her best to live, look and talk like a man.'

By then I was beside him and my arm was drawn back for the blow, but Jeanette shouted 'Lemmer!' and Wernich smiled in satisfaction. 'You're an inherent coward, Mr Lemmer,' he said. 'Just like your father.' And then I hit him.

He fell back against the glass and slid to the ground.

Jeanette got between us. She shoved me roughly back. 'Leave him,' she said.

'I'm going to kill him.'

'You're going to leave him alone.' She grabbed me by the collar.

Wernich wiped blood from his mouth and got up slowly. 'Before you go on, I think it's only fair to tell you that each of our offices is monitored by video. You might just want to deactivate the camera before you proceed. Otherwise it might look like cold-blooded murder.'

Jeanette kept a handful of my collar and said to Wernich, 'Don't be ridiculous. How many have you killed? Four, five, six? Let me see . . . Your partner? I see they call it a climbing accident. He didn't like the Machel affair, so you got rid of him? And the Le Rouxs, the conservationist, the gate guard . . .'

'You're going to jail,' I said to him.

'Would that be before or after you beat me to death?'

'You're going to do time, I promise you.'

He looked at me with a frown. 'Do you think so, Mr Lemmer? Do you really think so?'

'Yes, I do think so.'

He took a snow-white handkerchief out of his pocket and wiped his mouth. Then he walked slowly around to his throne and sat down slowly like a tired man. 'There's the minor problem of proof, Mr Lemmer.'

Jeanette shoved me into a chair opposite Wernich. 'The proof is sitting in a police cell in Hoedspruit,' I said.

He sighed. 'I can understand your limited intellectual capacity, Mr Lemmer. That is, after all, genetic. But not your naivety.' He looked at Jeanette. 'Please sit down, Miss Louw. We can't negotiate unless we are all calm and relaxed.'

'Negotiate?' she asked.

'That's right. But before we begin, let me ask, for interest's sake, how did you imagine things would proceed from here? Did you truly believe that Eric would voluntarily tell the police everything?'

'Last night Kappies sang like a canary, Quintus.'

'Very well, let us say Kappies tells them everything he knows. What then?'

'Then they come and get you.'

'There's nothing that connects me with him, Mr Lemmer. Nothing. He's not an employee, not on contract, nor has he ever been in this building. His knowledge is quite limited because we are not fools. Naturally, there are other options. Such as passing on certain information about Kappies' colourful history to the law enforcers. That would shed new light on his testimony. But in my opinion there's an easier way. We live in Africa, Mr Lemmer, where justice has a price. More so in certain provinces. Where is Hoedspruit again? Limpopo, if I remember correctly . . . Now what do we know about the general morals of Limpopo?'

'Are you going to bribe the press as well?' asked Jeanette.

His kindly face was back. He smiled as though a child had asked a cute but stupid question.

'And what are you going to tell the press, Miss Louw?'

'Everything.'

'I see. Let me get this clear. You are going to tell the press an incredible story based on the word of a highly unstable labourer at an animal rehabilitation institution who is wanted by the police for the mass murder of five innocent black people. In addition, you expect them to accept the supporting testimony of a man who has served four years for road rage murder?'

'Manslaughter,' Jeanette corrected him.

'I am certain the press will take the difference into account, Miss Louw.'

'The government is going to reopen the Samora Machel affair this year.' She said it without much enthusiasm. She realised, as I did, that he had a point.

'Aah,' he said. 'So if the police and the media don't work for you, there's always the government. And they will believe Misters Lemmer and Le Roux? Even though fifty-one per cent of our company will be in the hands of the black empowerment group Impukane in a few weeks? And a former ANC minister and three former provincial premiers on the board of directors? Miss Louw, from what I gather, you are a capable businesswoman despite your aberrations. I didn't expect naivety from you.'

'I'll get you, Quintus,' I said.

'You have an interesting thought pattern, Mr Lemmer.'

'You think so?'

'Not illogical. The concept of identifying a scapegoat who must be punished is very instinctive. But that leaves no room for nuances.'

'What nuances?'

'The nuance of a generous offer.'

'Let me hear it,' I said. Jeanette glared at me, but I ignored her.

'I understand your need for justice, Mr Lemmer. You feel that Jacobus le Roux and his family were done a great injustice, and that it should be rectified. Am I right?'

I nodded.

'Very well. I believe we can help. According to the evidence available to me, there's little doubt that Jacobus is responsible for the sangoma murders. But assume that I can rectify the matter, so that he is no longer a suspect. Would that be reasonable compensation?'

'It would.'

'And if I guaranteed that Le Roux could live his life freely, without fear of complications from the past; and if, furthermore, I offered to use the services of Body Armour extensively, in future, at a retainer of, should we say, fifty thousand per month?'

'A hundred thousand,' I said.

'No,' said Jeanette.

'Not now, Jeanette.'

'Seventy-five thousand,' said Wernich.

'Over my dead body,' said Jeanette.

I ignored her. 'On one condition. You answer all my questions.'

Jeanette stood up. 'Fuck you, Lemmer. You don't work for me any more.' There was more disappointment than dislike in her voice. She went to the door, opened it and walked out.

'I will answer your questions,' said Wernich, as though she didn't exist.

'Excuse me a minute,' I said, and went after her.

Louise followed me silently with her eyes as I crossed her office. I didn't wink at her; I was in too much of a hurry. Outside in the passage I saw my boss heading determinedly to the lifts. 'Jeanette,' I called, but she ignored me. I ran after her. She pressed the button on the elevator bank with vigour. The doors opened and she stepped in. I was just in time to prevent the doors closing.

'Jeanette, listen . . .'

'Fuck off, Lemmer, let go of the door before I *bliksem* you.' I had never seen her like this. The anger twisted her face.

There was only one thing to do. I grabbed her Armani suit and dragged her out of the lift towards me until her body bumped hard into mine. She was enraged. I put my arms around her and squeezed her tight with my mouth close to her ear.

I just had time to whisper, 'They've got microphones, Jeanette,' before she tried to knee me, but I was expecting it, knowing her background. I pressed my legs tightly together. She hit my thigh hard. I held her tighter. She struggled. She was a strong woman and she was angry. A dangerous combination.

'I won't accept his damn offer, I'll get him, just listen to me, please, we can't afford to let them hear us,' I whispered desperately in her ear.

I thought she was going to break free, but she relaxed slightly and hissed, 'For God's sake, Lemmer.'

'Microphones and video cameras. The place is wired, Jeanette. We can use that.'

'How?'

'You'll have to help.'

'Is it necessary to hold me so bloody tight?'

'Well, I'm starting to enjoy this.'

Jeanette Louw laughed.

I walked back to Wernich's office. Louise was on guard, her hands folded on her lap. Her eyes followed me with disapproval.

I smiled sweetly at her. It met with the same success as my wink. I would have to change tactics.

In his office, Quintus Wernich was on the phone. I heard him say, 'I have to go,' before he put the phone down. 'You seem to have lost your job, Mr Lemmer.'

'Do you think I can take her to the labour court, Quintus?'

Wernich smiled without humour. 'I would have offered you a position, but I think our mutual dislike wouldn't be the ideal foundation for a close working relationship.'

'In any case, I don't have the intellectual capacity for the corporate environment.'

'Touché,' he said.

We sat and looked at each other across the glass desk. He sighed deeply and said, 'So, where were we?'

I tried to guess whether Jeanette would have had enough time to do what she had to do.

'You owe me answers, Quintus.'

'For what it's worth,' he said.

48

'Were you there? In the Kruger Park in eighty-six?'

'I was there.'

'Who was the man with the moustache with you? The one who burned Pego Mashego?'

'That was our Chief of Security.'

'What is his name?'

'Does it matter?'

'It matters that you keep your part of our agreement, Quintus.'

His eyes drifted for a fraction of a second to the video camera in the ceiling. Then he said in resignation, 'Christo Loock.'

'What does he do now?'

'He is the Senior Manager of Human Resources.'

'Talented guy. Who were you working for when Machel died?'

'I don't quite follow your meaning.'

'Who contracted you? Who hired you to do it?'

'It was our own idea.'

'I don't believe it.'

'You will have to. It's the truth.'

'Why would a company that builds electronic systems want to assassinate the president of a neighbouring country?'

'Because we could, Lemmer. Because we could.'

He leaned back in his chair. 'You must understand the circumstances. When Nico and I left Armscor in 1983, we weren't popular. There were accusations that we didn't want to serve The Firm any more, that we were money-grubbers because we wanted to set up on our own. The thing that saved us was our knowledge. Excuse me if I sound arrogant, but we were the best of the best. They had to use us. But reluctantly. And frugally. Only when there was no other option.'

He stood up and went over to the windows. 'I admit that the accusations weren't entirely unfounded. We were financially ambitious.'

He looked out and folded his hands behind his back. I wondered whether he thought it looked dignified, the gesture of The Chairman. 'One of the reasons we left Armscor was that a parastatal institution seldom rewards performance over mediocrity. We'd had enough of that.'

'Get to the point, Quintus.'

'Forgive me. The fact of the matter is you can't run a technology company without capital. Research costs money, lots of money. We needed something to, shall we say, take our relationship with the government to another level. How? That was the question. But the Lord provides, Mr Lemmer, I don't know if you're a believer, but need teaches one to pray, and prayers are heard. I learned that.'

He realised that he was wandering and turned to stand with his back against the window, so the light made a halo around him. His eyes were elsewhere in the room.

'It was no coincidence that within the span of three days I heard about the government's dilemma with Samora Machel, and the Israelis' technology. It was providence. It was ordained. Nevertheless, we were working closely with the Israelis on several levels. We heard about their progress with VOR technology. That stands for very high frequency omnidirectional radio. Aircraft use it for navigation. A VOR beacon sends out a signal identifying which beacon it is as well as the pilot's orientation to the beacon in relation to magnetic north. Are you with me?'

'I understand you.'

'The Israelis developed the technology to create a false VOR, indistinguishable from the real McCoy. I will never forget it, Mr Lemmer. I was driving home late that night. When I pulled up in front of the garage all the parts seemed to come together. The minister's remarks about Machel, how it would be in the interests of the whole of Africa if he would just disappear. Then the new technology from Israel. I realised that there was a way. It would solve many problems.'

'So you offered your services.'

'That is correct.'

'So you could get into their good graces.'

'In a manner of speaking.'

'Although it would be murder?'

'Murder? Mr Lemmer, we were at war. Samora Machel was a communist, an atheist waging a civil war on the people of his own country with the help of the Soviets. He was detaining, torturing and executing his own subjects without benefit of trial, a dictator harbouring terrorists, so he could destabilise the entire region while Russia sat and waited.'

'Now those same "terrorists" are members of the board.'

'The fall of communism changed everything.'

'I see. And what about Jacobus le Roux? He was neither a communist nor an atheist.'

'He was there. My heart goes out to him; it was all unnecessary, a tragic clash of circumstances. Sometimes, Mr Lemmer, the fate of nations takes precedence over the individual. Sometimes one has to make difficult decisions, very difficult decisions, in the interest of the greater good.'

'Or the greater profit,' I said.

He came away from the window and walked past me to the desk. He crossed his arms and said, 'Who are you to judge?'

'I suppose you're right, Quintus.'

He nodded and went to his chair. 'What else do you want to know?'

'Where were you when the plane crashed?'

'On Mariepskop. At the radar station.'

'And when they murdered Johan and Sara le Roux?'

'It was a car crash.'

'Where were you?'

'I don't remember.'

'Really?'

'That's right. Is there anything else, Mr Lemmer?'

'I think I understand the rest. What I don't understand is why you are prepared to leave Jacobus now, to let him talk.'

'He won't want to talk now.'

'Oh?'

'Mr Lemmer, the day he walked into the witch doctor's hut and gunned down those people, he ceased to be a threat.'

'Then why attack Emma?'

'We were just lucky.'

'What do you mean?'

'At that stage we were not monitoring her calls. We didn't feel that it was necessary any more. When we heard that Cobie had murdered a witch doctor, we started listening to the police telephones, mostly to keep up with events. We heard Emma phoning. We knew then that she would be the new risk, if she should succeed in tracking down Jacobus.'

'But are you prepared to guarantee her safety now?'

'It depends on what her brother tells her. Or you. Should she recover fully, of course.'

'Of course.'

'Her safety is in your hands.'

'Unless I break your neck now.'

He looked up at the video camera. 'I think that would be very foolish.'

I got to my feet. 'Quintus, I want you to understand me very well. If the case against Jacobus does not go away, I will be back. If anything happens to him or Emma, ever, I will be back. I will show you, then, what kind of a coward I am.'

He nodded, not impressed. Then he leaned forward and swivelled the laptop so I could see the screen. 'Mr Lemmer, keep one thing in mind. Should anything happen to me, the following material will be handed over to the authorities.' He clicked a key and an image appeared on the screen in high resolution. I was standing in front of him with my back to the camera and I hit him. He fell back against the glass and sank to the ground.

Jeanette moved in between us and shoved me away. 'Leave him.' Her voice was as clear as glass.

'I'm going to kill him.'

Wernich froze the image on the frame, leaving me standing over him and Jeanette restraining me.

'Good sound quality,' I said.

'Our technology is top drawer.'

I had been leaning against the Porsche for ten minutes before Jeanette strolled up and unlocked the door. 'Let's go.'

Only once we were both seated did she take a DVD out of her pocket and drop it casually on my lap. 'There you are,' she said.

'Did you have any difficulty?'

'There's nothing like a nine-millimetre against a man's head to make him listen,' she said.

'You're wilder than a wild dog.' I plagiarised Dr Koos Taljaard's phrase.

She merely laughed, started the Porsche and drove off. Then she described it.

She had waited until I went into Wernich's office before asking Louise where the video control room was. At first Louise wouldn't cooperate. Jeanette threatened to break her fingernails. 'Her eyes were this big. Like I was some kind of barbarian.'

Louise reluctantly led her to the room to the rear of the building, the door unmarked. The secretary merely pointed a finger and walked away with huge dignity.

Jeanette had opened the door. The room was half dark, not very big. There was a bank of television screens encircling a man behind a control panel. The man was broad and strong with a bushy moustache; the hair that touched the top of his ears and collar was grey at the temples. She pointed the Colt at him and said, 'Who are you?'

'Loock.' He looked her up and down and said, 'You are Louw.'

'Only when I'm not high.'

He wasn't amused. 'What do you want?'

'Turn up the sound a bit, so we can hear what the men are saying.' She gestured at the screens that displayed Wernich and me in his office.

They listened to our exchange and watched silently in the twilight of the room up to the point where I left. 'I want a copy of that, please,' she said

He had snorted with disdain. She shot a hole through the first monitor.

'I didn't hear anything,' I said.

'His place is soundproof and dustproof. Probably waterproof too. Well, not any more. I had to damage the roof as well before he would make that DVD.'

She had shot three screens and a hole in the roof before he unhurriedly and mechanically burned a copy of the recording on a DVD. Then she hit him on the cheekbone with her Colt as hard as she could. His head jerked back and blood ran down his moustache.

'He lifted his head and looked at me like a python at a springhare.'

'Thanks, Jeanette.'

'No, Lemmer, I'm the one who should say thank you,' she said, and grinned in self-satisfaction.

I phoned B. J. Fikter. He said Jacobus le Roux had been talking to Emma for the past two hours. The police guard had been withdrawn.

'I'll come and relieve you tomorrow,' I said.

'Thank God,' he said, and ended the call.

'What now?' Jeanette asked.

'Now we are going to get your lovely receptionist, Jolene Freylinck, to make us a copy of this DVD.'

'Only one?'

'That's all we need.'

'Lemmer, I don't agree. We ought to give one to each prospective member of his BEE board.'

'Why? So they can fire him?'

'It's a start.'

'But not a good ending.'

'I suppose you have a better idea?'

'I do. It will cost you a plane ticket.'

'To Nelspruit?'

'No. A little farther than that,' I said.

'What's your plan?'

'I think it's better if you don't know.'

She thought it over and I suppose she agreed, although she wasn't happy about it. She banged the Porsche down a gear and floored the accelerator. The G-forces pressed us against the seats with an invisible hand.

The office looked out over the sea, but the antique air conditioner made too much noise for us to hear the breakers.

I faced a man the colour of dusk. He was deep in his sixties, hair snowy white, but the scar that stretched from the corner of his mouth to his ear was just as clear as when I had met him for the first time ten years earlier. His eyes were still vacant, as though the person behind them had died inside. He was a man who no longer cared about feeling pain and who felt a certain pressure to dish it out.

I slid the DVD case across the desk towards him.

'You will need an interpreter,' I said.

'For which language?' His accent was strong.

'Afrikaans.'

'You can translate for me.'

'I think we would both prefer an objective translation.'

'I see.' He reached for the holder and opened it. The disc gleamed, silver and new. 'May I ask you why you are doing this?'

'I would like to say it is because I believe in justice, but that wouldn't be true. It's because I believe in revenge.'

He nodded slowly and closed the case.

'I know,' he said, and put out his hand. 'We are like family.'

As I walked out into the oppressive heat of Maputo, capital of Mozambique, at noon, my cell phone beeped above the hiss of the Indian Ocean. I took it out of my pocket and beckoned a taxi. I checked the message.

Three words only: EMMA IS AWAKE.

49

I must confess that I had expectations about the moment I would walk into Emma's hospital room.

Not unreasonable expectations, such as Emma opening her arms and embracing me, whispering her gratitude and love in my ear. More along the lines of me sitting on the bed and she taking my hand and saying, 'Thank you, Lemmer.' That would have been good enough for me, a start, and a prelude to future possibilities.

But Jack Phatudi deprived me of that.

On Friday, 4 January he sent Black and White, the pair who had followed Emma and me a lifetime ago, to arrest me. The white one's swelling around the nose and eyes was not totally gone yet. They arrested me with great ceremony at the Kruger Mpumalanga International Airport for 'murder, attempted murder and defeating the ends of justice'. They allowed me to make one telephone call before locking me in the unbearable heat of the Nelspruit police cells, among a selection of colourful and antagonistic men.

B. J. Fikter came round on Saturday afternoon for what he called 'cell visitation'. After getting in a few wisecracks about my dilemma, he told me that Emma was being flown to Cape Town on Saturday on a SouthMed Health Care plane. Also that Jeanette said not to worry, she was working on 'my circumstances'.

By Monday morning there were threats about an additional charge of assaulting a fellow detainee, but I knew they would have difficulty finding credible witnesses. Then Black and White came to fetch me, cuffed my hands and feet, and took me to the magistrates' court for a bail hearing. They were unnecessarily rough when they shoved me into the back of their Astra.

The holding cells were below the courtroom, in the basement. A young white lawyer with a fat gold ring came to introduce himself as Naas du Plessis. He would be representing me at the request of Jeanette Louw. 'I will do what I can, but you have a former conviction,' he said gloomily.

I was the last one to be called, but the two uniforms didn't take me to a courtroom. They pushed me, shuffling to accommodate the chains and with my hands cuffed behind my back, into a tiny office where Jack Phatudi waited. They shut the door before leaving.

There were a couple of chairs, a table and a steel filing cabinet. I sat down. Silently, Phatudi directed a scowl of hatred at me. Then he punched a deep dent into the filing cabinet. The windows rattled. He came and stood in front of me holding his sore knuckles. His face was only centimetres from mine. For the first time I saw him sweat. The drops trickled down his dark skin, down the tree trunk of a neck into the snow-white collar of his shirt. I could tell by the look in his eyes that he would love to repeat the blow, this time against my head.

'You . . .' he said, but could not go on. He seemed to choke on the words massing behind his tongue. He turned around and kicked the cabinet. Another dent. He came back and grabbed my face with his right hand, fingers over my jaw and cheeks, and he squeezed with frightening force while he stared into my eyes. Then he shoved me backwards, making the chair topple over and my head hit the floor hard.

He made a sound of frustration and rage and said, 'Let me tell you just one thing. Just one thing.' He plucked me upright by my clothes and held me in front of him and said, 'They couldn't buy me.' We stood like that, Jack Phatudi and I, and I knew Wernich and his people had made Phatudi an offer which he had refused. And I knew nothing I could say would make any difference.

So I just asked, 'What do you mean, Jack?'

He let me go, so that I lost my balance and staggered backwards against the wall.

He turned his back on me. 'They came with money. They said I should drop all charges. Against the one you shot. Against Cobie de Villiers. I refused. They said my people would win their land claim, and they would give money. How much did I want? I said no. So they just went over my head. They bought someone else up the chain of command, I don't know who. But let me tell you now, I won't leave it here. I will get you. And de Villiers and Kappies. I'll get you.'

He turned on his heel and stalked past me without looking at me again. He opened the door and went out, barking some order down the passage in sePedi. The two uniforms came and unlocked the shackles and told me to go; the case against me had been withdrawn.

Emma had a room with a view of Table Mountain. When I arrived the door was open and the room was filled with people gathering around her, Jacobus le Roux, Carel the Rich and some of his children, Stoffel the Advocate, others I did not know. Peace-loving, attractive, successful people. The space was filled with friendship and joy. I stopped in my tracks before they saw me and stole one look at Emma in profile. Her face was thinner, but the lines were so unmistakably beautiful when she smiled, and I turned away and scribbled a note that I left with the flowers at the nurses' station.

I had to fetch my Isuzu from Hermanus. And then go to Stodels for the herb seedlings.

She phoned me the following day.

'Thank you for the flowers,' she said.

'It's a pleasure.'

'You should have come in, Lemmer.'

'There were so many people.'

'How can I ever thank you?'

'I was just doing my job.'

'Ai, Lemmer, you're back in your shell again. Where are you?'

'In Loxton.'

'What's the weather like?'

'Hot.'

'The wind is blowing here in Cape Town.'

'I'm glad you're better, Emma.'

'I have you to thank for that.'

'No, you don't.'

'I'll come and visit you. When I'm well again.'

'You're welcome.'

'Thanks, Lemmer. For everything.'

'It's a pleasure.'

Then we said goodbye, awkwardly, and I knew that the odds were ten to one that I would never see her again.

It was raining when I read about the deaths of Quintus Wernich and Christo Loock.

It was 14 February and I was sitting at my table reading the paper with thunder rumbling outside above the drum of fat raindrops on the corrugated-iron roof. The front-page article in *Die Burger* told the story of the suspected carjacking at Stellenbosch and a renewed outcry against the atrocious levels of crime.

I read it twice and then sat staring out of the kitchen window at the bright pools forming in my herb garden and thought about the man with the scarred cheek. Raul Armando de Sousa.

I saw him in 1997, just once, during government talks in Maputo. He called all the bodyguards together in a conference hall to discuss the procedures for the banquet on the final evening. By his eyes I recognised him as a brother-in-violence, but there was more to his dusk-coloured façade – a burden, an invisible weight he carried on his shoulders.

I asked about him circumspectly. They told me that he had been the man who guarded Samora Machel. He had been in the Tupolev 134A when it flew into the side of the Lebombo mountains. He was one of the ten they took out of the wreckage alive. I understood then. I wondered what it must feel like to wait your whole life to be defined, only to find when the crucial moment arrived that there was nothing you could do. Was it not preferable to remain invisible and incomplete?

It was of him that I had thought when Jacobus le Roux told me his story under a tree on Heuningklip. By then I knew how Raul Armando de Sousa must feel. And that sometimes there is a way out.

That was how I knew with total certainty that he had been there the previous night in Stellenbosch. De Sousa had pulled the trigger.

I read the rest of the paper without concentration. Until I spotted the small report on an inner page, a single column beside a Pick 'n Pay advertisement. Conservation groups have expressed their concern about the manner and extent of the settlement of the Sibashwa tribe's land claim in the Kruger National Park.

When I had finished, I took a walk around the garden to savour the divine smell of a wet Karoo. I thought about Jack Phatudi, son of a Sibashwa chief.

At five o'clock I went jogging on the Bokpoort road at a speed calculated to get me home in time to watch *7de Laan* on television.

There is a spot on this route, a rise beyond the last stock gate at Jakhalsdans, where millions of years of geological forces have piled massive rocks on top of one another like beacons. On either side the Karoo lies open, and I go and stand there to gain perspective of our place in the universe. We are all small, insignificant, invisible if you draw back, away from the earth, the solar system, the Milky Way.

But jogging back through town, sparkling and clean after the rain, people greeted me: Conrad at the Repair Shop, De Wit locking up at the Co-op, Antjie Barnard from her veranda, Oom Joe van Wyk pulling weeds in the garden.

'Afternoon, Lemmer. Nice rain, hey?'

Far down the street, right on the edge of town, was my house. I saw a green Renault Mégane, a cabriolet, parked in front of it, and I began to run faster.

ACKNOWLEDGEMENTS

Authors are often asked, 'What inspired you to write this book?'

My standard answer is that inspiration doesn't feature much. For me, perspiration is the name of the game – every story is like a house, and I have to build it brick by brick.

Blood Safari is an exception, however, to a certain extent.

As luck would have it, I visited the Moholoholo Animal Rehabilitation Centre below the Mariepskop mountain peak in Limpopo Province three times within twelve months while writing *Devil's Peak* a few years ago. Two of these visits were during motorcycle trips, and not intended as writer's research at all. But every time I listened to the presentations by Brian Jones and his personnel, I was inspired by their dedication, passion and sacrifice, especially the incredible work they do with vultures.

For this, and the fact that their struggle became the first brick of a new story house, I would like to extend my deepest gratitude. And may I urge the reader to both visit their website at *www.moholoholo.co.za*, and visit the Rehab Centre in person. Or even better, support them financially to help save our African vultures.

Which also means I can't deny the fact that the fictional Mogale Centre in the book is based on the geography, spirit and structure of the very real Moholoholo. But that is where the similarity ends. All characters in *Blood Safari* are fictitious, and definitely not based on any living human being – including the good people of Moholoholo.

I am also indebted to the following people: Tom Dreyer, for permission to quote from his excellent novel *Equatoria*, Keith and Colleen Begg, the world-renowned wildlife researchers, for permission to quote from their honey badger article in *Africa Geo-*

graphic (February 2005), Sarah Borchert, editor of *Africa Geographic* (definitely one of my favourite magazines), the archive staff of the daily newspaper *Die Burger*, Captain Elmarie Engelbrecht of the South African Police Services Psychological Investigation Unit in Pretoria, my agent Isobel Dixon and her colleagues at Blake Friedmann in London, my wife Anita, our children, Lida, Liam, Johan and Konstanz, and the ATKV for financial support of my research for the novel.

I would also like to acknowledge the following sources:

The Long Summer, Brian Fagan, Granta Books, 2004

Guns, Germs and Steel, Jared Diamond, Vintage, 2005

The Weather Makers, Tim Flannery, Penguin, 2005

Birds of Prey, Peter Steyn, David Philip, 1989

Roberts Birds of Southern Africa, 7th edn, Hockey, Dean and Ryan, Trustees of the John Voelcker Bird Book Fund, 2005

Slange en Slangbyte in Suider-Afrika, Johan Marais, Struik, 1999

Field Guide to Snakes and Other Reptiles of Southern Africa, Bill Branch, Struik, 1998

Sappi Tree Spotting: Lowveld, Rina Grant and Val Thomas, Jacana

Stormwind en Droogtes, Freek Swart, Litera, 2002

Skukuza, David Tattersall, Tafelberg, 1972

The Game Rangers, Jan Roderigues, 1992

Mahlangeni, Kobie Krüger, Penguin, 2004

Mashesha, Tony Pooley, Southern, 1992

http://www.contrast.org/truth/html/samora_machel.html

http://moholoholo.co.za

www.koerantargiewe.media24.com

http://www.geocities.com/lepulana2002/index.html

www.braininjury.com